Callatin Academy

#6

Shattered

By Melissa Logan

Thanks to Isaiah Guinzy for the use of his senior picture for my cover and Sarah Whipple of Sarah Whipple Photography for the amazing work. Special thanks to all those who answer my crazy questions for research.

This book, and series, touches on many different realities of our society today. I'm certain I cannot even begin to accurately depict life as a childhood cancer patient or their families, but I hope Jordan has spread awareness for this very real disease. A lot has taken place while revising this book and it's probably evident in my writing. I can only hope pointing out a small amount of the aftermath of suicide and overdoses will make someone realize there is hope outside of themselves and that others will ache for their loss and what could have been if they'd only reached out.

Chapter 1
Zack

My life would never be the same again. One month ago, I said goodbye to a friend and I don't think I'll ever recover. How can someone be so full of life one minute and be gone forever, the next? It's not fair. It's not right.

"What's up?" Caleb Donaldson, my best friend and roommate, asked as he sauntered into the room. I shrugged my shoulders, tossing a basketball up in the air as I lay on my bed. "You've got to leave the room sometime, you know?"

"I do." I mumbled.

"Zack…" Caleb cleared his throat and plopped down on his bed. "I'm not good at this stuff, but if you need to talk I am…"

"I know, Cale. Thanks." I continued focusing on the basketball, hoping I could figure out the hurt and heartache with the lines and spins.

"If you bail out of another class or practice, they're going to pull your scholarship."

"Basketball and classes don't seem that important."

"If they pull your scholarship, you won't be here anymore."

"I get it, okay? Your dad has been on my ass, just as Maddie and everyone else. I can't keep my head straight."

"We have a psychiatrist at the school for a reason."

"I'm not going to see a fucking shrink, I'm fine." I growled as I dropped the ball, climbed off the bed, and grabbed my hoodie and baseball gear before storming out of the room. None of this was Caleb's fault, he was struggling with everything as well and focusing on me was helping him deal. I didn't have that luxury.

I stormed towards the fitness center, ready to take my frustrations out in the batting cages. My brain flipped back to finding Jordan doing the same thing in here, trying to clear her head of Lance Bowman. My stomach plummeted and my heart hurt to see her gorgeous face pop into my memory. I groaned and picked up my pace as I jogged to the building. At this rate, my head would never clear itself of the grief and confusion.

Chapter 2
Caleb

I growled as I picked up my phone and called my fiancé, Maddie DeMarina. It was only seconds before her sweet voice answered.

"Hey baby."

"Hey." My anxiety lowered, Maddie was always capable of bringing me down a notch.

"You worried about Zack?"

"How did you know?"

"I could sense it." She sighed. "I know he's struggling."

"He skipped class and practice again today. He's failing all of his classes, which isn't a direct result of her death, but…"

"I know. He needs to talk to someone."

"I mentioned that and he stormed out of the room."

"Should I go look for him?"

"No, he'll know I called you and won't talk. He and Jo are more alike than I ever realized." Maddie giggled softly, then the line went quiet.

"This weekend if he goes out with us, I'll try to get him to talk to me. Maybe Alicia and I can help."

"He needs something, Maddie. I'm terrified they'll yank his scholarship."

"We won't let that happen." She murmured. "Why does everything have to be so hard, Cales? High school is supposed to be carefree and fun. We're not supposed to have to deal with death, grief and illnesses yet. It's not fair."

"None of this makes sense. What do they say? It'll only make us stronger?"

"Ellie was a big part of Zack's life for a short time and he's not handling this well, if Jo doesn't…"

"I think Jo's situation is the majority of his issues, but he's using his grief over his ex-girlfriend's death to mask it."

"Because he doesn't want anyone else to know just how deep his feelings for Jo run."

"Everyone, but Jordan, knows."

"I really wish he would tell her. I love how amazing Lance is being, but he's hurt her so much. I feel like he'll do it again and again if given the chance. Zack would never…"

"You can't say never." I interjected. "Shit happens. However, I do believe Zack is more perfect for her than either of them realize."

"I agree."

"It's extremely frustrating that Keller James is her boyfriend and he isn't even phased by everything going on in her life. Zack's distraught because of her uncertain future and Keller is more worried about what shirt he's wearing tomorrow."

"He doesn't deserve her. I hope Jo realizes that finally."

"If not, she is blind."

"She's blinded by all the wrong guys."

"Dad said she was having a rough day."

"A lot of pain?"

"Yeah, and vomiting."

"Poor girl." Maddie sighed softly on the other end. "We're going up Saturday, right?"

"Absolutely. Dad may be keeping us away during the week mostly, but he has no excuses for the weekends."

"He's trying to make sure we stay focused on school."

"I know, but what if…?"

"Jordan is going to beat this, Caleb." Maddie stated firmly. "Do not entertain the idea of what if, she needs all of the positive thoughts we can send her way."

"Some days that isn't easy. I'm terrified of losing my little sister."

"I know, baby. Look at all she has beat so far; the car accident where her and Lance both should have died and then surgery, with that mysterious bleed making her flat line for whatever reason. She won't give up easily, you know that, right?"

"I try to tell myself it often." I mumbled. "Why did *she* have to get it? Why couldn't I have gotten cancer, or Kyler? Why does Jordan have to be the one to deal with it?"

"Because she's stronger than any of us will ever know. She has so many great things lying ahead for her, don't ever doubt that."

"I don't know what I would do without you, Maddie."

"I feel the same about you." She giggled. "You are my sanity most days."

"I know the feeling." I was the luckiest man in the world to have found the love of my life in high school. We would be married in less than a year and would embark on our future together as husband and wife. I couldn't wait to be able to wake up next to her on a daily basis. We talked on the phone for almost an hour before I realized Zack was still gone. My stomach tightened with worry.

"You should look for him." Maddie instructed. "Text me when you find him."

"I'm certain he's at the batting cages."

"You're right, I'm sure, but it's still good to make certain he knows you're here if he feels like talking." I nodded, even though she couldn't see it. It never ceased to amaze me how well she could read me, without being in the same room.

"I love you."

"Love you, too." She giggled as she hung up the phone. I grabbed a sweatshirt and my room key, placing it and my phone in my jeans pocket as I scurried into the hallway and out the door. I prayed Zack was still blowing off steam in the fitness center, maybe it would get his head where it needed to be.

4

Chapter 3
Zack

Why is anyone faced with their own mortality at the age of sixteen? Why are people put on this Earth for only a small period of time? It seems like they get the short end of the stick compared to others who live for eighty or ninety years. You can have someone who is the life of the party, always smiling, always laughing, always kind and caring to others and they will perish before their life even begins. Then, you'll have the world's biggest asshole, who is always hateful and goes out of their way to destroy others and that person will live for almost a hundred years. It's not fair.

The pitching machine hurled a ball at me, I focused and connected my bat with it. It soared into the net. My muscles tightened with the exertion, but my anger and frustration slowly melted away.

Ellie Colvin and I had dated briefly. She was my first girlfriend at Callatin Academy, which quickly sent me from untouchable to attainable. The female population at our elite private school were known for wanting what they couldn't have, for being able to conquer the guy who can't be settled down. The problem is, almost every girl is certain in order to get a boyfriend you have to sleep with them immediately. I don't share their belief. My thought is that if a girl is worth me spending time with, she'll hold out and make me work for the good stuff. Ellie was the first girl at Callatin who was adamant she wasn't going to sleep with me until she was ready, therefore I immediately asked for a second, third and fourth date before we were a couple. I didn't date her so I could eventually get the sex, I was intrigued by her. She was cute, shy and an adorable dork in a way, which is a total turn on for me. Little did I know, once we did sleep together she became a completely different girl and not in a bad way. I cared about her, but I was never in love with her and she knew it. She loved me and it hurt that I didn't feel the same way. More than anything, it frustrated her to know I was infatuated with someone else, with someone who I repeatedly claimed to be just a good friend; my roommate's little sister. It got to the point where she was extremely jealous anytime I talked to, or about, Jordan Donaldson. In the end, she gave me an ultimatum and I chose Jordan. Ellie was away at college and I was pretty certain she had found a boyfriend while she was there, not that she would ever admit it, but I really believe she gave me the ultimatum so she didn't feel as bad for cheating.

The machine shot another ball towards me and I swung again, this time missing. "Shit." I grumbled, feeling my back tweak at the forced motion. I closed my eyes, took a deep breath and shook my head. I cracked my neck and got back in my batting stance to await the next pitch.

Ellie and I had a good relationship if we were in bed and that was it. However, that didn't mean it didn't hurt like Hell when I learned she had died of alcohol poisoning. She had always been one to go with the herd, so it shouldn't have been a complete shock that she was at a frat party with people she thought were friends. Her death is being investigated because of drugs that were also found in her system, making it seem as if someone laced her drink and it ended badly. She was found the next day alone, dead in a shower, where she had passed out and never woke up.

Some people were calling it suicide, others were saying there was foul play. All I know is the last time I had talked to her I was a complete asshole and I felt horrible for it. My guilt was swallowing me whole. She had begged me to visit, pleaded for me to meet her at a hotel somewhere when she learned I was in St. Louis visiting Jordan in the hospital. I basically told her I wasn't interested in someone else's throw away, she had her chance and she decided she didn't want it. She got pretty pissed, obviously, and then began bad mouthing Jordan. I snapped, my best friend had been about to undergo surgery to remove cancer and I had a nasty feeling about it. Ellie had threatened to kill herself then and very last thing she said to me wasn't nice and it was on replay in my head.

Another ball, another swing and this one arched high, causing the net to fly up with the force. I'd feel much better about things if I could see the distance I was getting on these balls, it might help my ego a little anyway.

Ellie didn't deserve to die in such a sad way and my heart broke for her. Her death was messing with me, but it was the fate of Jordan which had me going insane. We'd known of her cancer before she even did, but were told it wasn't serious. It took her passing out and going into convulsions before we learned they were wrong about her prognosis. Luckily, Lance called in his Uncle who is a well known Surgeon. Dr. Bowman, with a pretty fantastic team of doctors, was able to remove the majority of the tumor, but not all. She had almost died after the surgery due to a rare complication, she was actually legally dead for almost a minute or more. She was now fighting for her life in a St. Louis hospital. They were filling her full of chemo, radiation and drugs which were to control her pain. She was barely able to eat, barely able to keep her eyes open. I needed to be there with her, but her father was adamant we weren't allowed. Mostly, he was certain I belonged in school and not in his daughter's hospital room. He claimed I was like a son to him, but he knew my reputation and didn't want me anywhere near her. It probably didn't help that she was borderline genius and I was dyslexic and barely getting by in most of my classes, plus I was a scholarship kid and he wanted better for his daughter.

He would be more than happy to allow Keller James, her actual boyfriend, at the hospital if he actually cared enough to make an effort to be there for her. On a daily basis, he couldn't give anyone an update on her health, because he didn't care. Keller was the richest guy at Callatin Academy, he was also one of the smartest. He was captain of the soccer team, a damn good baseball player, captain of the debate team and always on the Dean's list. Every teacher loved him, coaches dreamed of him and every girl threw themselves at him for the chance at a life of luxury. He had probably slept with more females at Callatin than me, which is a lot, and many of them while he's been with Jordan. However, I'm assuming he's only with Jordan because it makes the snobby, jealous girls here want him that much more. His popularity has definitely skyrocketed since Jordan showed interest. Since Jordan was admitted into the hospital he had maybe shown up three times, but you know he loved her and shit. He's got a steady girlfriend on the side and I would give anything to be able to rat him out and then beat the crap out of him, but that was something Jordan definitely didn't need at this point in time.

Jordan's ex-boyfriend, Lance Bowman, however, was constantly at the hospital. Mr. D had told him he needed to be at school, rather than at Jordan's bedside, but since Lance attended a different school, it didn't matter what he thought. Lance was extremely respectful when he told him he would be there until Jordan told him to get the Hell out. Apparently, Lance already had all of his credits and more to graduate and as long as he wasn't falling behind in his classes Mencino County High School was allowing him to communicate online with his teachers and homework. Lucky bastard. I was certain Keller didn't know Lance was at the hospital day in and day out, because he'd be livid. Maybe he did though and was just lying in wait for the moment he could use it against her and everyone else. After all, it's what he did best, he was as underhanded as they came.

I slammed another ball into the nets, dropped my bat and pulled my phone out of my back pocket. I smiled when I saw a text from Jordan.

"*I need out of this hospital.*"

"*I'm pretty certain you need to be there.*"

"*Pshh, I feel fantastic. I'm ready to take on the world. Want to take my car and bust me out? I've got really good drugs I'll share with you.*"

"*I wish I could baby. I'm on lockdown.*"

"*You suck. Lance won't do it either, just keeps promising we'll go off into the sunset as soon as his uncle says it's safe to.*"

"*Dr. Bowman knows what is best for you.*"

"*I want to be at the beach, not in this hospital bed. If I'm going to die, I don't want to be staring at these boring ass green walls.*"

"*You're not going to die. Please don't say that.*"

"*It could happen.*"

"*Not to you. It's not possible, you're a vampire lol.*"

"*I wish that were true. How are you?*"

"*Good☺*"

"*Liar. I've been told you're skipping classes and practices and not doing so to come visit me, which pisses me off.*"

"*I'm not allowed to visit during the school week, you know that. If I could, I'd be there with you every day.*"

"*Then why are you skipping?*"

"*Who ratted me out?*"

"*Not important. Why?*"

"*Not important.*"

"*Zack.*" Immediately, my phone began ringing and Jordan's gorgeous smile flashed across the screen.

"Calling to yell at me?" I joked.

"No." She whispered. "I can tell by your voice if you're lying to me, I can't tell that via text."

"I'm not lying."

"Zack, I know you don't care about school, but it's not like you to skip practices. What's going on?"

"Nothing."

"Is it Ellie?" Her voice quivered on the other end, my heart tugged and I fell onto a nearby bench. "You can talk to me, Zack."

"We got into a fight."

"Were you back together?"

"No, *absolutely not*." I responded a little too quickly. Jordan was quiet on the other end, waiting for me to go on. "We were still friends and would text every now and then. I think maybe she saw on Facebook we were in St. Louis and she messaged me to see what we were doing. Long story short, she wanted me to meet her at a hotel so we could hook up." I could hear Jordan swallow on the other end. I closed my eyes and took a deep breath, I didn't want to tell her any of this, but I needed to tell someone. "I told her I wasn't interested and she got pissed,

7

started accusing me of cheating on her when we were together, attacking my friends and well, it wasn't a pretty conversation."

"You were fighting about me, right?"

"No, we…"

"Don't lie." She interjected with a sigh.

"Yes."

"She changed when you two became a couple, I know she hated me."

"She was threatened by you, that was her issue and not yours."

"I know. I also know you never cheated on her. You're an amazing guy, Zack and it's a shame she couldn't see it."

"I hate that our last conversation was so ugly. What if, what if that was why she…what if it was suicide and…?"

"Zack." Jordan sighed weakly. "Don't give yourself so much credit. I realize your ego is humongous, but…" She giggled and I smiled finally. "I'm going to repeat to you, what you just said to me. If she committed suicide it was because of her issues, not you. If she were a happy person, happy with herself, then she would have been able to see how lucky she was to have you. Clearly, she had self-esteem issues to accuse you of cheating, to believe you and I were any more than friends. What happened is so incredibly sad and unreal, but in no way, is it your fault. Please realize she is responsible for her life, not you."

"When you put it that way…" I murmured. "It's hard to tell myself that, even if I know it deep down."

"That's why you have me." She laughed.

"And I'm lucky for that."

"It's frustrating though."

"I am?"

"No." She snorted. "I would give anything to be a normal girl right now, to be healthy and in school. *Ellie had that.* Here I am fighting for my life, being pumped full of poisons to save me and she willingly filled herself full of it and took her future from herself." My heart broke and tears rolled down my cheeks. I hadn't thought of it that way, but she was absolutely right. Jordan's future wasn't set in stone. She may kick cancer's ass and die from the harshness of the chemo on her organs or from a simple cold or flu. People fight daily with everything they have against diseases, unseen demons and some people give up, let go and take their own lives. I no longer felt sorry for Ellie, I was pissed at her for taking her life for granted when Jordan couldn't.

"J, I don't…I don't know what to say."

"Sorry, I didn't…"

"Don't apologize. It's amazing how differently people see situations, though. I was feeling sorry for myself, for Ellie and now I realize she doesn't deserve my pity."

"I feel sorry for her, if she did commit suicide." Jordan admitted. "She was obviously fighting something stronger than we know. Alcohol is a depressant and didn't help her situation, maybe at that time it seemed like the only way. If it was accidental, it's upsetting to think we're all so careless with our own lives that we believe we're invincible, but I can't say much. I was the same way before I found out about the cancer. I'm sure there were times we were lucky to make it home alive after drinking and driving, or that none of us have ever gotten alcohol poisoning or something. We're never careful or smart."

"You *did* almost die from someone else's carelessness."

"But it didn't teach me anything. I don't know, maybe if I survive this it won't teach me anything either."

"It has shown you who your true friends are, I'm pretty certain."

"Definitely." She murmured. "I never realized how lucky I was before, I guess. I have this amazing support system and Ellie really didn't."

"Ellie alienated her support system." I grumbled. "She changed when she left for school."

"Maybe she was struggling with things before and we just didn't realize it."

"I should have."

"Not necessarily. It's not like you two were close before. Sometimes, girls are so terrified of getting hurt they don't open themselves completely. We push people away, we may love someone completely and still convince ourselves we don't need that person because of the power they hold over our hearts."

"Speaking from experience?"

"No, I read a lot." I chuckled and wiped at my eyes. "And maybe a little experience."

"Is Lance there tonight?"

"Every night." Her voice was barely a whisper, but you could tell she was in awe of the fact that Lance Bowman was at her side constantly.

"I wish I could be too."

"I know, Zack. You text or call me daily when you don't have to, it says a lot."

"It doesn't to me."

"But it does to me." The same awe was there and my heart fluttered. "Will you be here this weekend? I miss you."

"Nothing will keep me away."

"Promise you'll stop skipping school and practices." She breathed softly. "My dad won't let you leave if you fall far behind."

"I'm not…"

"Zack, please don't insult me by lying. Maddie and Caleb will help, if you would let them. I will be pissed if you can't come see me because you can't get over yourself."

"Jordan…"

"If you skip again and do show up, I'll ban you from my room."

"You…"

"Don't test me." She hissed on the other line. "I love you, Zack and I don't want you to fail because you're too proud to ask for help. If you fail they'll ship you back to New York and I…I can't handle not having you here."

"I wouldn't go back to New York." I murmured. I wouldn't be able to leave her, especially not in her current condition. If I did get kicked out of Callatin, at least Mr. D couldn't tell me I wasn't allowed at the hospital during the school week.

"Regardless, promise me."

"Tough love suits you." I chuckled. "I promise. I'll get my shit together and ask for help."

"Thank you." She sighed. "You are capable of amazing things, but it's hard for us to see that for ourselves sometimes."

"I'm really glad you called."

"Did I help?"

"Absolutely." I heard a noise by the door, Caleb was walking in.

9

"Good, I feel pretty helpless and trapped here. At least I had purpose today."

"You always have purpose J, don't ever think differently."

"Okay, okay, I'll stop feeling sorry for myself." She giggled. It felt good to hear her voice, her laugh, it was something I missed tremendously. My stomach tightened, remembering how sick she was. "Is Caleb there?" I laughed out loud and shook my head.

"Why yes he is, were you a decoy?"

"No, I can read you better than you know."

"Interesting."

"It really is. I'll talk to you later. Please remember to call or text me if you need to talk."

"I will. Thanks, J."

"Bye." She ended the call and I stared at my phone for a few seconds before I looked up at Caleb.

Chapter 4
Caleb

I watched Zack carefully. It was obvious he was talking to my sister from the serene look on his face. He'd been agitated and jittery for a while, distant and unfocused. His eyes darted up to mine before he finished his conversation. The room was quiet for a minute, before I started towards him.

"I take it talking to Jo helped a little."

"Usually does." He shrugged. "Is Maddie going to pop through the door in five minutes?"

"No," I laughed. "I sent her a text telling her I found you and that Jo was taking care of it."

"Is she my mom or something?"

"Jo?"

"I don't go to class or practices and you call to rat me out? Did you think she would ground me or something?"

"I figured Jordan could get through to you." I mumbled as I fell down on the bleacher beside him. "We were worried."

"If I tell you I'm fine,"

"Bull shit. The word fine is the most misused word in the English language. If anything, it is a red flag for anyone close to a person when it's used. You may think you're fine, but you're not. Zack Bentley hates school, but wouldn't skip and jeopardize his baseball career. For you to be so careless, so nonchalant about your grades and sports is a huge indicator."

"I can handle…"

"Sometimes, Bentley, you don't have to acknowledge the hand up, but you definitely need to take it. We are your friends and we will do anything to keep you around longer."

"I don't…"

"Just stop, okay?" I rolled my eyes, leaned back against the wooden bleacher and crossed my arms in front of my chest. I cleared my throat and shook my head. "If you repeat this, I'll deny it until my dying day." Zack's eyes widened as he looked at me from the corner of his eye. "I love you, man. You're my best friend, you're like another brother to me. There are four people in this world that will absolutely send me to the looney bin if I ever lose them. Maddie, Jo, Ky and you are my family, my life and I can't imagine not having you guys a phone call away. My baby sister's future is teetering dangerously close to being nonexistent, I'm trying not to focus on that, but it's hard not to. I can't worry about you and Jordan too." My voice broke and before I could continue Zack spoke up.

"I know. I can't fathom how my life would be if my parents had never given me this opportunity."

"Or if dad never took the job." I mumbled. Zack forced a laugh before shaking his head.

"Pretty crazy thoughts." My friend stood and began picking his gear up, I soundlessly followed. "You may never have met Maddie."

"Jordan and I probably wouldn't be so close."

"A life without knowing Jordan." Zack stopped what he was doing and looked down at the ground. "Not a cool thought."

11

"Thanks for mentioning me." I scoffed.

"Sorry, dude, but your sister is way cooler." He was grinning from ear to ear and I had to laugh. I wouldn't argue, because he was right. Not to mention, my sister had pulled my best friend out of his funk and that's all we wanted.

"Someday you'll disagree with that statement."

"Doubt it." Zack and I continued cleaning up before we left and headed back to our dorm room. It was nice to have my friend back to his goofy self. Now, if only we could get Jo back to school and healthy, life would be perfect.

Chapter 5
Lance

"What are you smiling about?" I asked Jordan as I walked back into her hospital room. She looked up at me and shrugged her shoulders.

"I was talking to Zack." My stomach tugged enviously. I was normally not a jealous person, but that had all changed the day Jordan Donaldson walked into my life.

"Is he doing better?"

"He's struggling, but talking helped, I think. At least, he took pity on me and pretended it helped."

"He wouldn't lie to you." She nodded her head slowly, her bright blue eyes watching me carefully. "Are you hungry?" She shook her head and snuggled under her covers. "Cold?"

"Yeah." She mumbled embarrassedly. In ten minutes, she'd be sweating and I'd have to turn the thermostat down again. I crossed over to the wall, changed the temperature and went back to her bedside. "You don't have to be here, you know?"

"Do you want me to leave?" I asked with a raised eyebrow. We had this same conversation about four times a day. She shook her head and I leaned down to kiss her on the forehead. "Then I'm not leaving until you kick me out."

"Your mom…"

"Is fine without me. I'm keeping up with school, the guys have the farm covered and my family can survive with me here. You're my first priority."

"What if…what if your dad shows up?"

"He's in jail, he's not getting out anytime soon. The guys are at the farm until late with the chores and Coop's brother makes certain to do a patrol out there every night he's on duty." She nodded slowly, worry filling her face. "If I were worried about it, about him, I would be there."

"I would…if something happened again and…" I took her fragile hand in mine before I sat down on the bed facing her.

"If the bastard ever comes back, it won't be your fault. My mom has to be strong enough to tell him no, to not buy into his lies." She looked down at our laced fingers. My father was abusive, he had been for the majority of my life. My twin brother had gone more than one round with him physically, before he finally ran away. I was all that was left to take care of my mom, two sisters, my nephew and niece. I had been hospitalized more recently for standing up to him, trying to protect Jordan from the sick bastard. He had been arrested the last time he attacked me, my family and friends. He ran from the police and there was a manhunt through town for him, when they caught him he was charged with a DUI. He was released and hit my family head on, my sister and unborn niece were almost killed and he's been in prison ever since. There wasn't a threat of him coming back anytime soon, but it was definitely something that always sat in the back of my mind.

"It's probably not as easy as you may think it is." She mumbled quietly. I squeezed her hand. "To get out of an abusive relationship, I mean."

"I'm sure it's not." Jordan's phone rang and I noticed Keller's face pop up on the screen. My entire body tightened in anger. He was her boyfriend and rarely checked in with her, had only visited her a few times. She closed her eyes until the ringing stopped. "You could have answered." She shook her head. I was grateful she hadn't answered it, but I had no right to voice my opinion on her life really.

"I'm tired." I pushed myself off her bed and felt her tug me towards her. "Please lay with me." I nodded eagerly, slid off my boots and climbed in beside her. "Thank you." I wrapped my arms around her, felt her scoot closer and place her head on my chest. She sighed peacefully as I rubbed her back slowly. It was only a few minutes before she was snoring softly.

I had met Jordan Donaldson on a camping trip in Tennessee. She was with her dad and brothers and I was with my friends. Our campsites were next to each other. I'd seen her from afar throwing horseshoes with her family, something about her melodic giggle wrapped around me and caught my attention. We were headed to the boat ramp when I heard her call for help. Well, I guess I didn't know it was her, but when you hear a female yell for help, you go. She wasn't in danger, just having problems reeling in her first fish. I immediately offered assistance without asking. The second our skin touched, I felt a zap of energy hit me and knew, I just knew she was trouble. She got up in the middle of the night to go to the bathroom and I asked her to join us while we celebrated my best friend Coop's birthday. We talked all night, never missing a beat. She told us she was from Texas and I walked away devastated that I'd never see her again. She was all I thought about, even months later.

My oldest sister got married and as my friends and I arrived at the reception, I came up behind a gorgeous auburn haired girl. It was Jordan. I couldn't believe my luck, couldn't believe my Texas angel was here in Illinois. She was the lead singer of the band my sister, Jenna, had hired to perform. If she wasn't singing, I was glued to her. She almost got away before I could catch her again. Her and her bandmate, Izzy, came back to a house party with us and I was enthralled. I had to touch her, to kiss her, to have her close to me at all times. She stayed the night, just hanging out with us and I took her virginity. And then she was gone. I had no way of getting a hold of her, I didn't get her phone number and couldn't remember her last name. I did everything I could to find her, knowing I needed her permanently in my life. It wasn't until a football game with our rival, Callatin Academy, where I found her in a cheerleading uniform and I was gone. We were a couple immediately, inseparable when we were able to be. We'd been through Hell, mostly because of my idiocy. I basically handed her right over to the asshole boyfriend, Keller James.

She was my first love, she'll be my only love. I need her more than I need food or water. I was acting as a friend right now, but I had every intention of winning her back. I may not deserve the girl in my arms, but I sure as Hell wanted her more than anything I'd ever wanted in my life.

Chapter 6

My phone vibrated in my pocket and I maneuvered enough to see one of my best friend's, Chopper, was texting me. I looked down at Jordan to make sure I hadn't woke her up, she was still sleeping soundly.

"How's our girl?"

"Sleeping. She's pretty wiped."

"We all plan on coming up Friday."

"I know, pretty sure she expects it. Lol"

"How are you doing?"

"Good, worried about her."

"Don't drive yourself crazy, she's going to get through this. She's a tough girl."

"It's hard not to think of the worst."

"And that is what will drive you crazy. At least you're there with her every day."

"I'm just grateful she wants me here."

"You're damn lucky she loves you. Lol"

"You don't even know, Chop."

"Oh, but I do. Will you text me when she wakes up later? I want to call and talk to her, check in."

"Absolutely. Thanks, bud."

The bond Jordan had formed with my close knit group of friends was amazing. Just like me, they all fell in love with her immediately. Throughout all the crap I've pulled, they've been there calling me on my BS and telling me how stupid I am for letting her go. Given the chance, I'm pretty sure any of them would snatch her away if they could. My cousin Drew was constantly trying and my girl repeatedly blew him off. My friends loved her, my family adored her and I was too stupid and proud to be honest with her. Every time I've let her go, it's damn near killed me but I had to protect her.

I watched her sleep and held her tightly. She snuggled into me and I felt her lips brush against my Adam's apple. I closed my eyes and relished the gesture. I kissed the top of her head as she sighed. I started praying again, because really I couldn't do that enough. I hated seeing her in so much pain, so exhausted and worried all the time. I would give anything to be able to switch places with her, to take it all away. She was too good to deserve any of this torture, she was too perfect for me. Our bond had strengthened throughout all of this, because we were away from the reality of our lives. I wasn't stupid enough to believe it would remain the same the second she was cleared from the hospital, until then though, I would do everything I could to prove my love to her.

Chapter 7
Chopper

"How's Jo?" Coop asked as he walked up behind me in the Bowman's barn.

"Sleeping." I answered with a roll of my shoulders. "Bo says she's pretty wiped."

"And going stir crazy."

"Pretty much." I chuckled. "I think the fence is broke down in the south patch."

"Yeah, Rob thought so too. He's headed out there now."

"He shouldn't have gone alone."

"I mentioned that. He has his phone, said he'll be fine."

"His phone won't do anything if Mr. Bowman is there." Rob was Jenn's husband, he knew the history of abuse in the family but I don't think he truly understood it. If he did, he wouldn't trust a jail cell to hold such a despicable man and he certainly wouldn't underestimate him.

"He's not getting out of jail anytime soon."

"Maybe not legally."

"I think about that all the time." Coop sighed as he went back to cleaning out the horse stall next to me. "It seems too good to be true that Bo and his family can live in peace finally."

"I wish there was a way to let Luke know."

"If he cared, he'd be back already."

"He cares." I growled. "Sometimes you have to take yourself out of a bad situation before it consumes you and you become it."

"And leave your family behind to fend for themselves?"

"He knew Lance could handle it." Coop shook his head and concentrated on his work. I was pissed at Luke Bowman for running away like a coward and leaving his family grieving and wondering. If I ever saw him again I'd punch him square in the nose for the pain he's put his mother through. It's been over a year and she still hangs Missing Person posters every Sunday after church. Her face lights up and falls just as quickly each time her phone rings, each time a car comes down the driveway. Lance will never admit, never let it show like his mom does, but he has the same reactions as well. Unlike my friends though, I understood why he left like he did.

"Rob said they lost their ass on the harvest." Coop mumbled. "They didn't get it in soon enough and Mr. Bowman ruined a lot."

"I know. Lance was worried about it, but I don't think they've told him yet."

"He doesn't need anything else to worry about right now. Do you think they'll be okay?"

"Hopefully the insurance was up to date. I'm pretty certain Mrs. Bowman has prepared for this though."

"I hope so. I feel like we should do something though. Lance needs to concentrate on Jo and nothing else. He's driving himself crazy as it is, adding this stuff to it won't help."

"Well aware." I murmured. "Mom's trying to get some info, see if we need to do anything." Cooper nodded.

"Surely if they were hurting for money she wouldn't be paying us."

"Yes, yes she would. Mrs. Bowman would sell everything to make certain we got paid for our work."

"If I realize she's selling stuff, I'll quit and sneak in at night to work." I laughed out loud and nodded. It didn't matter how many times we told Mrs. Bowman, or her daughters, that we didn't need to be paid for helping out on the farm, they refused to listen. The money was nice, but it wasn't why we were all doing it. With Mr. Bowman in jail, Lance always at the hospital it only left Rob to do the work and he couldn't do it alone. The hired hands weren't always reliable and the ones who were, should have retired a decade ago.

"Have you thought about what happens if Jo isn't better by graduation?"

"Then Lance won't enlist with us."

"He already signed the papers."

"He'll have to be medically cleared because of the accident. If she's still sick he will find a doctor who won't clear him. I know that without a doubt."

"I've always thought it would be the six of us in boot camp together, serving our country as a brotherhood. Drew bailed and Luke, wherever the Hell he is. I feel like if Lance can't...it won't be the same.'

"I never thought Drew was cut out for the military." I chuckled. "So, I'm not surprised. Lance won't back out unless Jordan isn't better. I sometimes think we'll show up at boot camp and Luke will be there too. He took our pact seriously, I can't imagine he wouldn't follow through."

"He took his family seriously too." Coop growled. I let the comment slide. We all were at different places with our emotions towards Luke's disappearance. I had realized I couldn't change what he did, I wasn't happy with him but I couldn't let it consume me. Drew and Coop were pissed off beyond words. Drew and Luke were inseparable though and the fact that Luke hadn't even hinted his plans to his cousin, had Drew reeling with hurt and rage. Sawyer had never been pissed off about it, I think he always kind of foresaw something like this happening. We've all know of the abuse throughout that family, so none of us really should have been surprised that one of them fought back and then took off. There were many times I woke up wondering if Mrs. Bowman got fed up, packed up the kids and disappeared into the night. Mostly, I always half wished she would. I would miss them like crazy, they were my extended family, but no one deserves that miserable, terrifying life.

"I think we're done for the day." I announced. Coop looked around and nodded his head, just as Rob walked into the barn, covered in mud.

"It's flipping cold out there boys." The tall, stocky blonde pulled his gloves off and rubbed his hands together before he began putting his tools up. "The fence is fixed though."

"Did we lose any?"

"Doesn't look like it, but there's too many to count." I chuckled and nodded in agreement. "You hear from Lance? How's Jordan?"

"Same, tired and miserable."

"How's he doing?"

"Worrying incessantly. He's driving himself crazy."

"He needs a break."

"I told him that too. He won't take one. He leaves to take a shower, get a change of clothes and check in, but that's about it. I'm surprised he hasn't started using the facilities there. He's terrified of leaving her and something happening."

"The whole thing sucks. Why should a child have to deal with a life threatening illness? Why should a seventeen year old guy be worried about his girlfriend's future, about his family, their livelihood? You guys should be freaking out over tests and curfews. Your biggest concern should be who the DD is for the next weekend or who you're taking to prom. This shit is for adults, not teenagers." Rob growled. "This is all bull shit."

"I couldn't agree more." I admitted. "They should be concerned about life after high school, not life in general."

"Lance has always had to be the adult though." Coop interjected. "But Jordan, it just doesn't…" He shook his head and looked down at the ground. "I can't even imagine having to deal with what she is. She is stronger than I ever realized."

"That's for sure." I agreed.

"Any more updates on her prognosis?"

"Just that she's healing well, she's responding to the treatment and they're taking things one day at a time."

"Which is a bull shit answer."

"Pretty much. I think Drew's dad is just terrified to give a better answer. If he tells us things don't look good, his whole family will hate him. If he blows sunshine up our ass and something goes wrong, they'll hate him again."

"Lance and Alicia definitely put him in a tight spot."

"I'm pretty sure if anyone else had taken her case though, she wouldn't be here." I shrugged. "The surgery saved her life, not to mention afterwards when she…died and he…I can't help but think other surgeons would have let her go. He brought her back and did everything possible to find out what happened and fixed the issue. He has saved her life twice now."

"You're right. I guess it's a good thing to have a close family." Rob nodded. "I guess I should get home and give Jenn a break."

"Give her a hug for us." I patted him on the back and watched as he hurried to the shower stalls Mrs. Bowman had installed in the garage so no one tracked mud and poop throughout her house.

"Bet he never imagined doing this after high school." Coop cracked as he shook his head. He started putting things away and I followed suit.

"I don't think he minds. It is how he and Jenn met."

"Yeah, but when he applied for the fall job I don't think he thought it would last this long."

"Or that he'd meet his wife here."

"Just like the country song." Coop laughed, as did I. "Isn't it crazy to think how one moment in our lives can determine everything?"

"What do you mean?"

"Well, if Rob never applied for the job would he and Jenn be married, would Ella exist? If we wouldn't have kidnapped Lance to go on the camping trip, would Jordan be in our lives right now?"

"If Drew and Lance weren't related, would we all be so close?"

"Yeah." Coop shook his head and looked around. "Think about it, Alicia said they found Jordan's tumor when they were performing surgery after the accident. If Jordan wouldn't have showed up at the party, if they hadn't left at the exact moment they did, if they hadn't been in that exact spot hashing things out then Jordan could have dropped dead, without any warning or chance."

"I try not to think about those things, it'll make us crazy."

"Probably why I haven't been sleeping well."

"Most likely." I chuckled. "I go back to that day in the hospital constantly. She was dead. Could you imagine our lives without Jordan in it?"

"Absolutely not. It's weird how we've all been friends forever and we're really bad about not letting others into our group. Jordan is different though. Even when her and Lance have been apart, she was still there, you know? Lance wouldn't survive losing her, I know that without a doubt. I honestly don't know if any of us could handle Jordan dying."

"You know she's something special if she holds such a big place in our hearts in such a short amount of time."

"I worry about things ending badly between her and Lance." Coop admitted. I nodded my head. Jordan was the only girl pal I had, she was easily my best friend. Considering Lance was like a brother as the rest of these knuckleheads were, it was a pretty big title for her to hold already. I wanted to beat the Hell out of Lance a dozen times for the crap he's pulled on Jo. She deserved better than he was giving her, but when he finally gave all of himself to her, it would be an amazing thing. A relationship everyone would envy. "He doesn't exactly have the best reputation with girls."

"That was how he dealt with Luke disappearing, with the problems at home." I shrugged nonchalantly. "Jo is different."

"She is, but sometimes I worry he doesn't see the same thing we do."

"He does. The problem with being told you're worthless all your life is that eventually you start to believe it. He doesn't think he's good enough for her."

"He's not." Cooper chortled. "At all. It doesn't mean she doesn't make him a better person. They're truly one of those couples you just know are meant to be together."

"Which sucks for the rest of us."

"Right? Pretty sure Drew kicks himself repeatedly over that."

"I'm certain he does, but I'm positive she wouldn't have given him much of a chance."

"Do you think she knows how much we love her?"

"She does, but it doesn't hurt to show and tell her often." Coop nodded his head and the two of us walked out of the barn and towards the showers.

"I called to tell your parents you were eating here tonight." Mrs. Bowman called out the door. I laughed. She was too good to us.

"You don't have to feed us."

"Yes I do." She gasped as if I offended her. "I normally have a full house for dinner, with farmhands and the boys and…" She trailed off sadly. "I tend to overcook. Please stay."

"We wouldn't turn down your home cooking for nothing, Mrs. Bowman." Coop interjected. "We are extremely grateful and hungry." Her face lit up and she looked like a young girl again. It had been a really long time since I'd seen a genuine smile come from her.

Coop and I went for the shower stalls. It had been a long day, a long week. My body hurt from the long, exhausting days we were putting in on the Bowman farm, but I wouldn't be anywhere else right now. The Bowman's would do anything for me and I would do the same for them.

Chapter 8
Jordan

Ensconced in Lance Bowman's strong arms is literally the best way to wake up. This would all end badly, but for now, I didn't care. My body was mush, my stomach felt like it was on fire and there was a constant metallic taste in my mouth. I wanted to go back to sleep just so all the pain and fear would disappear for a short time, but I hurt too much.

"The nurse brought your pain meds in, but she didn't want to wake you." Lance mumbled.

"How did you know I was awake?" I giggled quietly.

"You stopped snoring."

"I don't snore." I gasped.

"Yes, yes you do." His whole body rumbled with laughter. "It's not loud, just really cute."

"Snoring isn't cute."

"It is when it comes from you."

"Shut up." I sighed as I rolled my eyes and tried to push away from him. He laughed again and removed himself from my bed. I instantly felt the loss and closed my eyes to cover my sadness.

"Do you need a pain pill?"

"I wish I could say no."

"It's nothing to be ashamed of."

"I wish I could say no, because I wish I wasn't fighting this crap." I mumbled. "Why did…" Lance rushed to my side and engulfed me in a hug.

"None of it makes sense. It's definitely not fair, but questioning it will do nothing but make things worse. You have to be strong."

"I have no other choice, but to be strong." I sighed tearfully. "But what if I'm tired of being strong and fighting?"

"Then I'll be strong for you. I can't fight as well as you, but…" My heart absolutely melted into a puddle in the floor as more tears rolled down my cheeks.

"I hate you for saying that." I forced a laugh and let him hug me tighter.

"Sorry?" He chuckled before he pulled away. "You've got a full crew coming in for visiting rotation today. Maddie will be up in a second to help you with a shower."

"They don't have to ruin their weekends by coming here."

"Ruin? Really? They all love you, darlin' and they would be here daily if they could."

"I know. Can't you let me be a drama queen or something for one second?"

"Do you really believe it's ruining their weekends?" Lance roared with laughter.

"They all have better things they could be doing."

"Jo, if they had other things to do they would be doing them. They would trade…"

"Lance, I know." I mumbled. "I don't understand it, but I'm grateful for every one of them." He nodded and leaned over to kiss the top of my head. "It's pretty crazy that people who barely know me have been here constantly and yet my supposed boyfriend is nowhere to be found." I immediately regretted my words, bringing up Keller James was an asshole move. "Sorry, I…"

"Don't apologize. Unfortunately, he is technically your boyfriend." Lance sighed as he pulled away. "However, I'm pretty sure everyone here knows you better than he does." I nodded in agreement and reached out for Lance.

"You've been relieved of your hovering duties for the time being, Bowman." Maddie announced with a grin as she floated into my room. Lance chuckled, I dropped my hand unnoticed and looked down at the bed embarrassedly. I shouldn't be relying on him so much, it was going to hurt too badly when he broke my heart again.

"Hovering." He scoffed, she giggled and dismissed him with a wave of her hand. "I guess I'm being kicked out." He winked at me before he kissed me on the top of the head again. "You'll be okay?"

"Yeah." I murmured. He looked at me sadly for a second before he nodded and walked out of the room.

"Don't worry, J, he never goes far." Maddie smiled sweetly as she went to my overnight bag with clean clothes, grabbed some out and turned to look at me. "How you feeling?"

"Sore. Tired." I shrugged. "But my public awaits, right?"

"You don't have to take visitors." She sighed as she came closer to my bed. "You resting and getting better is all that is important right now. If you're too tired…"

"I'm fine, Maddie."

"Are you sure? I have no problem telling people to go away." I chuckled and shook my head.

"I'm sure…I'm going stir crazy. I look forward to today for just this reason." I also dreaded it for the simple fact that I would be absolutely drained by the time the day was over, but I would never admit it. Maddie smiled back at me as she put my clothes down and came to help me up.

Chapter 9

"Stop making me laugh, it hurts." I begged two hours later. I clutched my stomach as I continued to roar with laughter as Chopper reenacted a story of a camping trip he and Lance took where they'd fallen into a creek, gotten swept into a current scared for their lives, only to find out if they could get their footing the water wasn't very high. The most comical part was Chopper's imitation of Lance. "It hurts too badly."

"Is there a party going on in here or what?" Keller asked as he strutted into my room carrying a vase of gorgeous red roses. No one responded, everyone looked at him as if we were all sharing the same nightmare.

"What are you doing here?" I asked a little more rudely than I'd intended when I finally remembered I had a voice.

"Hey babe. How are you?" He put the vase on my bedside table as he bent down and touched my face gently. "I've missed you." He ignored the rest of the people in the room as he tipped my chin up and kissed me hungrily. When I pulled away quickly, I could only stare at him in muted stupor. He dismissed me with a smug grin as he plopped down on the side of my bed as if he'd been here throughout everything. "I thought there was a limit to visitors in the room. Aren't you breaking a fire code or something?"

"Keller." I began, my voice barely above a whisper.

"Why don't you losers bail out so I can spend time with my girlfriend?"

"Girlfriend?" Zack chuckled humorlessly, his eyes narrowed in disgust as he stood up slowly. "You suddenly remember that?"

"Fuck off." Keller aimed a warning glare at his roommate, but Zack barely noticed as he took another step towards my supposed boyfriend.

"Who the Hell are you to come in here…?"

"Zack." Maddie interjected as she stood up and placed a hand on our friend's arm. "*Now* is not the time." Zack's eyes flicked to her quickly and he noticeably calmed, but he didn't back down.

"Can you guys…?" I began, just as Wyatt came bounding into the room.

"Jordan!" The little brown haired boy's blue eyes danced excitedly as he carried in some of his artwork for me. Lance immediately shot out of the chair and intercepted his nephew before he could pounce on me.

"Jordan is sore, remember?" Lance asked as he scooped Wyatt up into his arms.

"You can't explode anymore?" He queried innocently. I shook my head and giggled while he cocked his head to the side. "Does your tummy still hurt? Can I give you a hug now?"

"Of course you can." I gripped the bedrails and moved myself over a bit before I patted the side of the bed. "You can sit by me if you want to."

"I don't think that's a good idea."

"I wouldn't have offered if I didn't think he'd be fine, Lance."

"Okay." He sighed exasperatedly. Lance looked back at Wyatt as he held him in his arms. "You have to be very careful, okay? If you move too much you could hurt her."

Wyatt shook his head eagerly as Lance set him down gingerly next to me in bed. The little boy handed me the two Scooby-Doo pages he had colored for me. He'd scribbled I love you across the top. I hugged the little boy and smiled back at him. Suddenly, he looked over at Keller and shot him a dirty look.

"Who are you?" He asked rudely.

"Jordan's boyfriend."

"No, *I* am Jordan's boyfriend." He stated before he looked back at me with puppy dog eyes.

"He's just for show, Wyatt. You're my *real* boyfriend." I answered as I half hugged him again. The little boy's face lit up and he seemed comforted by my answer.

"Don't lie to the little brat." Keller retorted snottily. My eyes grew wide as the entire room gasped in collective shock.

"Are you kidding me?" I hissed as I put my arm around Wyatt and hugged him close to me. "Name calling?"

"What is he even doing here? I thought there was an age limit. Why is he in my seat?"

"You're seriously jealous of a four year old?" Maddie asked drily from the corner. Keller paid her no attention as he waited for my reply.

"Jordan." Keller growled. I could not believe he was challenging a four year old. I was stupefied. Wyatt was the only one in the room who wasn't shocked.

"Is he bothering you, Jordan?" Wyatt asked as he reached up and patted my arm. "My girlfriend just had surgery and she doesn't need to be upset. You should leave." My mouth dropped open and I heard a snicker from the corner as Chopper hurried out of the room. Keller flicked an annoyed glance at Wyatt, but his angry eyes quickly came back to me. Wyatt got off the bed, walked over to where Keller was sitting and crossed his arms in front of his chest.

"You should leave. *My* Jo doesn't like you and you're making her upset. Leave." Wyatt puffed up and looked about four feet taller. Keller rolled his eyes.

"Buzz off, Squirt." Wyatt's face reddened as he pulled back and kicked Keller in the shin as hard as he possibly could. My boyfriend lunged and Wyatt stared him down.

"You little bastard." Keller hissed through clenched teeth as he clutched his leg. "I will kill you."

"You will not touch him." I spit. Keller spun around on his heel and glared at me. "Get the Hell out of here now." Keller shook his head. "I'm calling…"

"What's all the noise about in here?" Sonia, my nurse and one of the most gorgeous black women I've ever seen in my life, asked as she hurried into the room. Her eyes immediately went to Keller and she shook her head in disgust.

"I want him out of my room."

"Sure thing, honey." Sonia smiled as she gestured for Keller to go towards the door.

"You can't be serious. The little jerk kicked me, how was I supposed to react?"

"I don't know, like an adult? Or maybe just not like a stuck up ass wipe?" Keller's green eyes hardened. He nodded his head once, swallowed any words that were about to come out and followed the nurse out of the room. Once he was gone, I opened my arms and Wyatt hurried into them.

"Are you okay, buddy?" I breathed. "I'm so sorry."

"I took care of him." Wyatt hugged me tightly, not one inch of fear in the little guy. I pulled back and laughed.

"You're a trip, Wy. Where'd you learn that from?"

"Uncle Lance." He shrugged nonchalantly as he grinned proudly. "He protects mama and nana and you. He says you have to take care of your women, so I did." I fell back onto my pillow in a fit of laughter, the rest of the room roared as well. Wyatt just shrugged and climbed back beside me in the bed. I caught Lance's eye and saw that he was conflicted with anger at Keller and pride in Wyatt. I was having the same issues.

Mrs. Bowman quickly went to fussing over me like I were her own daughter, eager to bring her son's emotions within rein.

"Are you comfortable, sweetheart?" Mrs. Bowman asked sweetly. I nodded my head and smiled back at her. "Your bag is almost full, I'll let your nurse know." She scurried out of the room before I could respond.

"I seriously love her." I murmured as I looked over at Lance.

"Pretty sure the feeling is mutual." He chuckled. He noticeably relaxed, but his eyes darted to the door continuously.

"You ready for your meds?" Sonia asked as she floated back into my room. I looked around nervously, but nodded my head.

"Wyatt why don't you say bye to Jo, Nana said she was about ready to leave." Lance interjected. The little boy pouted, but did as he was asked.

"If that weirdo bothers you again, let me know." He whispered. I giggled, nodded my head and hugged him tightly. If only it were that easy. Everyone else cleared out of the room, leaving Zack behind with me.

"You don't…"

"You shouldn't be alone." He interjected. I was grateful, even though I didn't want him to witness my puking any more than he had to. Sonia checked my vitals, before she started messing with the bags and lines attached to me.

"What is your pain rating?"

"Twenty." I murmured, her smile turned into a frown before she checked my morphine drip.

"I'll be right back, baby." I nodded as she hurried out. Keller appeared in the doorway looking chagrinned.

"I apologized to the kid." He mumbled. "I was out of line."

"You think?" I rolled my eyes and glanced over at Zack.

"Leave Bentley, I want some alone time with my girlfriend."

"I didn't realize Sage was here." Zack retorted. Keller growled and took a step forward.

"Keller, knock it off." Sonia came back in the room with my pain meds and shot Keller a dirty look. "I don't feel like dealing with you right now."

"Out, now." Zack growled as he took a step towards Keller. The look they exchanged spoke volumes, but the two of them walked out. Zack turned to look at me sadly. "I'll get Lance to come in."

"Why in the…?" Keller hissed, his words were cut off and Sonia chuckled.

"I don't like to speak out of turn, but I really don't understand how that kid fits in with your group of friends."

"He's supposedly my boyfriend."

"You can do a Hell of a lot better." She smiled. "Lance is here constantly and…"

"Has been amazing." I finished with a sigh. He walked into my room and immediately went to the bathroom to get a cold washcloth for me. Sonia waited for him to return, before she injected the narcotic into my I.V. As the medicine took its toll, I was grateful to have Lance by my side. I may be repeating myself, a lot, but his constant presence was helping me in so many different ways.

24

Chapter 10

"I'm going to walk mom and Wyatt out. Will you be okay?" Lance asked nervously as he gently moved the hair out of my face. I was pretty drowsy, the medicine pulling me under quickly. I nodded my head. He bent down, kissed my forehead and smiled back at me. "I'll be right back, darlin'." I closed my eyes and heard him shuffle out of the room.

"It is absolute bull shit that I have to fight a crowd to see my girlfriend." Keller hissed from beside my bed.

"Girlfriend?" I laughed as I rolled my eyes inwardly. "If I were your girlfriend, this wouldn't be the first time in weeks that you've popped in for a visit."

"Probably because I don't want to deal with the Pathetic Patrol out there. Lance Bowman used you, cheated and…"

"Speaking of cheating, as if I've never walked in to find Sage on top of you." Keller took a step back, his eyes narrowed angrily.

"You're delusional. I would never…"

"Oh shut up! I've been told repeatedly that you're screwing around *and* I've witnessed it. I'm not an idiot, Keller. Do you really think so little of me that you believe I am clueless when you lock yourself in the bedroom with Sage or another of your groupies while I'm in the living room studying?"

"You're so pathetic." He hissed as he took a step forward, leaned down until he was inches from my face. He grabbed my hand in a death grip. "What kind of dumb bitch doesn't say a word when her boyfriend is in the next room screwing everyone but her? If you weren't so hard up for the loser plow boy I wouldn't have to look elsewhere. Do you really believe Bowman isn't doing the same thing while his friends run interference? You're an ugly, fat bitch trying to sleep her way to the top and you don't even know what you're doing. You're a dead lay. A…"

"Maybe if you were better…" I began, Keller grabbed a handful of my hair and yanked to shut me up. It worked. A wicked smile crossed his face as he balled up his fist and gently touched my stomach. He moved my shirt up, his knuckles brushing the bandage covering my healing incision site.

"I come to see you and you're cuddled up in bed with Lance Bowman as if he is something special. *You* are trash. *He* is trash. You've been fucking that bastard the whole time we've been together and you have the nerve to accuse *me* of infidelity." Tears rolled down my cheeks as he kept a vise grip on my hair, his other hand slowly adding pressure to my stomach before he was issuing as much force as possible. "He's only here for the pity sex he gets when he leaves. As soon as you die, he'll forget you ever existed." My head was throbbing and I made a noise, a grab for my call button. He chuckled as he blocked me from it, grabbed my other hand and sat on both of them, leaving both of his hands free. One covered my mouth and the other went back to my hair. "You are *my* girlfriend and have been for a long time, I'm not going to let you throw that away because the farm boy is pretending to be interested. I own you and I will not hand you over to that…" I bit his hand as hard as I could. "You fucking bitch." His tone changed to quiet and crazy, but he pulled away from me like I wanted. He was still blocking my call button. I closed my eyes, gathered all my strength and courage. I wanted to yell for my brother, for Zack or Lance but I also didn't want to bring them into the vindictive, narcissistic

25

world of Keller James. If they rescued me from him, he would focus on ruining their lives. "You deserve to die and the day it happens I will stand over your body and spit on your ungrateful, un…"

"We both know I am not your girlfriend." My voice was weak and Keller grinned proudly, as if he were winning.

"What in the Hell does that mean?"

"You lied to me and took advantage of my amnesia. I am not your girlfriend."

"Yes, you are." He spit, he reached down and grabbed my hand in a death grip again. I didn't even open my eyes. "You belong to me until I say otherwise."

"If you were my boyfriend this wouldn't be your third trip to visit me, as I said earlier. I almost…"

"Every time I come to visit you're snuggled up to the fucking farm boy. Do you have any idea how bad that hurts?"

"I'd answer with probably as bad as it hurts finding you and Sage in bed together." Keller's grip tightened to the point that I felt my fingers pop. "But I stopped caring. We're not a couple anymore."

"How…"

"I don't know why you won't let me go."

"I love you."

"No, you don't."

"Don't tell me…"

"Keller." I sighed.

"I will end you, Jordan. I will make your life Hell, I will ruin you at Callatin. You…" I burst out laughing and his hands went to my throat. I wasn't stopping.

"Newsflash Keller, in case you haven't noticed my life is Hell right now. I may never even return to Callatin, so who the fuck cares? I am fighting an invisible monster on a daily basis, you no longer scare me. You *can't* scare me anymore than I already am. I fear for my life every second of every day. Nothing you can threaten or do to me will compare to the Hell I live daily." Keller's eyes flashed dangerously as his thumb put pressure on my windpipe. "Leave, I am not your girlfriend anymore."

"You…"

"Is there a problem in here?" My Uncle asked as he took a step inside. He was as intimidating as Caleb and Kyler were, especially since he was wearing a police uniform. Keller barely moved, didn't remove his grip.

"Leave. There is no problem with me talking to my girlfriend."

"My niece asked you to leave." Calen asked taking a step towards us. I was fighting for air, Keller could kill me right now while my uncle stood five feet away completely clueless. I gripped the bedrail and started thrashing my legs.

"What the…?" Keller hissed as he let go. "Stop playing games."

"You need to walk out of this room, right now." Calen growled as he grabbed Keller by the shoulder and spun him around. Keller gasped and pulled back.

"Weird resemblance, huh?" I chuckled breathlessly. "Please leave, Keller."

"I believe my niece asked you to leave."

"It's a stupid game she plays. She's an actress and gets her kicks off making people…"

26

"I know what I saw. I also know the marks on her throat and hand are indicative of force, so unless you want me to escort you out of here in handcuffs I suggest you leave and never come near Jordan again."

"This isn't over." Keller whispered.

"I believe it is."

"Keller! What in the Hell is taking you so long?" Sage whined as she appeared in my doorway. "I hate hospitals, they smell horrible. You said it would only take a second."

"Sage." Keller pulled away from my uncle as if he were no longer crazy.

"I thought you were doing an obligatory pop in with Jordan, who is this freak?" Keller burst out laughing and I rolled my eyes. She's such a classy girl.

"You're hilarious, Sage." Keller grinned. "It's Jordan." Her eyes widened and then she began cackling.

"Yikes, you look like shit, which is nothing new." She looked back at Keller. "Can we please leave, I'm afraid I'll catch a disease from one of these freaks?"

"We can't get that lucky." Zack spit as he pushed into the room, careful not to get too close to Sage. Her voice immediately changed.

"Zacky, what are you doing here?" She took a step towards him, reaching out and not noticing he was avoiding her. "Why haven't you returned my calls or texts?" She pouted as she tried to put a hand on his arm. "Are you going to the concert with us?"

"Absolutely not." Keller hissed as he took a step towards Zack and Sage. "Sorry it took so long, Jordan isn't accepting me dumping her." I almost choked. Sage cackled loudly again.

"It's about time you ditched her." She flipped her fake blonde hair over her shoulder before looking at Zack. "Call me later."

"Not likely." Zack retorted. Keller grabbed Sage's hand and ripped her out of the room.

"It's so refreshing to know I don't have to deal with these lowlife bastards anymore." Keller spit loudly once they were in the hallway. Tears filled my eyes, not out of sadness, but pure relief.

"You okay?" Calen asked quietly, his eyes imploring mine. I nodded and looked away quickly.

"You dumped him?" Zack gasped, a grin filling his gorgeous face. I nodded again and looked at the door, waiting for Keller to return with a vengeance, or a machine gun. "Finally." I closed my eyes and inhaled deeply.

"That was your boyfriend?" Uncle Calen asked. "I thought…"

"It's complicated." I mumbled. His eyes flitted between Zack and me questioningly, but he didn't push and I was grateful. I was too embarrassed that he had somewhat witnessed me allowing Keller to hurt me, I would die if anyone else knew. Tears pricked at my eyes, my chest felt heavy and my breathing was still trying to regulate. I grabbed my morphine button, hitting it numerous times in hopes the pain throughout my body would go away soon. I was relieved Keller was gone, but I could feel the panic knocking on my door. It was too easy, I couldn't delude myself into believing it was all over.

Chapter 11
Zack

I couldn't believe she finally did it, finally cut Keller James out of her life. It almost seemed unreal. I watched Jordan carefully, she looked as if she were a mix of emotions and I didn't know if they were good or bad. I took a step towards her, needing to pull her into a hug, but I stopped.

"You okay?"

"Absolutely." She sighed, inhaling again before she opened her eyes and flashed a smile.

"Meds kick in?" I chuckled, she giggled and shook her head. She was acting, trying to throw me off any emotions tugging on her.

"I'm just glad it's over." She sighed. I watched her carefully, needing so badly to tell her everything I've been practicing since the day we met.

"You know…"

"Tell me I'm not imagining things." Chopper interrupted as he barreled into the room. "Did I hear the asshole correctly? Are you single?"

"Am I?"

"Hell no, this is the break I was waiting for! I won't let anyone swipe you from me ever again." Chopper grinned as he rushed to her side. "Let's go, Princess. I'm taking you to a beach somewhere." He was joking, I think, but I envied his approach. I wish I had the balls to just announce my feelings and whisk her off into the sunset. If she didn't feel the same way about me it would make everything extremely awkward and possibly ruin our friendship, he apparently didn't have that same fear.

"Please don't tease me." Her voice broke and we both looked at her in shock. Her Uncle slid out of the room, I should probably follow.

"I would never do such a thing." Chopper's face fell. "Jo."

"Don't tease me about taking me out of here, please. I just…I just want to be outside, to be at a beach watching the waves roll and forgetting that I..."

"Sweet girl, if I could break you out of jail and know you would have the medical care you needed."

"Fuck the medical care." She hissed. "I don't…I'm dying. I'm going to die. I want to die. I'm not…" This wasn't Jordan. Chopper looked up at me for help, both of us trying to figure out what was happening. "I don't deserve…I can't…"

"Jordan." I began softly. "Did…?" Her breathing quickened, she stared at the door as if she were waiting for something or someone. Keller exploded back into the room angrily, pulling something out from his back pocket. Jordan screamed and Calen flew into the room as if he had been lying in wait.

"I forgot my phone, dickhead." Keller hissed as he was thrown up against the wall, his face buried in the drywall.

"You mean, the phone in your back pocket?" Calen growled. "Make a move, pretty boy."

"One phone call and I'll have your badge."

"Not likely, but you can sure try."

"This is harassment."

"Jordan?" Chopper murmured, fear laced his voice. I turned to see she was ghostly white and not breathing, blood stained her sheets.

"Jordan!" Calen yelled, letting go of Keller before he ran out of the room to scream for nurses. The machines she was hooked up to began beeping erratically.

"Everyone out, now!" Sonia ordered firmly. I stood rooted to the spot, watching with fear as the medical staff rushed in and tried to save her life.

"Out." Calen instructed, grabbing Chopper and I by the arms and pulling us out of the way. "You can't help her, let them do their jobs." His voice was weak, filled with fear and pain. It shook me out of my confusion at the same time I heard Keller James laugh before he walked out in front of us. I saw red and I sprinted towards the bastard.

Chapter 12
Maddie

One second we're in the waiting room talking and laughing, excited that Keller was finally out of the picture. Calen had looked agitated, which in turn was making Caleb the same way as he watched his uncle pace the room. Cooper and Sawyer were telling jokes, possibly because they noticed the same thing I did. Our laughter was silenced immediately by Jordan's scream, followed by Calen's cries for help. We couldn't get into the room, didn't know what happened and I couldn't understand if Jordan was okay.

Keller walked out of the room with a cocky smile plastered on his face and before I could comprehend, Zack was rushing out of the room. He speared Keller from behind and slammed him into a wall with nothing but a sickening thud. There was a shrill scream and I turned to see Sage with her mouth open wide.

"Zack, stop! Stop, it's not Keller's fault. It's not!" Sage looked around for help. "They're fighting over me, someone stop them before he hurts Keller."

"There's no way in Hell it's over her." Cooper muttered under his breath. I looked at him in surprise, forgetting he was standing next to me. "He did something to Jo."

"What did you do? What did you do to her?" Zack was asking belligerently, his hands were wrapped around Keller's throat. Keller laughed and shook his head, trying to push Zack away, but Zack reeled back and punched him in the stomach.

"This isn't helping her." Calen growled as he grabbed Zack from under his armpits and yanked him off.

"It's all an act, you fucking idiot. She just wants attention, just wants to turn everyone against me so you don't realize the vindictive…" Zack charged again and landed a punch before Calen and Chopper were able to restrain him.

"Shut your mouth and leave." Caleb hissed as he got up in Keller's face and shoved him away. Keller stumbled, chuckled and shook his head.

"He did something to Jordan. She's not breathing. There was blood. So much blood. He did…"

"You got him?" Calen asked Chopper, he nodded uncertainly and Calen let go of Zack and went directly to Keller. He grabbed him by the elbow and didn't budge when Keller began fighting.

"What in the Hell just happened?" I mumbled. Zack was shaking, tears streamed down his face as he fought every urge he had to chase Keller James back down and do permanent damage. Caleb was warring with himself over following his uncle, helping his best friend or going to his sister. There was shouting coming from Jordan's room and they were racing beside her bed as they pushed her down the hall.

"What is going on?" Caleb asked one of the nurses who hurried to the desk.

"We're prepping her for surgery, that's all I know." She stated flatly, her eyes full of confusion and worry.

"Surgery…" I stood in the middle of the hallway watching my best friend being wheeled away from us, the last time she went through those doors we almost lost her. My fiancé was on the verge of a nervous breakdown and his best friend looked as if he were already there.

Chapter 13
Keller

"Take your fucking hands off me, pig."

"Not until you are secure in your car and headed off the premises."

"You have no right."

"Oh, but I do." The pig chuckled.

"I will end you. Do you know who I am?"

"A punk kid who likes to bully and threaten young girls because he's an insecure, privileged brat."

"She makes this shit up. I know you're new to the storyline, but it's what she does."

"He's right." Sage chimed in. "She's constantly making stuff up so people feel sorry for her. No one even believes this cancer crap."

"Her mom was the same way, right? She was fucking crazy, hearing voices and had multiple personalities. Jordan needs to be institutionalized before she kills someone. She doesn't even know she's crazy, says she's an actress and just playing parts." The guy tightened his grip on my elbow and audibly growled. Apparently, that's a weird, inherited trait because Caleb did the same thing when he was pissed off.

"My sister wasn't crazy, she was with a narcissistic bastard who made her think she was crazy." I chuckled inwardly, noticing the police officer's demeanor quickly changed with the mention of his deceased sister. His grip released and I took the chance to spin away from him.

"I'm sure that'll be Jordan's lie too." I laughed.

"You will stay away from my niece, do you understand?"

"Gladly, but not because you said so. She's too much drama for me." I would placate this jack ass, but he didn't scare me. By Monday, one phone call from my father with the mention of harassment and brutality this guy wouldn't be able to carry a gun or be employable as a rent-a-cop. If Jordan survived whatever happened to her in there, she would pay for this mess. She would pay for dumping me and hate her life more than she already should.

"Lay another hand on her, or any woman, and I will end you. Do you understand?"

"Threatening me is not going to help your situation." I grinned as we stood in the parking lot.

"Keep thinking that." The officer laughed. "I'll make certain the staff knows you're not allowed back in the hospital." He pulled out his cell phone, snapped a picture of me and walked back in the building.

"Bastard." I growled.

"Forget it, baby." Sage purred as she ran her hands up my left arm. "You dumped the bitch, you don't have to deal with her drama anymore." I looked back at the blonde beside me, she was ready and willing to take Jordan's spot. Even though I was disgusted by her touch and presence I allowed her to be there, because I would not let anyone know Jordan dumped me. I also wouldn't be seen alone. Sage Qualls had nothing on Jordan Donaldson for the simple fact that Sage will fuck anything and is about as smart as a turtle, but she was a warm body who would do whatever I asked of her.

"You're right. Life will be so much better without her around, hopefully she doesn't survive the night."

"No shit." Sage laughed awkwardly as she tugged me towards my car. I looked back at the hospital, cursing myself for not getting the cop's name. I'm sure it won't be hard to find out, but it was extra work I didn't want to have to do.

As soon as we were in the car, I felt under my seat for the bottle of pills I had stashed. I was livid Jordan had dumped me, that she was no longer scared of me and if I didn't relax I would take it out on Sage. I opened the lid, popped two of them before giving Sage one as well. She was a lot less annoying when she was high, I could handle her better.

Jordan and her loser family and friends may think she's done with me, but she has only just begun. We weren't over until I was done with her, regardless of what she says.

Chapter 14
Chopper

"What happened?" Lance questioned quietly, once they had taken Zack outside to calm down.

"I don't know." I muttered, still trying to process everything. "We were joking around one second and the next…she was near tears and then…"

"Why was she near tears, what did you say?"

"I didn't…I asked if she was really single and then said she wasn't, that I was going to whisk her away to a beach and…"

"She is constantly asking for me to break her out and take her to the beach." Lance mumbled, looking down at the ground. "That wouldn't have caused her to…"

"All I know is Keller came in the room pulling something out from behind him, then Calen came out of nowhere and threw him against the wall. As soon as Jordan saw Keller though, she screamed like she'd been shot and then…then I looked at her and she was white, she wasn't breathing and there was blood everywhere."

"He shot her?"

"No. I would've…we would've heard a shot or…"

"Zack obviously thinks he did something to her."

"I noticed…I don't know what happened before, when Keller was in there but I did notice marks on her throat and…"

"Marks?"

"Just leave it alone, boys." Calen instructed as he came in the waiting room. He looked around. "I took care of the situation."

"Obviously not if she…"

"The kid is out of the picture and I will make certain she is safe from here on out. If you go snooping, asking her what happened, she won't react the way you want her to. I have dealt with this numerous times, she will not tell the truth and she will close in. If you really want to help her, just let her know you support her and will never judge her or her choices. I guarantee, from what I've seen, you will not understand her decisions so far."

"You think he's abusive." Lance stated. "I know more about it than you think. Jordan knows…"

"Her reality is not the same as yours. What you and I think she should fully comprehend, is not correct." Calen grunted. "Drop it, do you understand?"

"No sir. If she's being hurt…"

"She will never be hurt again." Someone snapped from behind us.

"What does that mean?" I gasped.

"It means, that skeevy bastard will never come within two feet of her ever again." Caleb stated. Zack and Maddie were right behind him.

"Did you know he was…?" Lance growled as he took a step towards Zack.

"Not until today." He spit back.

"It's done. It's over. She kicked him to the curb, that's the biggest step."

"Any news?" Caleb asked his father as he walked into the room.

"They're not exactly certain of a lot. Dr. Bowman just arrived. As far as they can tell her suture site split, causing the bleeding. What was she doing before…?"

"Lying in bed…there is no way…" I mumbled. I shook my head and tried to wrap my head around everything. Why in the Hell would Jordan put up with someone hitting her? Why wouldn't she say something? We were missing something, this couldn't be right. She didn't seem like an abused person. I couldn't argue with the facts though and everything was pointing to Keller James being an abusive asshole who needed to die.

Chapter 15
Zack

"Any news?" Maddie asked with a sigh as she handed me a cup of coffee. I shook my head. Caleb and his family had been pulled back into a room over an hour ago. Dr. Bowman wouldn't allow any of us back. I was ready to crawl out of my skin. He had informed us she was sleeping off anesthesia in the post op room and she wouldn't be allowed visitors again until tomorrow. He thought we'd all go home, but we needed answers.

"Why wouldn't he just explain everything in here, like he has been doing?" Coop asked looking up at Drew worriedly.

"Because something changed." Alicia muttered tearfully. "I saw it in his face."

"He should have…" Drew started.

"It means they have to make a decision, you idiot." Alicia snapped. The whole room went silent again. I closed my eyes and began praying. It was really the only way I could hide the fact that I was crying. Maddie wrapped her hands around my arm and put her head on my shoulder.

"I can't lose her." She whispered, her voice catching on a sob.

"Me neither." I sighed. "She's going to be okay, she has to be."

"It isn't fair."

"I wish I could've…" Killed Keller for hurting Jordan, made Sage disappear into thin air so Jordan wouldn't have to deal with her, told J that I loved her and I was the one she was supposed to be with. So many things I should have done today, so many words left unspoken. When would I learn to say what was on my heart right then? Waiting was never a good idea.

Chapter 16
Caleb

"So you think Keller did something to her and we can't do anything about it?" I questioned angrily.

"I don't know who did it. It could have been a staff member for all we know. She says she doesn't remember much about today." Dr. Bowman answered. He looked at my uncle, then back to me. "She was alone with any number of people and her wounds are consistent with trauma of some sort. Keeping this on the down low is what is best for Jordan. If the person thinks they didn't get caught, then they will mess up the next time."

"Next time?"

"I didn't mean it like that."

"Caleb, I will not allow anything like this to ever happen again." My uncle interjected.

"You said that about my mom too, right?" I snapped. Calen's face paled, his jaw tightened and he nodded before he sat back in his seat.

"While she is here, her visits will be monitored with video cameras set up in the rooms. They won't be noticeable, so no one, not even the staff will know they exist."

"What about when she goes home?"

"We'll do the same at home." Dad interjected. "Whatever we have to do to make sure Jordan is safe." I rolled my eyes.

"You being home more would probably help."

"Caleb, attacking everyone else will not make things better." Dad retorted, giving me a dirty look. I rolled my eyes again.

"Explain to me again what caused this."

"We're not a hundred percent certain of what caused it." Dr. Bowman sighed. "However, your sister's hand is broken, she has faint bruises on her throat, wrists and hands. Her suture site was busted open by extreme force, she has a bruise on her stomach the size of a fist. One millimeter to the left and she would be dead. On anyone else, most of these bruises probably wouldn't be noticeable, but with everything go on in Jordan's body she's prone to bruise easily. These marks are indicative of someone intentionally harming her. Whoever did it, also didn't take into account how weak her system is or maybe they did. She suffered a small heart attack from the trauma."

"And even with all this, you're telling me to play dumb?"

"Exactly." Dr. Bowman nodded. "We can't accuse anyone without proof. We can't..."

"Jordan won't truly feel safe until this person is physically put away and kept away from her, we can't do that yet." Calen interjected. "I will make certain we fix that."

"You don't have a very good track record."

"Obviously, you don't either." He retorted. "Seeing me as the enemy is not helping your sister. If we work together we can catch this bastard and make sure he never comes near her again."

"Whatever." I muttered. I eyed everyone in the room carefully. The truth was, this was all about politics. If it was a staff member, it would be a media nightmare for the hospital and lawsuits would come out of the woodwork. If it were Keller James, my father was terrified of losing his job and of what the school would do to his career. I wasn't stupid, the James family was not someone you wanted to mess with. They didn't operate with the same moral conscience as the rest of us. I would play nice, work to make sure Jordan was safe, but I would do my own research, do my own security. I was the only person who could truly keep Jordan protected.

"Will she have long lasting damage?" Dad asked, dismissing me and everyone else in the room.

"The heart attack has me concerned. The cardiologist will be in later this evening to talk to you after he reviews her charts and bloodwork. So far, everything else looks normal."

"Except for the fact that someone tried to kill her." I hissed. Dr. Bowman closed his eyes, nodded and hung his head.

"That's all I have for now, if there's any more information I will fill you in as soon as I know." Everyone stood and began filing out of the room. I was grateful that it was only my dad, Uncle Calen, Uncle Kyle and me in the room. My cousin Cissy couldn't keep her mouth shut to save her life, she would blab to everyone that Jordan had been injured and they were monitoring her. I didn't trust my own cousin, which was sad, but over the years I have seen her do so many things to Jo out of spite. Maybe I overreact and it was always an accident, but she had pushed her in the water when they were six, knowing Jordan couldn't swim. She stood there watching while my little sister struggled, if it wasn't for Kyler walking by at the time my sister could have lost her life then. There were other times when she'd trip her when we crossed the road, pushed her out of a tree and caused her to break her arm. I think Jordan honestly believes it was her lack of coordination, but I know better and so does Cissy. They were rarely alone in the room together, but I'd realized my cousin was a very sneaky girl.

"Caleb?" Dr. Bowman cleared his throat. I looked up at the man as he motioned for me to stay. "I know you're worried about your sister, but I want to assure you that I, honestly, am too close to this case." He chuckled sadly as he looked down at the ground, then back up at me. "I had only met your sister a few times before Alicia begged me to take this case, so I didn't know much about her. I have come to know her extremely well and I know why my kids think so highly of her. She is an amazing girl. She is also my daughter's best friend, my nephew's girlfriend and I will do everything in my power to make certain she is safe and beats this cancer. You may have noticed that in our family, the important people take on a more important role and become part of our family, even if not by blood. Please know, I won't let this happen again."

"Is there anything I can do to help?"

"I have a friend in security who will be bringing me the cameras, when I get them I'll let you place them. You'll probably be more discreet than anyone."

"Thank you, sir." He nodded his head and gestured for the door.

"Your sister is safe now, I swear that to you." I wanted to believe him, but my head just wouldn't allow it. I shook his offered hand and headed out of the room.

Cancer was gunning for my little sister, now someone else was for whatever crazy reason. Whoever it is, won't survive the night if I catch them trying it again.

Chapter 17
Lance

I watched Jordan as she slept peacefully in her bed. She was still heavily medicated, pale and bruised. She was a smaller, fragile version of herself. My heart broke with the knowledge of the intense amount of pain and agony she was enduring, more than any of us even realized apparently.

"Lance?" I heard her murmur weakly.

"Yeah darlin'?"

"Will you hold me?"

"Absolutely." I responded as I shot out of the chair and was climbing in bed with her in seconds. "Do you need anything?"

"Just you." The instant my arms were wrapped around her, she was snoring softly. So many thoughts began flitting through my head as I listened for the rhythmic sounds of her breathing.

I didn't want to believe their accusations against Keller James. Yes, he was a cocky bastard but Jordan was too strong to allow someone to hurt her in any way. Not to mention, she knew my home situation so she should know she could come to me for help. There had to be another explanation.

My conscience was telling me I was an idiot, screaming at me to look at everything from a different point of view. Until recently, Jordan didn't know she could come to me with anything. Why would she? I've never trusted her enough to tell her my secrets, why would she open up and do the same?

Caleb had jokingly stated his sister's life had been in danger more in the last year than in her entire existence. That was my fault. Every time her life has hung in the balance, it's been my mistake. My father's threats, the car accident and now this. If Keller James is abusive, if he had injured her like this, while she sat on death's door in a hospital room then he had no fears and we were lucky he didn't kill her. *I* drove her to Keller James. *I* let him have her. I didn't fight for her. I turned my back on her when she needed me. I was raised to protect the ones you love and instead I was slowly killing Jordan, I wasn't good enough for her. She needed a white knight, a man who would put her before himself and all others and I was certainly not that man. I wanted to be, I needed to be, but I am obviously entirely too selfish for her.

Chapter 18
Jordan

"Are you driving me home?" I asked Lance softly. "Home…I didn't think I'd ever get to say that word." He chuckled and flashed a gorgeous half grin at me.

"Caleb wants to."

"But I want *you* to." I closed my eyes and regretted the need and whininess my voice showed.

"I want to." He mumbled as his hands found mine.

"I'll tell Caleb…"

"No, it's okay, darlin'. I've got a lot to do at the house, so…" I swallowed hard, closed my eyes and fought back the tears. I knew what came next. Damned my heart and damn Lance Bowman for betraying me once again.

"I'm sure you do." I stated flatly, my voice was even and all emotion was gone.

"And school work to…"

"I get it, Lance." I pulled away from him and climbed out of the hospital bed. I was thrilled to be going home, but now the emotion was dead. I wanted to cry and shout, wanted to do physical harm to him. However, I should have known once I was given the all clear our honeymoon phase would be over. It was my own fault, really, for ever believing his lies.

"Jo." He followed me off the bed, pulled me into him before linking our hands together.

"What comes next, Bowman?" I asked huskily as I clenched my fingers around his. His eyes went to mine, searching frantically for the answer.

"You've got a long road ahead of you."

"Will you be with me?"

"Will I?" He threw back. I looked down at our adjoined hands and shrugged my shoulders.

"I want you to."

"Then I will." His free hand went up to caress my cheek. "You'd have to get a restraining order to keep me away, regardless of your answer just then." I let out a breathy giggle before I looked around the room nervously. "However, I…I feel like I should back off and…" He closed his eyes and inhaled deeply. "You've been through Hell, basically since the second we've met. I've carelessly put your life in danger countless times and…"

"What are you talking about?"

"The car accident, my dad, Keller and…"

"Keller?"

"I know…" He began and my stomach convulsed. I wanted to puke. What did he know? What was he talking about? "We both have secrets that we don't feel comfortable sharing with each other. I need, we need, to take a step back and realize why that is. I'm suffocating you and…there's so much shit going on with my dad, the farm and…you don't need stress of any kind, especially the pressure of me pushing you to get back together. I can't risk your recovery."

"What?" I gasped. I thought we were back together, what in the Hell is he talking about?

"It's not for good. I told you I'm going to fight like Hell for you darlin' and I mean that, but I won't risk your health." He was a blessed idiot, he had me, all of me and he was too stupid to realize it. I needed him, but if he didn't feel the same way I sure as Hell wouldn't beg him to stay in my life. I was better than that. I deserved better, even if I didn't want anyone but Lance Bowman. I wanted to cry, wanted to scream and challenge him, but I closed my eyes, took a deep, cleansing breath and looked him dead in the eye.

"You contradict yourself, but you're absolutely right." I let go of his hands and moved away from him. I turned and walked towards the window. "It probably is for the best if you…" Lance didn't wait for any other words to come out; he silenced me effectively by planting a hot, passionate kiss on my open mouth. I melted into him and any words were quickly gone, forgotten, lost in the moment forever.

"I love you." He murmured into my ear once he pulled away and before I could get my bearings, he was out of the room like a dart.

I stared in muted stupor for what seemed like forever before I hissed; "Contradicting son of a bitch." But I would not cry. I could not cry.

"What's his deal?" Maddie queried with a strange look on her face when she floated into my room.

"Who the fuck knows?" I snapped. She knew better than to question my anger right now. So she sighed heavily before she finished putting my remaining things in the duffel bag. I looked around the room helplessly. I'd been locked away in this hospital for over a month, I'd almost died a few weeks ago from Keller's tirade and hadn't seen him since. Now, I was being discharged and all I wanted to do was climb back into the hospital bed and relive the safety here, especially since Lance had been by my side through it all. Now, I had to worry about Keller again and I didn't even have Lance Bowman to save me from him anymore.

Chapter 19

"How are you feeling?" Zack asked as he snuck in my room during his lunch break. I've been home for almost a week and he has stopped in to see me every morning before class, every lunch period and every night after basketball practice. My brother, Maddie and Alicia would mostly text or pop in daily, but Zack would text, call and swing by every chance he got. I was grateful, even though every time my door opened I was terrified it was Keller coming in.

"Bleh." I grumbled from under my pillow.

"Sounds fun." He chuckled as he came over and took the pillow off my head. "I brought you lunch and it is gorgeous outside, let's eat on the back patio."

"I don't…" His bottom lip went down in an adorable pout, I laughed and shook my head. "Please."

"How can I say no to that?" He winked as he grinned smugly.

"You might want to throw on some sweats."

"I still feel like I'm on fire from my treatment yesterday."

"I'll bring your blanket just in case. I have everything outside already, but we can bring it in the kitchen if we need to." Zack offered a hand and helped me out of bed. He didn't let go and I didn't want to. I did though, because I couldn't count on anyone but myself. Zack was being fabulous right now, but he would stop as soon as some pretty, rich girl caught his attention. As much as I longed for someone to stand beside me and protect me, it wasn't an option apparently.

"You don't need to do this, you know?"

"I want to." He shrugged as he grabbed mom's old quilt off my bed and gestured for me to go ahead of him.

"Well, I won't get used to it." I grumbled under my breath just as my phone chirped, notifying me of a text.

"I'll be over in an hour." Mrs. Bowman messaged. I smiled, grateful she hadn't abandoned me like her son. She had talked her brother in law into approving her as my in home nurse so she was here daily taking care of me. Sometimes staying with me for hours because my father was too busy to bother with me. Maybe this is what it felt like to have a mom.

"How can Mrs. Bowman be amazing and her son be a douche bag?" Zack chuckled and shrugged his shoulders as we made our way down the stairs and into the kitchen.

"Screw him, J." He hurried in front of me to open the back door and ushered me out to the patio. "He had you and let you go, *again.* He's not worth a second thought."

"I wish my heart agreed with that logic."

"You just need time." He pulled out a lounge chair and helped me into it before covering me up.

"Grill cheese and tomato soup?" I smiled.

"I figured you wouldn't be too hungry, but it's good for chilly days." I nodded my head, but wouldn't look at him as he handed me the plate of food. He was thoughtful and sweet and here in front of me, and all I could think about was Lance Bowman.

"You're pretty amazing."

"I try." He winked. He sat down next to me and began eating as well. "It's amazing how quiet you are with food in a close proximity." I gasped and swatted at him.

41

"Asshole." He roared with laughter and watched me carefully.

"Just trying to pull you out of the dark hole you're trying to jump in."

"I hate you for seeing that."

"Why?" I shrugged my shoulders. "What are you thinking about?"

"Lance...cancer...my mom."

"Don't waste another thought on Bowman." He grumbled on a sigh.

"I've tried. I'm just...I think I'm just dumbfounded by the whole thing and that's what bothers me the most. I feel like I can spot an ass from a mile away, yet he dupes me every time."

"Am I an asshole?"

"To ninety nine percent of the female population? Yes. To me, not always." He looked down at his plate, a mix of emotions.

"When am I an ass to you?"

"When you make comments about food." I giggled. "When you're blunt and honest with me." I shrugged, leaned back in the chair and looked up at the crystal clear blue sky. "But that's just you being a good friend. I appreciate it, because I hate being lied to. However, sometimes I want to throat punch you for it."

"Who else will call you on your shit, if I don't?"

"No one." I muttered.

"It's only because I love you."

"How can I be surrounded by so many people who love me and still feel so alone?" I queried tearfully.

"J." Zack put his plate down and moved towards me, in one swift movement he pulled me on his lap and wrapped his arms around me. "You're anything but alone, baby."

"I see that, but I don't..."

"Just because Lance is a fuck up and Keller is a bastard, doesn't mean the rest of us are the same." I shivered, not so much because I was cold as it was because I was wrapped in his arms. I didn't feel so alone now. He pulled the blanket up around us and pulled me in tighter. "The sooner you realize that, the sooner you'll see the amazing people right in front of you."

"I'm not ungrateful, please don't think that. I know how truly lucky I am to have you...guys, and Chopper and the others, and my Aunt Becky, my mom's family, Lance's mom and sisters. I probably sound like a whiny brat."

"No." He breathed. "You've got a lot going on, you're allowed to pout sometimes." He chuckled before he moved my face so I was looking directly at him. "Just open your eyes and see what is right in front of you." My heart stopped, I held my breath and let his words sink in. Was Zack Bentley putting himself out there? I've never known Zack not to come right out and say what he meant, so I was obviously reading too much into his words. He was talking about something, someone else. Right? For a split second, I convinced myself he wanted me and then felt my heart ripping at the realization he would never settle for me when he had five hundred girls clamoring for him. "Please, just..." His voice was low, soothing and I moved towards his lips. I just needed to know what it would be like to kiss him while he was holding me. There was a hundred million things I should be thinking about right now, things I should be focusing on rather than what it feels like to kiss the biggest player at Callatin Academy, who was also one of my best friends. My life was in a downward spiral and I was so desperate for a real, loving touch that I was latching on to unrealistic expectations. My text message notification sounded and I stopped moving as I realized what I was doing. I grabbed for my phone at the same time Zack did.

"Don't answer it, please." His voice was thin, pleading as his eyes bore into mine. I couldn't focus on that because I'd try to kiss him again. I couldn't lose my friendship with Zack. I couldn't ruin it all because I was lonely and depressed. Zack deserved better and he definitely didn't want me. I looked at my phone, but only saw tears as I spiraled back down into my dark hole.

"Look at me." He whispered. I closed my eyes, inhaled and shut off all emotions. When I glanced into Zack's green eyes they were filled with sadness. "I will always be here, just remember that." I nodded my head and watched him carefully. He did the same.

"Since I'm on your lap…" I began with a flirtatious grin.

"*Don't* tease me."

"It wouldn't be teasing if we." My text message indicator went off again, followed by Keller's ringtone. My entire body tightened.

"Why is Keller calling you?" Zack growled as he grabbed my phone.

"I don't know. I haven't talked to him since…" My chest tightened with fear and the air seemed to be slipping away from me.

Chapter 20
Zack

"What in the Hell do you want?" I hissed into the phone, ripping it out of Jordan's clenched fingers without even thinking.

"My girlfriend." Keller laughed cockily on the other side.

"Wrong number."

"You're an idiot, Bentley." Keller's voice was light and smug. "You don't honestly think she's going to go from me to a pathetic, scholarship loser like you, do you? She's got a perfect grade point average and you're barely getting by. She's too good for an ignorant delinquent like you."

"You talk pretty big from behind the phone."

"You can't even form a proper sentence, you're borderline caveman." Keller roared with laughter on the other end. If Jordan's phone didn't snap under the pressure of my grip, it would be a miracle. "So, does my girlfriend know what her daddy's been up to? I'm really concerned he's been making advances on her and Maddie, possibly even that townie Alicia."

"What the fuck are you talking about?"

"You don't know? Seems Mr. D has been giving extracurricular classes in his office."

"Whatthefuckever."

"Videos don't lie." My eyes widened as I watched Jordan carefully. Her face was white and her breathing was becoming more erratic. I hung up on Keller and threw the phone down.

"Jordan." I called loudly. "J, baby." Her eyes were round, unfocused and she gripped the table in front of her. She was having a panic attack, I think. I grabbed her head and pushed it between her legs. I'd seen people do it before, it seemed to work for them. It apparently helped because she slowed her breathing. When she came up, her eyes were glassy and wary.

"If you wanted me to go down on you, all you had to was ask, shoving my head down there is shitty."

"What?" I chuckled. She shot me a dirty look, grabbed her phone and hurried inside. "What in the Hell just happened?" I stared after her retreating figure long after she was gone. One second she's about to kiss me, then she closes in and blocks herself off, then she's flirting, having a panic attack and then pissed off at me. I couldn't figure her out.

I looked around and cleaned up our dishes. I shot a text to Caleb asking about Keller's claim, my phone immediately rang.

"Where in the Hell did you hear that from?" Caleb growled.

"Keller called J, I answered her phone."

"How in the Hell does he know?"

"It's true?"

"Absolutely not. Dad got an Express package today and when he opened it there was a flash drive with a typed letter. Basically, it's a video of someone who resembles dad, in his office, having sex with a few of the female students here. The letter threatened this would be released to the board unless the sender got what he wanted."

"What does he want?"

"Jordan." I nearly choked.

"Keller."

"Sounds like it."

"All he has to do is take that to the board with the threat."

"That's what I said. The sender says he has at least five female students and two teachers who will admit he has propositioned and tried to bribe them for sex."

"He's bluffing."

"Apparently, there are two female voices admitting, in detail."

"Do you think…?"

"Any chick who fucks my dad has issues." Caleb hissed on the other end. "He's hardly around so I don't know how he's propositioning anyone, but that's not going to be an alibi. It doesn't matter what the truth is, it's what it looks like to the board. Keller is pulling the strings."

"And Keller will do whatever it takes."

"Not if I have anything to do with it."

"What are we going to do?"

"Not we, me."

"I'm in this too, whether you want me to be or not. I won't sit on the sidelines and watch him take her down." I sighed. "So Keller is bribing your dad to get Jordan back…but why? Everyone knows he's with Sage."

"I don't know."

"What is it about Jordan that has him obsessed? I don't get it. He can have almost any girl in this school willingly, but he wants to force J? She's an amazing, beautiful girl but I…"

"That she is, but there's something we don't know. There has to be."

"Maybe she's that good in bed." I teased.

"I'm going to punch you the next time I see you." Caleb responded drily. I chuckled and brought Jordan's quilt back in the house with the dishes. I put her blanket on the back of a chair, washed the dishes quickly and listened to Caleb make a game plan. I brought Jordan's blanket back up to her room, but she was nowhere around.

"We need to figure out what he sees in her, what his motive is and take it away."

"I have this bad feeling that won't stop him."

"I hope you're wrong." I sighed. "Did Jordan have a treatment this afternoon?"

"No, she had one yesterday."

"She's gone."

"What do you mean, she's gone?"

"I mean, she was here because we had lunch and then she went through about ten different personalities in five seconds, took off inside and now she's not here."

"I'll call her. I'll text you when I find her."

"I have about fifteen minutes before I have to be at class, she's probably just hiding from me."

"What did you do?"

"Tried to tell her how I feel, it didn't go as planned."

"Chicken out?"

"Yes. I didn't come right out and say what I wanted to, I just kind of…"

"Chickened out."

"Screw you." Caleb roared with laughter and then sobered quickly.

"If she had you, Keller couldn't get to her, you know that right?"

"I do. If I fuck it up, push her too soon and…it'll ruin everything."

"Stop overthinking and just do it."

45

"Says the guy who took three years to ask Maddie on a date."

"I never said I follow my own advice."

"No one ever does." I chuckled. "Let me know when she says she's okay."

"Got it." He hung up the phone and I started hollering for Jordan. Caleb's words rolled throughout my brain. *"If she had you, Keller couldn't get to her."* It was the absolute truth, but she was so broken from Keller and Lance that she wasn't seeing reality right now. I could flat out tell her my feelings and she'd rationalize it was all a lie. I would do whatever necessary to prove I'm for real, because I would never forgive myself if Keller got to her again.

Chapter 21
Jordan

"What is it about Jordan that has him so obsessed? I don't get it." Zack's words were on repeat in my head. I'd ran downstairs to get mom's quilt and overheard his phone conversation. Nice to see I'm hideous to the asshole. Tears rolled down my cheeks. To think I'd once thought he was an amazing, sweet guy, that he was my friend. He's just another jerk like every other male I've ever known in my life.

I had also overheard something about Keller bribing my dad. That couldn't be good. My phone notified me of an email, when I opened it a video immediately began playing. Snippets of my father having sex with random classmates of mine.

"Oh, oh God." I gasped before I unloaded my lunch in the bushes. When I was done and got the video to stop I realized there was a message attached.

Unless you admit your mistake of dumping me, this will be released to the school board. Your dad will be finished, not to mention the scholarships you and your brother received will be pulled. One mistake on your part will ruin three lives. BTW using this as evidence won't help. I have enough dirt on everyone you love to ruin them forever. Zack, Alicia, Maddie, Chopper, Lance…everyone. When they all learn you're to blame for their misery, you'll be alone. No one will ever want you again. It's your last chance. I suggest you make your choice wisely. –Keller

I fell onto the porch steps and buried my face in my hands. How in the Hell had my life gotten to this point? How did I get in this situation, this relationship with a sociopath? No one could save me from myself, or from Keller. My phone rang and Keller's face flashed across the screen.

"Hey." I grumbled.

"All I need is for you to say you belong to me and all of this will go away." He stated with a smug grin.

"I…"

"Jordan, don't be an idiot. If you're holding out for Lance Bowman, remember he gave you up, repeatedly. He walked away from you at the hospital, didn't he? You haven't talked to him since, have you? Do you really want to ruin your dad's career, his good name because of some bastard who doesn't even realize your worth?" The tears fell faster as his words sank in. He was right. Lance Bowman didn't want me. No one did. I was damaged and broken goods, I was too much drama. I would forever be stuck in the Hell that Keller James has made for me and I just had to learn to live with that reality.

"I'm yours, Keller. I always have been."

"That's my girl." He laughed before he hung up the phone. My stomach heaved and I began puking again. My phone notification sounded alerting me to a text message. I picked up the phone and threw it as hard as I could. I was done with life right now.

Chapter 22
Lance

"Contradicting son of a bitch." Jordan had hissed before I'd gotten all the way out of her hospital room. Those words echoed through my conscience on repeat at least thirty times a day. I promised her I'd fight and then broke that vow just as quickly. It took everything I possessed to walk away from her, those words made it worse, but it was for the best. With me permanently in the picture it would only cause her undue stress and that's the last thing she needs right now.

"Joey is not going to text you back." Chopper hissed angrily as he plopped his tray next to mine before his plump body followed suit. "You'll be lucky if she ever talks to you again."

"I know." I placed my phone on my tray, just in case she did reply. Chopper rolled his eyes and dug into the disgusting taco salad in front of him, he'd doctored it with way too much taco sauce and ketchup, for flavor.

"Yeah, a text message is definitely the way to a girl's heart." Drew chortled as he took the chair across from Chopper and me. "The pussy's way out if you ask me."

"No one ever asks you." I growled as I narrowed my eyes at my cousin.

"I hate to admit this," Sawyer sighed as he took the seat next to Drew. "But I have to agree with Drew. She probably thinks it's just a courtesy check in."

"*You* think or Alicia has told you so?" I asked quickly, referring to his girlfriend who also happened to be Drew's sister and one of Jordan's best friends. Of course, Chopper happened to be both Jordan's best friend and mine, but he'd obviously taken Jordan's side recently.

"Both." He ducked his head to take a bite of his hamburger. "You went from being the golden child to the red headed step child again." He shrugged his shoulders. "Not only is Jordan pretty pissed at you, but so is her whole crew."

"Keller included." I snapped.

"Why? Are you scared of that smarmy bastard?" Coop asked in shock as he finished our table off by pulling an extra chair over.

"No way in Hell."

"Then why in the *Hell* would you back off? I thought you were over that crap."

"She's under enough stress as it is."

"And you're only concerned about her health, not *your* needs. It would be selfish of you to try and pursue her when she's so sick and going through so much." Drew recounted my exact words sarcastically. "Bullshit." He coughed.

"I really thought Jordan was *the one*." Coop sighed as he shook his head disapprovingly. "She had you chasing your tail boy, but obviously she wasn't enough for Bo. It's a shame really."

"I agree." Drew added with a shake of his brown head. "But if you're done then it just leaves her open for me, right? I mean, if you're *done with her* she's officially fair game."

"*I'm not done with her.*" I gripped my food tray so hard it cracked a little under the pressure. "And you will stay the Hell away from her."

"Nope." Chopper laughed with an exaggerated wave of his hands. "You ditched her three times. Actually," He tilted his head and mentally started tallying all my mistakes with Jordan in his head. "You let her go at the Lake without a phone number, that's one. Two was when you slept with her after Jenna's wedding and again, let her walk away. Three, was at the gas station when you saw her *again* and let her walk away *again*. Four was your big drama fest when she said the three little words, again after sex. Five was completely avoiding her after telling her you were still together. Six, not telling her anything about the drama with your dad. Seven, giving her up after the accident. Do I need to go on? Because, technically after the third time, she was fair game."

"Is this a new rule?" I asked drily.

"Yup, implemented per your stupidity." Chopper stated with a decided nod, a wide grin spread across his face.

"Fair game, huh?" Coop rubbed his hands together excitedly. "Well alright then, it just might get interesting around here boys."

"I think it might." Chopper agreed with a nod. I slanted my eyes towards my closest friend. The look on his round face was full of ulterior motives. I'm sure this new rule was his sly way of getting me to see what I'd given up; his way of lighting a fire under me to get Jordan back. He obviously didn't know the torture I'd been through on a daily basis since I walked out of her hospital room. I'd also be an idiot to not realize that Chopper had some feelings for my girlfriend that went way beyond friendship. What normal guy wouldn't? She was gorgeous, sexy as Hell, sweet and funny, smart, sexy, did I mention that? She attended the elite Callatin Academy which meant she was either rich, a genius or an athletic Goddess, her traits lay in the latter. Despite her crazy upbringing and her now high-ranking socialite status, she was as down to earth as they came; a tomboy, country girl who stole my heart the first day I laid eyes on her. I could go on for hours about how perfect she is, but that'd be boring and if you know her long enough, you'll figure it all out for yourself anyway.

"None of you will go near her." I announced in a quiet, chilly voice that usually caused most people to sit up and take notice, but not my friends. They weren't threatened by me anymore, thinking they were in the safe zone because they were practically my brothers. "Jordan is mine and none of you will touch her."

"Actually," Drew grinned as he drew out the word before taking a bite of his sandwich, then chewing, then swallowing and finally finishing his thought. "*She* is Keller James girl because you so easily disregarded her importance in your life. Maybe the idea of her happy, with one of us bothers you right now Bo, but eventually that jealousy will heal. Honestly, it's what is best for Jordan and obviously, it's not you if you can so easily toss her to the wolves."

"And I'd definitely classify Keller James as the wolves." Coop threw out offhandedly as he took a bite of his taco salad.

"Agreed." Chopper picked up his cell phone and read an incoming text message. Lunch was the only time we were technically allowed to have our cell phones during school hours, ninety-five percent of the students broke that rule on a regular basis of course, but at least now, we weren't afraid of getting caught with them. A toothy grin came across his face this time as he looked back at me cockily. "Speak of the angel. Looks like Jordan misses me."

I tried to keep my heart from dropping into my stomach, attempted to keep the jealousy squashed but it wasn't possible. She couldn't reply to me, but she could randomly text Chopper. I ripped the phone out of his hand before he could reply. Chopper grabbed for it, but I held it away and read the message.

"*IMY. I need a friend.*" She misses him? But she doesn't miss me. Chopper threw me a smug look before he yanked the phone back to him. His pudgy fingers flew across the keypad quickly before he hit the send button. His text indicator dinged seconds later and Chopper turned away so I couldn't grab it from him. I don't think he meant for me to be able to read her message, but I could and wasn't shy about doing it either.

"*Keller crap. Of course. I'm bored. Of course. And I miss your asshole bff. Of course. But don't tell him that. I'd die if he knew I was still pining away while I'm sure he's moved on. Way on.*"

"*Sad to say he hasn't. He misses you too, but it's not my place to tell you that. He's an ass & you can do better.*"

"*Will you love me Chop? Run away with me so I can forget about shittyness here.*"

"*After school?*"

"*I'll be packed. Lol. I'm counting on you to whisk me away to Neverland.*"

"*Ranch? No good, I might get molested.*"

"*That was wrong. Lmao. But thanks, I needed the laugh. Got anymore?*"

"*Tons.*"

"*You at lunch?*"

"*Yup.*"

"*Asshole w you?*"

"*Yup.*"

"*Punch him in the face for me. Please. And then tell him I love him. No don't really. I'll die. I might anyway.*"

"*None of that talk. Want me to swing by after school?*"

"*Yes. But no, Keller will probably be here & you know how much he loves sharing me w you.*"

"*Screw him.*"

"*I have been. LMAO. Joke. I'm just trying to avoid the never ending fights. That's all. Imy guys, all of u. Raincheck to play another day?*"

"*Just say the word and I'm yours.*"

"*Don't tempt me,Cchop. Lol. ILY. Thanks for the smiles. Go back to lunch & have a good day.*"

"*ILY2.*" My heart slammed against my chest this time at their easy banter and the terms of endearment. I should be the only one Jordan says those words to. Although I'm certain she sees Chopper as nothing more than a very good friend, stranger things have happened. I mean, why wouldn't she fall for the big lug? He was a giant teddy bear who treated her like a princess without fail.

"Jordan says she misses us." Chopper announced, making sure he didn't make eye contact with me. "Maybe we should throw a party soon, so we can all hang out together."

"But Bo is not invited." Coop interjected. "He'll totally mess up my game."

"You don't have any game." Drew roared with laughter. "Seriously, any girl that you get is totally out of pity."

"At least I have standards, Mister I sleep with whoever spreads their legs for me."

"That would be Bo." Drew snapped. "I just don't have a preference as to who goes down on me."

"Speaking of which," Sawyer gestured up with his eyes.

"Hey guys." Remy smiled as she pulled up a chair and plopped down at our table uninvited. Remy used to hang out with my group a lot growing up and until recently, she was one of my very good friends. Jordan never liked her from the beginning, telling me that my friend had the hots for me. Of course, I told her there was no possible way. But after our accident I found out Jordan was more intuitive than I gave her credit for. Not only did Remy

50

practically throw herself at me she attempted to attack Jordan, of course, Jordan handled it with the grace and poise of a Southern Belle and Remy had been too embarrassed and angry to look at any of us until now. "Hey Bo. How's it going?" I shrugged my shoulders and looked back at my friends for help. They all smiled as they stood up from the table, each making false apologies about needing to be somewhere. "You still hate me?"

"I don't hate you, Remy." I answered with an exasperated sigh as I fell against the back of my chair and reluctantly looked at her.

"I heard you and Jordan broke up again." She settled into her chair and attempted to cross her legs. I imagine she was trying to be sexy, but it really looked pathetic and forced.

"You heard wrong."

"So she's *not* with Keller James? The high powered big man of Callatin Academy?" She asked in a shocked gasp.

"Do you have a point, Remy? I really need to get to my locker before English class." I stood up quickly, my chair slamming back loudly.

"You two aren't together anymore. And obviously aren't going to be together again since, rumor has it, Jordan and Keller will be attending Harvard together in the fall."

"Jo's a junior."

"Supposedly, Keller's father bought her senior year so they can be together." She shrugged as if it were such an obvious answer as she stood up too.

"You can't buy someone's senior year."

"At Callatin you can. Besides, why would you want to start up with *her* again when you're leaving for Boot Camp in a few months?" I grabbed up my tray and took long, quick strides to the closest trashcan. If I moved quick enough maybe she'd get lost in the thrum of the cafeteria. Remy hurried behind me like an annoying little Chihuahua. "Seriously, Bo. Why go through that drama anymore? Besides, Drew told me you two were absolutely finished."

"Drew lies. You should know that though." I glanced at her sideways and saw her cheeks flush pink. It was a low blow, but I really had lost all respect for my former friend when she attacked Jordan. And besides, I didn't want to lead her on any more than I'd unknowingly done in the past.

"Well, I don't know what your hang up is with the bitch, but honestly Lance, it's not good for you. You're like a completely different person nowadays. And I don't like it." She harrumphed as she clucked her tongue.

"I don't really care, Remy." I spun around and glared at her. She backed up like a scolded dog, cowering as if I might hit her. I closed my eyes, took a breath, and with a shake of my head I dumped my tray in the nearest trash can and headed for the doors. Once through the swinging doors I bee lined to the right and straight for my locker.

"Well, this is my last offer, Lance. I'm willing to give you the rest of the school year. No strings attached." She stated with a shrug. "We're good for each other. *And* you know you've always had a thing for me, before SHE came along. Once graduation comes, we can go our separate ways and, if we're home at the same time, we can always hook up." My ears roared furiously. I couldn't believe what I was hearing. Not only was someone who I used to think of as a sister, throwing herself at me, but she was doing it pathetically. I felt bad for her. I wanted to smack her across the face, shake her and ask what happened to all her morals and self-esteem. But I didn't. I took a deep breath, stopped walking and turned to Remy. I closed my eyes and tried to find the right words, tried not to notice that she'd tried to dye her once brown hair to an auburn color, to match Jordan's.

51

"Remy, I'm not interested. I never have been and I never will be. I am in love with Jordan Donaldson and I don't see that changing any time in the near future. And yes, you're right, we aren't together right now, but we will be when the time is right. It would just be wrong of me to take advantage of you and lead you on."

"But I don't mind." She admitted quickly as she moved into me. I stepped back and put out my hand.

"But I do. You're like family. I can't do that. I don't want you as anything more than a friend. And I certainly don't want to be sex buddies with you at any time in our lives."

"I'm not good enough?" She hissed.

"I couldn't do that to you. You're a friend and I'd be scum to lead you on. I'm sorry." I walked towards my locker, ignoring the protests she was making to my back as I bent down to get my English essay out of the bottom of my locker. She was still talking as I made my way to my classroom, thank God, it was only a few doors down and she wasn't in the class with me.

"This conversation is over, Remy. If I can't have Jordan, then I don't want anybody."

Chapter 23
Jordan

At eight o clock, my phone rang. I gasped when I looked down at the caller I.D. and I just gaped. My finger involuntarily hit the answer button and I was forced to talk to Lance.

"Hey darlin'." I heard him drawl on the other end. "I was beginning to think you weren't going to answer."

"I was busy." I closed my eyes and tried my damnedest to reign in all my emotions. Eight o clock at night had been our designated phone date time when we were together, he would call me every night. I tried not to read too much into the fact that he was calling at the special time again.

"Too busy to talk?" He asked playfully, but I could hear the hurt and worry in his voice. He'd done so much for me while I'd been in the hospital and I loved him so much that I couldn't answer yes, I couldn't be a bitch. I could most definitely be a sucker though.

"No. What's up?"

"I miss you." He lied flatly. I sucked in a breath and held it. "Are you really surprised by that, Jo?"

"Yes." I mumbled, slowly exhaling. "Yes I am."

"You shouldn't be, just because I backed off doesn't mean…"

"I haven't heard from you since I was discharged." I snapped icily. "Yeah you were amazing while I was in the hospital, but I really wonder if I was right about your motives."

"Doesn't my calling and texting cause fights between you and Keller though?" He retorted. I remained silent. "That's what I thought."

"Keller and I only recently got back together so that's a piss poor reason, Bowman. You said you loved me, told me you'd fight for me, but instead you walked away like the pussy you are."

"Ouch." He murmured with an uncomfortable chuckle.

"I'm not trying to be funny."

"I know that, darlin'. I don't want to fight with you. I don't want to stress you out. I just wanted to call and hear your sweet, sexy voice. I'm going crazy without you, Jordan."

"How crazy?" I queried in a pouty voice, falling into his ridiculous trap,

"There is a dent in my wall from where I beat my head into it every night." He answered sincerely. "Mom is talking about sending me to a shrink so I can talk about my issues. Of course, she's hoping the doctor will be able to find out why I let you go, again. Maybe a medical professional can talk some sense into me, she says."

"I agree. I think you should see this doctor, see if he can get through that thick skull of yours."

"I don't need to see a shrink, Jo." He mumbled in exasperation. "I just need you. I'm doing what's best for you though and no one seems to understand that."

"Why would being apart from the person I *want* to be with, be what's best for me? Explain that to me, Lance."

53

"If you want to be with me, then why are you back together with Keller James?" He snapped. I was silent again, this time to let the tears fall down my cheeks as I sent up a prayer he wouldn't notice. "Why is it all on me?"

"Why should I waste any more time on you? All you do is break promises, repeatedly. Why should I take another leap of faith on you, when there's a huge chance that you'll turn your back like you don't even know me anymore?"

"Wait a second…who doesn't know who anymore?"

"You're an ass." I sobbed.

"I am. That was uncalled for. I'm sorry. I've just been getting it from all sources today. The guys, my family. It's not like I don't torture myself enough, but then to add them and now *you* to it."

"Then I'll hang up."

"Please don't." He begged, his voice unusually thick. "Please don't hang up. I'm sorry it's taken so long to actually call, but…I thought texting was better. If I don't hear your voice, then it's easier for me to back off. It's hard to be apart from you. You're my best friend."

"I know." I mumbled, closing my eyes again. "Lance? Do you really miss me?"

"Every second of every day, darlin'." He drawled in a tortured voice. "You have no idea."

"I do, actually. I miss you."

"Can I see you?"

"Not tonight." I looked over at my alarm clock and my stomach clenched. I wouldn't be able to talk to Lance for long. Keller had texted to say he'd be over around eight thirty so we could watch a movie before bed. Most of the time he was an hour later than he'd plan, but tonight, of course he'd be right on time because I was talking to Lance.

"Keller?" He asked, not attempting to disguise the contempt in his voice.

"Yes. I wish not, but that's exactly why. I wish I could explain things to you. I wish I knew how to…but I don't. I can't."

"Another time?"

"Maybe. I hope." I wanted to scream at him, tell him he had me and threw me to the side again and didn't deserve for me to acknowledge his presence anymore, but I couldn't. It was too nice to hear his voice, to feel the timbre of it wrap around me and fill in all the emptiness.

My conversation with Lance lasted another twenty minutes. He asked about my treatments and how I was feeling. He wanted to know when my next treatment was, when my doctor's appointments were and when I'd return to school. He basically asked a hundred questions, none of which, Keller ever seemed concerned about. But for my entire conversation with Lance I forgot about Keller James and the hold he had over me and I pretended Lance and I were back together again.

So when I finally hung up with Lance and Keller walked in the room five minutes later, my whole world shattered again. I was back in my depression, now deeper than I'd been before.

Chapter 24

Two weeks later, I was feeling worse and more depressed than ever. Lance would text just about every day and call every night. Keller was still staying the night with me, but he would sneak in around ten or eleven smelling of something I couldn't quite put my finger on.

The doctors decided they wanted to do an intense round of radiation; three times a week for four weeks and then I would go to once a week for four more weeks. My father, Caleb, Maddie, Alicia or Zack had actually been taking turns going with me. Keller never offered, but everyone else had been amazing.

Lately, I had been noticing more nests of hair left behind on my pillow in the morning but it had never been anything severe. Unfortunately, this morning was different. I woke up feeling nauseous, dizzy and just plain horrible. I immediately rushed to the bathroom and yakked into the toilet for twenty minutes before I stumbled back into my room. I gasped as I stared at a handful of auburn curls resting on my pillow as though they had just been misplaced. I fell into the floor and began sobbing uncontrollably. I'd be bald before the week was over and I didn't know if staying alive was worth walking around like a freak. No hair was a definite signal to the rest of the world that I was fighting cancer. I wouldn't be able to go anywhere without the sad, pitying looks of complete strangers. I didn't think I could handle that. Nor did I think I could handle seeing anyone while I looked like this. My auburn locks had always been what set me apart from others, had been my best asset, honestly. My hair was what characterized me as female, now I was nothing. I was an it.

Chapter 25
Lance

"Hey Lance." Alicia greeted into the phone around ten in the morning. I was at school, in between classes and when I saw my cousin's number pop up on my screen, I knew it had to be important. She should be in class as well.

"Hey Lish, what's up?"

"I was wondering if you could do me a favor, actually. I talked to Jordan earlier and she didn't sound very good at all, I was wondering if you could check on her."

"What happened?"

"I don't know." She admitted in a sad whisper. "I mean, her treatment yesterday was pretty intense. She barfed the whole way home and into the night. She just sounds tired and beaten down, like she'd been crying."

"Are you sure it's a good idea? Does she really want me there?"

"She won't admit it, but yes, she misses you."

"I miss her." I mumbled. The last few weeks had taken a toll on me. I talked to her every night, we texted all throughout the day, but I hadn't seen her since I walked out of her hospital room. In all ways she was still my girlfriend, but in the one way that counted. I couldn't even see her. She wouldn't allow it.

"I know. I'd go over there, but I have a test I can't miss. Could you run over there, please?"

"You don't have to beg, I'm already walking to my truck." I chuckled as I hurried to my locker, dumped my books into it and walked out the back doors to the parking lot.

"I figured. Thanks, Lance. No one is home but her, so just walk up to her room."

"Keller won't pop by to check on her?" I asked worriedly. Even if he was, it wouldn't stop me from seeing her, but I'd do my best to avoid a fight and the added stress for Jordan. Alicia gave a short laugh.

"That asshole barely comes to see her, he stays the night with her but doesn't get there until he's done partying for the night. Hell, on the weekends, he stumbles through the door around two in the morning. I don't know why she's still with him." My stomach clenched at the knowledge that he was spending the night with her, Jordan had said as much but it still hurt that it was really happening.

"Me neither." I grumbled lowly but it was drowned out by the sound of my diesel engine starting.

"Just text me and let me know how it goes." She added quickly before she hung up. Twenty minutes later, I was pulling through the Callatin gates with a bouquet of flowers, a blizzard ice cream treat and the newest book written by Charlaine Harris.

I hope she doesn't flip out when she sees me. Most of all, I hope I can keep my feelings in check. I thought to myself.

I grabbed the stuff off the grey cloth seat next to me and strutted to the door. The whole house was eerily quiet as I walked in. I looked around before climbing the stairs to her bedroom. I caught a glimpse of her in the bathroom mirror, she was sobbing hard as she took a pair of scissors to her beautiful auburn locks.

"Jordan? Jo, what's wrong?" I asked in a panic as I dropped everything in the hall floor and went to her.

"My hair." She choked out. There was a mess of hair splayed on the tile floor below her, hanging off the sink and her shoulders. What still remained on her head was cut raggedly halfway above her bare shoulders.

"Darlin', it looks beautiful." I whispered as I wrapped my arms around her and pulled her in tightly. And it did.

"I...I..." She stammered through her tears, but she couldn't form a sentence so she just buried her face in my chest again. I don't know how long I held her or how long she cried in my arms, but I didn't care. I'd hold her like this forever if I could. Eventually, she pulled away and wiped her eyes.

"I'm sorry." She murmured as she pushed past me and hurried into her room. She didn't slam the door in my face, so that was a good sign. I followed behind cautiously. As soon as I stepped into her brightly decorated bedroom, I realized what happened. There on her purple pillow was a tousle of hair, enough that it looked like she'd begun cutting on her bed. The radiation was assaulting her hair now and she had reacted quickly to the blow. My heart sank as she fell into the floor and leaned against her bed sadly. Knowing she needed to be alone for now, I wordlessly went into the bathroom to clean up the hair, stuffing it all into a Ziploc bag I'd found under the sink, as I did. Meanwhile, I texted my oldest sister, told her Jordan needed help and we'd be over soon.

I left the bathroom, picked up the things I'd brought her from the hall floor and took the few steps to her room. I leaned against the doorjamb and looked back at the beautiful girl before me.

"Hey sweetheart." I murmured softly before I walked over and plopped down beside her in the floor.

"What are you doing here?" She asked in an exasperated voice, trying her best to sound upset with my presence.

"I wanted to check on you." I smiled. "And I'm glad I did."

"Lance." She sobbed as she found her way to my arms again. "My hair. I didn't want you to see me like this."

"It's all right, darlin'." I chuckled, as I ran my hand softly over the back of her auburn hair. "Short is totally hot on you."

"Shut up, asshole, it's horrible."

"No, it's not." I tipped her chin up so her blue eyes were forced to focus on me. "C'mon, we'll head over to Jen's and she can straighten it out."

"It's horrible, Lance." She cried again. I shook my head as I stood up; I turned around and put my hand out to help her up.

"I don't want to go anywhere." She pouted as she pulled her knees into her chest, half hiding her face behind her arms.

"It's just Jen's house, no one else will be there. I promise." She tried to protest, but I wouldn't allow it. I glanced around the room to find a coat or something so she wouldn't be cold in the late March air. Immediately, my eyes landed on a Letterman's jacket. Keller's. I glared, hating what it stood for, that she belonged to someone else. I found a hooded sweatshirt nearby and handed it to her, then grabbed a throw off her desk chair and placed it over her shoulders. "Please? You'll feel better, I promise." She nodded her head and reached for my hand. I latched on to it and led her downstairs.

It was like old times as I picked her up and placed her inside the old farm truck. As soon as I climbed in beside her, she snuggled up as close as possible. I closed my eyes and savored the moment a little longer than I should have. I pulled onto the road and headed out of the Callatin Academy gates, I put my arm on her shoulders and pulled her closer. Out of habit, I found myself randomly kissing the top of her head and trying to soothe her crying as we drove to Jen's subdivision.

"Everything is falling apart around me." She whimpered. "Maybe the surgery was just prolonging the inevitable."

"Jordan, this is a completely normal side effect of the treatments." I squeezed her shoulders and steered into Jen's concrete driveway. "But for you, it totally works." I put the truck in park before I turned to look at her. My hands went to her hair carefully as I smoothed it out, cautious not to tug or let her notice when a few strands came out in my hand. I ran a finger down her neck and then to her collarbone. "The bare neck is incredibly sexy. I want to…"

My cell phone started ringing and interrupted my sentence. I silenced it, knowing it was Jenn. I looked back at Jordan sincerely before I tenderly kissed her neck. I knew I shouldn't go there, knew how vulnerable she was at this moment, but I couldn't hold back. She whimpered and I could barely focus on where we were or what we were doing.

"I know you may not feel like it, darlin, but you are the most beautiful girl I've ever seen." I whispered as I kissed her mouth softly.

"Lance." She sighed tearfully.

"C'mon, let's get inside before Jen comes out here to get you." I hugged her quickly and helped her out of the truck. It broke my heart to see how weak and fragile she had become. I felt the water brimming my eyes when she leaned in for support.

If only I hadn't been such an idiot in the past, I could constantly take care of her. I'd be able to take the brunt of her pain and ease her through everything, but I couldn't and I hated myself for it.

Jenn pounced on us the second we were on her concrete front porch and greeted Jordan with a giant hug, fussing over her immediately as if she were her long lost sister. Between the two of us, we led Jordan into Jenn's makeshift beauty salon in what used to be their garage. A few seconds later, my sister was shooing me out of the room proclaiming it a girl's only site.

"Ella's napping, but if you want to listen for her, that'd be great. Rob's in the computer room, playing Call of Duty or something." Jen advised. I nodded and looked back at Jordan for the okay to leave her alone with my big sister. She gave a weak smile silently telling me she'd be fine, so I bent down, kissed her forehead and went to find my brother in law.

"Hey Rob."

"How's it going? How's Jordan?"

"Not good." I answered with a shaky voice.

"Want a beer?"

"Yes, but I can't. If I start, I won't stop and I don't want to be drunk when I take her home."

"Good point." Rob smiled.

"Can you do me a favor? Or rather, can you help me with something?" I asked with a wide grin. Rob gave me a curious look and I pulled my brother in law into the bathroom.

Twenty minutes later, both of us emerged hairless. In a show of support, I decided I would shave my head until it was shiny and smooth. Rob decided to follow along and after a phone call to Sawyer, the rest of my friends were following suit. I even dialed Caleb's number to tell him about the events that had transpired before calling Alicia to do the same.

Rob had gone into the nursery to get a crying Ella out of her crib while I headed into the shop to see how my dream girl had fared at the hands of Jenn. My breath immediately caught in my throat as I viewed her from behind in the mirror. She looked gorgeous and sexy as Hell with an auburn bob that curled perfectly under her ears.

"Damn darlin'." I breathed. Jordan's eyes went up and her gaping mouth replaced her smile.

"Lance." She gasped as she stood up wearily. I lengthened my stride and tried to reach her before she exerted too much energy. "What did you do?"

"I got a haircut too." I chuckled nonchalantly. Her fingers went up to the skin on my head as she felt it, almost as if it weren't real. Tears streamed down her face and I forced a smile. "I never realized how misshapen my head was until I did this."

"It's beautiful." She whispered as she continued to feel the smooth skin. "You're beautiful. Lance…"

"*You're* beautiful." I smiled as I ran my fingers through her hair. "It looks amazing."

"Lance." She sighed as her hands went down my face and traced my jawline. "I love you."

"I love you too." I choked out so low that even I barely heard it. Of course, just because that's the kind of luck I have, as soon as I opened my mouth any sound was drowned out by the excitement of my beautiful niece's cries of excitement over seeing Jordan.

It was obvious she hadn't heard it by the disappointed look on her face, but the moment was gone. I never removed my hand from the small of her back, hoping she could just sense my emotions.

Chapter 26
Jordan

I couldn't take my eyes off Lance. I couldn't stop looking at what he'd done for me. When we left Jenn's an hour later I was drained from the day's events, especially since I thought I'd heard Lance whisper three special words to me.

What a day.

By the time we pulled in front of my dad's house I was passed out on Lance's shoulder. I didn't stir as he carried me out of the truck, up to my room, or as he gently put me into my bed and pulled the blankets up around me.

He was gone when I woke up.

"Hey sis." A bald Caleb grinned from the couch Zack had moved into my room. I smiled faintly, looking at the door with the hopes Lance would walk back in. "He went home. He didn't want you to be alone, he stayed while you slept until Zack got here. I probably shouldn't tell you that though, huh?" I shook my head, even though my heart was melting.

"Hey sleeping beauty." Zack grinned as he strutted into my room carrying pizza boxes. "You hungry?" I nodded and pushed myself up into a sitting position.

"You shaved your head too?"

"Duh." He chuckled, flashing me a wink. "The majority of the guys at Callatin shaved their heads for you today."

"It's amazing to see." Maddie gushed as she pulled out her phone, rushed to my side and began showing me all the pictures she'd taken of my bald headed male classmates. "Tomorrow, Jenn and some of her friends are coming to the dorms and doing a mass haircut. There's already like fifty girls signed up, all of the squad for sure."

"What? You guys don't have to do that."

"We know, but everyone loves you J and we want you to know you're not alone." Alicia interjected as she hugged me tightly and sat down on the other side of me. "And," She continued as she pulled a folded up piece of paper out of her back pocket and handed it to me. "It didn't just stop here at Callatin."

The paper had a picture of Lance, Sawyer, Drew, Cooper, Chopper and Wyatt all with soft, bald, shiny heads smiling at a camera. My heart melted and tears rolled down my cheeks.

"Aw J." Maddie chuckled as she began crying too. Alicia wrapped us both in a hug.

"Why do they cry so much?" Caleb asked in an exasperated voice.

"No clue, but why are we always excluded from group hugs?" I giggled and pulled away from my roommates. I couldn't have any better friends, I knew that, but I still felt lost without Lance. The five of us ate pizza for dinner while watching movies and talking. It felt good to forget about my reality and focus on being a teenage for a bit.

That night, around two a.m. when Keller snuck into my bed, he still had a full head of hair. I wasn't as shocked as I should've been I guess, mostly appalled and hurt that he didn't feel the need to show me any support, which really shouldn't have surprised me.

I knew Lance taking me to get my hair cut was all about soothing me, everyone, including me. knew it wouldn't be long until all my hair was gone and my head matched Lance and the others. However, I was still grateful he attempted to ease my pain.

Chapter 27

Despite the doctors protests, I was back in school two days later and there's nothing more embarrassing for a sixteen year old girl than her hair falling out in thick masses throughout the day. Especially when you have to check your seat after you get up from every class. Most people were great about it, pretending not to notice, but Keller's gaggle of girls couldn't wait to roast me about it.

"Gross." I heard Sage gasp as I stood up from my seat next to Keller at lunch. A thin pile of auburn hair had stayed behind on the top of the chair, looking like a small smashed rodent. "That's disgusting. Shouldn't she be wearing a hair net or something?"

"Sage." Brennan Brookman snapped disapprovingly. The snobby blonde shot him a dirty look before she snickered.

"What a freak. She looks like one of those mannequins they torture at the local beauty college." I squared my shoulders and bit my tongue. I wanted to fly across the table at the bitch, but I couldn't fight myself out of a paper bag right now.

"Knock it off Sage, it's not her fault." Brennan glared angrily at Sage and her girlfriends as they continued to make comments and laugh hysterically. I looked back at Keller for help, but he was laughing with the girls. He shrugged innocently as I gave him a dirty look, turned on my heel and walked to my next class.

"You okay?" Brennan asked breathlessly as he hurried next to me in the hall. He'd chased after me to check on me, my boyfriend was probably still in the cafeteria helping with the humiliating cracks about me.

"I'm fine." I sighed. "Those girls don't bother me." I let out a shaky breath before I shook my head and looked up at Brennan. Up was an understatement, he was a good foot taller than me, all arms and legs. "That's a lie, of course, but I'll be okay. Thanks for checking on me."

"They're just jealous of you. Sage wants what she can't have and she wants Keller so she'll do whatever necessary to make you look bad in front of him."

"She can have him for all I care." I grumbled. Brennan pulled back in shock and stared in disbelief. I shrugged. "Well, she can, but forget I said that."

"And forget when I say you can do a hell of a lot better than Keller James." He grinned.

"Forgotten." I giggled with a wink as I leaned into him. "Seriously thanks, Brennan." He nodded before giving a short wave and walking off to his next class. I stopped off at my locker where a note was taped to the outside.

Have I told you lately that you're smoking hot with the short haircut? Seriously. Meet me in the broom closet at noon. I can't restrain myself any longer.

I laughed aloud and tucked the paper into my book. It was 12:30 and I was certain Zack had never gone to the broom closet. It was a private joke between us from when I first came to Callatin. We flirted so much, got along so great that many people thought we were hitting it. Of course, Keller was pursuing me at the time and I wouldn't let him get close, Zack's closeness with me set him off. Zack ate it up, constantly telling me to meet him in the janitor's closet or the supply closet whenever Keller could hear.

"I knew that'd bring out a smile." Zack breathed in my ear, sneaking up on me. I jumped. "But I'm a little disappointed and hurt that you laughed at my offer. I was totally serious."

"Oh yeah? Well I was in the closet at noon, where were you?"

"Which closet? I will definitely be there tomorrow if you will be." He lied flirtatiously with a wink. He leaned back against a nearby locker as he watched me bend down to get a few books out.

"If I had the energy, I'd be all yours, but I'd rather our first time together be mind blowing."

"Oh it definitely will be." He drawled in his pronounced New York accent. I smiled and rolled my eyes playfully. "I'll do all the work; you just concentrate on the orgasms."

"Plural?" I cocked an eyebrow as I closed my locker door and started towards my next class, which Zack and I shared. "I think multiple would send me into a heart attack right now."

"Have you ever had multiple?" He asked in a low sultry voice as he slung his arm around my shoulders. I ducked my head embarrassedly, Lance was amazing at producing one or two at a time, Keller not so much and that was the extent of my sexual history. Zack leaned down and whispered in my ear; "When you're feeling better J, I can show you what sex is supposed to be like. Let you see how *you're* supposed to enjoy it the most."

"Zack." I gasped.

"I can make your toes curl; your eyes roll back into your head and send you into ecstasy." We walked into our classroom, Zack and me taking our seats all the way in the back of the room. Zack moved closer, whispering in my ear as his fingers played carelessly on my knee, drawing circles and lines seductively. "And that's before entering you, babe. I'd make love to you so thoroughly you wouldn't want to move for days, the only thing you'd think about was making love to me over and over again." My breath came out in short, ragged spurts as my body tensed, fighting the emotions his words were causing. There was a clearing of the throat from the front of the room and Zack pulled away slowly. My face was flushed, from excitement or embarrassment of getting caught, I'm not certain of which. I sat back in my seat and absentmindedly started fanning myself. I heard Zack snicker beside me, he flashed me a wink. I rolled my eyes at him.

"You are evil." I mouthed. He grinned back at me and I couldn't help but smile either.

But you forgot about the bitches in the caf? Right? He wrote on a piece of paper that he slid towards me when the teacher's back was turned. I forced a smile and nodded. I shouldn't be disappointed his interest was purely based on making me feel better, in a different way. I was stupid to think he'd actually be interested in me in a way other than as Caleb's little sister, his friend. I was in enough of a pickle as it was between Lance and Keller, so I shouldn't be disappointed his words were meant to soothe. I'd be an outright liar if I said I didn't wish they were promises for another day though. Damn, but I was a fool.

Chapter 28

A week later, I was shocked to find Lance at our front door. Alicia stood behind him, pushing him in and smiling excitedly. It was a Saturday night and I was home alone. Everyone else had plans to go out, except me. I had no clue what my boyfriend was doing tonight; I wasn't privy to his daily details. Caleb and Maddie were going out, Zack had a hot date, or three. Alicia and Sawyer had plans as did Chopper and anyone else who might want to hang out with me. The list was small these days. I'd planned on watching a movie in my pajamas as I buried my depression deep inside a lot of ice cream and junk food. But, honestly, my appetite was nonexistent these days.

"Hey, I wasn't expecting anyone." I gushed, hugging both of them tightly, and quickly realizing I was wearing a ratty tank top, no bra and dirty yoga pants.

"We won't stay long." Alicia looked around the room. "But Lance had a present for you and we thought we'd deliver it."

"I can talk for myself, Lish." Lance stated as he rolled his eyes.

"I know, but you usually fuck it up." She shrugged as she gave him a shove so he was closer to me. I stifled a giggle and watched Lance shake his head in disbelief.

"Who needs enemies when you've got family?" He nervously handed me the perfectly wrapped present.

"Lance, why would you…?"

"Don't…I wasn't completely alone in doing it. Actually, Jen, Lish, Maddie, Caleb and Zack helped too. They just thought I should…" He rambled as I started to unwrap the gift.

Tears streamed down my face as I pulled out an auburn wig cut in a bob which would fall halfway to my shoulders, like the haircut Jenn had given me days ago. Since that day, my hair had become pretty thin and pathetic looking.

"It's actually most of your own hair, from when you cut it that day." He started, ducking his head shyly. My heart melted at the thought that he'd gone to all the trouble of saving it for this reason.

"Lance." I sighed as I wrapped my arms around his neck and hugged him as tightly as I possibly could. I didn't want to ever let him go and I could tell he didn't want me to either. I gently kissed his mouth before I pulled away to hug Alicia.

"Don't kiss me." Alicia giggled.

"You can kiss *me* though." Zack offered with a flirtatious wink as he chuckled and picked me up in a hug as he walked in from the kitchen. Maddie, Caleb, Chopper and the rest of Lance's friends filed in after him. I turned my head and looked at them quizzically.

"Sorry, Lance is…"

"Amazing." Alicia gushed. "Don't let him fool you, he orchestrated everything. He's being so modest but, seriously, he's amazing."

"Not really." He shrugged.

"You didn't honestly believe we were going to allow you to be alone on a Saturday night? Did you?" Zack asked as he gave me another hug. I felt his lips on the top of my head, I was shocked but I played it off. I'm sure it was just my imagination.

"But I know *you* had three dates tonight."

"And your point is?" He asked with a careless shrug as he let me go and flashed me a wink. "Beer anyone?"

"I should go." Lance interjected nervously as he started towards the door. I grabbed his hand and tried to pull him towards me, but he shook his head.

"Thank you, again." I walked him to the front porch. "I just…I just don't know what to say. You've been…incredible." His hand gingerly held mine as he looked down into my eyes.

"You don't have to say a thing; I would do anything for you, Jo." He whispered desperately.

"I know, I just don't know that I deserve it."

"You deserve more." He pulled me closer to him. His arms instinctively wrapped around my waist and I felt my whole body melt into his. "I wish I could do more."

"You've done plenty, Lance Bowman." I grinned. "You're amazing."

"I don't know about all that." He chuckled modestly with a shy half smile. "I guess you bring out the best in me."

For a moment, we just stared into each other's eyes and the rest of the world disappeared into the chilly night air. Without hesitation, one hand went up to my face and he pulled me in for an amazingly passionate kiss. When he pulled apart, I was weak and breathless.

"I'll call you tomorrow." He mumbled as he kissed my forehead and then quickly made his way to his truck.

"Please stay." I begged. He glanced back at me, a pained look on his face as he shook his head.

"I want to. I do Jordan, but I can't. You have a boyfriend, I have to respect that. I can't…if I stay, I won't respect that."

"I don't want you to respect anything." I whined, my voice teetering dangerously close to a spoiled child.

"I know." He gazed at me intently over the top of his truck bed. "I don't understand any of this. If you love me, if you want to be with me I don't understand why you're not. I can't fathom why you're with Keller James over me. Being so close to you…if I stay Jordan, I'll get my hopes up but tomorrow you'll go back to Keller and I'm left to look like the fool. Frankly, my heart can't take much more of it." I nodded my head numbly. Words escaped me as my depression, pain and guilt enveloped me. Lance took it as the go-ahead, he climbed into his truck and he was gone. I collapsed onto the front porch and cried clinging to the wig he'd brought me, the only thing at this point that made me feel close to him. A houseful of people changed their plans for me, so I wouldn't be alone and I was outside crying, feeling like the most isolated girl in the world.

Chapter 29

On Monday morning, I walked into school on Keller's arm. My new wig was placed on my head, looking more natural than my own hair, really. Lance's gift couldn't have come at a better time, this morning the last of my hair had fallen out, I was completely bald. My confidence was back and maybe a little of that had to do with who had given me the wig. Which by the way, Keller thought was a gift from Maddie and Alicia. He'd never know otherwise either. I hadn't seen Keller all weekend, not until he came to the house to pick me up Monday morning and he said nothing about my new look. It was Maddie, who was skipping down the steps with Caleb in tow, who pointed it out. Keller still didn't comment.

I held my head high as my boyfriend walked me to my locker and made it a point to give me a completely inappropriate kiss while the majority of our school watched. When he pulled away, I caught a glimpse of Sage's enraged face before she stormed off, her entourage clacking at her heels.

I tried to be nice, I really did. However, the third derogatory comment Sage made to me in my History class, was the last straw. I popped off an extremely rude remark while smiling ever so sweetly. Her face was pale before turning bright red from the laughs that filled the room. The entire class was a ping-pong game of cattiness, I was definitely ahead. When the bell rang we all filtered out of the room. I headed down the hall to my locker with my friend Natalie beside me as we talked about our upcoming Spring Break plans.

"Hey, bitch." I heard Sage hiss behind me. "Where'd you get that hair, Wal-Mart or Dollar General?" She cackled, I ignored her and continued to walk. I felt a tug and my wig was gone, Sage was behind me holding it in her hands as if it were a dead animal. She was horrified at first and then she began to roar with laughter as she pointed at me. I watched as her gaggle of friends did the same, they even starting tossing my wig around as if it were a ball. I was furious, but I wouldn't let her know that. I'd pay her back on my own time.

"You're such a bitch." I heard Maddie gasp behind me as she lunged towards the girls. My auburn wig went flying through the hall, landing neatly on top of Keller's books. He yelped and threw it back in the direction it had come before laughing hysterically when he realized what had just happened.

"What a freak!"

"Look she's bald!"

"Oh my God, that is *so* disgusting!"

"Someone should've pulled the plug on her; I would rather die than look like that!"

"Oh, that is so sad."

"No wonder Keller is always with you Sage."

"Serves the bitch right." That came from Sage's mouth, along with a few other comments, but mostly her gaggle of girlfriends were chiming in to soothe their leader's ego.

"Oh look, she's going to cry." Sage laughed proudly. Her eyes were wide with excitement and she talked loudly hoping to get everyone's attention in the hallway. "What's the matter, freak? I mean Jordan, upset that people will see you for the loser freak you really are? Nothing great about you, is there?"

"I'm not going to cry." I laughed. "If anything, I'm just amazed at how jealous you are. Seriously, you think showing everyone I'm bald will make you more popular? It really just proves that you're a *sad, pathetic, bitch*." I shrugged my shoulders and walked off with my head held high. I would cry, but I'd be damned if it was now or anytime during school hours. Keller's mouth gaped open as I walked past him and to my locker.

"Jordan, you should really…you're not going to finish school like that, are you?" Keller mumbled in shock.

"Yes. Do you have a problem with it?"

"Well yeah, it's…it's…"

"It's a part of my cancer, Keller. It's a very real and very normal part of my illness. If you have a problem with that you can fuck off."

"You should at least apologize to Sage. You made her look like a fool in front of everyone." It was my turn for my jaw to hit the floor.

"You're kidding, right?"

"No. She's my friend and you…"

"Supposedly, *I'm your girlfriend*." I breathed slowly. "And you didn't even defend me while she tried to humiliate me in front of the entire school. And again, you can just fuck off, Keller." I turned on my heel and stomped away.

"I will deck that little bitch." Maddie hissed as she hurried beside me before I turned off into my Zoology class.

"I would like to as well, but letting her know she got to me will just fuel the bitchometer."

"You're just going to walk away and not…?"

"Oh she'll pay Mad, but when she least expects it." I shrugged. "Besides, the fact that I'm now walking around school without the safety of my wig burns her ass more than anything."

"She does look pretty livid."

"Understatement." Alicia chuckled as she met me in front of my zoology classroom. "She's seething. I heard Adrienne saying something about getting her medication so she calms down."

"Horse tranquilizers?" Maddie questioned with a raised eyebrow. "Better yet bovine ones, for the cow that she is."

"I'm more pissed about Keller having the gall to tell me I needed to apologize to Sage for embarrassing *her* in front of the entire school." Maddie and Alicia gasped and both stopped to stare at me in open-mouthed disbelief.

"You're kidding right? Tell me you're kidding."

"I wish I were. Apparently, their friendship is more important than our joke of a relationship."

"I will pulverize that son of a bitch the second we are out of the building." I heard Zack growl from behind me.

"I'll just smother him in his sleep." Caleb joined Zack. Both boys' faces were screwed up in anger. "Are you okay, sis?"

"I'm fine." I shrugged.

"I think you're still a thousand times more beautiful than her." Zack stated sweetly as he flashed me a grin. "And everyone but her little three person entourage just turned their backs on her."

"Except Keller." Caleb hissed as he turned around and saw my boyfriend comforting his friend. "Why in the Hell did you get back together with him?"

67

"As far as I'm concerned he can fucking have her, she can have him, whatever. He's really not that great of a catch for her to be so psycho over. In fact, I'll go right over there and tell her so to both their faces." I started towards the two of them. Sage was looking up at Keller as though he hung the moon. I should've been jealous but I was actually more disgusted than anything. Zack grabbed my arm and pulled me back into him

"It kills me to say this, but that's what she wants. Don't give it to her just yet. You'll just let her think she won." He squeezed my hand discreetly. I nodded my head in agreement before I said thanks to my friends and brother and then slipped into my classroom.

Throughout the day, I was bombarded with words of congratulations, support and admiration for my response to Sage. By the end of the day, I realized there were many people in this school who didn't care too much for the spoiled rotten heiress, which really didn't surprise me.

As for Keller, well of course, he wasn't well liked either, but if I was careful and planned correctly I could get rid of him for good and make him think it was all his choice.

Chapter 30

A few days later, my brother's roommate Grayson knocked on my bedroom door.

"Hey Grayson." I stood up and hugged the tall blonde. He flashed an award-winning smile at me and kissed me on the cheek.

"Hey Jordan, how's it going?"

"Could be better." I shrugged as I sat back down on my bed and then patted beside me for him to sit down. When he did, I softly touched the stubble returning to his head.

"I can't believe you did it too."

"Why wouldn't I?"

"Keller didn't." I grumbled.

"Unfortunately, that's actually what I wanted to talk to you about." He mumbled hesitantly as he began to rub his hands on his thighs nervously. "I don't want to do this, but…"

"What's wrong, Gray?"

"Keller's cheating on you." He blurted quickly and then immediately looked like he regretted the words that fell out. "I'm sorry. I didn't want to be the one to tell you this, but I can't pretend I don't know anymore. You don't deserve this; you shouldn't be treated like this."

"How do you know?" I asked, trying to pretend I was surprised. It was common knowledge to me, but in the past he had at least had the decency to cover up his indiscretions. It hurt that the rest of the school was seeing how stupid I was for staying with him.

"While you were in the hospital he and Zack got into a physical fight, or rather, Zack punched him. I overheard Zack and Sage talking that day, I heard Sage tell him. Then I also heard them arguing before Zack hit him, Keller admitted to it."

"Why wouldn't…"

"Zack didn't want to hurt you, J; he didn't want to be the one to do this. I didn't either but…Jordan, I checked into it too. I have pictures on my phone of Keller with Sage, Adrienne and a few other girls. I pretended like I wanted to get high with them and that's when I…"

"High?"

"Yeah. Pot, coke, and some other kinds of pills I didn't really recognize."

"How, how can I not…?"

"He's a pathological liar, a narcissist, a sociopath and a Grade A asshole. I just…I had to tell you because it's not fair that you're here going through Hell and he's taking advantage of your absence by screwing everything that walks."

"Thank you Grayson, I really appreciate you telling me."

"I'll go now." He mumbled as he stood up. "I'm sorry Jordan, I really am."

I didn't hear anything else; I didn't actually see him leaving because my room started spinning. There was a loud rush in my ears and without realizing it, I sprinted to the bathroom and heaved until my insides hurt.

When Keller climbed into my bed that night and kissed my forehead, I pretended to be asleep and prayed he didn't notice I was crying.

I honestly don't know why I'm upset; maybe for my naivety, my stupidity? I don't know. I was more frustrated with the knowledge that neither Keller nor I wanted to be with each other, but we were. I couldn't understand why he wouldn't let me go, why he threatened me every time I tried to break up with him, when he was out screwing all kinds of girls. It just didn't make sense.

Maddie was throwing a party a few days later. I wasn't in the mood for public appearances rather than school, mostly because I was feeling incredibly unattractive. I was still talking to Lance on the phone on a regular basis, but I hadn't told him about the wig incident, I was too embarrassed. Maddie had retrieved the wig for me, cleaned it up and put it back in my bedroom on its stand for me, but I decided I didn't need a wig or anything to cover my head. I was on a journey and covering it up would make people think it was easy, which is far from the truth.

I haven't been able to keep much food down and as a result I'd lost about forty pounds since my initial hospital stay for the cancer. My normally tone body looked frail and sickly. I was pasty, where I used to be tanned, and I had permanent dark circles under my eyes. Sometimes I looked in the mirror and would mistake myself for a corpse. Keller wasn't helping my self-esteem with the news of his infidelity and the fact that he rarely touched or kissed me, when he was even around, that is.

Maddie and Alicia had been at the house that afternoon, making me swear I would attend Maddie's soiree. They were legendary after all. They even picked out my attire. I walked downstairs in a sexy red, slinky dress and a pair of sling backs. My confidence was finally back, if even for just a moment.

"What in the Hell took you so long?" Keller huffed angrily. "It's not like you had to fix your fucking hair." I cringed at his dig, but I wouldn't let him see it bothered me.

"Damn J, you look fucking hot." Zack gasped as he walked down the stairs with Caleb. My brother punched him in the arm playfully. Keller glared as he grabbed my arm and yanked me down the stairs

"Whoa." Caleb growled as he lunged.

"What is your deal, Keller?" Zack grunted. "You have her, don't treat her like she's..."

"She tripped."

"Don't insult me." He rolled his eyes and looked past him, directly at me. "Say the word, J. He'll be banned from Maddie's house and you can ride with us."

"I'm okay." I murmured in a small voice. Keller's fingers were intertwined with mine in a death grip.

"Making up shit doesn't make you look better, Bentley."

"I'm not..."

"And you, of all people, should not be telling me how to treat a girl. How many times have you fucked and forgotten?" Keller cackled. Zack's eyes darted to mine quickly and I looked away. His sexual conquest list was no secret, but Keller was trying to make my friend the bad guy, rather than the hero he was trying to be.

"Let's just go." I pleaded as I tugged on Keller's hand. My boyfriend smiled smugly at my brother and friend before he pulled me out of the house without another word.

"Why in the Hell do you have to start shit every time?" Keller growled as he flung me away from him and stalked to his car.

"I didn't." I mumbled.

"And why in the Hell do you not wear that cheap ass wig anymore? It looks a lot better than you going bald. If you think I'm going to be seen with you at this party when you look like a fucking freak, you're wrong." I stopped walking. Tears stung my eyes as I stared back in

70

shock. I turned on my heel and stomped back towards the house. "Do not do this, Jordan. You will regret it."

"I could not possibly regret anything else in my life, Keller James." I stormed into the house and he didn't follow. Minutes later, I heard his car tear out of my driveway.

Chapter 31

"Why are you back?" Caleb asked with a cocked eyebrow.

"Because I don't want to deal with Keller any more than I have to." I shrugged innocently as I looked down at the ground quickly.

"I don't know how, or why, you put up with him at all." My brother grumbled.

"Lay off, Caleb." Zack interjected. "You know why…"

"He knows what?" I hissed.

"Nothing. Let's get out of here before Maddie shoots us for being late." I didn't want to argue and I sure as heck didn't want to be pressed on the reason I was with Keller. If they knew the truth, I wouldn't be able to deny their questions.

"What wonderful girl are we picking up on our way?" I asked with a forced cheerfulness to my voice."

"Excuse me?" Caleb responded before he climbed into the Tahoe.

"Who is your date tonight, Zack? Please tell me it's someone I can at least hold an intelligent conversation with."

"I don't…" He snapped as he opened the passenger door for me. He took a deep breath. "Are you saying I only date airheads or…"

"Sorry," I mumbled as I climbed in the truck. "I didn't mean anything by it. I just…I'm not in the mood to force conversations with some of the dimwits here, that's all."

"I don't have a date."

"You *always* have a date."

"I don't tonight." He shrugged nonchalantly. I turned in my seat to look at him while Caleb pulled out of the driveway and steered towards the Callatin Academy gates.

"Am I missing something?" Zack cocked an eyebrow and shook his head.

"Don't question it." Caleb grunted as he watched the road a little too carefully.

"I'll just be grateful I don't have to play nice."

"Is Keller going to the party?"

"Like he would miss one of Maddie's parties. Everyone will be there and he has to be seen where everyone else is."

"But without his girlfriend."

"What is that supposed to mean?"

"I'm just trying to figure him out, that's all." Zack responded with a shrug. "You really do look nice tonight." I rolled my eyes and focused on the radio.

"Holy crap, Maddie is going to roast me." Caleb moaned as we pulled up to the oversized brick home, the mile long driveway was already full with various cars and SUV's.

"She'll get over it." I giggled. "Just blame me."

"Do you need a jacket?" Zack asked as my brother hurried out of the truck and up to the house. I shook my head. I crossed my arms in front of me and tried not to shiver.

"I'll be fine once we are inside." Zack watched me carefully before he grabbed his jacket out of the backseat and tucked it under his arm.

"I knew that dress would look fabulous on you!" Maddie squealed when Zack and I walked into the marble floor foyer of her parent's house.

"The dress *is* amazing, even if I do feel awkward in it." I mumbled as my best friend hugged me tightly.

"You'll forget about that soon." She whispered. "Zack, can you help Cale with a table in the dining room?" He nodded and hurried away. Maddie smiled after him before she looked back at me worriedly. "If you start to feel tired or sick, just go lay down in my room, okay?"

"I'll be fine."

"I know, I just wanted to offer it." She sighed before she looked towards the kitchen and then back at me before pulling me down the hallway. "Steer clear of Sage and Jilly Zuckermann."

"What? Why? Since when are they friends?"

"Jilly was Zack's date." Maddie looked at me carefully as she let those words hang in the air. I moved uncomfortably under her stare. Jilly was an absolutely gorgeous girl with jet black hair and the cheekbones of an Indian Princess. She was the top female swimmer in the state and she had the body you'd see depicted in a cartoon about mermaids. She would look great on Zack's arm and my stomach tugged at the thought. "Keller walked in without you about twenty minutes ago, spouting lies about you being too dramatic so he ditched you. About five minutes later, Jilly walked in and checked her phone. Zack texted to tell her he didn't want to hang out tonight after all. She was pretty upset, about to leave and was explaining the text to a couple girls. Sage overheard and began blaming you."

"I didn't…"

"I know, *we* know that and there's no point in arguing it either. Sage is trying to turn people against you because she's threatened by you."

"How in the Hell can you be threatened by me? My life is Hell, I'm bald and sick *constantly* with an asshole boyfriend."

"She wants that asshole desperately." Maddie rolled her eyes. "Poor Jilly is so gullible that she is believing whatever bull Sage is feeding her."

"Lovely. I knew I shouldn't have come out tonight."

"Nonsense." Maddie waved her hand airily. "If they start shit I'll just kick the dumb witches out. Don't worry though, they won't get near you."

"I don't understand why I get blamed for everything. It's not my fault Zack ditched her."

"It's not, but it is." Maddie shrugged nonchalantly as she looked away quickly.

"What does that mean?"

"You're not that clueless, J. Just think about it and you'll see it too." I rolled my eyes and looked away. Caleb and Zack came out of the kitchen. My eyes locked with Zack's and his face broke into a smile, I couldn't help but return it. My stomach flipped ridiculously. I heard Maddie giggle beside me as she started towards my brother.

"I got you some water." Zack stated as he extended an ice cold bottle towards me. I took it, noticing he had one as well.

"You're not drinking?" He shook his head.

"I thought you'd appreciate sober conversation." He shrugged nonchalantly as he looked at my brother quickly.

"More than you could guess. Of course, you're more entertaining drunk."

"Is that so?" He chuckled as he cocked an eyebrow. "I get no love, Caleb."

"Get used to it. They like to bust balls."

"They?" Maddie asked as she crossed her arms in front of her chest.

"I meant Jordan." He answered quickly. Maddie shook her head and rolled her eyes as she leaned into my brother.

"If I didn't bust your balls then you'd think I was mad at you."

"Very true." Zack's eyes darted behind me, they grew clouded immediately.

"Who invited the freak? Didn't Keller tell you to stay home? Are you so psycho that you stalk him?" Sage's voice was high pitched and as irritating as getting stuck a million times with the same needle.

"She's with me." Zack interjected as he stepped in between the overdone blonde and me. Sage's pink mouth went into a straight line as she squinted in anger.

"You're an idiot." She rolled her eyes and flipped a look back at her entourage. "Keller will end you."

"I'd like to see him try." Caleb hissed.

"You can do so much better than her." Sage stated, rolling her eyes again. She let out an exaggerated sigh as she turned to look at Jilly. "Didn't I tell you Jordan was behind Zack ditching you? She is such a whore."

"Says the girl who offers me threesomes on a regular basis." Zack spit. I felt nauseous from his words as unwanted scenarios began playing out in my head. Sage sputtered for just a second, her cheeks a bright pink with anger and embarrassment. She looked back at me and a wicked smile crossed her mouth immediately.

"You've never turned me down though, have you?" Her voice was syrupy sweet as bile rose in my throat.

"I have…"

"Why would you text me that you didn't want to hang out and then show up here?" Jilly asked, her chin raised defiantly. "Jordan made you ditch me?"

"Jordan…"

"Is a whore." Sage cackled. "And a freak."

"Jealousy is unbecoming."

"I am not jealous."

"Keller doesn't want you, because he's with Jordan. He doesn't want Jordan and she doesn't want him, but he'd rather be miserable in a fake relationship than be in one with you. You are so threatened by her and the beautiful, amazing person she is that you are attacking someone who is sick and fighting for her life. She has friends, you have people who bow to you, because they're terrified to be the next person on your pathetic hit list. No one likes you Sage, no one, not even your own family. How many times have they gone on vacation and left you behind?"

"Zack." I mumbled quietly. He was going too far.

"That's why she's better than you." He continued. "You are a hateful, psychotic bitch towards her and she is trying to stick up for you." Tears rolled down Sage's cheeks and Zack just glared at her. "You can think you're the queen of this school, but it's all in your head. You are nothing, Sage. Keller doesn't want you. I don't want you. No one wants an easy, manipulative, psychotic, drug addict trying to be a mean girl. You've had more plastic surgery and…"

"Zack, stop." I stated loudly as I grabbed his arm and pulled him back. "She's not worth the breath, but she also doesn't…you're just sinking to her level by humiliating her like this. Her words don't hurt me, please stop." He looked at me with wide eyes

"Keller will end you." Sage hissed before she stalked away.

"She deserves worse for…" Zack started. "

74

"If I let her bother me, then she wins." I shrugged. "I hate losing." Zack shook his head and chuckled.

"I'm sorry, J. I didn't mean to…" I shook my head and started away from the view of the party.

"Zack." Jilly interjected. "If you want to be with Jordan, then by all means, be with her. You need to come to terms with your feelings though, because leading me and every other girl in this school on, makes you an asshole. And Jordan is too good to be with a jack ass coward who lacks the balls to speak the truth to her or to some other idiot who thought she caught the eye of a nice guy." She turned on her heel and stalked away.

"Burn." Caleb coughed from behind me. Zack turned around slowly, his face drawn in mortification. I couldn't face what came next so I hurried towards the bathroom to let the nausea take over.

Chapter 32
Zack

"Did she run because of what I said to Sage or because of what Jilly said?" I asked on a loud sigh as I ran my hand down my face. I could not get anything right today.

"Jilly. Maybe. Maybe both." Maddie responded with a roll of her shoulders as she bit her bottom lip and watched her roommate scurry away. "Sage deserved it, but…"

"I was sticking up for J."

"She knows that and she'll be grateful when she processes it all."

"What did I miss?" Alicia asked warily as she approached our group. I was incredibly leery about anything I said in front of Alicia Bowman, she was Lance's cousin after all. Her loyalty would lie with him and if she learned my true feelings for Jordan and told Lance, it might cause him to resurface. It seems like he only remembers Jordan when she's taken by someone else. No matter how much of a jerk Lance was to Jordan, she repeatedly took him back without hesitation. I treat her a thousand times better than he ever has and she doesn't notice it, apparently. Lance needed to remain out of the picture for me to ever get a real shot with my friend. Her eyes would never open to other possibilities with him lurking in the shadows.

"Sage was starting crap, but Zack put her in her place." Maddie answered with a light laugh.

"Is J okay?" Alicia responded worriedly.

"She'll be fine, she just needs a minute."

"I'm going to look for her." I interjected as I started in the direction she had left. After Jilly's words, there was no better time for me to put it all on the line. Not telling her what was on my heart was only putting her in harm's way, repeatedly. I was overthinking everything, she needed to know so she would stop choosing jerks to fall in love with.

"Why don't you let us?" Maddie offered as she grabbed my arm and tugged me towards her fiancé. "She needs time to process everything. She honestly is clueless as to why anyone would be interested in her at all."

"It pisses me off that she's so conditioned to believe she's worthless." I hissed. "Maybe if she'd stay away from the assholes she chooses." My eyes flicked to Alicia's.

"I can't change who her heart wants."

"But you could stop sticking up for the bastard and quit filling her head full of lies about how much he loves her."

"I have never lied to her."

"Bull shit."

"Zack." Maddie interrupted quietly.

"Every time he ditches her, you show up telling her that he loves her and misses her and you just can't understand why he's blowing her off. Sound familiar? It's all a load of shit that he fills you full of so you help him use her. He doesn't love her, if he did…"

"You know nothing about Lance and the…"

"I know he is a worthless piece of shit who is using a beautiful, amazing girl and brainwashing her to believe she is nothing."

"Zack, you are not having the best of luck with the ladies tonight. Maybe you should rethink the sobriety thing." Caleb joked as he stepped in between Alicia and me. "Jordan makes her own decisions and Alicia has nothing to do with it. Accusing her is not helping."

"If she thinks he loves her, she holds on. When Alicia lies to her about his feelings she holds on to this stupid hope he'll take her back. She needs to let go."

"We all agree she needs to let go of Lance. He's not good for her, but we can't force her until she's ready. You will push her away by preaching to her about her love choices. If you want to protect her, to save her from her reality then you have to surround her with love and positive vibes. She needs to be reminded that she is a beautiful, amazing and vibrant soul who deserves to be treated like a queen." Maddie smiled sadly. "Trying to keep Lance and anyone else away from her isn't going to fix the bigger problem."

"She doesn't want to…"

"Until she wants to let him go, she won't. You don't want to start a relationship with her when she's holding onto someone or something else, right?" I nodded my head. I hated when Maddie was right, but it happened often. I didn't apologize to Alicia, even though I probably should. However, she needed to know that her falling for Lance's lies made Jordan do the same and he was not good for her. She deserved better. She deserved me.

Chapter 33
Jordan

"You're here with Bentley?" Keller hissed. I swear I had locked the bathroom door behind me. I closed my eyes and continued to hide in the corner of the porcelain filled room.

"I rode here with him and Caleb."

"Sage said…"

"Sage Qualls is a dramatic bitch who likes to make shit up so she feels better about her sad, pathetic existence."

"That sounds more like you, than her."

"I guess she lives in the same warped reality as you, I forgot."

"Stand up when you talk to me."

"I'm not. I don't feel good." Keller made a weird sound before he stalked over and yanked me up by my arm.

"You will do as I say." I was so tired that I didn't fight him. It was almost like I was watching the whole thing take place from afar as he screamed and hit me.

Chapter 34
Alicia

"What crawled up his ass?"

"Sage. Keller. Jilly. Everything?" Maddie chuckled in response. "Men have PMS just like women, now is Zack's time of the month."

"He has no right to attack my cousin. He did nothing. It's not Lance's fault…" Maddie held a hand up quickly.

"I know you're pissed at Zack for jumping on you, but we both know you don't agree with that. Lance is at fault for at least part of Jordan's insecurities."

"That's not what I meant." I sighed, realizing it definitely sounded like that was what I meant. "Zack knows nothing about Lance and the Hell he has been through. He comes from a fucked up home with a reality most people couldn't fathom, Zack included. He is who he is because of it and he can't change that. He genuinely loves Jordan and is trying everything possible to be the man she needs him to be, the problem is that he never thinks he's good enough for her."

"And maybe right now, he isn't. I'm not saying he won't ever be, just…she needs someone who is mature and secure in his love for her. That's not Lance, you can even admit that." I sighed and nodded my head. "I'm not saying Zack is that guy, we know Keller sure as hell isn't, but if we don't take a step back and continue to throw our two cents in, even if we think we're right and know what's best, she will never find the guy she needs."

"So, you think I should stop telling her about Lance too?"

"I know it hurts you to not make two people you love happy again, but Zack does have a point. If she believes there's hope with Lance, she'll never heal from how he's hurt her. She can't grow if she doesn't and she certainly can't break this horrible cycle she's in with him and Keller. Do we really want to be sitting here twenty years from now while she's on another break up with your cousin or with Keller? No, we want her to be happy and healthy and in a love like she deserves. If she doesn't stand up to Keller *or Lance*, this crap will never stop happening to her and they and others will just continue to take advantage of her huge heart."

"I don't think Lance is using her. He seriously is in love with her, but you're right, he's not mature enough to understand what he's doing to her." Maddie smiled as she gave me a quick hug. This girl never ceases to amaze me. She grew up with more money than four countries, she's been pampered and protected her entire life, but she is wise beyond her years.

"We just need to make it about her and not the guys in her life. It's easy for us to say because we have two amazing guys, but she needs to see she doesn't need a man to survive."

"She's doing just fine on her own."

"But she doesn't see that. She is dependent on a relationship, even a horrible one, for whatever reason."

"I wonder where she even ran off to."

"We'll check my room first." Maddie grabbed my hand and we hurried down the corridor and up the stairs towards her bedroom. How do you make a girl see how amazing she is when it's apparent to everyone but her?

Chapter 35
Brennan

"Who is in the bathroom taking a shit?" Will Cabrio asked in an exaggerated whine. "They've been in there for twenty minutes, at least."

"Do you hear anything? Maybe they passed out."

"The party just started, no one is that pathetic to pass out already."

"You know as well as I do there is more than alcohol at this party." Will's eyes widened as he looked at the door worriedly.

"I'll find another bathroom." He practically ran away. I moved closer to the door, listening for someone on the other side. I heard feet scuffling, heavy breathing and something crashing to the floor. Someone was screwing on the other side, nice. I chuckled to myself and started away.

"You are a worthless bitch, Jordan. You verbally attack my friends, you fuck every asshole that'll unzip their pants for you and…" I wasn't hearing this correctly, was I? Keller was on the other side berating Jordan?

"Please stop, you're hurting me." Her voice was weak and barely audible, but I didn't need to hear anymore. I pounded on the door.

"Go away, it's occupied." Keller hollered from the other side.

"You've been in there too long."

"Brennan, seriously, go away." I closed my eyes, knowing he wouldn't take me seriously on the other side. I heard more scuffling before there was a loud crash, I heard Jordan whimper and I wasted no time. I tried the door knob, it was locked so I took a step back and kicked at the expensive wood. He splintered easily.

"What the fuck, Brookman?" Keller gasped in shock. He looked at me with wide eyes before he stepped in front of Jordan, to block my view of her huddling in the corner. "You seriously have to go that bad?"

"I heard you yelling at Jordan." I stated breathlessly. I inhaled deeply and tried to calm myself down. Keller rolled his eyes.

"Couples have arguments."

"True, but they normally don't result in the female huddling in the corner covered in blood and bruises."

"Don't fall for her shit. You're smarter than this, Brennan. She's rehearsing for a part, she pulls this crap all the time. I would never."

"C'mon J, I'll get you out of here." I offered her my hand without stepping around Keller. She didn't move, so I did. Blood ran down her face from a cut on her forehead, bruises were already forming on her wrists. "Jordan?"

"Get the fuck out of here, Brennan." Keller hissed, his voice was full of more venom and warning than I'd ever heard before in my life.

"I'm not leaving her in here with you. Do you want me to find Caleb and tell him what I found?"

"You will tell no one anything. I will ruin you."

"I don't care, unlike you status isn't on my priority list."

"Don't fuck with me." I rolled my eyes and pushed past Keller. I bent down so I was in front of my friend.

"J?" Her eyes flitted to mine as if she were only just now seeing me. Her eyes darted to Keller's fearfully before she reached for my extended hand.

"Jordan, don't bring this stupid Hoosier into your bull shit games." She didn't respond and neither did I, we just walked out and left Keller seething. I knew Maddie's bedroom was close by, so I led her in that direction. She was in shock right now, at least in there we would have privacy for her to clean up and realize where she was. She was barely putting one foot in front of the other, but carrying her the thirty feet down the hall would pull too much attention. "Why don't you try to take a shower and I'll find you a beer?" I asked two minutes later when she fell onto Maddie's overstated canopy bed. She nodded her head and looked around the room. I closed the door behind me and hurried downstairs to find her a drink. Surely, it would bring her out of her shock.

Chapter 36
Zack

"Hey Brennan, have you seen Jordan?" I asked the lanky giant before me. He looked at me warily before he shook his head.

"Well, actually, she's in Maddie's room. She said she didn't feel good and needed a shower."

"Why didn't you come find me?"

"She told me not to." He lied with a shrug. I watched him carefully, noticing he couldn't look me in the eye which was a sure sign he was lying. Brennan Brookman always looked anyone and everyone straight in the eye when he was talking to them, unless he was lying.

"What's going on?" Brennan shook his head before he looked me dead in the eye.

"She didn't feel good. If she wants you to know anything else, she'll tell you. It's not my place to run my mouth about her." Brennan grabbed two beers out of the large metal tub someone had filed with ice and various bottles.

"How long ago did you leave her?"

"Five seconds? I just ran to get her a beer."

"She can't drink with her meds."

"I...I know, but she..."

"I don't care if she asked for it, you could kill her."

"Understood." He shot me a dirty look before he brushed past me and started towards Maddie's room.

"I can take it from here, you obviously don't know what you're doing."

"You know, condescending jack ass comes pretty easily to you, obviously, but it's not a good look for you." He hissed. I stopped in my tracks and looked up at him. Brennan was well known for being a pushover. Well, he was an extremely nice guy and hated to rock the boat. I must be a world class jerk right now for him to stand up to me.

"I'm sorry. I'm having a bad day apparently." I stated. "Thank you for taking care of Jordan. I just worry about her."

"So do I." I nodded my head and the two of us fell into stride next to each other. As we cleared the top of the stairs there was a group of people trying to get into Maddie's bedroom. Luis Garcia, his sister Adrienne, Sage, Nathan Lousch and Ben Seetar were gathered in a huddle passing around a bottle of vodka. Adrienne was passing a bottle of pills to Sage.

"Maddie's room is off limits." I hissed from behind them.

"Sorry, Bentley." Luis chuckled, his eyes already bloodshot and far away. "Didn't realize it was Maddie's room."

"It probably isn't, he's just being an ass to me." Sage shot. "Where's your bitch girlfriend anyway? She crawl in a corner and die finally."

"What is that annoying sound?" I asked Luis nonchalantly. "Do you hear it? That high pitched whine."

"Yeah." He answered slowly. "Like nails on a chalkboard. Hideous." I chuckled. He was so stoned he fell into my trap easily. Sage gasped and huffed as the others laughed too. She practically ripped the lid off her pill bottle as she grabbed Adrienne's arm and tugged.

"Save some for the rest of us." Ben spit as he ripped the bottle out of her hand as she began emptying it in her mouth.

"Hi, Brennan." Adrienne smiled, batting her eyelids innocently at him. "You coming with?"

"Maybe later." He responded automatically. He barely noticed she was hitting on him. Although, Adrienne was gorgeous and could have any guy she wanted easily she was a lot like Sage and thought she needed to throw her body and vagina in everyone's face.

"When did that happen?" I chuckled as he opened the bedroom door.

"What?"

"Adrienne was hitting on you."

"She's just being nice to me until Keller tells her differently." He shrugged as he rolled his eyes.

"What are you guys doing in here?" Jordan asked as she came out of the bathroom wearing a very small towel.

"Checking on you."

"I was hot, I took a cold shower. Why does that require someone checking on me?"

"Bren said you didn't feel good. I was worried."

"I'm fine." She replied flippantly as she made a shooing motion with her hand. "Y'all can go now. I'd like to get dressed."

"What's stopping you?"

"You."

"We'll go." Brennan responded quickly as he lightly tapped me on the arm. I didn't look at him, my eyes were glued to Jordan's. She wasn't ready to address what Jilly had said so she was attempting to be a bitch in hopes that I'd step back and give her space. I wouldn't, I may not get another chance.

"I'll catch up."

"Don't be an ass, Zack." Jordan pleaded. Brennan watched us carefully before I motioned for him to leave. He obeyed and shut the door behind him. Jordan's dress was laying on Maddie's bed, which I was standing in front of. I grabbed it up without thinking and watched as a pair of red lace panties fell to the floor. I stared at them, images rushing thought my mind. When I looked up at her, her face was bright red.

The door burst open and two giggling freshman came tumbling into the room just as I picked up the panties. The red head's face dropped as her cheeks turned a bright pink.

"Oh my God, I'm so sorry. We were looking for the bathroom."

"Aren't you Keller's girlfriend?" A mousey brown haired girl asked. Her face was filled with freckles and her brown eyes were full of excitement. "And you're in here with Zack Bentley…"

"It's not…" I began.

"It's really none of our business." Red smiled awkwardly as she grabbed her friend's arm and pulled her out of the room. Brown sputtered in protest, but Red wasn't listening.

"Fucking fantastic."

"Who cares what they think or say? Maybe Keller will finally get the hint and leave you alone."

"I care what they say." She hissed. "I'm already known as the school freak, I don't want to add slut or be next on the Bentley Dupe List."

"Dupe List?"

83

"Don't act like you don't know."

"Enlighten me." She rolled her eyes before she crossed to me and snatched her clothes out of my hand.

"You know damn well there is a rapidly growing list of heart broken girls who you make believe are something special just to get in their pants and then once you do, you trash them like a used condom. Jilly was just added to it."

"Jilly and I never…" I began. I stopped and took a deep breath and watched her carefully. This was her defense mechanism, but why didn't she use it on the guys who actually treated her like crap, rather than me.

"Those girls aren't innocent. I'm a pawn."

"You're a bastard, blaming them when you pretend to care, pretend to be a friend."

"I have never pretended to be anyone's friend."

"Whatever." She snapped before she spun on her heel and stomped into the bathroom. I didn't yell after her or even follow like I wanted too. Instead, I sat down on Maddie's bed and made myself comfortable. She'd come out soon and I'd be ready.

Chapter 37
Jordan

I was shaking.

I felt like I was close to passing out or having a seizure. What in the Hell was happening today, has everyone gone absolutely crazy?

I dropped my towel in the floor and gawked at my own reflection. I was barely recognizable. I was emaciated and my skin was littered with welts, bruises and cuts mostly from Keller. I was sore, nauseous, weak and exhausted. I should have stayed home in bed with a tub of ice cream and Reese's cups. If Alicia and Maddie really cared about me, they would have left me alone.

I didn't need all of this stress and drama right now. It was making everything worse. Fuck Zack for being an ass and pretending to be innocent. Fuck my so called friends for thinking only about themselves. And fuck Keller James for being the arrogant, psychotic asshole he is.

I looked around for my phone. It wasn't in the bathroom, it was still in Maddie's bedroom. I would text Chopper, ask him to come get me and within the hour I would be back at my house, laying in my nice warm bed.

I slid back into the dress and left the bathroom. Zack was laying on the bed, his eyes closed as if he were asleep. I looked at him a little longer than I should, studying the gorgeous planes and angles of his face. He was beautiful, and unfortunately, he knew it. I wanted to hate him for that and so much more, but I couldn't. I absolutely didn't want to admit how I hoped Jilly's words were true, but I knew it wasn't possible.

I let out a small sigh before I tiptoed to the foot of Maddie's bed. My phone was lit up, laying on an antique wooden trunk with intricate carvings decorating it. Zack moved slightly and I froze, when he remained quiet I continued.

"Don't think you're going to sneak out of here without us addressing what Jilly said." I gasped, shocked he was really awake.

"What are you talking about?" Playing dumb seemed like a good option, I couldn't bear to hear him say he only wanted me as a friend.

"J?" Alicia called as she burst through the door. She stopped immediately and gaped at Zack and me. It was obvious what this would look like to someone expecting the worst, especially if she had overheard what Jilly said or listened to Maddie's ridiculous thoughts on my friendship with Zack. "I…uh…um…Maddie needs you downstairs." My roommate wouldn't look me in the eye. I wanted to cry, could this day seriously get any worse?

"Are you fucking kidding me?" Keller growled from the doorway. "My roommate and my girlfriend? Unreal." Zack was off the bed and by my side in a flash. I didn't have time to process what was happening.

"Keller…"

"If anything did happen, it wouldn't be near as bad as what you do with half the female population at Callatin." Zack retorted. "Don't start…"

"How about you keep your fucking mouth shut, Bentley?" Keller took a step into the room, his entourage close at his heels. They wouldn't do anything other than instigate a fight and exaggerate it when it was over. "How dare you go after my girlfriend."

"Your girlfriend? You only remember she holds that title when you're trying to make her life miserable."

"Jordan?" Keller's voice changed immediately as if he were about to plead with me. His eyes were dark, hunter green and they were narrowed in anger. "How could you ruin what we have for one night with the biggest player in the school? You know it won't go anywhere."

"Nothing happened." I responded through clenched teeth. "I'm not the one who cheats."

"Accusing me when it's obvious you're at fault makes you look bad." I rolled my eyes and started past him. I felt his hand snake around my wrist before it tightened like a vise grip. "We are not done."

"Maybe not, but I am. I have been accused of enough bull shit today." I walked out of the room, sending Chopper a text as I did. I pushed through the crowd that had formed in anticipation of a fight. They weren't getting the show they wanted so people started to get rowdy. And stupid.

"Maddie still needs you."

"I'm not in the mood, Alicia. I just sent Chopper a text to come get me."

"What? Why? You can't leave."

"I can and I will. I should have never came and you and Maddie should never have forced me too."

"It's not good for you to lock yourself away in your room and…"

"But it's fantastic for my health to be subjected to more drama and stress than I've dealt with in a year?"

"I can't help that."

"It doesn't matter. Everyone just thinks of themselves and not me."

"Apparently, I should have stayed home as well." She snapped before she turned on her heel to leave. "Go down or don't, I don't care, I'll tell Maddie your alter ego, the bitch, is back"

"Fuck you." I snapped as I stormed in the other direction. I was running out of places to hide. I smacked right into Zack's chest. His arms went to my elbows to steady me and I looked up into his emerald eyes, he cocked an eyebrow and waited for my response. "And fuck you." I spun back around and headed down the stairs.

Chapter 38

"Come outside." The text message from Lance caused me to stumble down the last few steps. I was hoping for Chopper, but Lance would do.

"I'm not home."

"I know. Come outside." I smiled as I scurried outside. Lance was in the driveway, standing near the elaborate water fountain and he was grinning from ear to ear.

"Sorry, I know this probably seems weird. I...I just wanted to be with you when the clock struck midnight." He pulled a single white rose from behind his back. "Happy birthday."

"Birthday." I repeated. What kind of airhead forgets her own birthday? I was too caught up in my misery and drama that I'd forgotten what month it was. Lance sauntered towards me and grabbed me by the waist. He pulled me close and when his watch beeped the hour, he planted a seductive kiss on my mouth.

"Jordan!" Maddie called from inside the house, I could see her searching for me worriedly through the huge floor to ceiling windows of the front room.

"It's your party." Lance leaned down and kissed me on the forehead. "Go. Have fun. I'll see you tomorrow, with your present."

"Lance."

"I have to go, darlin'. I just couldn't let your birthday go without...I love you."

"Jordan!" Caleb hollered from the doorway. "Come on, Maddie's got something for you." I nodded at my big brother and then looked back at Lance; imploring him with my eyes, begging him to stay with me.

"I can't stay, I'm sorry."

"What? Why not?"

"I'll see you tomorrow." Lance repeated as he hugged me quickly, wished me happy birthday again and hurried away to his truck just as Zack was yanking me inside the house. Of course, Maddie had an enormous birthday cake and candles glowing in the polished living room of her parents' house. My friend's gathered around saying surprise and singing happy birthday. I should have been grateful for the thoughtful gesture, for the fact that they threw this elaborate party in my honor. I wasn't.

In the midst of Maddie's incredibly sweet gesture, I realized how pathetic my life had become. I was currently with a guy who basically didn't care about me and was cheating on me. Then there was Lance, I was still madly in love with him but, at this point, he was playing games with me. What was up with him showing up, planting an awesome kiss on my mouth and then taking off without another thought? Not only was I confused, but I started to become depressed which only made me angry.

I walked outside to the pool; found a quiet spot near the Carriage house and pulled out my phone. I immediately dialed Lance's number, without any regard for the fact that it was after one in the morning.

"Jo, are you all right?" Lance asked worriedly as soon as he answered.

"No. I am not all right."

"What's wrong? Do you need me to come get you? What happened?" He rambled awkwardly.

"No, I don't." I sucked in a big gasp of air and continued with everything I'd practiced in my head. "Where in the Hell do you get off just showing up here, kissing me and then leaving without another word? Are you fucking playing games with me?"

"No, no, no. I'm not playing games, I just…"

"Dammit, Lance Bowman! You pull this shit all the time and I want to know why."

"I can't really talk right now, Jo."

"I found it Lance, are you ready?" I heard a very feminine voice say in the background at the same time Lance cursed.

"Are you fucking kidding me?" I screeched. Tears stung my eyes and I thought if they began to fall down my cheeks, I might hear sizzling from the heat of my skin. "You fucking come here, kiss me and then go back to some fucking whore? What in the Hell is wrong with you? Better yet, what in the Hell is wrong with me? Here I am, like an idiot, still in love with you and you're just messing with me? Maybe Keller was right, maybe he's telling the truth and *you* were making everything up. What is this? Is this your way of beating him? You want to trick me into getting back together with you, just so you can laugh in my face and then shove it down Keller's throat that you won *again*?"

"Jordan…Don't do this. Don't do this now. I can't…"

"Can't or won't? Admit it, you'd rather stay with your little slut, get some, instead of rushing over here to prove me wrong. Obviously though, I'm not wrong, because if I were you'd be protesting."

"I can't right now, I can't do this right now, Jo. I'm sorry but you *are* wrong, so wrong. I just…"

"Fuck you, Lance. Just stay the Hell away from me from now on. I never want to see you again in my life." I cried, before I punched at the end button and ran to the bushes to puke. My stomach was cramping, tears raced down my cheeks from the pain in my heart and my body. Why in the Hell did I ever leave my house?

Chapter 39

I turned the pain into anger. I would channel all this bull shit into something good. I was going to find Keller James and make one area of my life better anyway. I went straight to the bathroom, cleaned myself up and then marched up the stairs.

I heard voices in the large library that Maddie's father used as an office sometimes. I moved closer and recognized Keller, Sage, Brennan and a few others. I slowly opened the door and poked my head inside.

"There you are." I gasped, feigning sweetness and a playful smile. "I've been looking for you all night." Keller jumped up from his seat near Sage and hid something behind his back. He immediately looked guilty. I peered at him questioningly. "Am I interrupting something?"

"No, we were just hanging out. It got a little too crowded out there."

"Crowded? Since when doesn't Keller James like crowds?" I scoffed. He shrugged his shoulders and looked back at his friends nervously. I looked around the room at all the vacant eyes, and then back at Keller, whose eyes were cloudy. It was then that I noticed the pungent smell filling the room. Pot. They were in here smoking pot.

"I…I…" Keller stammered as he backed away from me. All eyes were waiting for me to flip out, so they could all run out of the room and tell the whole school about how I was a goody two shoes. This could make or break me socially, so I did what I thought I needed to do and it was the biggest mistake of my life.

An hour later, I lay on the couch with my head resting on Keller's shoulder. I had forgotten about Lance, forgotten about Keller's infidelity, I didn't even remember that all my hair had fallen out or that I had cancer. All I knew is I felt amazing, floaty and carefree.

I was finally relaxed.

Chapter 40
Lance

I have to go see her. I have to fix this. What the Hell was I thinking telling her I couldn't talk about it right now? Like the babysitter would've cared about listening to my saga. I tried to be romantic and it totally backfired on me.

I was pacing the small living room of the house I was born and raised in, wearing a hole into the floor as my mother always did. My niece Ella had been asleep on my chest and Wyatt was on the other end of the couch when Jordan had called and that's why I didn't want to discuss anything with her. I was afraid of waking them up and I really had no clue how to get them back to sleep. Now an hour later, I couldn't take it any longer. I carefully put Wyatt and Ella in their coats and carried them to my truck before I headed back to Maddie's house.

"Lish, you have to make her come outside. You have to get her to talk to me so I can explain this. Once she sees the kids she'll understand. I just...I can't let her think what she thinks."

"I don't even know where she is Lance. She's probably asleep somewhere, like I was, it's like two in the morning, you know?" Alicia asked bitterly, her voice still full of sleep.

"I know, I know. I'll owe you big, monster big."

"Fine, I'll go look for her. I'll make sure she's out front in fifteen minutes, jerk. You know if you thought things through better this wouldn't be happening."

"I know, I know." The wheels were in motion, but a jolt of fear hit me when I realized Alicia was right. Fifteen minutes was not enough time to think my spiel through, especially for someone who sucked with talking and couldn't get words right unless I wrote them on paper. My stomach knotted tightly. Why was I such an idiot?

90

Chapter 41
Jordan

"Alicia, I don't want to go outside. I'm fine." I mumbled groggily.

"No, you're not. I think you need some fresh air." She retorted angrily as she snatched me out of the pot filled room and pulled me downstairs and outside.

"Fresh air, smesh air." I started giggling.

"I cannot believe you."

"Oh screw off. Don't act like you're so much better than me. I have cancer, I am dying and it is perfectly legal for me to smoke marijuana."

"You're not dying."

"Says you." I folded my arms across my chest. "If you don't like it then just fucking go away."

"I'm not leaving you alone." I rolled my eyes and suddenly became extremely tired, so I plopped down onto the lush, green grass and lay down. I pretended to be looking up at the stars, but I could feel my eyes growing heavy as the cold slipped into my dress.

"Jo, are you all right?" Lance asked as he stood over me. "Have you been drinking? You know you're not…"

"Fuck off, Bowman." Lance held out a hand to me, but I ignored him. So he bent down and scooped me up in his arms instead.

"Bastard." I cut as I glared at him, but I was too tired to argue or fight anymore. Lance chuckled as he carried me past his truck, slowing so I could look in the windows at the two sleeping children in back. Then he sauntered to the open tailgate and placed me on it. Before I could get my bearings, he grabbed my face in his hands and kissed me passionately. I felt my body go weak and seconds later, he pulled away.

"I showed up earlier because I thought I was being romantic. I thought you'd be swept away that I blew off my friends so I could be here with you, to kiss you at midnight. I wanted to be the first to wish you happy birthday."

"I would've been more impressed had you shown up at the beginning, not the end, like I was your last resort or something." I mumbled as I crossed my arms in front of my chest and stared down at the ground.

"I know." He responded slowly, I could feel his eyes on me. "Jo?" He reached towards me and put a finger on my jawline before he tipped my chin up. "Look at me." His voice was soft, soothing and I wanted to get lost in it. I looked at him, but my eyes were so heavy. "Jordan, were you drinking tonight?"

"No." I looked away quickly.

"Are you high?" I didn't move. I was frozen with the realization of how stupid I was. He grabbed my face in his hands and forced me to look at him again. "Are you high?"

"Get off your fucking soap box, Bowman." I retorted as I glowered at him. "I'm dying, I have every right to self-medicate."

"Are you in a lot of pain? Is your stomach bothering you again?" He asked hurriedly, his voice full of worry. My eyes went downcast, I felt really bad for making him worry.

"Not anymore."

91

"If you're having problems, you need to tell your doctor and they'll try to help you. You do *not* need to be getting high."

"Oh fuck you." I tried to fight free of his grip. "Who the fuck are you to judge me, to tell me what I should or shouldn't be doing?"

"Where did you get it from? What did you take?"

"I just smoked a little pot, it's no big deal. Everyone does it."

"I don't."

"We can't all be as perfect as you." I snapped in a syrupy sweet drawl.

"Don't start this shit. Do you have any idea what that stuff can do to you?" I looked away and stared at the lush green grass of Maddie's perfectly manicured lawn. It looked so soft and inviting. "Jordan, who were you smoking with?"

"It doesn't matter."

"You're right, it doesn't. I'm taking you home so you can't do it anymore." Lance picked me up and threw me over his shoulder.

"Put me down, you bastard!"

"Stop it; you're going to wake up Wyatt and Ella." He warned as he sat me down in front of the door.

"I'm not going anywhere with you." I hissed.

"Yes, you are. You're high *and* vulnerable; I'm not leaving you alone here for someone to take advantage of that."

"Too late, I already fucked Keller, if that's what you're trying to avoid." I lied angrily. Keller barely touched me, he hadn't in a long time, but I knew it would upset Lance. He took a step back and I pushed past him. I needed to get away from him and fast. Guilt was seeping in, no matter how much he deserved it.

I had gotten to the back of the house when my world began to spin. Nausea overtook me as heat flashed through my body. I fell onto the wet, cool grass and closed my eyes.

Chapter 42
Lance

I was not leaving Jordan here alone. I don't care if Keller is her boyfriend on a technicality, I wouldn't leave her so she could sleep with him again. Maybe that makes me a possessive psycho, but I don't care. He obviously couldn't take care of her, if he was allowing her to smoke pot and drink, knowing mixing her medication could kill her.

I stalked in the direction she had scurried off in. Hopefully she hadn't gone far, because the house and grounds in this place were massive. It could take me hours to find her if she didn't want to be found.

"Jo?" I heard a cell phone singing and followed the sound. The music stopped and then immediately started back up. A red heap lay in the wet grass. There she was passed out hard, snoring and flailed out in the grass, exposed to anyone and everyone. "Damn it, darlin'." I swept her up in my arms and carried her to my truck. I would take her home, let her sleep this off and then we'd have a nice long talk about her poor choices.

"What in the Hell do you think you're doing?" Zack Bentley growled behind me.

"Taking Jordan home." I murmured as I opened the car door, placed her on the seat and shut the door.

"No, you're not." I crossed behind the truck and strutted to the driver's side door. Zack took a step forward. "She needs to be here with Caleb and her friends. She needs to be protected from jack asses who take advantage of her vulnerability."

"She needs to be protected from me?"

"Absolutely." Zack strode to the passenger side of the car and reached for the door handle.

"*Do not* touch my truck." I hissed. Zack chuckled and didn't stop. I don't know why I'm being so crazy possessive right now. I wanted to pulverize Bentley for trying to take Jordan from me though. I took a deep breath and reminded myself of where I was.

"Did you kidnap these kids too?"

"Excuse me?"

"It's considered kidnapping when you take an unconscious person and put them in your truck."

"She wasn't…"

"I saw her pass out, I was coming to get her."

"Well, you're too late."

"I'm not going to let you take her. She's vulnerable and…"

"How are you going to stop me? Vulnerable? I'm not the bad guy here, I'm trying to protect her. She's trashed or high or something…she passed out in the wet grass twice, if I wouldn't have been here she could've died come morning."

"*Why are you here?*"

"You're not surprised she's drunk?"

"Answer my question."

"None of your business."

"Actually, it is. Caleb will be thrilled to know you're trying to kidnap his unconscious sister." He pulled his phone out of his back pocket and started dialing. This was about to get out of control.

"I'm not kidnapping her."

"Evidence shows otherwise." Zack hung his phone up when it went to voicemail. He reached for the door handle again.

"She needs to be away from this place and the dangers."

"I can protect her."

"Obviously not. She's so high she couldn't even keep her eyes open."

"You exaggerate." Zack rolled his eyes just as a shrill voice began screaming from inside the house. "Shit, that's Maddie." His eyes flitted to Jordan, to the house, to me, then back to Jordan. It was obvious he didn't know what to do.

"You can't help Maddie if you're carrying Jordan." I stated smugly. "And she's not going to be easy to wake up."

"Do not leave." He spit as he sprinted to the house. I waited until he had disappeared and then I climbed into the truck, backed up and steered it out of the driveway. There was no way I was allowing Zack Bentley to take care of Jordan tonight, I would deal with the repercussions tomorrow.

Chapter 43
Zack

"What in the Hell is going on?" I asked breathlessly as I skidded to a stop right beside Caleb and Maddie. My eyes went to where they were watching in open mouth disgust. Brennan was covered in blood, naked and lying unconscious in the floor as Adrienne writhed on top of him while kissing Sage. Luis was laying ten feet away, also unconscious and bloody. Sage and Adrienne were oblivious to their audience. The few people who were still at the party were all gathered around, watching and unsure of what to do next.

"There's so much blood. Who does this?" Maddie mumbled.

"What happened?" Sage looked up at me with hooded eyes.

"My stupid brother thought Brennan was getting too rough, so they got into a fight." Adrienne moaned, not changing her rhythm as she spoke. The two girls were completely out of it, high as a kite.

"It was so hot. Brennan is a sadist." Sage chimed in.

"Just the way I like it." What? My eyes darted to Caleb's in confusion, he seemed to have the same look. Brennan Brookman would not even swat at an annoying fly, there was no way his personality would change so drastically in the bedroom.

"You do realize you're screwing an unconscious man." I stated flatly. Adrienne giggled.

"He loves it, he especially loves it when Sage and I are together."

"Doesn't that piss off Keller?"

"Keller likes to watch." Sage stated breathily. What? Am I high off the contact buzz? This whole scene cannot be real, their words and demeanor can't be reality. Caleb kicked at Brennan and I did the same to Luis, he started to rouse before Brennan. Luis looked around, his hand went to his head where blood was oozing out of a small cut.

"What in the Hell happened?" He grumbled as he took in the site of his sister riding his friend and making out with a girl at the same time. "Jesus, Adrienne, what is wrong with you?" Both girls giggled hysterically, just as Brennan came to his senses and shoved them away from him.

"What? I don't know…" His voice was gruff and weak, his words slurred and slow. A door down the hall flung open and Keller stumbled out with a black eye, cuts and welts all over his normally flawless face. He lunged at Brennan as he tried to sit up. Caleb grabbed him by the shirt collar and flung him backwards.

"He attacked Jordan!" Keller screamed. "He wanted to fuck her and when she said no, he attacked her and then went after me. He's on steroids and went psycho." Caleb audibly growled as he dropped Keller and took a step towards Brennan, who looked like he might piss his pants.

"Whoa." I interjected as I held up a hand and stepped in between my best friend and Brennan. None of this was making sense. Brennan had gone to great lengths earlier to take care of Jordan, he wouldn't do that and then attack her later on, would he? "None of this sounds like Brennan. "Why don't we talk to J, get the whole story and then attack the problem."

"Where is J?" Fuck. I'd forgotten all about Lance and Jordan downstairs. Caleb glanced at the group, before looking back at me. "Why don't the five of you get the Hell out of here? None of you are ever welcome back either. How in the hell can someone be so disrespectful to start fighting and fucking in the hallway of someone else's house?"

"Caleb, I'm sorry. I don't know...I can't remember anything and..." Brennan stammered.

"You can't kick me out." Keller hissed. Luis knew better than to mess with Caleb so he nodded, mumbled an apology and grabbed his sister on his way out. Adrienne grabbed Sage, who grabbed Keller and the freak patrol headed for the doorway.

"Bren, why don't you sleep it off. You're in no shape to drive or ride." I offered when the others were gone. He looked as though he were ready to cry, so I opened the door to the room I would have stayed in and motioned for him to enter. "We'll take you home in the morning if we need to." He nodded his head and stumbled in the room.

"Why did you do that?"

"None of this makes sense. Think about it. However, if Jordan says he attacked her well then he's close for us to pulverize him." Caleb nodded his head and looked around.

"Where *is* Jordan?" I sprinted outside and wasn't surprised to find Bowman was nowhere to be found. "You going to tell me what your deal is?"

"I saw Alicia and J go outside, so I followed. I got sidetracked and then looked out a window and saw J passed out on the front lawn. When I got down to her, Lance was loading her up in his truck and she was completely unconscious."

"Unconscious. Why was he here?"

"I don't know. He wasn't exactly forthcoming with details. I told him he wasn't taking her, but when I heard Maddie scream I knew I couldn't wake her up and I'd be no help if I was carrying her." Caleb nodded understandingly.

"Let's go check on Maddie. Alicia is with her and maybe she'll know what Bowman's deal is." I didn't wait to see if Caleb was following as I stomped back into the house and up the stairs.

"On second thought, why don't you just give me the keys? I'll find her." I queried, as I turned around at the top of the steps.

"Zack, you don't know where Bowman lives and you won't find them." Caleb admitted. "Just talk to Alicia." By the time we reached Maddie's bedroom, I was livid and strung as tight as a violin.

Chapter 44

Lance

As my phone began ringing, I ignored it while I carried Ella and Wyatt inside the house. When I returned to get Jordan, it was still ringing. The Caller ID said it was Alicia and I contemplated not answering. I knew she'd be worried about Jordan, but I didn't want to deal with her questions.

"Everything okay, Lish?" I questioned innocently.

"I don't know, is it? Where are you? Is Jo with you?"

"Yes."

"Get off my phone, Zack!" Alicia hollered on the other line.

"Where in the Hell is Jordan?" Zack hissed.

"With me."

"I told you not to leave with her."

"Yeah, you did. Funny thing though, you're no one."

"I told you not to leave with Jordan. That's kidnapping. You kidnapped an unconscious girl so you could…"

"She was not safe there." I hissed. "I didn't kidnap her."

"Yes, you did."

"She is safe at my house sleeping off whatever she put in her body. I will bring her back first thing in the morning, when she wakes up."

"You will bring her home now."

"No, I won't." I hung up the phone and then shut it off. I grabbed Jordan's phone and did the same thing. I wasn't about to deal with that asshole anymore. I slowly opened the passenger door and pulled Jordan into my arms. She didn't flinch which was probably not a good sign.

"Oh darlin'." I sighed as I smoothed her hair before I kissed her and carried her into the house. I put her in my bed and covered her up, she rolled over and snuggled under the blankets. Jess walked into my room and cocked an eyebrow.

"What's going on?"

"She got high, I didn't feel safe leaving her there and…"

"Alicia called, said something about you kidnapping Jo."

"She was passed out in the front lawn, it's not…I saved her life."

"I'm not accusing you and neither is she, but Caleb and the others are pretty livid."

"Not my concern, I only care about her." Jess looked back at Jordan sleeping peacefully in bed and then looked back at me.

"Give me a shirt and I'll get her out of that dress." My sister offered. I found a tee shirt, handed it to my sister and walked out of the room. Ten minutes later, Jess was outside with a strange look on her face.

"She's covered in bruises, is that normal with her treatments?" I shrugged. "Old bruises, new bruises. She didn't even stir while I changed her. I don't remember Luke bruising so easily."

"She's pretty out of it. Their cancer isn't the same." My thoughts automatically flew back to the accusations of Keller abusing her, but I immediately pushed them to the side. However, as controlling as Zack Bentley was just over an hour ago, maybe he was to blame and

Keller was the scapegoat. Maybe I just wished that was the scenario because Zack Bentley was a threat to me.

"Did she fall or something?"

"Not that I know of. Both times I found her she was passed out in the grass. I'll ask her if…"

"Is she eating?"

"I don't know."

"If you truly loved her, you would know these answers." Jess snapped.

"I'm not around her, that's her choice."

"No, it's not." She rolled her eyes. "You shut her out first, whether you want to admit it or not. Someday you're going to push her too far away and you'll lose her for good." I shook my head. Jess didn't understand our connection, Jordan knows I love her, knows we will be together soon. "She makes you a better person little brother, that's rare and I hope you realize that soon."

"I do. I just…"

"If you're not ready, you're not ready, but pulling her along for the ride while you mature into the person she needs you to be will do nothing but alienate her. You already know how bad it sucks not having her, do you want to live your entire life without her, only knowing a mediocre happiness?" I shook my head and tried to move past her. She stepped in front of me. "Then get your shit together." My sister has had one relationship in her life and he was a dirt bag, so she was nowhere near an expert, but she certainly believes she is. I moved past her and began to close my bedroom door.

"Idiot." She grumbled as she disappeared down the hallway. I climbed into my bed with Jordan and wrapped my arms around her tightly. She may wake up tomorrow and believe I kidnapped her too. This might be the last chance I have to hold her and I will relish it.

Chapter 45
Jordan

"Wh…where…?" I opened my eyes slowly, already feeling my head pounding like a jackhammer. The bed didn't feel like mine, the room didn't smell like Maddie's house, the body against my back definitely wasn't Keller. I closed my eyes and tried to remember yesterday.

Maddie's party, fight with my boyfriend, Jilly, fight with Keller again, Brennan rescuing me, Zack trying to be an ass, Alicia getting pissed at me, another fight with Keller, Lance showing up, a fight with Lance, and finally I remembered finding Keller again to give him the boot, only to get sucked into some pot. The headache definitely made more sense.

"Happy Birthday." Lance's deep drawl in my ear sent goosebumps racing down my body. Why was I here?

"How…?" My mouth was dry and didn't want to cooperate with my brain.

"How ya feel?"

"Confused." I took a deep breath and rolled over.

"About what?"

"Why I'm here. You left, I called and bitched you out. I called Chopper for a ride home, not you. I can't…"

"I came back to talk to you, to explain and I found you passed out in the front yard, twice."

"Twice."

"I brought you home so I could watch you, make sure you were okay."

"So I was passed out and you took me from Maddie's house without…"

"Okay, it sounds bad when you say it like that."

"Does anyone know where I'm at?"

"There may have been a standoff with Zack." He coughed.

"A standoff. What?"

"He didn't think you should be alone with me. He was needed inside and I left when he went to see what was wrong. Alicia called before I got you in the house, so they know you're here."

"What was wrong?"

"Maddie screamed. That's all I know."

"Maddie screamed." I repeated. I pulled away from him. I needed to make sure Maddie was okay, it wasn't like her to scream for the heck of it.

"Where are you going?" He asked in a strained voice.

"I need to make sure Maddie is okay." I rolled out from under the covers. "Did you undress me?"

"No, Jess did. You didn't wake up." I nodded and climbed out of the bed. I looked around his room for a second before I glanced back at him.

"Where's my phone? My purse."

"You didn't have your purse. Your phone is on the dresser by mine." I walked over to the dresser and hit the screen to wake it up.

"Did it die?"

"No, I shut it off. I hung up on Zack and didn't want to deal with them calling all night. I wanted to make sure you got your rest."

"Do you realize how stalker you sound right now?" I teased nervously. I'd never known Lance to be so overprotective of me when it came to my own family. He nodded and looked down at the bed.

"I told them I'd have you back this morning, but I was kind of hoping you'd want to hang out with me a little longer."

"I need to get home." My phone powered on and I waited for the messages and voicemails to activate. There were at least five of each. Mostly from Zack, he seemed to be freaking out as well. Why were the two of them acting so weird?

"Okay." He slowly climbed out of his bed. I stared at his naked chest, it was nice. I closed my eyes and forced myself to turn around. "I'll get you a pair of shorts to throw on with my shirt."

"You don't..."

"Jess already took your dress to the dry cleaner." I nodded slowly. I heard him rummaging through his drawers before he handed me a pair of athletic shorts.

"Sexy." I grumbled as I quickly slid them on.

"Can I ask you something?" I nodded and Lance moved so he was standing in front of me. Thank goodness he had pulled an old Mencino High tee shirt on. "What happened last night?"

"You obviously know more than I do." Keller's ringtone began playing and I instantly froze.

"Jordan, please." Lance begged. As I glanced up, I could see the worry in his eyes and hear the concern in his voice.

"Can we...I'm just going to call Zack for a ride."

"No! I...I can take you home, you don't have to call anyone. I just...I know you were high last night and I just want to know why...where you got it and why you would..."

"Why the inquisition? Are you my father?"

"Jordan." Lance sighed, almost with a pleading tone in his voice.

"What Lance?" I exploded as I glanced down at my phone and saw three missed calls from Keller. "What in the Hell do you want from me? Do you want me to say thank you for rescuing me...again? Or thank you for bringing me back to your house, just so I could completely embarrass myself in front of your family? I adore your mother and now I don't know if I can even look her in the eye."

"Mom's not home." His eyes searched the hardwood floor for words. "Jess is the only one who knows."

"Thanks Lance, thanks for letting your sister see me like that. Did you let Wyatt in too? Did you tell him what I did so he could be disappointed in me as well?" I had no control of the tears rolling down my cheeks.

"Wyatt probably doesn't even realize you're here. Stop avoiding the question."

"What do you want from me? I can't..."

"I want you to talk to me, tell me what's going on. Why were you high? Why risk everything you've worked so hard for, for that? Why would...why are you covered in bruises?" His eyes searched mine for the truth and my breath caught on his last question. My tears stopped and I glared at him.

"You have made it more than clear that you don't fit into my life right now, therefore your inquisition is invalid."

"It's…" Lance let out a long breath. "It's not like that and you know it. I am not the only one who made a choice, Jo. You don't have room for me in your life, that's your choice."

"Maybe if you would ask me, rather than assume I don't have room for you."

"Obviously, you can't answer questions." He moved so he was in my face. "I love you. I am worried about you and regardless of how you feel about me, you are my friend and I want to help you. I can't do that if you shut me out."

"I am not your friend, I see how you treat your real friends and I am not in the same classification. Your friends are treated like family, you would take a bullet for them and for me, you'd probably take a shit on my grave."

"How…what?" He stammered. I spun on my heel and stomped out of the room.

"This conversation is over." I hit Zack's speed dial number on my phone and waited for it to begin ringing.

"Hey Jordan." Jess smiled from the kitchen. I hung up my phone.

"Jordan!" Wyatt squealed as he catapulted himself from the kitchen chair and sprinted to me.

"Careful, bud." Lance interjected as he stepped in front of me.

"Stop!" I hissed. "I am not made of glass." Lance's eyes widened and he moved out of the way, just as Wyatt jumped into my arms and wrapped his arms around my neck.

"I missed you." Wyatt admitted. "Can you play with me this morning?"

"Well, how about we play for a bit while I wait for my ride to get here." He grinned and nodded his head.

"I will take you home." Lance stated gruffly, Wyatt cocked an eyebrow at him before he grabbed my hand and tugged me outside. My phone began vibrating and I looked down to see my brother's face on the screen.

"What's up?" I mumbled into the phone.

"You okay?"

"Yes, I'm fine. Is Maddie okay?"

"Yeah, why…"

"Lance said Maddie screamed and Zack ran inside."

"She's fine, just saw more than anyone should ever have to see of the skanks in this school."

"Um, I think I'll need more detail than that."

"When you get home Maddie will fill you in." He chuckled. "You need a ride?"

"No, Lance is adamant he's taking me home in a few minutes."

"Are you sure you're okay?"

"He's harmless, Cales….physically anyway."

"Keller said Brennan attacked you last night, is that true?"

"What? How ridiculous…I don't…no, it's not true! Brennan would never hurt me."

"We know that, but I had to ask for my own piece of mind."

"Why would…?" I didn't need to finish the question, because I knew the answer already. Keller was trying to punish Brennan for rescuing me from him yesterday, apparently it backfired.

"Something got a hold of Keller." My brother chuckled. "He looked rough last night and said Brennan did it. I'm starting to wonder if the ass doesn't do it to himself to try to get people in trouble." I forced a laugh, my brother was smarter than he even realized. "We're leaving Maddie's house now, so I guess we'll be at the house about the same time."

"K, see you in a bit." I hung up the phone and allowed Wyatt to tug me out to the barn.

"We have a new baby horse, Uncle Lance said he can be mine."

"Really? That's awesome, buddy."

"Yeah, I don't know how to take care of it, really, but Uncle Lance is going to teach me. He's really smart. He knows everything about everything." I giggled, just as his direction changed to the fence where the mom and baby horses were standing tall.

"Awww, how precious."

"Handsome, not precious."

"Sorry." I smiled down at Wyatt and watched as he climbed up on the wooden fence to get a better look at the two animals. He held his hand out and his face lit up when the baby came over to him.

"We're having lunch at Jenn and Rob's house, you were invited as well." Lance informed as he walked up behind us. Wyatt's smile grew even broader as he looked up at me hopefully. Lance knew I would tell him no, but I would have a hard time telling his nephew the same thing. I took a deep breath and looked back at my ex-boyfriend.

"I can't. I'm sorry. I really need to get home. I have a lot of homework to catch up on and…"

"I understand, I thought I'd try." He rolled his shoulders and looked back at the old, black farm truck a few feet away. "If you're ready now…"

"I am." I bent down and gave Wyatt a giant hug. "I'm in Beauty and The Beast at school, opening night is next week, do you think you'd want to come watch it? I know it's not…"

"Yes!" He exclaimed as he wrapped his arms around my neck. "It's mommy's favorite and mine too." My heart melted as he gave me a tight hug and ran towards the house to tell his mom.

"I'll text Jess later to give her the info." I mumbled as I scurried to the truck.

"Am I invited too?"

"You've never been to one before, have you?"

"It wasn't…" I immediately felt bad for snapping at him, but I closed my eyes, inhaled deeply and brushed it off. He jogged ahead of me and opened the passenger door. I climbed in and when he stood in the door staring at me, I pretended to be intrigued by my phone. He took the hint, shut the door and took his time walking to the driver's side door. When he got in and started the beast with a rumble, I was ready to break and apologize for being so hateful.

"I want us back together, Jordan." He whispered softly. "I miss you so much and I'm not…I don't think things through until after, that's what happened last night. What always happens. If I'd stuck with my initial impulse we'd be okay, but I always talk myself out of following up. I want you to come back to me because it's your decision and not because you feel like you have to or something. I want you to leave Keller because you want to."

"Keller and I…there's not…but I still…I can't risk dumping him for you, when you're so good at ditching me." I prayed he couldn't see the real cowardice behind my decision. Lance nodded his head and looked around the truck quickly. I felt a pang of guilt as he did because I knew he was only doing this so I couldn't see the wetness in his muddy brown eyes. He put the truck in drive and we lurched forward.

"Things will be different, Jo, I promise you. I understand if you still don't trust me. I'm not giving up though, I'm still here and always will be. I just want you to know that I aim to win you back and I won't stop until I do."

"Lance." I gasped, I continued without thinking before I spoke. "I still love you."

"I know and I do too."

"You still what?" I asked quickly as I grabbed his arm. He looked back at me nervously as a smile played on his lips.

"I still love you. I always have Jordan Donaldson, I'm just not good at saying or showing it." He mumbled. I gasped as my hand went up to my mouth in shock, I'd dreamed of this moment for so long and now that it was reality I didn't know what to do. New tears streamed down my face as I stared back at him in shock.

"That's not how I wanted to say it. I've said it before but it's always bad timing because you're passed out, asleep, or someone interrupts."

"I know. I thought…I thought I heard you in my dreams when I was in the hospital."

"I did say it then. I'm sorry I said it now."

"What? Why? You can't take it back!"

"I'm not taking it back." He chuckled, flashing a dimpled smile at me. He laughed again and reached across the seat to take my hand in his. "I'll never take it back. However, you have a boyfriend and it's not me. You're with Keller. I should've said it a long time ago and we wouldn't be in this situation right now. I loved you the minute I met you Jordan, I was just too stubborn and frightened to realize it."

"This changes everything."

"No, it doesn't."

"Lance."

"Listen to me, Jordan." He started as he tugged me closer to him. "I realize last night could have just been a lapse in judgment or it could've just been the first time you got caught…"

"What?"

"You have to stop. You can't do drugs anymore. My girlfriend will not be a fucking pothead. I will not allow you to…"

"Hold it right there, cowboy." I snapped as I yanked away from him and dropped his hand. His accusation hurt. "I am not your girlfriend or someone you can control."

"Stop." He reached for me again.

"Fuck off. Don't touch me."

"Jordan, stop. Come on." He leaned over, grabbed my hand and tugged me back towards him. The movement caused him to steer us into the ditch and he immediately stopped and put the truck in park.

"Why are we stopping? Put the car in drive and go or I'll get out and walk."

"Stop being stubborn and listen to me, please."

"I hate you." I growled.

"Great. Because I'm starting to feel the same way about you." New tears stung my eyes as I pressed myself against the door. I should bail out of the truck. I should get out, call my brother to come get me and walk away from Lance Bowman forever. It was not natural for someone to play so many games with a girl's heart, there was obviously something wrong with him mentally. Maybe, I was the problem for allowing it to continue. I looked back at him and when our eyes locked I fell against the door and began sobbing controllably. He slid across the seat and wrapped his arms around me.

103

"I'm sorry. I don't hate you." He mumbled. "I was angry and…I just worry about you so much."

"It was a mistake, Lance. A onetime mistake, that won't ever happen again. I know how bad I could've fucked my whole life up in one night."

"I hope you do, because it's not worth it."

"Stop lecturing me." I sobbed.

"Okay." He pulled away and looked back at me. His eyes darted around the truck, settling sadly back towards his house. His brown eyes grew darker and sadder than I'd ever seen them before. "I just…there's something…you know what? I should probably get you home."

"Yeah." I agreed, somewhat relieved. "I have a lot to do today."

Chapter 46
Lance

As I started down the driveway, I glanced at her nervously. There was so much to say, but the words wouldn't come out of my mouth right. I needed to put pen to paper and let my hands work the magic. If I told her what was in my heart, none of these ridiculous games would continue. She snuggled into me and I put my arm around her shoulders. Her head rested on me, her eyes closed as we drove. I pulled her hand to my mouth and gently kissed it.

"I miss that." She mumbled drowsily.

"Me too." I whispered. "Hey Jo? I meant what I said earlier."

"I know, Lance. I promise I won't do it ever again. A girl is allowed to experiment, right?"

"No, that's not…" I objected before letting out an exasperated groan. "It's okay to experiment. I just wish you were with me, or Alicia, or someone who'd take care of you, look out for you, you know?"

"I was with my boyfriend, Lance."

"Yeah." I gritted my teeth and gripped the wheel tighter. I hated when she called Keller her boyfriend, that's what he was, but the thought of it made me sick to my stomach. "Where was he when I got there?"

"Alicia was with me."

"Only because I called her, woke her up and begged her to find you so we could talk." She rolled her eyes and moved away as we passed through the Callatin gates. My first impulse was anger; did she pull away because she was embarrassed to let anyone see her snuggling up to me? Or was she just ticked and that was her way of showing it? Most likely, she was nervous word would get back to Keller about our coziness. I'd bet on the latter, mostly because I'd noticed a strange cast to Jordan's face, to her shuttered eyes when Keller's name was mentioned; fear, something I'd unfortunately known all too well from living with an abusive father. Maybe there was more to the accusations than I was ready to admit. "I hate to think of what would've happened if I hadn't showed up."

Two minutes later, I looked ahead and saw Keller's orange Hummer parked in front of Jordan's house. She saw it too and her body tensed immediately as she started to fidget nervously.

"Do you want me turn around?" I grabbed her hand again. I knew she'd think I was trying to rescue her, but; truthfully, it was only because I didn't want to hand her back over to that jerk. She looked up in shock and smiled. "I could take you to Alicia's or we could just drive off into the sunset."

"I wish it were that simple, but thanks."

"Seriously, I can turn around and we can drive to the beach or Mexico, wherever your heart desires, darlin'. I know you hate confrontation and I'm about to drop you smack dab in the middle of it and it's all my fault. If I'd never messed up or I just stayed away like I promised…then…"

"It's not your fault, it's mine." She squeezed my hand and looked up at me with her gorgeous blue eyes. "I don't want you to stay away. I want you to fight for me, to sweep me off my feet again, Lance."

I nodded and stared ahead for a moment. My whole body was tense as I clenched my jaw tightly.

"When I said I still…love you, I meant it."

"I know. I wish…I wish it were enough." My heart dropped and my stomach ached as if someone had just punched me in the gut. I had delusions of grandeur; thought the minute I uttered those words everything would be better, that she'd take me back and we could start right where we'd left off as if I'd never been an idiot. I guess it was a stupid thought.

"I mean…you have no idea what it means to actually hear you finally say those words to me, but maybe it's too late. No, I mean, I just need action behind those words." She rambled. I took a deep breath as I slowed the truck down, it was times like these that I didn't like living on a dairy farm, where all the vehicles were loud, auspicious beasts meant for hauling and ruggedness, it was too hard for them to blend into the scenery.

"I know. I'm new at this Jo, but I'm trying and I'll never *stop* trying."

"Trying isn't good enough." She shrugged sadly; her normally bright eyes were wet and incredibly heartbroken. I wanted to stop the truck and take her in my arms, but I didn't. "I deserve better. I need what you gave me in the beginning. I want flowers and kisses and I love you constantly. I merit romance and to be swept off my feet. I am worthy of *all* of you, Lance Bowman and I won't settle for less."

"I know." I repeated numbly. "You deserve more, better than I can give you, but…I'm going to show you that I can give you all of the best of me."

"I can't wait." She answered with a sad smile as she squeezed my hand. We were in front of the house now, I put the truck in park and Keller charged outside. She looked up at me as my hand went to the door handle. "Lance, please don't start anything, just ignore him okay?"

"I won't." I promised as I opened my door and then turned around to help her out of the truck. Despite Keller's angry face looming nearby she hugged me tightly and kissed me on the cheek.

"Thanks for last night." She whispered in my ear.

"Are you fucking kidding me?" Keller bellowed as he grabbed her arm and yanked her away. I lurched instinctively, but held back when I saw her pleading eyes.

"Get the fuck out of here, plow boy before you're leaving on a stretcher."

"Shut up, Keller." Jordan hissed, obviously annoyed by his tough guy attitude. By this time Caleb, Maddie and Zack had found their way outside, but the two boys were allowing the scene to play out.

"Fuck you!" Keller screamed. My fists clenched at my side as my whole body tensed. "I barely saw you last night and after I finally spend some time with you, you disappear and I find out from Sage that you went home with this fucking joke?"

"Whose fault is it that you barely saw me last night?" Her eyes narrowed accusingly. "You certainly didn't seem to give two shits about my whereabouts then."

"I can't help it that you think you're better than everyone else and none of my friends like you. Or maybe the fact that I caught you fucking Bentley made me want to puke at your feet." He cut as he yanked at the shirt she was wearing, my shirt. "Go inside, take off the hick's clothes and bring them back out now." Fucking Bentley? What was he talking about?

106

"Fuck off." She retorted nonchalantly. She turned around and flashed a forced smile at me. "Thanks for the ride and taking care of me last night. I really appreciate it."

I nodded, but didn't take my eyes off Keller. I had a feeling the rich boy didn't like being shown up by me, especially not on his own turf.

"Get his fucking clothes off now!" Keller yanked again, this time causing her to stumble.

"Keller!" She screamed as he tugged harder and almost knocked her down. I lunged, but Zack yanked me back as Caleb flew at Keller.

"Get your hands off my sister." He growled as he pinned him against the truck.

"I didn't touch her. I'm just trying to get all the redneck stuff off of her. My girlfriend will not be seen in some fucking hick's clothing."

"Well, I wouldn't be in his clothes if you'd taken care of me last night."

"Had I known you were going to call your ex asshole then I would have."

"So when Lance is around is the only time you can bother with me?"

"Stop turning this around on me. *You* are the one who hooked up with your ex, not me. How many guys did you fuck last night anyway? Brennan, Bentley *and* this fucker?"

"I haven't fucked anyone in months, which can't be said for you. I am not an idiot, I know about you and Sage." She cut. Her eyes had turned to fire and ice as she glared. "I know what and who you were doing when I was fighting for my life in that hospital."

"Jordan, I told you. I told you that wasn't true. How can you accuse me of something so horrific? I would never cheat on you, I love you. I love you, baby." Keller lied desperately as he stepped forward and tried to touch her. She shrugged him off too and continued to glare.

Punch him. Punch him in the face and tell him to get lost. Or I will. Punch him before I can't hold back anymore. I thought to myself, praying that now would be a good time for us to develop mind reading skills for each other.

"Why in the Hell do people throw that word around like it means something?" She snapped. "I have heard it a dozen times in the last few days and it is bull shit. *Fuck that word.*" Keller took a step back and looked at her in shock.

"Who else said it to you?"

"Who all have you said it to within the last hour?" She snapped.

"Keller, maybe you should leave."

"Fuck off, Bentley." Jordan and Keller hissed in unison. Zack's eyes widened before he looked directly at Jordan.

"I'm trying to help you."

"You're trying to help yourself, not me."

"Attacking…"

"I am done." Jordan snapped as she put her hand up in the air before spinning on her heel and stomping inside the house. Keller started after her, but Caleb grabbed him and flung him backwards.

"You'll be leaving now."

"I…"

"You're leaving. You're not welcome here, *ever*."

"Is that really what you want, Caleb?" Keller cocked an eyebrow as he started to smile.

"What I want is to pulverize you until you no longer exist, but since that isn't possible, this is the next best thing. Stay away from my sister."

"I try, but she always begs me to come back."

"Bull shit."

"Eliminating me from the equation still won't give Bentley a shot with her. Honestly Caleb, I would think you'd want better for your sister. If you think he's not going to dick and ditch her, well then you're a bigger idiot than I ever thought." Caleb lurched forward and Keller ducked. Zack roared with laughter.

"He's baiting you, Caleb. Let him go, don't give him anything else to use against us." Caleb glared at Keller before he listened to his friend and let him go. Keller scurried to his Hummer and tore out of the driveway in a matter of seconds. Zack turned and pinned me with a steely glare.

"If you ever take off with Jordan again, I will hunt you down and…"

"She could have died with *you* watching her."

"Nothing would have happened to her. I was going to get her when…"

"Are you sure about that? She's not supposed to drink with her meds and she reeked of alcohol and she was high as a kite, all on your watch. I will not…"

"Let's get something straight." Zack took a step towards me. "You chose to remove yourself from her life, despite swearing you were back for good. She trusts you, for whatever reason, and loves you, and you continuously take advantage of her. Not only does she have to deal with normal teenage girl bull shit, but in case you forgot, she is battling a deadly disease and all of it is taking its toll on her. The last thing she needs is a pussy who can't decide if he wants her or not. You are not her bodyguard, you are not her friend, you are nothing but an ex-boyfriend who broke her heart. You are a memory and nothing more. So, in the future, when you believe you have an important place in her life, remind yourself of your own stupidity, of ignoring her and ditching her repeatedly. You are nothing to her, do her and the rest of us a favor by getting lost."

"Pretty certain she doesn't feel the same way you do, Bentley." I chuckled with a roll of my shoulders. I wanted to deck the cocky jerk in front of me, but it would only hurt my chances with Jordan in the future. "I will always do what is best for her even if you don't agree with it. I'm the one she talks to, the one she confides in and calls when she needs something, not you. Until that changes, stay out of my face." I turned on my heel and strutted away. I climbed into the truck and left before I let my anger overtake me and I gave Bentley the black eye and broken nose he deserved. He was definitely competition and I could only pray Jordan didn't fall for his empty promises.

Chapter 47
Keller

"How dare you?" I hissed as soon as I was in the safety of her room.

"What? You left, where…" I chuckled. The security in this place was a joke and the idiots out front were too busy marking territory to realize I had pulled around back and snuck in. I grabbed the Mencino High shirt she was wearing and yanked at it. I was disgusted by the cheap feel and the shitty smell of her clothes, *his clothes*. "You have the gall to accuse me of screwing around when you're constantly with that loser fucktard? I caught you alone with Brennan *and* Zack yesterday and…"

"Why are we together if we're screwing other people?"

"You fucked him?" I roared as I ripped her shirt off, sending her into a spiral onto the bed.

"No, not last night, but…"

"What is wrong with you?" I grabbed her off the bed and looked into her eyes. I was sick of the disrespect, the lies and especially of the assholes she associated with.

"I don't want to be with you, for one." I threw her against the wall and watched her slide down.

"I'm not fucking around, Jordan." I was hung over, still a little high and sore from my escapades with Sage and Adrienne. Those girls were crazy and a lot kinky. However, they worshipped me and I couldn't disappoint. Maybe the confrontation with Bowman and Caleb had my blood flowing, maybe it was the Monster energy drink I'd had twenty minutes ago, combining with whatever pills Sage had given me. Whatever it was, my whole body was strung tight and I was seeing red.

"You are, but I'm not." I grabbed her arm, pulled it behind her back and held her there until she stopped struggling. "You're hurting me."

"That's the point, maybe you'll stop disrespecting me."

"I don't…just let me go, please." I shoved her away, feeling her arm crack as I did. Tears rolled down her cheeks as she stumbled. "I don't want to be with you." I shoved her again, this time she fell and cracked her head against her dresser. She didn't move. Shit. I picked her up and searched for a way to cover my tracks. I could make it look like she passed out downstairs, maybe. They'd find her when they come back in. She was dead weight in my arms and as I got to the edge of the stairs, the front door opened. I dropped Jordan, watched her hit one step and then begin rolling. I was gone and racing to the guest bedroom, out the window, down the tree and into my car before anyone could realize I was to blame. That bitch wasn't going to take me down with her.

"Happy birthday, Bitch." I chuckled.

Chapter 48
Zack

"I want to pulverize that MoFo." I hissed as Bowman rumbled out of the driveway.

"Which one?" Caleb snapped.

"Both. I would give anything to break both their faces."

"Stand in line, Keller is mine first."

"Why does she have such shitty taste in guys? What do they have that I don't?"

"It's not you." Maddie interjected softly.

"He freaking kidnapped her last night, there's no telling what he could have done to her and she said thank you? Keller cheats on her, treats her like shit constantly and she acts like he's a king." The more I rambled, the angrier I got. My heart hurt to hear her mimic Keller's words. My stomach was in knots from fear, jealousy and plain outrage. How dare Bowman act like a God? "She needs to know what..." I stomped towards the house. Jordan needed to know about the real Keller, needed to know Bowman was stringing her along and she needed to be told, by me, that I was in love with her.

"No." Maddie jumped in front of me and put her hands up in the air. "Now is not the time. You are not going up there to lecture her about her boyfriend choices. Especially, when you're not speaking from your heart."

"I am, I'm worried about her."

"Zack, we know that. We're all worried about her, but you're jealous."

"I am not." I snapped. Maddie cocked an eyebrow and looked at me directly. After two minutes of silence and fidgeting under her glare, I took a step back. "I am." I am extremely jealous of the fact that Lance Bowman got to Jordan before I did, that he woke up with her this morning and took care of her last night. I hate he knows her in a way I might never know her.

"Her intuition is freaky sometimes, right?" Caleb chuckled.

"That's a big word for you, Cales."

"I know, Maddie made me learn them for my college applications." He shrugged nonchalantly. "It makes me sound hellasmart though, right?" I laughed and shook my head as I caught Maddie rolling her eyes and hiding a smile.

"Is it wrong for me to be jealous?"

"No, it's healthy, in a way. It shows you care, shows you're insecure about your part in her life though. However, if you go up there and bad mouth Keller and then Lance and then say you love her, she'll have already shut you out and not hear a word you say." I nodded slowly, knowing she was right. I hated that she was right, but grateful she stopped me from making a mistake. "She needs you to support her, to be her friend and show her how important she is to you. Words are kind of moot for her at this point." Maddie moved and opened the front door. I followed her in just in time to see something rolling down the steps. Maddie's shrill scream pierced through the house.

"Jordan!" Caleb hollered as he rushed to his sister as she landed with a sickening thud on the laminate floor at the foot of their long staircase. I sprinted after him. She was laying at a strange angle.

"She's not breathing." I muttered as I heard Maddie pull out her phone.

"I need an ambulance at Callatin Academy, 22 Mustang Way. Now. She's not breathing."

"Jordan, Jordan." Caleb was in panic mode as he kept shaking his sister, hoping she'd wake up and everything would be okay. Nothing looked okay right now. I don't know why I remembered the Health class where we learned CPR, other than Jordan had been my partner for the mock trials. It was an immediate thing for me to start chest compressions.

The town's First Responders flew in the front door within minutes. A blonde bulky guy immediately went to Jordan and felt her neck.

"She's got a faint pulse. Good work." A tall, lanky blonde came up beside him, they put a neck brace on Jordan before sliding her onto a backboard expertly. She was out of the house within seconds. When Maddie, Caleb and I raced after them, a campus security guard stepped in front of us.

"Let them do their job." The older man grunted. "And why don't you tell me what happened."

"We don't know." Maddie murmured. "We walked in and she was rolling down the steps. She was fine ten minutes ago, I watched her walk inside the house."

"Was anyone else in the house with her?"

"No, it's just us. She...we...we were all outside and..." Tears rolled down Maddie's cheeks as they slammed the doors on the ambulance.

"Is she...okay?"

"She's breathing. You probably just saved her life." The bulky blonde nodded at me and then jogged to the ambulance. They were racing out of the Callatin gates a minute later. The security guard continued to stare.

"I need to call my dad."

"He's already been notified."

"I still need to call him." Caleb growled. The guard looked at us long and hard before he nodded and took a step back. Maddie closed the front door and the three of us hurried to the truck. How was this happening? And why did this stuff continue happening to Jordan?

Chapter 49
Maddie

"No one else was in the house with her?" The police officer asked for the fifth time.

"Not that we know of." Caleb repeated gruffly.

"Did you just get into a fight?"

"No."

"Does she have a boyfriend?"

"I guess."

"Did they break up? Did they have a fight and she was upset?"

"If you're insinuating that my sister threw herself down the stairs, you're way off. She is battling cancer with everything she has. She wouldn't go through all of this Hell, just to dive down a set of stairs because her boyfriend is a bastard. She wouldn't commit suicide." The officer nodded as he wrote in his tiny notebook. Caleb's entire body was tense, he was ready to come unglued and I couldn't blame him.

"Aren't you an Illinois State Trooper?" Zack questioned.

"Caleb?" Mr. Donaldson interjected as he came through the emergency room doors. "What happened?"

"I don't know." He mumbled as he dropped his head. "She went inside, five minutes later we went in and she was rolling down the stairs. I don't know...I don't know what happened."

"Are you the father?" The police officer asked. "Where were you when this took place?"

"I...I travel a lot for work, I just got into town after Caleb's phone call."

"Where were you?"

"In Belleville." Mr. D snapped. Belleville? He was supposed to be in Chicago for two weeks of conferences that the Academy was sending him to. Mr. Donaldson's eyes flitted to Caleb's before he looked back at the officer. "What's going on?"

"That's what I'm trying to find out."

"Mr. Donaldson?" A nurse called. "Can you follow me?" My soon to be father in law disappeared into the emergency room.

"Caleb? Is she okay?" Calen asked breathlessly as he skidded into the waiting room, in full uniform.

"I don't know."

"Is your dad here yet?"

"Just got here." Calen looked around the room, his eyes landing on the officer.

"Can I help you?"

"No sir, just doing a courtesy check in on the young girl. I see the kids have family here so I'll be heading out." He was gone quickly.

"Why was a State Trooper checking on Jordan? I thought you said it happened at the house."

"It did."

"Did State respond because County wasn't close?"

"I don't know."

"The car that responded said Mencino County, this guy was waiting for us when we got here."

"Something isn't right." Zack interjected. "I asked if he was a trooper and he ignored me. He shouldn't have been asking questions, right? It should have been a county cop."

"You're correct." Calen answered as he stood up and hurried out the glass doors to the parking lot.

"I don't understand."

"If this had happened within city limits, it would have been a city cop's jurisdiction. Since Callatin is outside of city limits, it means we are within Mencino County's territory. State usually handles highways and more major things. It would be understandable if we needed an officer and there wasn't a county officer close, but that wasn't the case. I should have realized he was a state boy sooner and told him to buzz off."

"Why would you have realized that?"

"My entire family is practically in law enforcement, I should have known the difference."

"You have a lot on your mind." I mumbled with a roll of my shoulders. Calen came back in the hospital.

"He was already driving off when I got outside but I got his patrol car number. I'll do some research as to why he was here. Was he asking questions?"

"Yes, he was insinuating Jordan attempted suicide, he was asking if she got into a fight with her boyfriend."

"Did she?"

"Sort of." Caleb shrugged. "It was a weird deal. She got into it with Keller last night, he accused her of cheating on him with Zack and then Lance. Somehow Lance took her home last night because she was out of it. When he brought her home this morning Keller was here and flipped out."

"How did he flip out?"

"He got kind of rough, we stopped him and I told him to leave. Before then, Jordan was kind of arguing with Keller, then snapped on Zack and Lance and went in the house. Five minutes later, we went inside and she was rolling down the steps by herself."

"Where were Lance and Keller?"

"Bowman had left as we were walking in, Keller a few minutes before."

"Are you sure they both left? Is there a way for either of them to get inside?"

"Positive." Caleb stated. "There is, but they would have to know their way around campus."

"Which means it wasn't Bowman." I interjected. "Keller has been going to Callatin since kindergarten, he knows every inch of campus. Maybe…"

"Do you think he would try to kill her?" Calen asked me directly. I shook my head.

"He acts like a badass, but I don't think he has murder in him. Maybe she passed out from the stress or…I know she didn't attempt suicide, so there has to be some explanation." Calen nodded his head and looked at each of us carefully.

"Why isn't there an alarm system on the Headmaster's house?"

"There is, I think dad disarmed it permanently when Cale and I came so people could come and go as they pleased."

"Does that still happen?"

"Dad's rarely there and since Jo got sick, it's just us mainly."

"I think we should have it re installed without broadcasting it."

113

"You honestly think someone pushed her?"

"I know I have a bad feeling about this whole situation and the cop in me is saying to protect her from outside sources."

"He's right, I have the same feeling. Something doesn't feel right with the whole Keller situation."

"Why do you feel that way?" I stood up and walked away. I'd been through every detail about Keller and Jordan's relationship and I didn't understand any of it. The boys would fill Calen in on everything and maybe his training would help us find something to go on. As of now, we just had a lot of hunches and no solid evidence against Keller. By the time we figured all of this out though, it may be too late.

Chapter 50
Zack

Jordan had been sedated for almost two days. The fall had caused her some pretty major injuries and her body needed to work overtime to heal. Things were slow going but the doctors were pretty certain she was on the mend and would be fine in no time. It was hard to watch her laying in the bed, sleeping and motionless. People were in and out constantly, everyone taking time out of their day to sit with her, except Keller. He had not shown up since she was admitted, in fact he had gone into hiding. Supposedly, his parents had whisked him away to a remote island for a few days to rejuvenate. It only made me more certain he was to blame for Jordan's predicament.

"I thought she'd be awake by now." Calen invaded my thoughts when he walked in the room.

"Me too. They scaled her meds back yesterday and thought it'd be pretty quick."

"She's probably exhausted." He murmured. "I need to head out, my shift starts in an hour. I let Caleb and Maddie know I'd be nearby if they need me." I nodded my head and watched as he squeezed his niece's fingers. He shook his head and forced a smile as he walked out of the room.

It sucks that they finally have their niece and nephews back in their life and have almost lost Jordan twice.

I moved back over to the bed, sat down beside Jordan and pulled one of her hands into mine. It was rare that I was alone with her, just because so many people were always in and out and Mr. Donaldson wouldn't let us skip classes or practices to be here.

"I would give anything to hear your sweet voice right now." I mumbled as I reached up and touched her cheek gently. "Even if you are just telling me to leave you alone." I watched her carefully, praying for a change soon. "There's so much I need for you to hear from me. You may not be ready, I may not be ready, but I still need to tell you. I can't keep losing you over and over again. I feel like this is all my fault. If I would just force you to listen, to believe that I love you well then maybe you'd stop going back to Keller and Bowman. If we were together, you wouldn't continue getting hurt. I would protect you. I won't hurt you, J. I wish you would believe me." I leaned down and kissed her mouth softly. "I love you, J." I mumbled against her lips. I pulled away and wiped at my eyes. I guess I had hoped she would come alive under me, but Prince Charming's kiss didn't awaken Sleeping Beauty this time. "Dang it, J. Come on."

"Nothing?" Maddie questioned warily as she walked into the room, followed by Caleb. I shook my head. "Give her time."

"How much time are they saying?" Jordan's fingers moved in mine and I stared down in awe.

"Did she?" She tightened her fingers around mine before moving her head.

"Jordan? J?" I squeezed back, thinking she needed reassurance to open her eyes.

"Did I get hit by a truck again?" She whispered.

"What?" I moved closer until I was millimeters from her mouth. Her voice was weak and strained.

"Did I get hit by a truck again?"

"No, you fell down the stairs."

"I fell." Her eyes remained close. "I don't…"

"It's okay, babe. There's plenty of time to remember what happened." I still held her hand and gently touched her cheek. "Do you need anything?"

"Can I have water?"

"I'll ask and tell the nurse you're awake." Maddie interjected as she hurried out of the room.

"Do you hurt anywhere, sis?" Caleb asked.

"Everywhere."

"They'll probably give you some pain meds soon. Uncle Calen just left."

"Is dad here?"

"No, he is recruiting in Washington State." Caleb's whole body tightened with his response. I realize Mr. D is a single dad trying to raise two kids, but there comes a time when you tell your job no. His daughter was battling cancer, had to be sedated to heal from the wounds of a mysterious fall and he chose to help scout and recruit, to go to numerous conferences rather than be a support system for his children. Once they had told him she was okay, he bailed out. Fortunately, his brother in laws had really stepped up to be here for Caleb and Jordan. Mrs. Bowman had done the same, she was here daily and would stay for hours. I wanted to hate her for it, but I couldn't, she was too nice and Jordan needed all the support she could get.

"Go figure." Her voice broke and I squeezed her fingers gently.

"We're here, that's better anyway."

"True." She giggled, she stopped immediately and groaned. "I am so sick of hurting."

"Pain meds will come soon." A nurse announced with a smile as she came into the room. "The doctor wants to do a thorough exam before we put you to sleep again."

"I don't want to sleep anymore."

"You need your rest, child."

"What day is it?"

"Tuesday."

"I've been asleep for a whole day, that's long enough."

"Um, it's actually been almost two days." I coughed.

"Two days. I missed, I missed dress rehearsal for the play and…" She looked down at the thin white sheet covering her and then looked up at me. "Why does this keep happening?" Her voice was so weak and strained that I reached for her and pulled her into a hug. I wish I could answer the question, but I couldn't. It was a question we'd all asked at least a dozen times a day.

"It'll get better." I promised as I held her tightly. The on call doctor walked in the room with a wide smile as she floated to Jordan's bedside. She gestured for us all to leave, so Maddie and I obeyed. Caleb wasn't leaving his sister though.

"She's exhausted." Maddie mumbled as we made our way into the waiting room.

"I wish I could take away all her pain, all the shit that keeps happening to her."

"We'll get the other stuff to stop."

"How? She's not talking and we're not…"

"She'll talk or we'll just do some investigative work." She rolled her shoulders and looked back at me. "I won't let anyone hurt her anymore." We've never let anyone hurt her, I can't fathom why anyone would want to hurt her, but someone was out to get her and until we confirmed who it was, she wasn't safe."

"Guess it's about time for me to stop denying what's in my bloodline and embrace it so we can protect her." Maddie cocked an eyebrow and shot me a funny look. "I grew up around New York's finest, I may have picked up a thing or two." Her mouth turned into a Cheshire grin in a matter of seconds and it was obvious she was putting a plan together. I can only hope we figure this out before it's too late.

Chapter 51
Jordan

I was finally released from the hospital at the end of the week, but I wasn't allowed to return to school for obvious reasons. I was too weak anyway, I fell asleep so often I would be in detention constantly if I were in school.

I sat in my room alone, plowing away into my Trigonometry book. My mind was elsewhere, of course, yearning for Lance Bowman and dreading the hours until Keller arrived. I'd only been home a few days, but he'd been there every night after everyone went to sleep. Our relationship had bloomed into one of convenience, unfortunately, he would bring something to relax me every night and we would pass out in a drunken or high stupor. If anyone really knew what we were doing behind closed doors, they never mentioned it and I was grateful. I was ashamed of myself enough, having my family and friends the same way would probably push me even farther over the edge.

"Hey." Alicia greeted as she slowly came into my room Wednesday morning.

"Hey Lish, what are you doing here?" I asked hesitantly. It was the middle of the school week and technically, she wasn't allowed here.

"Lance's dad passed away this morning. Lance just found out an hour or so ago."

"Oh my God, that's horrible." I gasped. "What happened?"

"He hung himself in his jail cell." She shrugged. "I thought you'd want to know."

"Thank you. Have you talked to Lance?"

"No I'm headed over there now."

"Will you hug him for me? Do you think it's bad to call him right now?"

"I don't know. I think he'd appreciate it."

"I'm sorry, Alicia." I hugged her tightly before she left. I stared at my phone for five minutes wondering if I should call. Finally, I did. Lance picked up on the first ring as if he were waiting.

"Hey. I talked to Alicia. I'm so sorry. Is there anything I can do?"

"Thanks." He mumbled in a broken voice.

"Are you okay?"

"Yeah, yeah I'm fine. I'm just a little shocked, I guess. It's good to hear your voice though." We talked for a few more minutes before he rushed off. I knew it was because he was upset and didn't want me to know. I texted him immediately after to let him know I was here if he needed me and I'd be free to talk at any time.

Two days later, I attended Mr. Bowman's visitation. Alicia walked through the line with me and I thought Lance might cry when he saw me.

"Jordan you didn't have to come, you've been sick, darlin." He hugged me tightly. I shrugged nonchalantly. Lance clasped my hand as he took me through the line so I could see his mom and sisters. A few minutes later, he walked outside with me, still clutching my hand. "You're something else, do you know that?" He walked me to my Mustang convertible. "You have no idea what this means to me."

"I do, actually, and that's why I'm here." I hugged him tightly. "If you need to talk once this is over tonight, or any other night, don't hesitate to call."

"Thanks, but I'm fine *really*. It's not like…"

"Just thought I'd offer." I mumbled, hurt by his brush off. Lance nodded his head and opened my car door for me. He leaned down and kissed me on the lips quickly without thinking.

"You really are amazing." I was frustrated with Lance, but I knew he would text me tonight. He may think I'm clueless, but I know him better than he realizes.

"*Dad says you can't stay the night with me anymore.* ☹" I texted Keller. It was a complete lie and, most likely, he knew that.

"*Suddenly he doesn't like it?*"

"*Yeah, go figure.*"

"*Guess I'll see you tomorrow then.*" I let out a quick breath, relieved he didn't push the issue.

Three hours later, Lance texted to see if I could meet him somewhere. Twenty minutes after that, I had pushed through an opening in the gate just behind our house and met Lance on the side of the road.

"I guess you get a little more leeway now that you're not in the dorms?" Lance asked nervously as he drove to an empty field road and parked.

"Yeah, it helps dad was already in bed." I shrugged nonchalantly.

"Thanks for…this." I rolled my shoulders again and looked out the window. I wanted to be wrapped in his arms, but he was gripping the steering wheel tightly.

"It's what friends do."

"Not always."

"It's what I do. It's how I was raised." He nodded his head and looked down at the steering wheel.

"He was a bastard and I'm relieved he killed himself."

"That's understandable." I responded slowly.

"No, it's not. It makes me *like* him."

"How?"

"Because he was a cold hearted asshole and not feeling anything…"

"Tomorrow will be different, I think. Tomorrow is the finalization and that's when it will become real."

"I made the arrangements. I identified the body. It doesn't get more *real* than that." I gasped and looked back at him in shock. I was appalled Mrs. Bowman would even ask him to do it.

"Why?"

"Mom was distraught and felt horrible. I didn't…I am the man of the house, it's my job."

"You're the man of the house, but some things aren't meant for a teenage boy to do."

"You wouldn't understand."

"We found my mother in a pool of blood, my brother covered her up and called the police. Kyler is still not right from the whole thing."

"He was a lot younger."

"Age doesn't mean anything. No one is ready for that job, especially a child."

"I'm not a child."

"That's not what I'm saying." I sighed in exasperation. "I just wish you didn't think you have to take the world on, all alone, that's all."

"I kind of have to, especially now."

119

"You don't."

"Our lives aren't the same, Jo." Lance mumbled before he looked back at me sadly. "I am all my family has. I am the only one who knows the ins and outs of the farm. I've been working it since I was five, it's my entire life. If it fails, we have *nothing*. My father believed a woman's only worry should be the children, the house and the kitchen. Mom knows nothing of our finances, the payroll…"

"Who did all of it?"

"Dad and me."

"Why would…?"

"It's how I was raised, I'm sorry it's different than you, but…"

"Stop being so defensive." I snapped. "I grew up without a mom. I was responsible for juggling schedules, the checkbook, laundry and housecleaning since I was six years old. I know there is a certain idea as to the roles in a home. There is no need for you to jump down my throat for just asking questions." His eyes widened, he nodded his head and stared out the window.

"It's all on me."

"Obviously, it's not. You have help. If not, you wouldn't have been at the hospital with me every single day."

"I have help, but…it's not their responsibility, it's mine."

"So, you're priorities have changed." When I was dying I was a priority, now I no longer matter.

"Not by choice." He mumbled.

"It is though. Your pride is too…"

"Jordan."

"Lance." I mimicked. "You have help. You have amazing friends and family who will help with everything. They know you are going to college and can't…"

"I'm not going to college." He laughed.

"What?"

"I have no desire to stay in school any longer than I have to. I will have my Associate's degree when I graduate in a few months, that's all I need." Lance Bowman was, honestly, one of the smartest people I knew. Some people saw him as a dumb hick, but they were wrong. He had a perfect grade point average, knew the mechanics of every engine known to man and had rigged some pretty impressive feeders throughout their barn for the cattle. He knew medical jargon most teenage boys couldn't spell. Just a conversation with him would show you how intelligent he is. I was floored he had no desire to further his education, but I wouldn't comment because it would lead to another argument.

"I guess I always thought you'd be leaving for college someday." I murmured. He shook his head, opened his mouth to say something and then closed it. The truck was quiet, except for the faint sound of country music coming out of the radio.

"The prison gave mom his personal belongings, there was a suicide note where he blamed her for everything. He basically said she put the rope around his neck."

"And so she's struggling to remember she's not to blame?" He looked at me in shock, then nodded his head. "I've heard it's hard to get out of that mindset when you've been blamed for everything for a long period of time."

"I really feel like he committed suicide out of spite. You know, one last chance to make mom and the rest of us feel worthless."

"He probably thought you guys wouldn't survive without him."

"But we are."

"And that probably bothered him more than anything." Lance nodded his head and then chuckled.

"I should get home."

"You've got a long day tomorrow."

"Jo?" I looked at him, tears running down his cheeks as he gripped the steering wheel tightly. "I'm sorry I've been such a bastard. I didn't mean to jump down your throat this whole time and…"

"Lance." I sighed as I opened up my arms and felt him fall into me. I hugged him tightly. "I know what it's like to put up a wall so people don't see your emotions, so I get it." He didn't respond just wrapped his arms around my waist and held me tight.

An hour later he pulled away, put the truck in drive and wordlessly drove me back to the spot he'd picked me up at.

"Will you be okay walking back?"

"Yeah, it's my backyard." I mumbled. He nodded his head. When he didn't move towards me, didn't say anything else, I slowly put my hand on the door handle.

"I'll see you in the morning."

"I don't…you don't have to come. I mean, I want you there but I don't, either. I need to focus on mom and my sisters. I can't…I don't want you to feel ignored."

"I wouldn't." I snapped. I took a deep breath, closed my eyes and nodded. "I understand."

"Thanks, Jo." I nodded, climbed out of the truck and scurried into the dark. The whole night was weird, but I couldn't take all of it to heart either. Lance was under a lot of stress, he'd just lost his father and he was unsure of his feelings about it. He would come around.

Chapter 52

For the next week, Lance and I had a secret rendezvous every night. I was finally seeing a softer side of my ex-boyfriend as he confided in me about his anger and sadness towards his dad and his death. It was nice that he trusted me enough to share so many emotions and secrets with me.

"Do you know what's really bothering me?" Lance asked, his voice tinged with aggravation one night. "I hated my dad, I still do."

"No, you don't."

"*Yes,* I do. He caused nothing but hurt and misery for my family. What did he ever do for us?"

"Lance, your dad helped make you who you are. You have his smile, his mannerisms. He taught you how to be a hard worker, polite and respectful. But sweetie, he also showed you how you *didn't* want to be. You saw your dad's struggle with his temper and alcohol and *you* learned to control it. You don't hate your dad because, despite all of his faults, he was still your dad. He made mistakes and he taught you to learn from him and *not* follow completely in his footsteps."

Lance just nodded his head and stared out into the darkness surrounding us. I leaned over, nudged him with my shoulder, and flashed him a sweet smile. Lance chuckled and grinned back at me.

"So you could've snuck out the entire time we were together and didn't? I'm hurt." Lance teased.

"I just found out I could. Maddie and I would sneak out a lot to meet Caleb and Keller."

"How are things going anyway?" His body tensed. We were sitting on the tailgate of one of his old farm trucks. He had put a blanket down for me to sit on since it was covered in crop dust, among other things. He pulled his knees up to him, rested his elbows on them as he looked out at the world around us.

"I don't know. Fine I guess." I shrugged nonchalantly. I hoped he wouldn't press the issue, but I wasn't that lucky.

"You can talk to me about it if you want. I don't mind. It's a little weird, but I can handle it."

"Lance." I sighed.

"I'm your friend, remember? Well, I'm trying to be a better friend than I have been, at least." He gripped the tailgate tightly under his legs.

I stared out into the trees surrounding us and contemplated telling him about how much I hated my relationship with Keller. I wished things were different and that Lance and I were back together but I couldn't tell him that, could I? I looked down at the ground and then up into Lance's brown eyes.

"I guess I'm a little disappointed because I think he should at least offer to go to my appointments or treatments with me. Zack has, but Keller never has." I rambled sadly, forcing a smile.

"Did you tell him that?"

"Hell no. I don't want him to feel like he *has* too."

122

"He should be there." Lance mumbled and I ignored the comment as if I didn't hear it. I looked back at him and watched his facial expressions. It was amazing how many things I could read from just looking at his gestures and movements. He was biting his lower lip gently and I knew he was holding back comments.

"He doesn't handle my puking or…" I took a deep breath. "The port, or my hair loss, well at all."

"I guess it's hard for some people."

"I guess." I shrugged. Lance fidgeted nervously on his truck's tailgate.

"It isn't easy for me to see you struggling. When I met you Jo, you were this vivacious force to be reckoned with. You took on life without any hesitations and then when you fell into my arms…seeing you so helpless at the hospital almost killed *me*. I mean, you're better now and that's obvious, but it still sucks knowing I can't help you get through it all."

"But you have." I mumbled softly as I leaned into him.

"Do you know, other than mom, you're the strongest person I know? You're going through Hell, fighting like Hell for some sense of normalcy and you're actually more worried about *me* and my problems."

"That's because I love you." I responded without thinking. "That's what friends do for each other."

"I'm kind of surprised Keller lets you meet me like this."

"Yeah." I looked away quickly.

"You haven't told him?"

"There's nothing to tell."

"Yeah, but if he finds out he won't believe that."

"It's not a big deal."

"Yes, it is. I'm making trouble again."

"No, you're not. You're the only thing keeping me from falling apart." I argued.

"I should get going, I have to be up early to feed before school."

"It's not a big deal."

"Mom will be worried." He wouldn't look at me as he jumped off the tailgate and closed it when I slid off. He immediately went to the driver's side door and climbed in. He was upset, but he wasn't going to talk about it. He was done. I wanted to argue, to tell him it didn't matter because Keller never showed up until two in the morning when he was done partying for the night. If Lance wouldn't talk to me I sure as heck wasn't going to pour my heart out to him and show him how truly pathetic I was.

"Sweet dreams, Jo." He mumbled as he dropped me off in the driveway. I threw a wave over my shoulder and hurried inside so he couldn't see me crying. I wasn't surprised that he didn't call me the following night or any night after that.

A week later, my Nana passed away. Lance called to offer the same support I'd given him, but I declined anything more than phone conversations. I confided that Keller wouldn't be traveling with us to the funeral and he offered, but I wouldn't let him. Lance's family sent flowers to the memorial service and I talked to him on the phone every night we were gone. I wasn't so much upset about my Nana's death as I was about my mom's ghost continuing to sneak up on me and Lance was great about talking me down. Keller knew nothing about my grief or problems, because he never bothered to ask. If I was compiling a pros and cons list about the two boys, Lance's pros would seriously outweigh Keller's. However, just like I expected when Lance realized Keller didn't know we were talking again, he stopped calling and texting and went dark. Just like that, I was miserable and depressed all over again.

Chapter 53

Keller and I were hanging out at the house, watching a few college soccer games. This is all we ever did together, we never went out in public and he would bring me something to help with my pain and we'd sit in the basement watching sports.

"My last treatment is tomorrow." I announced proudly.

"Cool." He mumbled without taking his eyes off the television.

"I thought maybe we could celebrate."

"We are. There's a huge party at the lake Saturday."

"Not exactly what I had in mind." I fell back against the black leather couch. I was digging for excitement. I was pathetic, I wanted some type of validation from him, or anyone really so I knew I wasn't fighting this battle alone, for myself.

"Then I'll take you to dinner before." He rolled his eyes, thinking I couldn't see him.

"Never mind, Keller. Not a big deal. Getting trashed is a great celebration for me. Maybe it'll help me forget that my boyfriend is a big fucking jerk." I mumbled as I stormed off to my room.

"Dumb bitch." I should have turned around and throat punched him, but I didn't have the energy. Why did he still latch on to me? He hated me, I hated him, and this whole thing is ridiculous.

As soon as I was in the sanctity of my bedroom, I grabbed my phone and immediately texted Lance to share my good news. I knew it wasn't good that I was constantly falling back on Lance to pick up Keller's slack. I was getting myself in over my head, but I didn't care because it was so easy to be with Lance and I just wanted him back.

"That's awesome! Want some company?" He replied.

"I'd love some."

"Great and then I'll take you out to celebrate afterwards."

"I may not feel up to it."

"Then before? Or next day?"

"Next day?" I responded, grinning from ear to ear. I heard the front door slam, then heard Keller start his Hummer and tear out of the driveway. My grin grew, I didn't have to deal with him anymore today and I would be spending the day with Lance tomorrow. My life was definitely looking up.

"I know it's Maddie's turn to go with you tomorrow, but since it is your last treatment, I was hoping to go with you." Zack stated as he walked into my room and propped himself against the doorframe. I looked up at him in shock, I didn't know anyone else realized it was my last.

"Were you working out?"

"Yeah, why do I smell? Sorry."

"No." I giggled. He was drenched in sweat, but he still was gorgeous in a sleeveless shirt and athletic shorts. "I…uh…Mrs. Bowman offered to take me." It wasn't a complete lie, she had offered, but she wasn't taking me.

"Oh. I'd really like to take you, if that means anything."

"It actually means a lot."

"Do you have a few minutes? I was hoping we could talk."

"We talk all the time." I laughed nervously.

"This is different." He took a few steps towards me, his whole body was tense and he couldn't look at me.

"Zack?" Caleb called down the hallway. "Get in the shower, we're leaving for the movies in fifteen minutes." My friend let out a sigh.

"I'm talking to J." Caleb was outside of my door in a flash.

"Oh yeah? Pretend I'm not here."

"Don't be an idiot."

"What? I need a front row seat for this."

"Hello?" A male voice called from downstairs, drawing out the word.

"Anyone home?" Another one bellowed. Chopper and Cooper, my heart smiled. Zack let out another sigh as Caleb moved to the stairs.

"I guess we can do this another time."

"Is everything okay?"

"Yeah, will you rethink letting Mrs. Bowman take you tomorrow? I really want to be there for you."

"You're always here for me, Zack."

"Tomorrow is different." I nodded in agreement as I heard my friends coming up the stairs.

"Hel-lo Princess." Chopper grinned as he strutted into the room and rushed to engulf me in a hug.

"What are you guys doing here?"

"Thought we'd celebrate a little early with you since Lance has already stolen you for tomorrow." My eyes flitted to Zack's, he made no attempt to hide the disgust in his eyes. He turned around and walked out without a goodbye.

"How'd you know? I just texted him."

"We've known it was your last for a while. Mrs. Bowman was going to pretend she was going with you, but Lance was going to take her place." Coop shrugged as he hugged me tightly. "Lance just called to tell us it wasn't a secret anymore."

"Lish and Sawyer are on their way over."

"We brought pizza, beer, movies, cards and a good time." Chopper flashed a grin and a wink. "We figured you could use some excitement since you're confined indoors."

"You guys are amazing." I gushed.

"All the credit goes to Maddie, really." Caleb interjected. "It's always her brainchild when there's a party involved."

"I didn't think anyone realized it was my last treatment." I mumbled.

"Of course we did. It's a huge milestone."

"Is Lance coming?"

"He didn't want to cause problems." Zack was finished with his shower and walked out of Caleb's bedroom in a fitted tee shirt and shorts. I let out an involuntary sigh and then looked down quickly. I hope no one heard me. Zack looked up at me, shot me a dirty look and then glanced down at his phone and began texting. He didn't acknowledge anyone as he went down the stairs.

"You ready to have some fun?" Chopper asked me, no one else seemed to notice Zack ignoring us. I nodded, but watched after him. I shouldn't have lied to him, he deserved better and apparently, he was going to make sure I realized it.

Chapter 54
Zack

"Oh Zack, thank goodness." Maddie smiled as she stood in the foyer with her arms loaded down. "Can you help?"

"What is all this?"

"Snacks, drinks. I might have gone a little overboard."

"Might?" I chuckled.

"It's a big deal, I just…I feel so helpless with everything and I know I can do something with this." She rolled her shoulders and looked down embarrassedly.

"It is a big deal. Do you know who she chose to go with her tomorrow?" I took most of the bags out of her hands and started to the kitchen.

"I didn't know it…"

"Bowman." I interrupted with a growl.

"Mrs. Bowman?" Maddie put her bags down on the kitchen table and started emptying their contents.

"No, Lance." I put my bags wherever I could find an empty spot and she began emptying them as well.

"Lance is going with her tomorrow? I guess I just assumed Caleb would go."

"I asked if I could go and she lied to me. She lied right to my face without batting an eye."

"Zack." Maddie stopped organizing and turned to look at me.

"I'm sick of this shit. Why does she constantly choose him, over me?"

"To be fair, she doesn't know you're an option."

"It doesn't matter." I shook my head, turned on my heel and left the kitchen.

"Where are you going?" Maddie questioned as she scurried after me.

"Out." I stomped out the front door.

"You can't leave. It was your idea and…" Maddie closed the door behind her.

"I'm not going to sit here all night and pretend like I'm okay with her allowing Bowman to be there for her tomorrow."

"Then tell her that, if she knows…"

"There's no point."

"If you love her, there is." Maddie put her hand on my arm and gave me a sad smile. "I know you're frustrated, but Lance won't be here tonight and if you bow out to him, then you're giving him the edge."

"All he does is use her, ditch her and then lie to her to get back in with her. He kidnapped her for God's sake and she came home and fell down a flight of stairs. Why are we even allowing him anywhere near her? He's not good for her. He's not safe."

"It's not your choice to make."

"I can make the decision for her."

"And you'll regret it every second for the rest of your life. She's holding on for the normalcy, for the memory of how things were before she got sick."

"No."

"Zack, how many girls know you aren't interested in a relationship with them and yet they still offer you everything? It's the same thing. Some girls want what they can't have and others believe they are the one to change a guy. Sometimes they are and sometimes they aren't. Jordan won't see you until she realizes Lance Bowman won't change for her unless he wants to."

"How can she not see it?" A car pulled into the driveway, Alicia and Sawyer were here and our conversation was over. Sawyer turned around to let someone out of the backseat and I took a step forward. I would pulverize Lance Bowman before I let him walk through this door.

"It's Drew." Maddie murmured softly as she put a hand on my shoulder. "He's not coming, I didn't invite him and I made certain Alicia and the others knew it."

"Thank you."

"I didn't do it for you, I did it for Jordan. She deserves better than he's giving her and if we accept him and allow it, she won't see it without distance from him." I nodded, it's what I've been saying for a while. Things would be better if he would disappear permanently, then she would be able to heal and get over him but every time she comes close to moving on, he pops back into her life. "Please, just hang out and celebrate with us tonight. She needs you, she needs every one of us tonight and tomorrow especially. Don't ditch her now, because she'll never see past all the bad to the good."

"I'll stay." I sighed as I opened the front door for Maddie.

"Was she surprised?" Alicia greeted excitedly.

"Yeah." I mumbled. Lance's friends were cool and nice guys. They treated Jordan like a Princess, but they were like brothers with her ex-boyfriend which meant them being around so much wasn't helping her heal either.

"Let's get this party started!" Chopper bellowed when we were all in the living room. And that's just what we did. Jordan didn't drink, but she was smiling and laughing more than I'd seen in a long time. It felt good to flirt and just hang out again.

"I'm sorry about earlier." Jordan murmured when only she and I remained with Caleb and Maddie.

"About what?"

"Lying to you about tomorrow. I knew, I knew you wouldn't be happy about Lance going with me and I was avoiding a fight. I shouldn't have lied to you though." I shrugged my shoulders.

"I don't want him to go with you, I don't trust him. I don't like him. I want to be the one to hold your hand tomorrow, but it's your choice, not mine."

"He's…he's a good guy, some day you'll realize that."

"He strings you along like popcorn at Christmas, I will never believe him to be good." She sighed and nodded her head.

"I should go to bed, I have a long day tomorrow." She stood up, kissed me on top of the head and hurried out of the room. I should have followed after her, told her why I really didn't like him, but she had enough on her plate right now. I couldn't ask her to choose between Lance, Keller and me, it wasn't right.

128

Chapter 55
Jordan

Lance picked me up early the next morning and we didn't speak a word until we got to the hospital. He held my hand throughout the entire treatment as if it were nothing. I felt fine afterwards so he took me to the mall where we ate soft pretzels and got some ice cream. It was fantastic.

I don't understand how he can be so perfect one minute and then the next he ignores me for weeks. I wanted to call him out on it, but my stomach was in too many knots to acknowledge anything.

Saturday afternoon Keller flew me to San Francisco for a fancy dinner in the bay. On the plane ride there and back, I was trying to make out with my boyfriend, but he wanted no part of it. The private plane was playing another basketball game and Keller was more interested in it than my, apparently, disgusting body.

We met up with my brother and friends at the lake cabin to party. I wasn't really into the whole thing and because of all I'd been through I had two beers, smoked with Keller and his friends and I was done. I excused myself from the group, climbed into the back of our SUV and passed out. Zack and Alicia came to check on me ten minutes later.

According to Alicia and Maddie, my boyfriend didn't even notice I was missing until almost midnight. When he was told where I was he didn't bother to check on me and just continued to party.

Our relationship had become extremely strained because he just didn't care anymore. It was always about his needs and what he thought were mine. Unfortunately, Keller was the only one in our circle who didn't notice we were having problems. I guess he thought he wasn't doing anything wrong and I tolerate it.

I'd also allowed myself to fall into my mother's old patterns. I had turned to marijuana and occasionally some pills Sage would pass to me on a regular basis. It just seemed easier to deal with my feelings for Lance, my loveless relationship with Keller, and the pity I'd been receiving from everyone at school. I may have been finished with all of my cancer treatments, but I was still torturing my body with poison in the hopes it would make me better. It wasn't working.

Chapter 56

Alicia was having a party at her house, she assured me her brother and his friends wanted no part of an Academy beer bash and wouldn't show up. I half hoped Lance would, wished he'd whisk me away from the horror my life had become, but as the night wore on, I just figured he had moved on. I'm sure he wasn't still pining away for me. My reality set in and I allowed Keller to talk me into smoking with him and the others in one of the bedrooms. I was half lit when I realized we were in Drew's bedroom and I started looking at the pictures hanging on his bulletin board.

"My room should be off limits." Drew bellowed from the doorway. I looked up in shock as I stared back at Alicia's older brother. He flashed a smile at me before glaring narrowly at everyone else. "Y'all should get the Hell out now and take your *bullshit* with you." He nodded at the bag of pot and pills laying on his desk and the bowl in Keller's hand. My boyfriend staggered off the bed and towards Drew.

"Oh chill out *townie*, we're just having a little fun."

"In *my* bedroom and I don't appreciate it." Drew stated blankly as he moved closer.

"Keller, he's right. It's not cool." I mumbled, as I tried to pretend to be sober. "Sorry, Drew. We're out."

"*You* can stay." He flirted as he tugged at my hand.

"*She* goes with me." Keller yanked me away from Drew as hard as he could. He was off balance though and sent me flying into the wall. I felt my head hit hard against the doorjamb before I slid into the floor, dazed.

"Sorry, babe." Keller laughed as he stared down at me. Drew tried to help me up while Keller stood there stupidly. As I went to take his hand, Keller's temper flared.

"Get your hands off her." He pushed me back down and away from Drew. He shot Drew a look, as if he were the one who'd knocked me into the wall, before he grabbed my wrist tightly and yanked me up. As I stood there, willing the ground to stop moving, I barely noticed Keller's grip was sending searing pain throughout my arm.

"Stay away from these fucking townies, Jordan." He growled inches from my face. "We're leaving."

"I'm staying with Lish tonight."

"Like Hell you are." I guess he thought Drew had stepped out with everyone else as his hand went up to my hair and he yanked my head backwards. "I won't take the chance of you slumming on me again. You make me look like a fool when you talk to these fucking townie losers."

"Hey now. I think you should back off." Drew interjected tightly, as he started towards us with a pleased grin on his face. He was itching for a fight and Keller would definitely scratch it.

"This is between *me* and *her*." Keller yanked my head again.

"Not when you're in my house, it's not and definitely not when the girl you're manhandling is Jordan. I suggest you get the Hell out of here now. I can take you out, right here, right now, but you should know that four of my buddies are headed up here and I *know* they won't hesitate to kick the shit out of you either. Especially when they learn you're messing with Jo."

"You want a fight, then you'll get one." Keller drawled with a laugh. "You touch me, and you'll have about fifty guys on your ass."

"No, he won't." Zack announced from the doorway. Before Keller knew what was happening his best friend had put himself in between us. He stood in front of me protectively as he glared at Keller. "I suggest you get the Hell out of here before Caleb finds out you laid a hand on Jordan."

"Fuck off, Bentley." Keller laughed. "Why are you protecting these fucking rednecks all of a sudden anyway? Your pathetic upbringing finally rearing its ugly head?"

"I'm protecting Jordan, no one else. Get the Hell out of here." Keller didn't move. He glared at Drew and Zack for a minute before he looked back at me.

"Come on, J." He held his hand out as if nothing had happened. I shook my head and moved closer to Zack, grabbing the back of his shirt and hiding behind him. Rage filled Keller's facial features instantly. I was terrified and my resolve was slowly slipping away.

"You're *not* going to make a fool out of me."

"You know." Zack started as he pulled his cell phone out of his back pocket with a wry smile. "Not only do I have pictures on here Jordan might want to see, but I also have some that your dad, the police, or maybe Coach Jakzen might be interested in." Seconds later Zack laughed and flipped his phone to a picture of Keller doing a line of cocaine. "Get the Hell out of here or I'll make sure the whole school *and* your dad gets a copy of this before the night is over." Keller huffed as he glared at his best friend.

"This isn't over. I'm going to make your life Hell."

"Bring it on." Keller stormed out of the room and Zack immediately turned around to me. "Are you okay?" I nodded numbly and slunk into the floor. I buried my face in my hands and wondered how everything had gotten so bad, so quickly.

"You want to return that to your friend?" Drew asked, handing the bag of pot to Zack.

"Jordan." Zack sighed. "Please tell me you weren't doing this too."

"Zack." I sobbed. "Please don't…"

"Jordan." He fell down in front of me. "What in the Hell, girl?"

"Don't judge me." Zack wrapped his arms around me tightly before he pulled away and stared down at the bag.

"I'm going to flush this, okay?"

"What the Hell did you say to the pretty boy to get him all riled up?" I heard Lance's voice laugh from the hallway.

"Hide that." I tried to grab the bag out of his hand. It was too late though; Lance had already walked into the room and caught me red-handed. My heart sank as his eyes filled with disappointment, anger and sadness.

"Jordan." He spat as he stared at the bag. His eyes flashed from the bag, to my face, to the gash on my head from Keller's temper. I could see the war inside him, the one where he was fighting the urge to come to my aid, and then the desire to heal my pain and that he was so angry, so hurt, and so disappointed in me that he didn't want to look at me. I thought about lying, but his face said he already knew it was a lie. He always had a way of staring into my soul and at that moment, I was sure it was blocked by bloodshot and distant eyes. "You promised me."

"Lance please, it's not…" He shook his head disgustedly and flipped around on his heel. He stormed past his friends as I raced after him.

131

"Please stop." I sobbed once we were outside. I grabbed for his arm, but he ripped it away angrily. I fell to the ground in a fit of hysterical tears, when I looked up Lance was standing at his truck glaring back at me. I felt so small and worthless.

I still sat there, sobbing, twenty minutes after his truck disappeared into the night. People stared at me, some offered to help but I didn't move until Alicia coaxed me into the backyard.

"You'll have some privacy okay?" She offered as she helped me up and walked with me. She was wrong though, Sawyer was standing by an old swing, waiting for me.

"Are you going to make me feel like shit too?" I asked angrily.

"I just came to see if you were all right." He motioned for me to sit down on the wooden swing. When I did, he sat down next to me and Alicia went inside. "Drew told me what happened."

"Great." I mumbled sarcastically. "Not only does Lance hate me, but now all of his friends think I'm a pothead with an abusive boyfriend."

"Lance doesn't hate you. And I, *none of us*, think anything bad of you. Actually, we all think you hung the moon."

"Whatever."

"Everyone makes mistakes." Sawyer shrugged. I barely nodded as I stared out at the neighbor's house. I really wanted to be too drunk or high to remember this point in my life. I couldn't face Lance or anyone now that they all knew what I'd been doing. I was humiliated Drew had seen Keller knock me around, that he saw me so weak. I'm not a feeble person, unless Keller James is involved.

"Did Lance ever tell you about Luke?" Sawyer grabbed a hold of the metal chain by his arm and stared into the darkness. I nodded my head. "How much did he tell you?"

"That Luke and Mr. Bowman got into a horrific fight, Luke climbed out the bedroom window and never came back." I mumbled tearfully.

"Did he tell you Luke was high?" I nodded my head. "Did he tell you *he* was high?"

"What?"

"Lance is worried about you." Sawyer admitted tightly as he continued to stare into the night. He let out an exasperated sigh. "He worries about you constantly. When he found out about the cancer, he told me he was afraid *this* would happen." He leaned forward and looked back at me sadly. "Drew and Luke had been experimenting before Luke was diagnosed with the tumor. When we found out it was back, the second time, the rest of us thought we'd experiment as well. I didn't know it at the time but Lance had already started, it was how he dealt with everything. The bag of pot his mom found, it *was* Lance's but Luke took the fall, he told me Lance was the Golden child and he was on his way out anyway so there was no reason to ruin his brother's rep."

"Lance said…"

"He thinks he killed his brother, Jordan. Lance and Luke smoked some stuff laced with downers or something. Luke snuck out when he thought Lance had passed out. When he came back in he was so depressed and out of it that he went looking for his dad, got a beat down, stumbled into his bedroom, climbed out of the window and ran away from the only home he ever knew. Lance was awake, saw him leave but was so blasted that he didn't think it was real. Luke said something to him, but he was too high to do anything. He could have told him where he was going and Lance doesn't remember."

"Sawyer, I don't believe you." I gasped as a sob escaped my throat. "That's horrible."

"Why would I lie?" He shrugged. "Lance stopped cold turkey after that. He thinks if he wasn't high he could've saved his brother's life. Drew lit up recently and Lance flipped out. He threatened all of us that if we ever smoked or did any of it, he'd turn us in and wouldn't speak to us ever again."

"He would've told me that."

"*No*, he wouldn't. He only told me because he was so fucking drunk he couldn't stand. He's ashamed and he wouldn't tell you because he'd be afraid you'd think he was a murderer too. He's convinced Luke is dead somewhere and it's all his fault."

"He's not…"

"*We know that,* but he…he doesn't really. He just wants to protect you and he's afraid of what will happen if he can't. He will die if he loses you too." Sawyer leaned back and took my hand. "That boy is in love with you, more so than he'll probably ever let on. When you were in the hospital, he didn't sleep or eat, he closed in to himself. He slept at the hospital every single night, did you know that?" I shook my head. "When Luke disappeared, so did part of Lance and if you died, then there wouldn't be anything left. Do you understand? He's fucked up in the past and I know you're not together now, but…you are his entire world." I nodded in understanding, tears falling down my cheeks faster than before. If I thought I felt bad earlier, I was lower than dirt now.

"Will he forgive me?" I asked softly almost ten minutes later.

"In a few days." He shrugged. "He won't come to you though."

"I'll go to him." I leaned back into Sawyer. A few minutes later as we sat in the cool night air in silence, I turned around to look at Lance's friend. "If he loves me so much then why won't he fight for me?"

"He does Jordan. He fights himself every freaking day." He chuckled. "He doesn't think it's right because of what happened with Luke, doesn't think he deserves to be happy and in love. He doesn't believe he should feel this way now, when we're all so young. And he sure as Hell doesn't think he's worthy of loving you, he doesn't think he's good enough for you and *that's* his dad's fault."

"Do you think we're too young?"

"Don't ask *me.*" He laughed. "I'd marry Alicia tomorrow if it were legal."

"You know, you're a lot sweeter than I ever knew." I giggled.

"Yeah, but sweet doesn't exactly get you very far these days." He laughed as he let me fall back into him again.

"Ah, but it does Teems. You have your dream girl waiting for you inside, what more could you ask for?"

Chapter 57
Lance

I couldn't sleep. I tossed and turned as I stared into the corner of my bedroom where Luke's bed had once sat. I'd rearranged the room not long ago, but the memory, the ghost of the way the room used to be, haunted me on a daily basis. Even more so now with what was happening with Jordan. I shouldn't have stormed out on her, I should've stayed and talked but I was just so upset and I acted on impulse.

"Lance, honey, you have a visitor." Mom smiled from the doorway at about ten o clock in the morning. I shot her a funny look as she nodded for me to follow. "It's Jordan, she said she'd wait on the porch for you."

My heart soared and then fell. What was she doing here? Had she come to tell me to mind my own business or had she come to explain her actions? I was terrified of what this visit might mean to my heart, but mom wouldn't let me linger as she shoved me out the door.

"Hey you." Jordan smiled sadly, as she turned around when I opened the screen door. I folded myself down to sit next to her on the front porch steps. She was leaning with her back against a post as she watched me carefully. I couldn't look at her, but only because I was afraid of what she would say when I did. "Can we go for a drive or something?" I nodded and silently stood, I turned to go inside and get a set of truck keys. She grabbed my wrist lightly before dangling her keys in the air. With the other hand, she laced her fingers through mine. "It's a nice day out, you can drive the Stang." I nodded dumbly and followed. Without any words, I walked her to the passenger side, opened the door and helped her in before heading to the driver's side. We drove down the field road beside my house in silence for a few minutes before she spoke.

"I see you're not going to make this easy on me." She sighed. There was so much I wanted to say, but I didn't know where to start. I looked back at her questioningly, she smiled sadly and continued. "I'm sorry, Lance. I made a promise to you and I didn't keep it. I'm so incredibly sorry." Again, I just nodded. Out of the corner of my eye, I could tell she was watching me, trying to read my body language and waiting for some type of response.

"You're killing me, Bowman." She leaned her head against the back of her seat. "Say something to me, please?"

"I'm sorry too." I mumbled as I put the car in park when we were at a secluded spot by the pond.

"Sawyer told me about Luke. He told me why you were so freaked out by me and my... new habit." She crossed her arms in front of her chest self-consciously. "I wish you would've told me."

"I couldn't."

"I know. I just...if you had then..." She stammered. "Oh Lance, I'm sorry. I won't do it anymore, I swear. I promise you. I didn't realize it would hurt you so bad and that's the last thing I want to do."

"I just want to know *why* you're doing it. You have this whole future ahead of you, but this could rip it all away."

"It's easier for me. It's how I deal." She mumbled.

134

"But it's only going to make things worse."

"I know. Every morning when I wake up, after I've done it, I'm worse off than I was before." She cried. "I just wish everything were normal again."

"Me too." I whispered as I turned in the seat and grabbed her hand.

For the next few hours, we sat there under the sun and talked about everything that went wrong and how we could fix it. She poured her heart out to me about Keller and about how she didn't want to be with him anymore, but she didn't know how to end things. She also told me how much she still loved me, and like an idiot, I didn't return the sentiment. Instead, I sat back, never interrupting and never offering more than was safe for my heart.

When she finally left late that afternoon, after I'd forced her to come in and eat lunch with my family, I planted a passionate kiss on her mouth and promised we'd be back together soon. For the first time in a while, I really believed it to be true.

Chapter 58
Jordan

Keller had already committed to Washington University in Missouri to play soccer. It wasn't a huge division one school like he'd expected to go to, but they had a great psychology department. He said he chose Wash U because it was close to me and that's all that mattered to him. He was seriously full of crap and my stomach hurt to think I would not be done with him as soon as I had hoped.

"So, dad planned a last minute trip for him and me to visit Harvard this weekend."

"Oh yeah? That sounds like fun."

"Not really." He grumbled. "I know we had plans for tomorrow night and…"

"Don't worry about it." I rolled my shoulders and went back to my homework.

"I could make it up to you right now."

"Keller, I really have to finish this tonight. It's due tomorrow and they're not giving me the leeway you might think."

"Whatever." He growled as he stormed out of my room. I wasn't upset about him leaving and it apparently bothered him. I was hopeful our time apart would let him see what else was out there and give me the privacy to decide how to get rid of him.

I was debating the best method of dumping him when Alicia walked into my house before classes Friday morning.

"So, Lance is having a huge party Saturday night." She announced with a sly smile as she plopped down on my bed.

"I know. He told me."

"Good, because I already told him you'd be there if I had to tie you up and drag you behind the Civic."

"Alicia."

"Jordan." She mimicked. "It'll be fun. Lance misses you. Everyone misses you. Keller's gone. We can dress inappropriately, get drunk and have a blast. Sawyer will take care of us, okay?"

"I don't want to be a third wheel."

"Whatever. You could never be a third wheel. We have too much fun when you're with us."

"Fine." I sighed, pretending she was twisting my arm.

"S-weet!" She jumped up and down excitedly. Alicia pulled her phone out and immediately started texting as I followed her downstairs. "The guys will flip." A few seconds later, her phone beeped and she let out a laugh. "The guys are ready to start partying now." My phone went off as well and I pulled it out to see Chopper had texted me too.

"Ditch and let's make it a rowdy weekend together!" I read off the screen with a giggle. Alicia squeezed my arm and flashed an excited smile.

"*We*, as in us girls, will make this an entire weekend thing. Seriously, you minus Keller the jerk, equals great fun for all." I laughed. She made it sound like she was joking but I knew she wasn't.

Today was my first day back to school full time, now that my treatments were over. I was super excited, but nervous. I wasn't up to par, by any means, but I was able to convince my doctor to clear me to play softball this year. I had already sat out my entire cheerleading season, and I felt like I was getting lazy.

That night, Maddie, Alicia, Quinn, Natalie, Leyna and I had a rare girl's night out. We went to the mall immediately after school where we shopped, goofed off and ate dinner. We took in a chick flick before we headed back to my house for a sleepover.

"Wow what a surprise Caleb, you didn't tell me *all* the girls were staying the night here." Zack drawled innocently as he flashed his sexy, dimpled grin.

"Sure Zack." I giggled. "We're going to play cards and drink some beer, you in?"

"That's a stupid question, sis. Girls, cards and beer are three out of Zack's four favorite things."

"What's the fourth?" He winked at me and bent down to whisper in my ear.

"Maybe you'll find out for yourself someday. I can guarantee, one time with me and it'll become your favorite thing too." I rolled my eyes as my face turned bright red and I pushed him away playfully.

In Keller's absence, Zack and I flirted relentlessly, okay so maybe we did it when Keller was around too. The two of us had become even closer than before. He was crazy and would do anything for attention or to get a laugh and anymore, I would too. We had definitely been getting into a lot of trouble together, which usually involved starting crazy challenges or games. After cards, I snuggled up on the couch with him while everyone else was strewn throughout the house. Eventually, I fell asleep on him.

"That's the first time I've ever slept with a girl and not tried anything." Zack laughed the next morning. He was absolutely gorgeous. I was self-conscious because I was certain my breath stank and my makeup had probably run, but Zack's sweet smile made me forget my insecurities.

"I don't know if I should be flattered or not." I giggled.

"It was nice." He smiled with a wink. "And I totally would've made a move if you weren't Keller's girl."

"Good to know. And I would totally let you take advantage of me, Keller or not."

"Really? Well, I think I've made it pretty clear you can do better than Keller. He treats you like shit. I'm constantly telling him that too."

"I know and I've heard it from people other than you. But Keller loves me."

"He loves the idea of being with you, there's a difference." Zack stated rudely, his arms still wrapped around my waist as I looked up at him. "I really don't know why you put up with him. There are fifty guys alone at CA who would give their right arm for a shot with you."

"And forty are assholes just looking to score."

"Which leaves ten of *us* who aren't. Seriously J, I'd treat you better in one date than he has in a year."

"Zack." I sighed sadly.

"You know I'm right." He whispered as he tipped my chin up to kiss me. Our lips were millimeters apart when my phone sounded Keller's ring tone.

"How's that for irony?" Temptation sucks. Zack Bentley was freaking hot and his thick New York accent made him a hundred times more attractive. He was sweet, sexy and good to and for me. Keller was the only thing that kept me from jumping on Zack right then and there. I knew what my boyfriend was capable of and I couldn't put Zack at risk. We still had a year left at Callatin and Zack was here on a scholarship, I wouldn't jeopardize that. I wasn't worth it and I would be devastated if I lost Zack's amazing friendship.

"I miss you." Keller lied quickly.

"What's wrong?" I asked awkwardly, avoiding lying to him.

"Nothing, I'm just stressed from being with my dad."

"Sorry."

"So big plans for tonight?"

"I'm staying the night with Alicia." I stated nonchalantly.

"Really? What are you going to do?"

"Hang out. Party hop, maybe. I don't know."

"Townie parties?"

"I don't know. We haven't really planned anything."

"Oh." He mumbled. "Dad's got some things planned so I guess I should meet him in his room. I love you."

"Bye." I hung up. Is it weird that I barely noticed I was talking to my boyfriend while encased in a hot, shirtless guys arms?

"So you won't be here tonight?" Zack asked sadly.

"No, we're going to a party at Lance's."

"Why didn't you tell Keller?" He raised an eyebrow.

"What he doesn't know won't cause a fight." I shrugged. "You want to come?"

"Hmm, not that the thought of hanging with you isn't tempting, but going to would be like walking into the lion's den."

"Lance wouldn't let that happen."

"Yeah, until he realizes I'm putting the moves on you."

"You're putting the moves on me?" I gasped as my eyes flashed.

"Trying." He smiled as he tried to kiss me again.

"Not now Zack. I've got enough to deal with as it is. I'm flattered and extremely intrigued but…"

"I get it." He mumbled. "Bad timing, with everything." His arms loosened around my waist, but he didn't remove them and I didn't move away from him.

"Are you sure you don't want to party tonight?" I didn't want to leave the safety and warmth of Zack's embrace. Truthfully, I'd forgotten all about Keller and Lance while I was with him, I was finding it hard to remember their faces actually.

"Maybe another time." He shrugged as he let me go and stood up. "All good things are worth the wait." He walked off as if it were no big deal either way, which of course, sent me reeling. I was tempted to go after him, just because he'd walked away. A few minutes later, I escaped upstairs to the sanctity of my room where I hung out with the rest of my girlfriends for the better part of the day.

Chapter 59

Alicia and I got ready at her house for the party. We both looked hot in micro skirts and cleavage bearing tops. It's not exactly something you'd wear to an outside party, but we didn't care. Our goal was to make every boy within a fifty mile radius drool excessively over us.

"So I didn't tell Lance we were coming." Alicia announced mischievously as we drove to the party. "And I made sure Sawyer and the others didn't either."

"What? Why?" I asked as we drove down the familiar driveway.

"Just wanted to surprise him. Oh and maybe show you how pathetic he is." She giggled as she steered into the grass between two cars.

"Huh?"

"Lance has all kinds of girls after him, but doesn't care."

"Alicia, I don't think I can handle seeing him with someone else." I whined as we parked and started to climb out of her Honda Civic. She popped the trunk and we pulled out my rolling cooler.

"That won't be a problem. Seriously. You'll see, Jo." She took a hold of my arm and the two of us made our way towards the large group of people who'd gathered around the pond on Lance's property.

"Wow." Sawyer commented as he hurried over to us and immediately took over pulling our cooler. "This party just got a Hell of a lot better." The tall red head hugged the two of us eagerly as he grinned. Minutes later the rest of Lance's close friends all engulfed us in hugs.

"Where is Lance?" Alicia asked.

"Around here somewhere. He was dealing with some stupid shit." Chopper answered with a shrug. The heavy set, brown haired boy hugged me again with a huge grin. "It is *really* good to see you."

"Hey, darlin'." Lance whispered in my ear as he snuck up behind us. His arms wrapped tightly around my waist as they drew me close. I closed my eyes as I felt his lips brush my neck before he kissed me sweetly on the cheek.

We were amazing together. It felt fabulous to be in his arms until I suddenly remembered he wasn't mine anymore. My eyes flew open and I immediately pulled away. I quickly turned around and eyed him carefully.

"Hey you." I smiled. "How's it going?"

"A lot better now." He flirted. "I thought you weren't coming."

"Alicia tricked me." I giggled. "She invited me to stay the night and instead brought me here."

"She's full of it." Alicia interjected. "I didn't even have to beg."

"Is Keller showing up later or something?" He asked worriedly.

"No, he's at Harvard with his dad. They're checking out the school." I smiled coyly. "So I'm *all alone* this weekend."

"Is that so?" He grinned with raised eyebrows.

"Harvard huh?" Sawyer asked in amazement. I nodded my head and started to reply but Lance wrapped his arms around my waist again. I felt his lips brush tenderly against my left ear.

"I'll have to keep you as close as possible so you won't be lonely."

"Lance Bowman, you better behave or I'll be forced to leave." I warned playfully, but not removing his arms from me, it felt too nice. "I have a boyfriend, remember?"

"Unfortunately, I do. It doesn't mean I can't try though."

I rolled my eyes and continued to flirt with my ex-boyfriend. I hung out with everyone and had a blast. I quickly forgot about Keller and continued to slip back into how great it was to be with Lance.

"How cold is the water?" I asked Lance a few hours later.

"Too cold." He chuckled.

"Have you been in it lately?"

"Hell no, it's Spring time!" I shrugged and made my way to the dock with Lance following curiously. "What are you doing?"

"I'm hot."

"No shit?" He teased. Lance grabbed my hands and pulled me towards him. "I'm dying to kiss you. It's so hard to be this close and not."

"I'm not the one who messed up."

"I know, I know. It's just…" He rambled before he tried to kiss me. I wanted to feel his lips against mine more than anything. Keller wasn't what was stopping me this time though, it was the fear of falling for Lance all over again and then getting burnt, all over again. Unfortunately, I couldn't stop myself; I was already head over heels.

I still loved him and longed to be with him again. I missed his arms constantly wrapped around my body. I yearned to feel his lips on mine every few minutes. It was too scary though. It was too frightening to jump back in and experience heartache all over again.

Keller was a jerk, but he wouldn't dump me like Lance did. Keller was sort of safe. I guess that was because I didn't really love him in the same way I loved Lance, which meant I couldn't really get hurt.

Lance, on the other hand, was amazing and usually treated me like royalty. Unfortunately, he let his insecurities get the best of him and he walked away too easily. Those insecurities had a way of hurting me. Lance Bowman could be my soul mate if he'd only give me all of himself instead of just some

Before Lance could kiss me, I giggled and quickly gave him a playful shove. He teetered backwards and landed in the pond with a yelp.

"Is it cold?" I laughed. I couldn't tell if he was pissed or not. I dropped my phone on the pier and took my shoes off before I jumped in after him. I stayed under the water a little longer than I should've and when I popped up; I could see Lance looking around for me. I swam up to him from behind and leaned towards his ear.

"Are you still feeling frisky or did the water do its job?"

"It did, until now." He whipped around and grabbed me in his arms as his brown eyes flashed suggestively.

"Do you ever give up?" I moved closer to him and felt his arms tug me to him.

"I will if you want me to." He whispered as my legs instinctively wrapped around him. "If you don't want me to try and kiss you anymore darlin', I won't. But I think you want me back as bad as I want you."

"Of course I do." I sighed. "I'm just not sure of *what* you want. Are you just looking to get laid? Do you just want to steal me back from Keller only to let me loose again? Or do you want *all* of me Lance? Do you want to go back to how great we were *before* you broke my heart?"

"I want *you* Jo, every inch of you. I *want* my girlfriend back."

"Then prove it, Lance. Prove to me I'm not just someone to keep you from being lonely tonight." I whispered in his ear before I let go and swam back to the pier. Lance stayed there dumbfounded until I began to climb out. He hollered for me and rushed to help.

When we were out of the water he could've kissed me, but he didn't. Instead, Lance Bowman laced his fingers through mine and led me back to our friends. For the rest of the night he held and snuggled with me while we hung out. It was amazing and horrible at the same time because I was slipping back into the belief nothing had changed between us.

"Are you cold?" Lance questioned when he noticed I was shivering and no matter how tightly he held me it wasn't slowing down. "Come on, let's go up to the house and I'll get you something dry to wear."

"Won't your mom…?"

"My sisters kidnapped her for a spa weekend. She won't be home until Monday." He led me to his truck and gently brushed his lips against my hand.

"I have to pee." Alicia announced quickly as she rushed to follow behind us. Sawyer made up some excuse as well and climbed into the truck after he helped Alicia in.

"You are so beautiful." Lance breathed as he opened his door and started to help me in.

"Yeah, I probably look like a drowned rat." I laughed awkwardly.

"No, you've never been more beautiful." He kissed my forehead before helping me in. We pulled up to the dark, two story home and Lance proceeded to help me out. While his cousin and best friend followed, Lance led me into his room but left the door wide open so I didn't feel uncomfortable. He handed me a pair of flannel pants and then went to his dresser to find a tee shirt.

"Mmm, this is my favorite shirt." I breathed as I fingered a blue and white checked button down shirt in his closet. "I love how it looks on you."

"Really?"

"Can I wear it?" Lance nodded his head and left me to change. I stripped down as soon as the door clicked shut. I toweled off and stepped into his dry clothes. As I inhaled his familiar smell, I got lost in the past and imagined the clothes were actually him holding me again.

I lingered in his room for a few minutes searching for proof that he did indeed still have feelings for me. On his bulletin board there was a picture of us from his sister's wedding, only the second time we'd ever hung out. I couldn't help but smile as I remembered how perfect that night had been. It wasn't proof of anything, but it gave me hope I didn't need. I opened the door and walked out.

Lance was standing in the kitchen looking through the refrigerator for something to eat when he glanced up at me. Immediately, his smile faded and I grew self-conscious.

"I was wrong earlier." He admitted as he rushed towards me. Lance's arms wrapped around me again and he searched my face for the go ahead. "You've never looked more beautiful than you do *right now*, in my clothes."

My heart melted and without hesitation, I grabbed him in an emotional kiss. There was no turning back now, but I didn't care. All I wanted was Lance, and for now, I finally had him again.

Lance picked me up and carried me, while we kissed, into his bedroom. Our mouths and hands raced to get reacquainted with the other's body. I couldn't get enough of him and I just wanted more.

"I missed you, Lance." I whispered.

"I know darlin'. You're all I think about." He admitted as he continued to kiss me hungrily. "I want you back."

I misunderstood his last word and thought he said he wanted me bad. I made a mental note for the time being. Right now, I didn't care if I was just sex for tonight and nothing more tomorrow.

"Is this okay? Is it okay we're doing this?" He asked between kisses.

"No, but I don't care. I don't want to think about it. All I know is I want you more than anything right now."

"Me too." I began to unzip his pants and pull them down as he sweetly unbuttoned my shirt. His mouth kissed skin underneath each button. If Lance just wanted sex, he was doing an excellent job of convincing me otherwise. We spent the next hour engaged in an intense make out session. Amazing sensations and emotions shot through my body as he continued to make love to me.

"*You* are amazing."

"That was better than I remembered." I breathed.

"I was thinking the same thing." He smiled and squeezed my hand.

"We should probably get dressed. You have a party going on outside, remember?" I began to throw his clothes back on. My stomach hurt. It wasn't regret, but most likely a premonition for what would happen tomorrow.

"I don't want to be anywhere but here, Jo." He pulled me back into his bed with him. "Unless you…"

"I'd rather stay in bed with you." I was still wearing his unbuttoned shirt as I climbed underneath the covers with him The two of us snuggled, held hands, talked and stole sweet kisses for a while.

I had forgotten about Keller James and the consequences that would surely follow if he ever found out about this night. Instead, I focused on how great it was to be back in Lance's arms. He had a habit of breaking my heart every chance he got, but he was a good friend regardless. It was so easy to talk to him, to laugh and be myself around him. He was perfect, if only he would realize that.

"Are things going to be weird when we leave this room?"

"I don't know." I mumbled as I thought quickly about how I could ever win Lance back. I was starting to doubt everything. If he still wasn't interested after the amazing sex we'd just had, then I'd definitely have to step up my game. "Let's just not ever leave the room. Or at least, not for a while. Although, I bet Lish is ready to kill me. She's probably been ready to go for a while."

"I'm sure she's asleep on the couch with Sawyer."

"Cute." I shrugged. "But I should go…"

"Stay, please. Please just stay with me tonight."

"Why?" My voice was dangerously close to breaking and revealing the weak, needy girl I was. I could play a tough girl, but the truth was I wanted Lance Bowman so badly that I would continue to let him hurt me, over and over again, because I couldn't live without him.

"Because I don't want to let you go." He admitted as he wrapped his arms around me tightly and pulled me back down into bed with him.

"Then don't." I whispered, fighting back tears. I snuggled up next to him and lay my head on his bare chest, closed my eyes and prayed things would be like this forever.

Chapter 60

The next morning I woke up still in Lance's arms. I watched him sleep for a few minutes, his breathing changed and his eyes opened slowly.

"Good morning, beautiful." He drawled with a grin. "I didn't want to wake up because I was scared last night was just an amazing dream."

"Nope, it was real." He moved to pull me closer and kiss me.

"You okay?" He asked as I backed away.

"I don't know." I climbed out of the bed.

"Can we talk about it?"

"I don't know."

"Jordan, please?"

"Lance, last night was freaking amazing, but today, I'm so confused. I'm still in love with you and I can't handle if you tell me it was just sex and nothing more. But I don't know if I can handle what I want either."

"What *do* you want?"

"*You.* However, I'm terrified of you wanting the same thing. I can't handle the heartache again and, let's face it Lance, you're pretty good at breaking my heart."

"Jo."

"*Don't.* Please just let me leave. I'm sorry. I'm sorry I can't have sex with you and not have feelings. I shouldn't have come here last night." I rambled tearfully. "I have a boyfriend, for God's sake, and I just cheated."

I started to leave the room as Lance stood there speechless. I stopped, spun on my heel and scurried back into his arms. I pulled away, grabbed the back of his head and pulled him in for a knee weakening kiss. When I broke the kiss I leaned my forehead against his.

"I would never forgive myself if I hadn't…I'm sorry."

"Jordan!" Lance yelled after me as he raced out of his bedroom in just a pair of flannel boxers. Alicia and Sawyer were snuggled on the couch, talking quietly. I skidded to a stop in front of them. Tears streamed down my cheeks as I looked at my best friend's shocked face.

"Can we go?" I asked in a weak voice. She nodded, jumped off the couch and took my hand.

"Jordan, please?" Lance begged as he reached for me. I yanked out of his reach and scurried out of the house. The boys followed and I jumped into Alicia's car, she followed.

"Let her go for now." I heard Sawyer say.

"But I don't…" I didn't hear anymore because I slammed the door and buried my face in my trembling hands.

"What's wrong?" Alicia started the car, but didn't put it in reverse.

"Just drive. Please just go and I'll tell you everything." She backed out of the driveway. "I shouldn't…I shouldn't have come last night. I shouldn't, I can't say no to him and he may not care, but I can't…"

"He cares."

"No, no he doesn't. Lish, if he cared for me half as much as I care about him, he wouldn't keep backing off."

143

"Being with Keller, you're sending him mixed messages too. Why didn't you stay and hear what he had to say? Why do you always expect the worst? I know he loves you. I *know* he wants you back too."

"That's what I'm afraid of."

"Why? You love him, he loves you and the two of you are perfect together."

"But I'm with Keller now."

"Who cares? Lance has been there for you and Keller hasn't. You know Lance is a thousand times better than that fuckhead."

"But Lance dumped me without a problem, not once, but repeatedly. How do I know it won't happen again?"

"I guess you don't." She shrugged. "He's learned from his mistakes, but I know what you're saying, I know you're scared."

"I love him Lish, but if I dump Keller to run back to him and he does it again, then where does that leave me?"

"There are better guys than Keller out there."

"Not any who want me."

"Are you blind or just stupid, Jo, seriously?" Alicia asked in disbelief. "There were at least five guys at the party last night who would've made a move if it weren't for Lance. My *brother* is totally crushing on you. Not to mention all the guys at CA who are dying for the day you dump Keller James."

"You exaggerate."

"I wish I had half the guys chasing me that you do."

"You have *one* amazing guy who already caught you. I would give anything for that." I interjected quickly. Alicia's phone began ringing, she picked it up and showed me the screen. It was Sawyer, of course.

"Hey baby." She breathed softly in a voice meant only for her boyfriend. "We're headed back to CA now." She was quiet as Sawyer talked. She made a face. "Yes she told me, no I won't tell you. And if Lance wasn't such a moron he'd know for himself. Tell him to figure it out on his own. He's a big boy and he shouldn't need someone else to make phone calls for him."

I laughed and silently wished I could be more like Alicia. I admire how brave she is, I was a coward next to her.

"Hungry?"

"Starving."

"Burgers and shakes?"

"Absolutely." I giggled as my friend hit her blinker and turned into a restaurant drive thru. We placed our order and when we pulled back out on the road she turned to look at me.

"I realize Lance has a horrible track record when it comes to you, but, I do know he loves you. It's probably not easy to believe him when he says so, but he really does mean it. I wish you two wouldn't fight it so hard."

"I don't want to fight it, but it's hard to convince my head and heart not to run at the first sound of his sexy voice."

"Always go with your gut." Alicia sighed. "Even if that means breaking my cousin's heart, because your instinct is always right." I nodded. She was right, it was something I told myself often. However, it was easier said than done. If I followed my gut, rather than my heart, Lance wouldn't be the only one holding a broken heart.

144

Chapter 61

"Why are you wearing Lance's clothes?" Zack questioned hesitantly when I walked into the house. He tried to hide the disappointment in his voice, but it was evident. Alicia shot him a funny look.

"Because I went swimming and my clothes were soaked last night."

"You went swimming *with* your clothes on?"

"I will only go skinny dipping with you, Bentley." I giggled.

"That needs to happen soon." He took a step towards me and Alicia grabbed me by the arm.

"Did you still need help with your Trig homework?" She asked innocently.

"Definitely." My eyes flitted to Zack's face, he was shooting Alicia a dirty look. I wish I knew when their friendship went sour. I definitely didn't like the tension in the room right now. "You going to be around a while?"

"Yes." Zack answered. "Cale and I are working out in a bit, but we'll be close." I smiled, nodded and hurried up the stairs with Alicia.

"Did you hook up with Zack sometime?"

"What the fuck?" She gasped. "Why would you ask that?"

"I can't understand why suddenly you two hate each other."

"We have never hooked up. He tends to jump down my throat when anything doesn't go his way. He's either blaming me or Lance for everything."

"Like what?"

"When Lance picked you up after your birthday party, it was supposedly all my fault." She rolled her shoulders and her eyes. "He's extremely envious of Lance and he takes it out on me. I'm done playing nice. He has no room to badmouth my cousin when he knows nothing about him." I nodded my head. Her words didn't make sense, it certainly didn't sound like Zack but I had been preoccupied lately and may have missed it.

"He's been pretty stressed with…" I began. Alicia didn't want me to stick up for him though and it was obvious when her eyes narrowed. I stopped talking and shook my head. "I'll talk to him."

"I'm not worried about it."

"I am though, I don't want my friends fighting. You and Zack are huge parts of my life, I can't, I don't want there to be tension all the time." This time she nodded.

"Maybe I am overreacting sometimes." I knew how that was, I did it a lot, especially when it came to Lance and his hidden meanings. I walked over to my desk and grabbed my trig book and notebook before carrying them over to my bed.

"And he probably is too. I'll smack him around and tell him to stop being an ass." She giggled and went through my notebook to find my most recent work. As I went to the assignment I was having the most trouble with, my phone began ringing.

"It's Lance, what do I do?" I practically threw my phone off the bed as if it were toxic.

"I don't know. Answer it." She laughed.

"I'm not ready to talk yet."

"Then don't answer. If he's smart, he'll keep calling until you do." She shrugged. It went to voicemail and Alicia pretended as though nothing had happened before she began explaining where I'd gone wrong in my work. Twenty minutes later, she was headed home and I was staring at my phone, daring Lance to call me back. The phone rang again and Keller's fake grin flashed on my screen. I let out a low groan before I answered it.

"Did you have fun last night?"

"What…what do you mean?" My stomach hurt as fear rushed through me. How in the Hell did he know about last night?

"Spending the night with Alicia, did you guys have fun?"

"Oh, oh yeah. We just hung out at her house all night. Low key, but it was nice."

"Good. Big plans for tonight?"

"Staying in and watching movies by myself probably." Sadly, I wasn't lying. I was hoping Caleb, Maddie and Zack would be around, but they were probably going to a party or something. "What about you?"

"Dad has some dinner meeting planned with business partners and I have to go for appearances. I'm sure it will be incredibly boring."

"Probably not." I laughed.

"I have to go. I'll see you tomorrow." I heard Keller's dad call for him and my boyfriend hung up before I could respond. Not that I'm complaining though, I'm just glad we're not forcing a conversation anymore, for now.

Lance called and I ignored it again.

I tried to take a nap and was unsuccessful as the memories of last night continued to replay themselves in my head. Two hours later, my phone rang with Lance's number again and I finally answered it.

"What do you want?"

"You." He blurted.

"Excuse me?"

"I want *you*, Jo. I want you back. I want to start over and forget about everything that happened before."

"You mean last night?"

"No! Jordan, the only thing I regret about last night is that you have a boyfriend and it's not me. I'm sorry. I shouldn't have kept trying, but I'm glad I did. Last night was unbelievable and I just miss you even more now."

"I miss you too." I pouted. "But…"

"I wish I could take my mistakes back. I'd never let you go if I could. I've changed darlin', I'm not letting you go without a fight and that's why I've been calling all day."

"Calling is only *one* thing."

"I know, but it's more than I've done in the past, isn't it?"

"Yeah." I mumbled. "I can't get hurt again, Lance."

"That's not my intention. It never is. I just…I know if you give me another chance I can make things right."

"I want that." I whispered. The line was silent for almost ten seconds before Lance spoke.

"You know, it's pretty lonely in this house all alone."

"Oh, is it?" I giggled. "Why don't you have one of your buddies come over and keep you company?"

"They're all with girlfriends or just busy. Sawyer has a hot date with Lish tonight."

"I'm well aware."

146

"I wish there was some hot girl who'd come over and keep me company tonight." He hinted again.

"You're a big boy. I'm sure you'll be fine."

"I'll be scared. I'm terrified of being home alone *and* the house is haunted. You don't want me to be scared, do you?" He whined on the other end. "What if something gets me?"

"You want *me* to protect you? Isn't that backwards?"

"So?" He laughed. "Actually, I rented some horror movies and I was hoping you'd come over and hold me through the scary parts. Sawyer was supposed to, but he *obviously* got a better offer."

"The mental picture of you and Sawyer holding each other is just frightening." I teased. "*And* you're a freak."

"Only with you. Are you going to come over and protect me or not?"

"Lance." I sighed. "I can't just go over to your house again, everyone will wonder."

"Then tell them you're staying with Lish again. Okay wait…" He backpedaled. "Just say you're going to watch a movie with Alicia and if you decide later to stay the night with me, you can tell them you're staying at her house again."

"I don't like to lie."

"Then tell them the truth, I don't care if the whole world knows."

"Lance." I sighed again.

"Please darlin', if you don't come on your own then I'll kidnap you."

"Whatever."

"I'm serious. I'm not playing games. I want to see you again and I'm not taking no for an answer. Besides, my house *is* really scary alone."

"Fine."

"Now?" He asked excitedly. "Just wear whatever you have on and get over here *now*."

"Thirty minutes." I hung up the phone. I took a deep breath, closed my eyes and thought about what I had just agreed to do.

I stood up and a prom picture of Keller and I caught my eye. I immediately flipped it over before I could feel guilty. Then I flipped through my photo album on my phone to the picture I'd taken last night of me laying on Lance's chest. It was incredibly stupid to have evidence of my indiscretion, but the moment was just too perfect. My dad was actually home for a few hours this afternoon, only to take off for a conference again tonight. I poked my head into his office.

"Hey, I'm staying at Alicia's again tonight. I'll be back tomorrow morning."

"Again? You two live together, isn't that overkill?"

"No." I giggled. "I'm just making up for my lack of a life for the last few months."

"Fine. Have fun and be careful." I bounded down the steps and out the door before I ran into anyone else. I didn't want to lie any more than I already had. I was also certain Zack would talk me out of my decision to go to Lance's. I climbed into my car, started it and called Alicia as I was backing out of the driveway.

"Alicia, I'm an idiot."

"You're going to Lance's aren't you?"

"Yes."

"Then you're not an idiot, just a whore." She teased with a laugh. "No, you're just following your heart, sweetie. And I guess you're headed to my house for parental purposes?"

"Yes. Thank you. Will you stop by before, during or after your date? I'm nervous and…"

"Say no more, we will be there. Good luck and stop overthinking things." I smiled as I hung up the phone and drove through the Callatin Academy wrought iron gates.

Her directions to not overthink, was having the opposite effect. I shouldn't be going to Lance's. I should break up with Keller, because I was cheating on him and even though he was doing the same thing, it didn't make it right. What was I thinking? I've been cheated on so many times before and here I am, doing it myself. What's wrong with me? Why can't I break up with Keller? Why can't I follow my heart and jump back into Lance's arms wholeheartedly? Was that a bear? I stopped the car and realized I was in the middle of the road, so I pulled over to the shoulder and looked around. Whatever I had seen was now gone and it started sprinkling. My fears were not though. My phone began ringing, Lance's gorgeous face flashed across my screen and I hesitated to pick it up, but I did.

"Second thoughts?"

"How did you know?"

"Because I can see you at the end of the driveway." He chuckled. "I can't force you, Jo. I guess I can just tell you how badly I want you here with me. I'm crazy about you and I just want you back."

"Lance, I have a boyfriend."

"I know and it sucks. Nothing has to happen; we can just watch the movie and hang out *as friends*."

"*But I want something to happen Lance.* I want you to kiss me and hold me."

"Then why are you still on the side of the road?"

"Because I'm an idiot."

"No, you have a conflicted conscience. Come on baby, please? I miss you so much, I just want one kiss and then you can leave if you want."

"Okay." I started down the road again, knowing damn well he didn't mean I could leave if I wanted. I wouldn't want to and he would talk me out of it if I pretended I did. I was driving at a snail's pace, because it was raining harder and I was trying to talk myself out of going through with this. Parking in this driveway wouldn't be good for my heart.

I stopped and was about to throw the Mustang into reverse and peel out of the driveway just as Lance jogged down his front steps. The rain was coming down in sheets, but he still hurried out to open my door for me. My stupid heart melted.

"Come on." He held out his hand for me to take.

"No." I murmured as I stared straight through my windshield. "Tell me why I'm here, Lance. Show me I'm not as stupid as I feel right now."

Without hesitation, he squatted down so he was eye level with me. "How can I do that when you won't get out of the car and give me a shot?" He held his hand out again and this time I took it. When we were both standing he pulled me into an amazing kiss. I was breathless and speechless when he pulled away.

"How was that?" He asked hopefully. I made a funny noise, unable to form a rational thought as my spine tried to straighten. Lance chuckled before he looked around quickly. He pulled me away from my car, shut the door and then put up a finger.

"Wait, right here." He sprinted to his truck, rolled down the windows and started it. He turned the volume all way up on the radio just as a slow song by Alabama filled the air.

"Will you dance with me?" He asked as he held his hand out to me again. I took it, nodded my head and fell into him as he wrapped his arms around my waist and pulled me close. Lance sang the song in my ear as we slowly moved with the music. When the song ended, he began to kiss me hungrily. Within seconds, he was leaning me against my car as we made out.

My throat tightened and my stomach hurt. Did he just bring me here for sex? Is that all I am, just a booty call? Did he know I would come right over with just a few sweet words? Was I really so easy to read? Tears filled my eyes before I pushed him away and turned to get back into my car.

"I'm sorry, I didn't mean to *attack* you. I've just wanted to kiss you since you left this morning." He admitted sheepishly. He looked back at me nervously when he realized I was upset. One hand was on my waist while the other went up to my face where he tipped my chin up gently.

"Do you know how beautiful you are right now?" My face grew red and he continued. "You're the most beautiful girl in the world Jordan and I'm in awe that you're in front of me right now."

"Lance." I breathed, all rational thought flew from my brain as my body went to mush again. I was so easy.

"I'm glad you came. I'm not going to mess up again." He whispered in my ear. "Let's get inside out of the rain. I don't want you to get sick."

"Lance, I…" Should go, should get the Hell out of here and never look back. His hands fell away from my waist as he jogged over to the truck, rolled the windows up and shut the beast off. He was back in front of me in a matter of seconds.

"Did you eat lunch yet? There's not much food in the kitchen, but we can order pizza or something." He grabbed my hand and tugged me towards the house. I started to dig my heels in, but I couldn't. I was hooked on him. I wanted him too badly and I deserved to have this night, just in case it never happened again. You never know when the last time you would see someone, I wouldn't let this night pass and have it as a regret for the rest of my life.

"Lance." He must've heard something strange in my voice as he stopped and turned around just at the foot of his porch steps. I yanked him towards me and kissed him. Yeah, I wasn't going anywhere.

When I pulled away, he was grinning from ear to ear which caused my face to break out in a smile as well. My whole body tingled with anticipation as he tugged me up the porch and into the house.

"Let's get you into some dry clothes." He started towards his room, but I pulled him back and held up my dripping wet backpack.

"I brought some." I unzipped the bag, pulled out a tank top and shorts and dropped the backpack into the floor, out of the way. Lance took the clothes out of my hand and put it on the nearby table before he began helping me out of my clothes. It was the sweetest, sexiest gesture, but I couldn't let it go there right now. I kissed him gently before I ducked away, grabbed my clothes and scurried to the nearest bathroom. I changed into a black tank and red cotton shorts and then headed back into the living room.

"Are you hungry?" He asked nervously as he ran his hand against the back of his head. "I can order the pizza now and it'll be here in thirty minutes. Or, I have leftovers. Mom overcooked knowing I'd be home alone or thinking the guys would all be over here and…well, there's a variety of food."

"Leftovers sound like Heaven." I sighed. Lance cocked an eyebrow. "What? The closest I get to home cooked meals is grill cheese sandwiches."

"I can do better than that." He chuckled as he went to the refrigerator. "And I'm not going to let you choose either, you're going to have some of mom's chicken and dumplings because you won't find anything better."

"I haven't had those in forever." Lance grinned back at me as he pulled a container out of the fridge. He went to the cabinets and pulled out two plates and some silverware.

"Sit."

"I can help."

"No, sit. I'm perfectly capable of throwing food in the microwave." I giggled and sat at the old wooden table in the nook of their kitchen. Minutes later, Mrs. Bowman's chicken and dumplings were steaming in front of me. They definitely looked amazing. Lance didn't take a bite until I did.

"You were right." I mumbled after the first forkful. "This is amazing." He grinned proudly and began eating as well. I was almost finished when my phone began ringing, it was Keller. Normally, I wouldn't be so rude but I also knew Keller would continue to call until I answered and when I did, I would get an earful.

"I have to…" I stammered. Lance nodded and wouldn't make eye contact. I got up from the table and went into the living room for some privacy.

"Hey you." I mumbled into the phone.

"Hey. Sorry I'm calling again. I just miss you. Besides you sounded…weird earlier. I didn't know if it was because you missed me too or because you were tired."

"Tired."

"So you're staying at Alicia's again tonight?"

"Yeah, Drew's throwing a party and he wanted us to be there." I lied.

"Will Lance be there?"

"It *is* his cousin, but I don't know." I shrugged as I looked into the kitchen nervously. Lance was clearing the kitchen table and moving the plates to the sink. I turned back around and heard the water come on.

"Great. Now I have to compete with other guys too."

"What do you want me to do, hide in my room while you're gone?"

"Yes!"

"Screw you." I muttered angrily as I contemplated hanging up on him.

"I'm sorry. I'm not being fair. It's just hard to be here, when you're there. I trust you though, so go have fun, I guess."

"I would anyway."

"I know, *that* was just to make me feel better." He laughed. "I have a surprise for you when I get home tomorrow."

"What is it?"

"It wouldn't be a surprise if I told you. Our flight gets in around noon so I'll come by afterwards."

"Okay, how's the trip?"

"Not bad. Dad is tolerable at least so it's better than I thought it would be."

"He hasn't talked you into breaking up with me yet?"

"You're off limits, that was one of my conditions when I said I'd come."

"That's pathetic, Keller."

"I know and I'm sorry."

"It's just a little disheartening. I wish it were different, maybe we…never mind, I'll see you tomorrow."

"Yeah, okay." He mumbled as he sensed there was trouble on my end of the line. "I love you." I hung up the phone without repeating the sentiment. I closed my eyes and inhaled deeply. Why couldn't I just finish the sentence and break up with him?

I heard a dish fall into the sink and I turned around to watch Lance. He pretended not to notice I was done with my phone call. I slowly made my way into the kitchen, looking at all of the family pictures decorating the rooms. It was nice and homey, I envied that.

"Wyatt looks like you when you were little."

"That's what mom says, but I don't see it." He laughed as he joined me in the hallway. Lance stood behind me and wrapped his arms around my waist as he looked at the photos with me.

"I wish mom would take these down, they're embarrassing."

"No, they're perfect." I smiled. "Do you know there is not one family picture hanging up at my house? I don't even know if dad has any of my old pictures."

"I'm sure he does. Guys just aren't as good at decorating as women. I guarantee these wouldn't be up if it weren't for mom."

"Is that Luke?" I asked pointing at a photo of a young boy. He favored Lance, but they really didn't look a lot alike. "I thought you were twins."

"Not identical." He laughed. "People usually say Jess and I should've been the twins."

"I could see that."

"Are you ready to watch movies?" I nodded my head as his hand found mine and he led me to the couch. "I got three, which one first?"

"Surprise me." Lance shrugged his shoulders and put a DVD in the player before he dove next to me on the couch.

"You better hold my hand. I heard this one is pretty scary." he laced his fingers through mine and flashed an amazing smile.

"I don't know how I'm supposed to protect *you* when I'm a big wuss when it comes to scary movies."

"Want to know a secret?" He whispered in my ear before I nodded. "I actually knew that."

"You tricked me, huh?"

"Yup. I like being the one you bury your face into or you grab when you're scared."

"Me too." I admitted with a grin. Lance calmed my fears about just being sex by cuddling with me while we watched the movies. It was nice spending the entire day with him again.

It was between the second and third movies that there was a knock on the door. Alicia and Sawyer were just starting their date and she had forced him to check on us.

"What are you kids up to?" Sawyer asked as he grinned at Lance.

"Watching movies." He answered with a shrug as he shot his friend a dirty look.

"Exciting. You really know how to woo a girl, don't you?"

"You're on a date and you come to *my* house. Where do you have room to talk?"

"See what happens when you try to be a good friend and do a checkup?"

"Checkup?"

151

"We thought Jordan wouldn't show and that you'd be depressed and miserable." Sawyer responded. Alicia quickly slapped him playfully before she grabbed my hand and yanked me into Lance's bedroom.

"How's it going? Are you okay?" She asked warily as she closed the door behind us.

"It's good and I'm fine. I was worried at first, but...he has a way of making me forget my insecurities." Alicia smiled back at me before she walked over to his laptop. She hit a key and caused the computer screen to flicker on. There was a picture of Lance and me on his four wheeler. I was sitting behind him, holding him tightly as we both grinned. A second later, the picture changed to one of us at Homecoming. For the next few minutes, a slide show of photographs of the two of us together and just of me played.

"If he didn't care about you, would this be his screensaver?" I swallowed hard trying to process what I was seeing. It didn't seem normal for him to still have our pictures displayed if he didn't still care, right? Alicia started looking through the notebooks and papers on the desk before grinning as she cleared her throat and began reading out loud. "I don't understand why I can't say the words. I don't know why I can't tell her what she means to me. I hope someday I can make her mine again and I'll never let her go. How hard is it to let her know how much I love her?" She put the yellow note pad down and continued snooping.

"Alicia, I don't...I don't feel right doing this."

"Oh please, if you only knew what Luke, Lance and Drew all put me through growing up. At least I'm using it for good rather than evil. He does love you; he just has a hard time saying it. I'm not pushing you towards him though, because I know how bad he's hurt you in the past. When the time is right Jo, you'll be together. Maybe that's now and maybe it's not. I just know you shouldn't be with Keller."

"I know that too. It's just...it's not as easy as it seems to cut him loose. Lance is...amazing until...he's not anymore." Alicia nodded understandingly.

"I think you and Lance are perfect for each other, if you two would stop overthinking it."

"It's complicated."

"*Only* if you make it."

"You look great tonight, by the way." I smiled, changing the subject because I was uncomfortable.

"Thanks." She blushed. "Sawyer's told me that five times already."

"Aww, he's so sweet." I gushed. "Thanks for coming by." I gave her a quick hug.

"You've done it for me." She rolled her shoulders and started out of the bedroom. "Think about what I said, what you saw and follow your heart." I nodded and trailed her out of the room and into the living room. Sawyer and Lance had been talking quietly, but stopped immediately when we came out.

"Are you done talking about us?" Sawyer joked.

"Or snooping?" Lance queried.

"We were doing both, and yes." Alicia laughed.

"Most likely *you* were doing both." Lance retorted as he cocked an eyebrow and watched his cousin carefully. "Find what you needed?"

"Possibly." Alicia rolled her shoulders and moved closer to Sawyer. He took Alicia's hand and looked adoringly back at my friend.

"Ready to go?" She nodded, moved to give me a hug and threw a wave over her shoulder. "I'll have my phone with me if you need something."

"Thanks Lish, have fun guys." Sawyer gave me a quick hug too and they were out the door in seconds.

"They are too cute." I giggled as I plopped back down on the couch.

"We are too, you know?" Lance fell beside me.

"But we're not together."

"We could be. We should be." Lance whispered flirtatiously in my ear. "I want us to be."

"So do I." I mumbled as I fell back against the old, blue cloth pillows. I didn't want to talk about our future yet so I quickly tried to get out of it by grabbing the remote and turning the movie back on. "Are you going to come over here and hold me while we watch the rest of the movie, or what?"

"Hell yeah!" He moved closer and put his arm around my shoulders. I snuggled into his warmth and closed my eyes. This was Heaven.

"What time is curfew?" Lance asked after the movie ended.

"Eight o clock tomorrow morning."

"Really?" He asked excitedly. "You're going to stay the night with me?"

"Technically, I'm staying the night with Alicia, but I guess I can stay here if I have to."

"Yeah, I really don't do well in this house alone at night. I need someone to hold when the ghosts come out."

"And just who do you hold onto when I'm not around?"

"I hide under the covers."

"Yeah, I bet." I answered sarcastically as I rolled my eyes. "I highly doubt Lance Bowman spends many nights alone." He made a funny face as he looked down at the ground.

"Jordan, you're the only girl I've ever stayed the night with." He mumbled.

"But not the only one you've had in your bed, I'm sure."

"Actually, yeah you are. Where are you going with this?"

"But I'm not the only girl you've...been with."

"And I'm not the only guy you've been with. Those other girls were *just sex,* Jordan." He looked up at me, watching for answers. Suddenly, he knelt down in front of me and looked up into my eyes sadly. "And you think that's all you are to me?"

I nodded and Lance looked perplexed. He took a deep breath and searched for the right words to say as I waited for the truth.

"You could never be *just sex* to me. I've never brought a girl to meet my family or inside my house before. I haven't been on a date since you. If I'm interested in a girl, it's just like it was before I met you, we hang out, party, hook up and that's it."

"Like us, last night."

"No!" He stood up quickly and clenched his fists in frustration. He knelt back down and grabbed my face in his hands. "I'm usually gone before curfew and I, sure as Hell, wouldn't have called to hang out today if that's all you were to me. Any other girl is just casual sex. You're different. With you I take my time, I fell for you and *then* I made love to you. It's not just sex when I'm with you."

My heart fluttered and I ignored his comments about casual sex with other girls. All I heard was the word love and I was done. Tears streamed down my face as I looked back at him.

"There's no one else I want darlin', you're perfect."

"No, I'm not."

"You are to me and that's all that matters." He muttered as he kissed me sweetly. As if to prove a point, he stood up and sat back down next to me on the worn in couch. He pulled me close to him and snuggled me while we continued to watch the movies. I sighed and relaxed into the security of his strong arms. I really was a sucker. It didn't matter if everything he said was a blatant lie, I believed every word because my heart couldn't take anything else.

Chapter 62

"Good morning, beautiful." Lance drawled as he smiled back at me the next morning. He kissed my forehead sweetly. "You look like a perfect angel when you're asleep."

"As opposed to a monster when I'm awake?" I cracked. "What time is it?"

"Six. I guess you have to go soon."

"Yeah."

"I don't want you to, though." He whined as he pulled me closer to him. "Kiss me." I did, because the perfection was about to end. The second I walked out of his house, reality would set back in and this amazing weekend would be nothing but a bittersweet memory.

"Why don't you jump in the shower and I'll make you breakfast?"

"Breakfast?"

"Bacon, eggs and toast?" He offered, as he kissed my bare stomach.

"You're amazing. You're so good to me, Lance."

"Of course." He laughed cockily. "How else should I be?"

"You want to take a shower with me?" I asked flirtatiously.

"Darlin', I'm exhausted. A man needs a break sometimes. Besides, I *really* want to make you breakfast."

"I know I'm being redundant, but you're amazing and incredibly romantic."

"I'd do anything for *you* and *only* you." He whispered before he kissed my head and got out of bed. I followed and headed to the shower after I slapped his tight, bare butt on the way.

"*That* is nice." I giggled as I eyed him approvingly.

"And so is this." He spun around, picked me up and kissed me intensely. "You do things to me Jo and it makes me want to do things to you that are triple x rated."

"Care to demonstrate?"

"We'll have time later." He chuckled.

"You're no fun." I whined.

"Unfortunately, you have practice in an hour otherwise I'd still be in bed with you."

"I don't believe you." I teased before I went into the bathroom. After my shower, Lance and I ate breakfast and twenty minutes later, I was headed out the door. He grabbed my hand and walked me to my car.

"I don't know what's going to happen when reality sets back in so there's some things I need to say before you go."

"Lance, you don't have to. I'll be back, I mean I'm not…"

"I should've told you this a long time ago." He kissed me sweetly. "*You* are the best thing in my life. I would do anything and everything for you. It kills me when we're apart, but it destroys me to see you hurting in anyway, especially when I'm to blame. I wish I could protect you from everything."

"Lance." Tears filled my eyes. This sounded an awful lot like goodbye, again.

"Even if you leave here and stay with Keller, I'll still be here. I'll be devastated and disappointed but having you in my life, in any form, is all that matters to me. I'll wait forever for you, Jordan."

"I'm not going anywhere." I whispered as I kissed him passionately. I climbed into my car and left for practice. I couldn't stop smiling.

"Someone had a good night, I take it." Alicia teased as we started grabbing our gear after practice was over.

"Amazing." I gushed. "How was yours?"

"Perfect." She grinned. "Who would've known *Sawyer* could be so perfect."

"That's awesome, maybe we can double."

"Talk to me again once Keller gets back." Alicia retorted. "It's great now, but it's not going to be easy later."

"Do you always have to burst my bubble?"

"Unfortunately, yes. Someone has to be your voice of reality and reason."

"I have homework I need to finish." I mumbled as I waved and started towards my car. It was easier to run away from the truth, rather than deal with it. I could only hope Keller's father had bribed him to break up with me, so this could be easy. Lance Bowman was all I wanted and it was about time I made certain Keller was aware of it.

Chapter 63

"Hey babe." Keller smiled from my doorway, abruptly shattering my sweet fantasies. He was wearing a white polo shirt and a pair of plaid cargo shorts, a white baseball cap rested backwards on his head. He was always dressed up even though he didn't have to be. His eyes sparkled as he started towards me. As he bent down to kiss me he handed me a gift and whispered.

"I missed you."

"What's *this*?" I shot him an uncomfortable and questioning look.

"I missed you, isn't that enough of a reason for a gift? I don't show you how much I love you enough." I slowly opened the package, worried about what his intentions were.

"Don't worry about ripping the paper." He grumbled as he ripped the paper open, pulled out a black jewelry box and then opened it to display a gorgeous silver diamond pendant necklace. He pulled it out and put it on me. I was speechless. "My girlfriend deserves the best." He grinned. "We've been together for so long, I thought you needed something to show a little more commitment."

"Keller, I can't…I don't understand."

"You're part of my future and I guess…the necklace is my promise to you." He beamed. I burst into tears. What had I gotten myself into? We were both cheating on each other and he thought we needed more commitment? Was he that clueless? I had to stop this right now before I was fifty and still in this Hell.

"I love you, J and I'm here for good." He wrapped his arms around me and tried to kiss me. I pulled away and cried harder.

"I can't do this, Keller." His body tensed, but he didn't let go of me. "I don't love you. You don't love me. This is ridiculous." I tried to take the necklace off, but Keller grabbed my hands and squeezed.

"Don't be an idiot."

"Keller, I was with Lance all weekend. We're back together and…"

"I'm not stupid." His voice was tight with anger as he pushed me away from him and stood up. "I was hoping you'd get him out of your system."

"I'm in love with him."

"No, you're not."

"Please, I…"

"You will not leave me for the Plow Boy, do you understand?" Keller's voice was calm now. He flipped my television on, put it on a local news channel and chuckled as they showed the aftermath of a massive traffic accident on the interstate. "This is your punishment, you're warning for being with him this weekend and lying to me."

"I don't…" That's when he pointed to the black SUV in a ditch. The front was on fire, but he was pointing at the license plates that clearly read BWMN…Mrs. Bowman's car. I gasped, flew off my bed and got as close to the screen as I could.

"Don't fuck with me, Jordan. I don't lose."

"Is she…are they okay?"

"They are for now, just got ran off the road and caused a ten car pileup. The next time they won't be so lucky."

157

"Keller, how can you…?"

"I always get what I want." He shrugged as he pulled me up to him. "Now, why don't we consummate our commitment to each other?" I could feel the bile rising in my throat as he began kissing me. He pulled away, shut my bedroom door and came back for me. He pushed me down on the bed.

"Keller, no. I don't…I can't."

"You fuck that filthy bastard all weekend and you can't stand for me to touch you?" He growled.

"Please, don't." I begged as I fought, but he was stronger and took what he wanted while I cried.

When he was finishing, my phone began ringing. I knew it was Lance by the ringtone and I sobbed even harder. Keller fell on top of me with a grunt, grabbed my phone off the nightstand, looked at it and threw it at me.

"Finish that bastard now." He growled as he got dressed. I ignored the call. "You will end it or trust me, you haven't seen anything yet. He strutted out of my room. I curled up in a ball and cried. What else could I do?

Chapter 64

"Is everyone okay?" I texted Lance later that night. *"Sorry, I just got your message."*
"They're fine. Shaken up, but home. Thanks for asking."
"Do you need anything?"
"A hug? Lol"
"Can you meet me near campus in a bit?"
"Sure, twenty minutes?"

"I'll be there." I was already waiting for him when I sent the text message. I didn't want anyone to realize what I was doing. I needed to be alone with Lance. Keller had spies everywhere, obviously, since he knew my every move before I did. If I sat alone in this clearing long enough then his spy would get bored and move on. At least, I was hoping that was the case.

Lance pulled up and I burst into tears. When he climbed out of the truck, I rushed to give him a giant hug.

"I'm sorry I wasn't there for you earlier."

"There's no need to cry, darlin'." He chuckled. "It's okay."

"No, it's not." Lance's body tensed as he realized I was crying for a different reason.

"Jordan." He sighed sadly.

"I'm sorry, I'm so sorry."

"It's okay darlin', I kind of already knew."

"Lance." I sobbed.

"Take a deep breath and just tell me what happened." He led me to his tail gate. I couldn't tell him what happened, because he would hate me. I was careless and put his family's life in danger.

"Keller, he...he changed his life for me and...I can't...He is what is best for me."

"What about me? What about us?" He mumbled. "Don't I get a say? Don't I matter?"

"Lance, I love you but..."

"I love you, but...*no,* you don't love me. If you did, we wouldn't be having this conversation right now. Am I a joke or what? Or wait...was this your way of getting back at me for everything? Did you just want to watch me hurt like you did? Here I am Jo, fucking broken."

"Lance."

"You broke me, Jordan. You broke my heart and *everything* in me." He pushed off the tailgate and began to walk away. He spun on his heel and glared with angry, disappointed eyes. "Seriously, am I just a game?"

"Lance, no." I sobbed. "I can't hurt, Keller. You don't know him."

"But you can hurt me?"

"This is killing me. Please believe me. I never meant for this to happen. I should've stayed away...I shouldn't have went to your party. I can't hide or control my emotions when it comes to you." Lance wasn't coming anywhere near me. I felt empty and alone, I hugged myself insecurely.

"Funny, it doesn't seem that way."

"Please don't hate me." I jumped off the tailgate and tried to grab his hand, he shook me away.

"I don't understand any of this."

"Me neither."

"If you love *me*, why stay with Keller?"

"Because I have to."

"He treats you like shit, he's constantly…and …"

"*You're* constantly breaking my heart."

"I thought we were past that."

"It's not that easy. I'm terrified of it happening again, I guess it's why I can't break up with Keller." I lied; when in doubt blame someone else.

"But you can spend the last two nights screwing me?"

"It wasn't screwing to me, Lance, but I guess the truth comes out." I laughed angrily.

"It wasn't for me either. I thought I proved that to you."

"No, you proved you're a damn good actor!"

"Like you have any room to fucking talk." He growled as he got up in my face. "I never know from one minute to the next if you're for real or just rehearsing for a fucking soap opera! Are these tears even real, Jo? Is there a video camera around somewhere? Are you shooting a movie about a dumb hick who falls in love with the spoiled princess, who's clearly out of his league?"

"Lance…please."

"What does it matter? You've obviously made your decision."

"It does matter."

"Go back to your rich boyfriend. You're not the girl I thought you were. If you choose him over me because he can buy you a fucking necklace than *I'm* the fool." Lance screamed angrily. His eyes were wet and he looked like he might cry at any minute.

"I'm not…" I began quietly. I was so surprised and touched by his display of emotions that I rushed to him and wrapped my arms around him. He tried to push me away but I held on tighter. Finally, I fell to the ground in a fit of tears.

"I'm sorry, Lance. I'm sorry. I never wanted to hurt you. I never dreamed I could."

"What?" He scoffed. "You're fucking unbelievable."

"Lance, I can't get hurt again. Damn it, but I am anyway."

"*I* won't hurt you again." He whispered, his voice full of pleading.

"You are though. You're hurting me just by being angry with me."

"Shouldn't I be angry? I'm disappointed and hurt. I knew this would happen, I just got my hopes up and …"

"I did too."

"I have to go."

"Please don't."

"Jordan, don't drag this out. Seriously, I'm over it." He cut.

"Well I'm not." I cried as I stormed off. Lance chased after me, grabbed my arm and yanked me back to him before he kissed me passionately.

"You're breaking my heart, Jo." He whispered.

"Lance." I breathed as I kissed him again. Then I turned on my heel and sprinted away. I rushed back to the dorms without looking back. If I stopped for even a second I'd have found myself back in Lance's arms and complicated matters even more.

Keller got what he wanted and I was miserable. How did things get so out of control?

Chapter 65

Sitting here, with my feet dug into the cool Florida sand enjoying beautiful weather on a private beach next to a gorgeous guy; I should've been thrilled, counting my blessings or something, but I wasn't. I was dreaming of someone else, of being somewhere else entirely.

"You need another beer?" Keller asked as he stood up from the chaise lounge he'd been laying in beside me. I slowly opened my eyes, half hoping I'd heard the wrong voice, but I knew better.

"Of course." I smiled.

"You want something else?" He asked coyly as he cocked an eyebrow. There was a time when I would've thought my boyfriend was hinting about sex but lately, I knew better.

"I'm good. You go ahead though." Keller had recently introduced me to recreational drugs and since his father was one of the wealthiest men in the Midwest, he had access to a multitude of anything he wanted and it was always at our immediate disposal.

"Are you sure?" I nodded and went back to sunbathing. I heard Keller head up towards his father's beach house and I let out a sigh.

It was Keller's birthday, which allowed us to skip school for a few days so his father could whisk him to their beach house in the Florida Keys. He'd planned for the whole week but at the last minute my doctor had called to schedule an appointment for Friday morning, they said it had to be Friday morning. Keller was not happy. In fact, he threw a fit that would make a two year old jealous. While our location was beautiful, the company was terrible. We barely talked.

Keller had started hanging out with a different group of friends; the trust fund group of our prestigious private school. The group was well known for their addictions and partying. I knew Keller was cheating on me daily, the whole school knew it, but he didn't protest the rumors because it hid the truth about his new habit.

The trip was just for show, a way for him to make people believe he was the perfect boyfriend. Keller and I hadn't been intimate in months, he rarely kissed me either, actually. When we hung out, we were usually getting high in some way, fighting, or not even really talking. The drugs had changed Keller into an even more aggressive, possessive person, which is something I could do without. His insecurities were loud and mostly in the shape of handprints all over my body.

So far, we'd been alone for an entire day and we hadn't so much as held hands, we'd barely talked on the private flight down, we'd only drank, he'd smoked pot, but there hadn't been any angry episodes. Sure, he'd taken me shopping and bought me an insane amount of clothes and shoes, but that was normal. Keller was always taking me on shopping sprees to make up for his jerkish ways or he'd go out himself and come back with thousands of dollars' worth of the best things as gifts for me. That's right, thousands of dollars.

"Any chance I could get into those dreams?" A male voice asked.

"Doubt it." I cut, without opening my eyes. "What are you doing here?"

"Keller invited us." Toby Clive smiled smugly as I opened my eyes and glared back at him.

"What?" I asked, realizing now that a group had come down the beach. All the kids made up Callatin's elite, the wealthiest teens at school and Keller's newfound friends. I let out a sigh and turned around just in time to see Keller walking down to me, carrying two beers and flirting with Sage and Adrienne, his hoes.

"I didn't think y'all would be here so soon. Sage said you wouldn't get in until tonight." Keller laughed as he high fived his friend. "You don't mind do you, babe? I invited everyone thinking they'd get here tomorrow, after you left."

"The more the merrier." I mumbled dryly, pretending not to be upset that he wouldn't be returning to Illinois with me.

"I knew you wouldn't mind." He smiled as he handed me the bottle of beer. It wouldn't matter if I did and we all knew it. He then shook his baggie of marijuana at me and the rest of the group nearby, "Are you sure you don't want some?"

"I'm good. I'm feeling a little run down as it is." I lied. "You go ahead, I'll be fine." Keller shrugged and, thinking I couldn't see it, made a funny face at Sage. He led the others back up to the house so they could smoke in private while I remained on the beach, alone. I wanted to be furious, I probably should've been but in all honesty, I really didn't care we couldn't spend time together. I guess he'd finally noticed I wasn't into the whole trip.

I was relieved the next morning when Keller dropped me off at the airport, although I was doing my best to mask it.

"You're not going to see me for a week, maybe we can have a quickie on a back road somewhere." I teased, knowing he wouldn't take the bait.

"You'll miss your flight."

"It's private, not commercial, they leave when I get there, isn't that what you've said a thousand times?" Keller nodded his head but did his best to push me away.

"Sorry J, I'm just really wiped. Last night was wild, I'm sorry I didn't come to bed until four."

"No biggie. I'm used to it." I fell back into the passenger seat and pouted.

"I'll make it up to you."

"That's what this whole trip was supposed to be about and instead, you invited your whole brew crew."

"*You* are leaving me, what was I supposed to do?"

"I stupidly thought you would be coming back with me!"

"Why in the Hell would I cut my birthday trip short, for you?"

"You know they are going over my bloodwork with me tomorrow. They're either going to tell me the cancer is gone or it's still there. I don't know why I thought my boyfriend would be there for me. We all know you haven't been there at all for anything else though, so I shouldn't be surprised."

"That's not my fault. Maybe, if you didn't have such asshole friends, I wouldn't feel threatened when I'm with you."

"You feel threatened?" I cackled. "Oh that's hilarious! My friends are fantastic, they don't like you because you treat me like shit."

"You're an ungrateful bitch." He hissed. I rolled my eyes, shook my head and turned to stare out the window. This car couldn't get me to the airport fast enough. My phone began beeping, alerting me to a text message.

"*What time does your flight land?*" Zack had typed. "*Can't wait for you to get here, we need someone to liven up the party.*" My fingers flew across the keyboard with a reply before I sank back into the plush leather seats of the rental car.

"Which boyfriend was that?" Keller asked, grabbing at my phone. "Why the fuck does he need to know when your flight lands? And what does he mean by *liven up the party*?"

"Get over it, Zack and I are really good friends." I rolled my eyes. Keller was furious and threw my phone down into the floorboard. When I leaned down to pick it up, I felt his fist connect with my head before I slumped against the window in shock.

"I will *not* get over it! You're *my* girlfriend and you spend more time with Bentley or the farm boy than you do with me."

"And you're with your gaggle of dimwits, Sage and Adrienne, more than you are with me." I narrowed my eyes at him. "You fuck them more than your so called girlfriend."

This time I knew I shouldn't have opened my mouth just as soon as Keller backhanded me there. I let out a shriek and grabbed my face, trying to stop the stinging sensation. I felt something wet and salty trickle down into my mouth and knew I was bleeding. Tears stung my eyes.

"Keller." I cried. I heard him curse, watched as his hands gripped the steering wheel as he focused on the road ahead of him. I turned my back to him, leaned against the seat again and cried until we stopped at the airport. He didn't say a word as I opened the door, went around to the trunk and pulled my luggage out or as I started towards the small private plane his father's company owned.

"Jordan! J! Wait baby, please wait!" Keller hollered as he raced after me, barely catching me as I started up the steps into the jet. He put his hands up to my face, gently touching the tender spot he'd caused. "I love you." Keller leaned down and kissed me ever so gently and I forgot why I was mad in the first place. "Don't think of doing anything stupid while you're at home without me." His eyes danced as he smirked. "I have eyes everywhere." I nodded. "Zack will be the first one I go after."

"I shouldn't have argued, I'm sorry." I whispered.

"I love you." Keller repeated. "Are we okay?" I nodded my head, let him kiss me again and then boarded the plane. I took a deep breath and let it out the second I was in the safety of the lush confines of the jet. When did he become such a sadistic bastard and why had I not realized it sooner?

Chapter 66

A few hours later, the plane had landed at a small airport near school where my friends and my cousin Cissy awaited me. It was obvious no one was thrilled about her being there.

"Cissy, what are you doing here?" I asked as I hugged her. Her hair was dyed platinum blonde, she was wearing way too much makeup and had recent plastic surgery done to her chest. She was not shy about showing them off either.

"Oh you know mom, as soon as she hung up with you we were in the car headed here for your appointment tomorrow."

"I told her I didn't need her to do that."

"You should know by now mom never listens." I chuckled as I hugged everyone else. "I hope you don't plan on living in a depression zone after your appointment tomorrow, because mom has tons of shopping plans and I need new clothes."

"I...uh..."

"Actually, *we're* going to celebrate after her appointment." Zack interjected as he slid his arm across my shoulders.

"Where are we celebrating?" Cissy asked flirtatiously.

"I didn't invite you."

"Zack!" I gasped. He shot me an apologetic look as he opened the SUV door for me and mumbled.

"I'll explain later."

"What's with all the stuff in the back?"

"We're headed to a Lake House. A new investment for our aunt and uncle." Caleb explained over his shoulder as he climbed in the driver's seat. "Aunt Becky thought it would take your mind off things, plus it's a little closer to your doctor."

"I was kind of looking forward to being in my own bed."

"Seriously? What's wrong with you?" Cissy rolled her eyes and harrumphed as she got placed in the back seat.

"Why are you being super bitch?" I retorted as I turned and pinned my cousin with a glare. "What did I do now?"

"What are you talking about?"

"You're making snide comments. Not to mention, Zack wouldn't have been rude to you unless you were being a bitch to him."

"He's just pissed I wouldn't screw him." Zack and Caleb roared with laughter.

"Not with someone else's dick, honey." Cissy narrowed her eyes before making a comment under her breath.

"That wasn't necessary, Zack."

"*Yes*, it was." He turned around and looked at me meaningfully. "I'm sorry. She has done nothing but throw herself at me and bad mouth you, all day. I'm sick of listening to her." My eyes flitted back to my cousin. She wasn't normally like this, before I moved to Illinois she and I were like sisters. She was rolling her eyes.

"Who are you going to believe, your cousin or the douchebag up front?"

"Zack doesn't throw himself at any girl, we all know that." Maddie threw over her shoulder. "If he was trying to get you in the sack, you wouldn't know until your legs were

164

spread for him."

"Whoa." I coughed as I looked at Maddie and burst out laughing.

"That's probably the best compliment I have ever gotten." Zack chuckled from the front seat. Caleb looked in the mirror at his fiancé, then at his best friend next to him before he punched Zack in the arm as hard as he could.

"Why would she know that?" Caleb asked.

"Girls talk, Cales. Not to mention, I've seen him in action a million times." Maddie rolled her eyes as she smiled and looked over at me. "Will you help me with wedding stuff this weekend? I'm feeling so overwhelmed."

"Absolutely. It'll be nice to focus on something good for a change." I grinned back at her. "If we're at the lake then we'll be super close to some great stores."

"Remember our budget?"

"What does that word even mean?" I teased.

"I stashed a lot of my best whiskey, Caleb, it'll be all right. We'll drink to forget about their spending habits." Zack offered.

"I'll get alcohol poisoning before that happens."

"If that happens, you'll have to answer to me."

"Like I would let anything happen to my bro."

"Your relationship is scary." I giggled.

"Speaking of which, how was your trip with Keller?"

"Fantastic, especially when the asshole brigade showed up yesterday."

"All of them?"

"Except Brennan. He's been laying low since my birthday."

"I think Keller banished him."

"Not completely." I shrugged. "He's still around when I am, but Keller gets pissed anytime he talks to me. I've asked Brennan about it a few times and he gets all weird."

"He has been acting distant lately." Maddie agreed with a thoughtful expression.

"Probably has more to do with embarrassment than anything. You did catch him in a pretty bad position." Caleb interjected. I nodded. He'd caught me in a pretty bad position as well. My brother was right, the awkwardness was probably equal on both of our parts. The car grew quiet for a minute as my brother turned on the road leading to the secluded, more expensive lake houses in the area. It was breathtaking, but my aunt and uncle's lake house was secluded and the road leading to it is gorgeous with tons of flowers and foliage. I rolled down the window and leaned out.

"You may not have much hair, but I do and you're wrecking it." Cissy snapped from the back seat. I rolled my eyes.

"Sorry, I love the smell of honeysuckle and I just…I needed to smell it."

"You'll get plenty of it when we stop, the nasty stuff is surrounding the house. Roll up your window now." I began to roll it back up when Zack and Caleb both rolled down theirs, Maddie followed suit. "Are you fucking kidding me?"

"Here's something you need to understand." Maddie began sweetly as she half turned in the seat. "Whatever your issues are, they are not Jordan's fault. We deal with mean girls on a daily basis and you are way out of your league. You should play nice, because if you make another snide comment to my friend I will give it back to you a thousand times." Caleb put the car in park and opened his door. When I looked up, my aunt was already hurrying over to the car. Cissy didn't respond, she just pushed past me to get out.

165

"Aunt Becky." I gushed as she engulfed me in a hug. "You really didn't need to come."

"Nonsense, tomorrow is important. I thought before your appointment we could do some shopping. You've lost so much weight and probably need all new clothes."

"Aunt Becky, I'm fine. I don't want anyone to go to the appointment with me." The mosquitoes were already biting so my aunt began tugging me inside the house. "I don't even want dad to go, but it is apparently not an option."

"You need your family."

"Most people might, but…" Aunt Becky opened the front door and gestured for me to walk in.

"She doesn't want anyone fussing over her." Zack interjected from behind me. When we were standing in the large living room he slung his arm across my shoulders. "She is expecting the worst and doesn't want anyone there because she thinks she has to take on the world alone. We all know they are going to tell her she beat the cancer and we'll be ready to celebrate."

"I won't fuss, I promise." My aunt stated in a tiny voice.

"Weakest argument ever." I giggled. "You are like the queen of fussing."

"It's only because I love you."

"I know." I gave my aunt another hug. "I just…I need to do this alone."

"You don't need to, you want to." Zack murmured. "You think you need to, but you don't."

"Who is ready to go out on the boat?" My uncle asked with a wide grin as he came into the room.

"Let's go!" Caleb shot towards the back door before anyone else could chime in.

"You know, there's no one really using the house this summer, Jo." Aunt Becky smiled. "You guys are more than welcome to use it, if you need to escape or something."

"Excuse me?" Cissy gasped as she sashayed down the stairs wearing barely a bikini. "You said it was occupied. Why does Jordan get to use it and I don't? I am your daughter and you treat her better than me."

"We have given you every opportunity in the world, Cissy and you always throw it away. You got two DUI's in two days. You were caught with drugs both times. You skipped out of rehab. You flunked your sophomore year and then you were expelled. At this point, you're lucky we let you pee alone." My eyes went wide.

"That cop was a bastard!" Cissy shrieked. "He only gave me those DUI's because I wouldn't fuck him! He tried to rape me and…" She made a weird noise as her eyes set on the large Smart TV in the living room. She smirked as she made her way to one of the priceless heirloom vases my aunt had displayed. She picked it up and before anyone could grab her she heaved it and watched it slam into the television screen as both objects shattered easily. "You think Caleb and Jordan are so perfect, if you only knew all the trouble they've been in lately. Keller…"

"Keller? How do you…?" I interrupted as I took a step towards my cousin. Her mouth clamped shut, she made a strange screeching sound and stomped up the stairs. I started after her. How did she know my boyfriend and why were they talking?

"Let her go." My aunt sighed, fighting back tears. "Everything out of her mouth is a lie. She was so stoned when she got pulled over, both times, she offered sex in exchange for a get out of jail free card. The officer refused and she became irate. When they arrested her, she began accusing him of rape. He was wearing a body cam and had a dash cam in his car and they both showed her throwing herself at him. Before then she accused the football coach and some players of raping her as well." Tears raced down her cheeks now. "She's so angry and…" I wrapped my arms around her in a hug.

"I can talk to her, maybe figure out what's going on." I offered.

"No." My uncle interjected as he came towards us. "She's got it in her head that you're the enemy. She's been dating the Atler boy since you left and I think he has something to do with that."

"Zane?" My stomach clenched at the thought of my ex-boyfriend. He had been Kyler's best friend since birth and I've always had a crush on him. When my dad and brothers left for Callatin Academy and I was left behind, my aunt cleaned up the geeky tomboy I used to be. Zane and I began dating. I wasn't ready for sex, he was and found it elsewhere. When I caught him I immediately dumped him and he proceeded to make the last few weeks I had at home, absolute Hell. Obviously, I have horrendous taste in guys.

"I still think…"

"Not everyone has to like you, J." Zack stated quietly. My eyes flitted back to him. It was one of my insecurities. I couldn't handle people not liking me, especially when I didn't know what I did wrong.

"We should probably get out on the boat." My uncle gestured towards the back of the house.

"You guys go ahead. I've got some things to clean up here." My aunt stated halfheartedly.

"You're not going?"

"No, I get sea sick." She was a liar and most likely staying behind to babysit her seventeen year old daughter.

"I guess I'll run upstairs and change into my suit then." I murmured.

"I already staked out our room." Maddie grinned as she took my hand and pulled me up the stairs. "I know you had suits with you, but I brought a few more and some cover ups. You've lost so much weight I didn't know what would still fit you."

"I haven't lost weight. I'm so bloated it's ridiculous. Keller says…"

"How about you ignore everything Keller says to you? And let's not talk about him or Lance or any other guy all weekend." I shot her a funny look. "I'm sorry I didn't mean to sound bitchy. Cissy really grated on my nerves earlier." Maddie took a deep breath and shook her head. "I just want you to relax and celebrate this weekend. You are an incredibly strong woman and I want you to remember that, to realize you have amazing people supporting you and that you don't necessarily need a guy to make you happy."

"I do know that."

"I already have my suit on, so I'm going to check on the guys. Cissy really did a number on Zack earlier, I just want to make sure he's not plotting her death."

"What did she do?"

"He can tell you." She shrugged uncomfortably before she hurried out of the room. Well that was weird. She shut the door and I dug through my suitcase for one of the suits Keller had gotten me on our trip. Most of the clothes he bought me looked more like something out of a high priced call girl's closet. This bathing suit was more modest and covered my port and the scars from my surgeries, which was the only reason he allowed it. I looked like a freak right now and he didn't want the rest of the world to see it too. I changed into it and stared at my reflection in the mirror, I was nowhere near the girl I used to be and it broke my heart. I was grieving for the healthy, happy and gorgeous Jordan who would probably never return.

Chapter 67
Cissy

"Your girlfriend just had a mental breakdown." I whispered into the phone to Keller.

"Oh yeah?" He chuckled. "I'm not surprised. She's got one foot in the asylum."

"Mom told her she couldn't take the boat out and she threw an heirloom into our seventy inch television. She's psycho."

"Jordan threw a temper tantrum? That doesn't sound like her."

"Well she did. Are you coming to see me while I'm here?"

"I'm in Florida."

"You said if I..."

"I know what I said and I always keep my promises. Tell you what, why don't you send me some naked pictures again and I will set you up at the spa near the lake."

"I don't..."

"Didn't your parents cut you off?"

"Yes." I grumbled.

"Then take it. I'll make it up to you next time I'm in Texas, I promise."

"Will you call me tonight?"

"Of course."

"I love you, Keller." He hung up the phone without returning the sentiment.

"I'll be down in a minute!" I heard Jordan holler down the stairs, before her pathetic self appeared in my doorway. "Hey, you okay?"

"Do you care?"

"Of course I do. Why would you even ask that?"

"All you care about is yourself."

"Cissy, what's going on? Those things your dad said and...this isn't like you."

"You know nothing about me."

"Apparently, you're right. The girl I know would never throw a tantrum like that or accuse..."

"You think you have everyone fooled, don't you?" I hissed. Her face dropped. "We all know it's just a matter of time before..."

"J?" Zack called from the hallway. I wanted to punch her and Zack in the face. What in the Hell could he see in this freak before me? He chose a sick bitch over me? Me?

"I'm in here." She answered over her shoulder. "What happened to make you hate me? To make you so angry?"

"You stole my mom because yours was a..."

"Shut your mouth." Zack's New York accent was thick as he growled and was in between Jordan and me in a flash

"What are you going to do about it?"

"Certainly not what I'd like to do." He hissed. I smiled coyly, ready to start the sexual innuendo. There was a dark look in his eyes and I knew he wasn't flirting. His hand instantly went to Jordan's and she grasped it without hesitation. I hated her for having friends, for having guys who would protect her instantly. I had no one. My own parents had turned on me. "Let's

168

go, J."

"Zack."

"No, J, now. They're going to leave without us." Her eyes flitted to mine sadly before she looked back at the hot blonde.

"Cissy, please talk to me."

"Fuck off." I spit. Zack tugged her out of the room and they were gone. I hated her and everyone around her. If it wasn't for Jordan I would have a normal life. My parents would have no one to compare me to. I was nowhere near the perfect angel she had them fooled into believing she was. Keller James was the best thing that could have happened to me though, he was compiling an entire list of Jordan's truths so we could take her down completely. When we were through with her, there would be nothing or no one left for her.

Chapter 68
Zack

"Please stay away from her." I murmured when we were at the foot of the stairs. Almost everyone else was outside and Becky was hiding somewhere.

"She's my cousin."

"I know and it's hard for me to comprehend too, but she is not your friend."

"She's family."

"J, there is something wrong with her. I don't…she needs medication or something."

"Why would you say that?"

"When you were in the hospital, she threw herself at every single person she wasn't related to. As soon as she realized our friendship she tried to turn me against you. She did it with everyone."

"If I could just get her to talk to me," She started to go back up the stairs. I grabbed her hand again and tugged her into me.

"She's not going to talk to you."

"We're like sisters."

"You may have thought so, but she's been fooling you for a long time."

"I don't…"

"Jordan." I sighed as I looked down at her sadly. "Remember the things Zane said to you at the beach house? How you couldn't figure out where he'd heard them or why he was even here? He came with Cissy, she paid for them to stay in a condo nearby. He's actually down the road again. He also learned all those hurtful things from her."

"I don't…"

"That's how she knows Keller, I think. Somehow they became friends and that's how he's gotten some dirt on you, as well."

"She wouldn't."

"She would. I've doing some research, baby, I have proof." She pulled away from me, shook her head and walked towards the back of the house. I knew she wouldn't believe me, which is why I collected the physical proof. I also knew she wouldn't want to see the proof until she was ready. Ever since Caleb admitted they thought someone had hurt Jordan in the hospital, I'd been doing as much research and investigative work I could do. Keller had made three trips to Texas to visit Cissy, but so far I hadn't been able to catch him doing more than other girls. Police work was in my DNA though, so it was only a matter of time before I nailed him or Bowman to the wall for hurting her. "I don't want to hurt you, I hate having to tell you something like that, but I need to protect you and…"

"I can protect myself."

"Oh, trust me, I know that well." I smiled as I tugged her into me. "I want to protect you, J. Wouldn't it be nice to lean on someone else for once?" She didn't answer, but moved in to allow me to hold her tight. I closed my eyes and relished the feeling. "You don't have to face the world alone, I'm here to stand beside you." She wrapped her arms around my waist and squeezed almost as if she didn't want to ever let go.

"No more touchy feely crap." Caleb groaned as he came through the open French doors that led out to the pool and dock. "Let's go have fun." I tried to slide my hand down to hers, but she was officially closed off. I knew she wouldn't be sleeping tonight and I had every intention of sneaking into her room and laying it all on the line.

Chapter 69
Jordan

"Your bloodwork and scans all came back clean." Dr. Bowman grinned as he gave me the biggest news of my life.

"So I...?"

"You're cancer free, my dear. You kicked cancer's ass." I giggled as I looked at my father and Dr. Bowman.

"I wasn't expecting this."

"Alicia told me. You can't always expect the worst."

"So I'm done with everything?"

"We'll do rechecks every six months to be safe, but everything is completely clear. You're a tough girl and I have high hopes for your continued health."

"Thank you so much." I hugged my friend's dad quickly and bounded out of the room. I felt as though I was floating on air. This was the best day of my life.

"Do you want to grab something to eat?" Dad asked as he made an appointment for six months from now. I shook my head.

"Can we grab burgers and brats and grill out? I just want to hang out on the water and breathe."

"Absolutely. I'll call Beck and see what we need."

"Let me call Zack first." I stated as I pulled my phone out of my pocket. "I mean, he'll be with Caleb and Maddie so I'll get all three of them at once." My dad smiled and nodded as I dialed Zack's number. Why was I so nervous about calling my friend? And why was he the first person I wanted to tell my good news to?

"You're on speakerphone." Zack answered his phone with a laugh.

"Take me off." I instructed in a flat tone.

"What? Why? There's no...it's not possible." There was a muffled sound as he took me off speaker.

"I'm cancer free." I whispered.

"What?"

"I'm cancer free." I giggled.

"You ass, I was terrified." He chuckled.

"I wanted to tell you first, now put me on speaker."

"You did it? You kicked cancer's ass, J!" Maddie squealed. "Oh my goodness, this is amazing!"

"Congratulations sis." Caleb laughed. "I hope you're ready to celebrate"

"Hell yeah."

"And pay for giving me a heart attack." Zack interjected. I giggled, nothing would take the smile off my face. Dad led me out of the doctor's office and to his SUV. I called Alicia and Chopper to tell them my news and even though I was leery, I called Lance as well. He picked up on the third ring.

"Congratulations."

"Hey, how did you know?"

"Lucky guess." He chuckled. "I figure if it were negative you wouldn't want to talk to anyone and you would've texted."

"You know me well."

"Are you on your way home? Want to celebrate? I can take you to dinner and then, Chopper was planning a celebration just for you and this phone call."

"He was?" I gushed. My heart melted. Why hadn't Chopper mentioned that when I just talked to him though? "We're actually headed to the Lake House. My family came up and Zack, Maddie and Cale and everyone are already there waiting for us."

"Oh, oh, yeah I guess you would want to be with your family. Rain check? Will you be home on Sunday?"

"Yeah, I will. Can I...can I call you when we get home?" I took a deep breath and exhaled slowly. I'm sure Lance was clueless as to how hard it was for me not to take him up on that offer. I couldn't let him see my latest bruises from Keller though, and there were a lot of them. Because if anyone could see the truth, see through my lies, it would definitely be Lance Bowman. I could wear a cover up and extra clothes at school, with my family, but that wasn't possible with Lance.

"Absolutely. I'm so proud of you, Jo, so happy for you."

"Thanks." My phone beeped in my ear and I pulled it back to see Kyler was calling. "Hey, that's Ky, I'll talk to you later." I switched over quickly.

"I gave you ten minutes. Ten minutes to call me rather than hearing it from someone else first."

"I'm a horrible little sister."

"Yes, you are." He chuckled. "I see how I rate." How could I have not remembered my oldest brother?

"I...um...never know when you're in class."

"Shitty excuse, but I'll let you slide. This is huge, sis."

"It's pretty amazing."

"I wish I could be there with you."

"Me too. You'll be missing one Hell of a celebration, I'm sure."

"I'm sure. Maddie was going about a mile a minute in the background when Zack called."

"I can only imagine. You'll be home for the wedding though, right?"

"Absolutely. I've already got it approved."

"Good, for some reason we miss you."

"Same here. I've got muster in five, so I got to run."

"I have no idea what you said, but I'll talk to you later." When I looked up my dad was pulling into the lake house driveway.

"Becky already has everything we need. She always anticipates everything." I giggled and nodded my head. She really did. Dad put the truck in park and as I opened my door I was bombarded with hugs. I had an amazing life.

173

Chapter 70

"Where's Cissy?" I asked later that night. "I would have thought she would have come down to eat at least."

"She left." My aunt answered as she stood up from the hammock she'd been resting in.

"What do you mean, she left? I thought…"

"She snuck out sometime in the middle of the night."

"What?"

"It's not a big deal. She does this all the time. She'll be back." The flatness of my uncle's voice broke my heart. Their daughter ran away on a regular basis and they were no longer worried about her. Someone could legit kidnap her and they wouldn't start looking for weeks probably.

"The attention wasn't on her and she can't stand it." My aunt sighed. "I'm beat and headed in for the night. There's alcohol in the fridge and all keys are safely hidden. Have fun." She leaned down and kissed me on the head. "Congratulations, baby girl."

My dad had disappeared a long time ago. My uncle followed my aunt inside. I looked over at my brother.

"Did you know she left?"

"I heard them talking about it this morning."

"Did they call the police?"

"No, she took off in one of the cars with Onstar, they can track her."

"Why would she leave?"

"She wasn't getting what she wanted." Caleb shrugged. "Don't worry about her, Joey. She's fine. She's down the road with Zane and a bunch of the guys from Lakewood."

"How do you…?"

"We just do." Caleb wouldn't lie to me and I was assuming they checked things out for their own peace of mind. My brother stood up and went to the large bar that had been set up around the pool. "She was trying to take the attention from you today and put it all on her. Don't let her win."

"Does Zane know we're here?"

"He does. We ran into him at the marina yesterday before you arrived. He won't be coming anywhere close." I nodded and hugged myself. I didn't want Zane Atler anywhere near me, ever. I leaned back into the lounge chair I was sitting in. Maddie was talking about wedding plans while Caleb and Zack goofed off in the pool. I was only half paying attention. I couldn't understand how my cousin could be dating Zane Atler, knowing he cheated and tortured me afterwards. I also couldn't fathom why my current boyfriend was making trips to visit her. I really hoped Cissy was okay and knew what she was getting herself into with both boys.

"Let's head down to the lake, just walk through the sand for a bit." Zack offered a few hours later when Maddie and Caleb were half asleep in the hammock.

"I don't…"

"C'mon J, it'll clear your head. I see you heading down the dark hole."

"I hate when you see that." I sighed. He winked and held a hand out to me. I took it and let him help me up. He pulled me into a hug I wasn't expecting.

"Sorry, I've been wanting to do that since you called this morning."

"I guess everyone else was hogging me." I giggled. His hand went to mine and he laced our fingers together. "I will never get over how amazing this place is."

"It's unreal." We passed the pool and hot tub and made our way down a set of rock steps leading to the lake. It was a gorgeous and warm night, the water and the sand between my toes definitely helped me focus on the good in my life, not the questions.

"How are you feeling?" He queried as he brushed his shoulder against mine. I winced, my whole body was still tender from Keller's attack.

"Tired. Happy. Confused. Exhilarated. It changes every five seconds."

"Understandable. What are you confused about?"

"It would be a shorter answer if you asked what am I not confused about."

"Well?"

"I'm still sorting it out in my head. I'll tell you when I'm ready." He nodded before he moved in front of me with a giant smile on his gorgeous face as he tugged me into him.

"No one would ever know if we went behind a tree over there and celebrated."

"Zack Bentley, are you trying to seduce me?"

"Maybe."

"We're drunk and barely dressed, all you had to do was kiss me." I giggled playfully.

"In that case." He smiled as he pulled me tight and found my mouth with his. He kissed me hungrily and my whole body melted into him.

"Whoa." I gasped when he pulled away and the shock of the amazing kiss hit me. "Zack."

"Speechless is good." He chuckled, as his green eyes looked deep into mine; I felt his hand caress my cheek. "Why don't we do that more often?"

"We can't." My voice was breathy and unsure.

"Why? Keller?" He backed away. "It's not something he…." He stopped suddenly and I could see he clearly regretted what he almost let slip.

"What? Finish the sentence."

"Nothing. I just, he treats you like shit and it's hard for me to understand why you would even care how it would look if you and I hooked up."

"First of all, that's not what you were about to say. I know he's cheating on me, I'm not an idiot. Now that I'm done with cancer and the treatments things will be different. And second of all, Zack Bentley, I am not like the rest of the girls at this fucking school. I don't hook up with just anyone, I don't just kiss anyone either. If I kiss someone, it means something. We can't, because I will not be another one of the loser girls in the Zack Bentley fan club or black book, okay? I care about you too much."

"Jordan…" He moved closer to me.

"Don't. Just back off, okay?" Zack took a deep breath and shook his head.

"I care about you too much not to."

"Don't do this." I turned to leave. I couldn't listen to anything else. Zack was the first person I wanted to call and tell my good news, most of the time he was who I went to bed and woke up thinking about. I was confused about my feelings, about the new place he was taking in my life, but I was mostly terrified of these thoughts.

"Please stop and just listen." He grabbed my arm and my knees buckled from the pain. I was pretty certain Keller had sprained it or something in his tirade when I left, I'd been babying it since I got on the plane. "What's wrong?"

"Sorry, they just…they…" I rambled as tears rolled down my cheeks. Zack's face was sad as he moved closer. I flinched as he touched my arm again. He took my hand in his before he pulled the sleeve of my cover up away.

"What in the Hell happened?" My entire arm was littered in bruises, some deeper and darker than others.

"I fell."

"When?"

"In Florida, it was stupid really, I tripped down the steps leading to the kitchen and fell on…"

"Those are fingerprints." He gasped. He tried to look at my other arm and I yanked away from him. "Jordan, who…?"

"No, no they're not. They…"

"Did Lance do this? When did you see him?" Zack's jaw was working back and forth in agitation as he tried to make sense of my injuries.

"I haven't seen Lance in weeks. He wouldn't…"

"He has a history."

"He wouldn't hurt me physically."

"Did Keller do this?"

"I barely saw Keller." I lied. Zack watched me carefully. "I wouldn't lie to you."

"You're lying right now."

"I am not."

"I will go up there right now and wake up everyone in that house if you don't tell me who is hurting you."

"It's the chemo, the treatments, Zack. I bruise easily. I'm a klutz and walk into things, trip a lot. Don't make a scene, it'll only make us both look bad."

"Who are you protecting?" I rolled my eyes and shook my head, before I hurried away from him. He was close on my heels and I decided to distract him with ridiculous accusations.

"Who are you protecting, Zack? I know you knew about Keller cheating on me long before I knew. Why didn't you tell me?"

"Jordan." He sighed, his eyes finally found mine. Zack's gorgeous face was sad as he tried to put a hand to my cheek. I stepped back and glared at him.

"You knew…you've known all this time and you never told me?" I yelled. "You fucking knew and you've let me look like an idiot?"

"You've been through Hell lately. I didn't want to make things worse on you."

"And letting me think my relationship is perfect is better?"

"Come on, you know…"

"Fuck you, Bentley. I thought you were my fucking friend and all this time you've been lying to me. You lied and sided with Keller. You're just as bad as him!" I shoved him backwards and stormed off.

"I did not side with Keller." He protested as he regained his balance and chased after me.

"Don't touch me."

"Come on Jordan, don't be like this. I was trying to protect you."

"Well, you failed. You hurt me even worse. I trusted you." Zack was speechless and I stalked to the house, praying he wouldn't pursue this in front of my family. I was up on the porch of the house, ready to go in when Zack caught up to me.

"Come on J, talk to me please?" He begged. I didn't answer because I could see someone looming inside the house. It was Keller and Cissy, there were a few others fully

176

clothed in black. I flew backwards, praying he didn't see me. "What are you doing?"

"Sshh, shut up, shut up." I put my hand over his mouth and peeked inside. They were unplugging things and carrying it out of the house. Stealing? Why would any of these guys be stealing? "There are people inside, they're robbing the house."

"What?" Zack pushed me behind him and peeked inside as well, he made a move to go in but I yanked him back. I scrambled for my phone and dialed 9-1-1.

"Please do not go in, Zack. What if they have guns?"

"It looks like a bunch of kids." I gripped his arm tightly and shook my head.

"There's a break in." I informed the operator as I rattled off the address. "We're outside the house, the robbers are inside but my family is in there sleeping."

"How many do you see?" The dispatcher asked.

"Five? Maybe. They're in and out, taking stuff out the front door, but they're all wearing the same thing."

"There's an officer nearby, just stay where you are. Do not try to go in."

"I'm going around front, see if I can get a license plate number." Zack informed me as he pulled away.

"No." I whispered loudly. My stomach instantly knotted. Why in the Hell did he think he needed to be a hero? "My friend is an idiot and just went to get a better look. I need to go. Please make the cops hurry." I dropped the phone and scurried after Zack.

"What are you guys doing?" I heard a distant voice ask incredulously.

"Shut the fuck up, Brookman!" Keller's voice was unmistakable. I was hiding in the bushes and saw him going towards Brennan. "Mind your own business."

"We're just taking back what they took from us." Cissy interjected. "They have guns, so shut up before you get us killed."

"You're going to rob your own parents?" Zack questioned loudly as he stepped out of the shadows

"Zack, no!" I screamed without thinking. I watched as Keller's hand left his waistband, his arm went up. I sprinted towards Zack, screaming for the idiot to move. Brennan let out a wild yelp as he lunged at Keller.

"Jordan!"

"I told you not to bring these fucking kids along." A deep voice growled from behind. There was a series of loud gunfire before a shrill scream and the sound of a police siren. I could hear feet hitting the ground as people began running.

"Are you hurt?" Zack asked in a terrified, hushed tone. I looked down, only now realizing I had tackled him. I shook my head.

"No, are you?"

"You might have dislocated my shoulder." He teased as he moved slowly. I hurried off him.

"Sorry, I...I saw a gun and I..."

"Brennan." Zack leapt off the ground and sprinted towards where we had last seen our friend. He was laying on the ground holding his side. He was wearing a black hoodie like the others, something I hadn't noticed before.

"He shot me. I can't believe he shot me." Brennan murmured as he tried to sit up.

"Don't move." My father was behind us suddenly, along with Caleb and my uncle. Caleb ripped his shirt off and put it on the wound while my dad called for an ambulance.

"What happened?" My uncle asked.

"Cissy…" Zack began.

"She was right by you, where is she?" I interjected. I didn't want to rat Cissy out just yet, I needed to know what the Hell had just happened. She was by Zack, but I was certain she was long gone. My aunt and uncle gave Cissy everything she wanted and needed without hesitation, there was no reason for her to be breaking and entering.

"I don't…" Zack stuttered as he looked around. "Oh shit." I followed his line of sight and there laying on the ground was a black clad figure, barely moving. My uncle sprinted to the body.

"Daddy?" Cissy gurgled before my uncle began wailing in protest. There was a flash as more police officers arrived, with an ambulance and first responder. Caleb was pulling my uncle out of the way and Zack was holding onto me tightly.

Chapter 71

"Don't think of doing anything stupid while you're at home without me." Keller's eyes danced as he smirked at me. *"I have eyes everywhere."* I nodded. *"Zack will be the first one I go after."* Keller's words rang through my head over and over as tears rolled down my cheeks. My cousin was dead and my boyfriend had murdered her, because of me, because I had kissed Zack Bentley.

Once the hospital had announced Cissy's death my dad quickly ushered us out, explaining one of my Uncle's would meet us at the house to make sure we were okay. Uncle Calen and Uncle Kyle were waiting on the front porch when we pulled in. I wasn't in the mood to talk so I pushed past everyone and beelined for the backyard. Behind the pool and hot tub, stood an old Weeping Willow tree that I would sneak off to when the cancer and Keller became too much. I went straight to it and hid under its foliage.

My phone beeped, I looked down to see I had fifteen text messages and four missed calls. I swiped the screen, cleared the notifications and shut my phone off. I wasn't in the mood to talk to anyone. I couldn't answer questions because I couldn't be certain of what my answer should be.

Brennan was in surgery to remove two bullets and repair the damage. Dad wouldn't allow us to stay and swore he would notify us the second he was in the clear. Tears rolled down my cheeks, but I made no sounds as I stared off into space. My cousin was dead and Brennan was fighting for his life, all because of me. Keller was out there somewhere and there was no telling what he would do next. Every noise caused me to tremble with fear, every thought sent me further into an anxiety attack.

I should have learned my lesson a long time ago, but I continued to put the people I loved in danger. Keller punished Lance's family because of me, and now he did the same to my own family. When would I learn to love him and no one else? What did I have to do to get rid of him?

No one was safe and I knew if I took what I saw to the police that it would only make matters worse. Keller James was a sadistic bastard and he was untouchable. I was stuck with him. I almost envied Cissy.

Chapter 72
Zack

"Are you going to go talk to her or just watch her from the window like a perv?" Calen asked from behind me as he poured himself a cup of coffee. His nephew sounded more like him than I'd realized.

"She saved my life. She pushed me out of the way and her cousin died because of it."

"There were five shots fired. Two bullets into the young male, one bullet into Cissy, which leaves two bullets." How did he know that? "All the witnesses said they heard five shots."

"Meant for me and Jordan?"

"Possibly, or he was just a bad shot."

"He was a teenager or young, anyway. I don't know who it was, which is why I can't figure out why Brennan and Cissy were there. It wasn't Zane Atler, I would have recognized his voice. And if it were Zane, why was Brennan there? Why was Brennan even at the Lake House? None of it makes sense."

"It'll make more sense when the shock wears off." He took a long drink from his coffee mug. "Do you want some?"

"I'm not a coffee person."

"You should be today, it'll calm the nerves." He turned around and pulled out two Styrofoam cups. "Jordan will definitely need some. The fact she didn't say a word and just went directly outside means she shouldn't be alone."

"She's been through so much, I don't understand why this shit keeps happening."

"Can you remember back to when these things started happening?" Calen began pouring the brown liquid into one of the cups.

"Since she moved here." I shrugged. It was a general reply, but it was the truth. If I had to pinpoint an exact time though... "When she started seeing Lance Bowman."

"What was the first thing you remember happening?"

"First time she brought Lance around she was almost raped, he was attacked by a couple of guys. Then there was the car accident where they both almost died."

"So, Lance is the reason most likely."

"He's responsible. He's the one who is hurting her, it's in his blood."

"You said they both almost died in a car accident, he wouldn't kill himself. What do you mean it's in his blood?"

"His dad was abusive."

"Was?"

"Suicide in jail. He beat the Hell out of Lance when he was trying to protect Jordan, or so they say."

"What about the rich kid? Keller?"

"He's a pompous ass, but I don't think he's smart enough to come up with half this stuff."

"People can be very surprising when they're driven by pride and jealousy." Calen murmured thoughtfully. He filled the second cup, placed lids on them both and handed them to me. "Don't ever let your pride and jealousy allow you to overlook facts. Never rule out a suspect or underestimate them."

"What are you saying?"

"You've got dirt on Keller James, correct? At least, the last set of research showed you did. He was visiting Cissy even though they shouldn't really know each other. I'll look into it more. In the meantime, go out there and be her friend."

"I *am* her friend." I argued. Calen chuckled and nodded his head.

"Never said you weren't. It's obvious how you feel about her and she's lucky to have you in her corner. However, she doesn't you need to be asking twenty questions about what she saw. Just comfort her and let her do the talking."

"You're not that old to be this wise." I joked.

"I've had a lot of time to look back on my mistakes. I can't change my past, but I can help others not make the same mistakes." I nodded and went out the door. He was right though and I was grateful, because I had been headed out to ask what she saw, what her thoughts were on what happened. There was no doubt we would be questioned a hundred more times about this morning's events.

I'd never seen her go out to the Weeping Willow before, I don't think I've ever actually noticed it. She seemed to know it well though, because she had found a small opening and disappeared inside as if it were her own personal clubhouse.

"I brought you some coffee." I announced in a low tone, hoping not to surprise her. I heard her gasp and when I looked through the limbs she was cowering against the trunk. "Sorry, J. I didn't...Calen thought coffee would calm the shock of everything."

"I'm not...it's okay. I just...I need to be alone."

"You want to be alone." I began. She closed her eyes and I stopped talking because I sounded like I was preaching to her. "Sorry. I don't want you to be alone. I was hoping to hang out with you, even if we don't talk. I really don't want to be by myself, so I guess my motives are purely selfish." I handed her the coffee and plopped down beside her. I looked down and realized she was sitting on an old blanket, I hadn't seen her go back in the house. "Um, you develop magic powers or something? Where'd this come from?"

"The tree." She responded softly as she pointed up. "I came out here a lot when the cancer got bad. It kind of made me feel like I wasn't alone." She shrugged embarrassedly and looked down at the ground.

"I can see why."

"He was aiming for you. He tried to kill you."

"We don't know that."

"*I* know. He warned me. He told me and I didn't..." She rambled, her words were slurred and it was then that I noticed the bottle of whiskey, almost empty, laying in between her legs.

"Who warned you?"

"Keller. Keller shot you. Keller."

"He wasn't there, J. It wasn't him."

"Yes, it was." She whispered. "I saw him." I shook my head, but I wasn't going to argue with her. There was a reason behind her accusations and I had to find out what.

"How did he warn you?"

"He...he..." There was a noise behind us and she went completely rigid as she looked around nervously. "I don't know."

"You don't have to tell me yet, I'm here whenever you're ready." I reached for the

181

whiskey bottle and she handed it to me slowly. I took a swig and leaned back against the tree. "This is an amazing spot." She nodded and looked around again.

"I need…I need to go inside." She stood up quickly, scurried to stash her stuff. I handed her the liquor bottle and she stared at it. Maybe four shots remained, she put the bottle to her lips and finished it off in one long drink. She didn't shudder, just turned around and stashed the bottle inside of the blanket. This was not a good sign. I picked up her backpack off the ground and handed it to her. She opened it, dug through it for a second and pulled out her cell phone. She turned it on and stepped out of the sanctity of the tree.

"Do you want to watch a movie or something?" She turned to look at me, a small smile played on her gorgeous mouth. She opened her mouth to respond just as her phone started ringing and beeping. She silenced it and I noticed it was Keller calling. Her face was pale as she turned back around.

"I need to be alone. Just…just leave me alone."

"Jordan, you saved my life and I can't just sit back and watch you fall apart."

"Stay away from me." She stated as her phone beeped again. "Please." Tears rolled down her cheeks. Her whole body shook with sorrow or fear as she spun on her heel and hurried inside. I chased after her.

"I can't, J. Please don't shut me out."

"Zack, stop it! Just leave me alone, I don't want…" Her voice cracked and she let out a wild scream as if she'd seen a ghost. I reached for her, but she shoved me away.

"Jordan?" Lance Bowman's voice echoed throughout the backyard as he barreled outside of the house. He rushed to us and pulled her safely into his arms. He placed himself in between her and me, as if I were the danger. "Are you okay?"

"No, she's not okay."

"I'm fine. I just want to be alone and…" She looked up at me sadly. "He's just trying to be a good friend and…"

"Why don't you take a hint, Bentley? She's been through a lot."

"I was there. I know what she's been through."

"Then you should…"

"Shut up!" Jordan screamed as she covered her ears and pushed past Bowman. She sprinted into the house and ran straight into her Uncle Kyle.

"Whoa, whoa, what's going on?"

"I can't…I can't do this. It's my fault. It's all my fault. I called the cops. I told them to come and Cissy, Cissy is dead and…" She was looking all around the kitchen as if there were more than just the four of us there.

"It's not your fault. You didn't know she was there."

"I did. I saw her in the house. I saw all of them. I saw the gun, I saw him aim and Zack and I couldn't…I couldn't let him die and I…the bullet hit Cissy. I saved Zack and let my cousin die. I love him, but I…" She was slurring and rambling hysterically, but I latched on to those three words. "He warned me. I kissed him and he…he was going to kill Zack. He killed Cissy. He tried to kill Brennan because of me. He…"

"Who is he?" Lance interjected. Jordan looked over at him, her face turned a greenish color.

"You can't be here." She whispered, her eyes went to me. "You can't be here."

"Jordan?" Keller called from the living room. Jordan's scream should've shattered every glass object for twenty miles, but instead it caused her to fall back into her uncle's arms. Caleb and Calen sprinted into the room at the same time Keller appeared.

"What in the Hell is happening?" He growled.

"Everyone out!" Calen hissed.

"Jordan." Lance's voice was broken as he reached for her. Caleb, Calen and Kyle rushed out of the kitchen while Maddie ushered us out of the kitchen.

"I'm not leaving until I found out what in the Hell is going on." Keller spit.

"She just lost her cousin, who was like a sister to her. She's having a hard time dealing with it." Maddie snapped as she shoved him towards the door.

"What in the Hell is the redneck doing here?"

"I heard what happened, she wasn't answering her phone for anyone so I came over. I shouldn't have, but…I was worried about her."

"She's no longer any of your concern, plow boy."

"Keller, get the fuck out of here." Maddie's voice was laced with pure venom as she shoved him towards the door.

"Not until he leaves."

"Oh for…"

"I'll go, I'm sorry. I shouldn't…I didn't…" Lance rambled. He shook his head as he looked up the stairs towards Jordan's room. She was screaming again and you could tell it was killing him to walk away. He put his head down and hurried out the door. Keller rolled his eyes and followed behind him.

If Lance Bowman was hurting her, he was a damn good actor because he had just convinced me he was innocent. It didn't mean I liked him or his place in Jordan's life though.

183

Chapter 73
Jordan

"How are you feeling?" Keller asked in a hushed voice as he appeared in my room sometime in the middle of the night. My eyes and brain were fuzzy, my mouth was dry and my head was hammering out a symphony. Was he even really here or was I in the middle of a nightmare? I grumbled a reply and rolled over. "After earlier, I wanted to check on you. I also brought you something to take the edge off." He placed a prescription bottle on my nightstand. "I am so sorry about Cissy, Jordan. I just…I can't understand how someone can steal and murder and still sleep at night." My eyes widened, but I hid my reaction. He wanted a sign, he wanted to hear me say I knew he was there and what he did, so he could end me right here and now.

"It doesn't make sense."

"Death rarely does, babe. I guess you're headed out in the morning."

"I don't know." I murmured. Keller reached forward and grabbed the pill bottle up. He twisted the cap off, shook out two pills and popped them in his mouth. He grabbed a bottle of water off the nightstand and washed them down. He shook out two more pills and handed them and the bottle of water both to me. It was safe if he'd just taken them right? If he was trying to poison me, he wouldn't have just taken them. I sat up and took the pills from him down and then swallowed some water. "Thanks."

"I know this can't be easy. I just wanted you to know I was here for you. I've already been threatened if I was caught here so I'll head out." I nodded. If he wanted to be here, he wouldn't let my brother or uncles keep him away. I knew he was lying in hopes to pit me against my family. If they really banned him, I was grateful. I'd be happier if there were a way to keep him out of the house and my life for good. "By the way, why was Bowman here earlier? Did you call him?"

"No. I haven't talked to anyone since it happened. He just showed up, like you did."

"I am your boyfriend."

"I cut him out of my life, Keller. I can't help that he heard about what happened and was worried about me. It's just how he and his friends were raised. If you don't believe me, check my phone."

"I already did." He chuckled. "Maybe you just got smart enough to cover your tracks."

"My heart is literally in shreds right now and you're going to question and accuse me of bull shit?" I gripped my sheets tightly, readying myself for his backlash. "I get it Keller, you don't want me and no one else can have me. I am stuck in this Hell until you decide to let me go. I am okay with that. I am done with anyone who is not you."

"I need actions, sugar." He chuckled with a cocky grin, his hands went to his pants.

"I'm not…"

"Are you afraid your boy toy will get pissed if he wakes up and catches you?" His jaw ticked as he turned and looked behind him. Zack was asleep in the recliner in the corner of my room. I couldn't tell you when he even came in.

"I…"

"It's a good thing I spiked your bottle of whiskey with a little something special. He won't be waking up for a long time."

"Keller, I didn't ask him to come in here…I…"

"Doesn't matter, you need to get rid of that pesky mother fucker too. He's asking too many questions to the wrong people. Do you understand? If he ever wakes up, I have a lot more in store for him. Too bad he wasn't hit instead of Cissy, I heard it was a pretty close call." I gasped involuntarily. "Get rid of him." Keller strutted out the door seconds later and I didn't release my breath until I couldn't hear his footsteps anymore.

"Zack?" I murmured quietly. He didn't move. "No." I forced myself off the bed, realizing the pills were doing their job as my legs felt like dead weight. "Zack?" I drug myself closer to him and collapsed in front of him. "Zack." My voice was a whisper as I moved my hand to his knee. He didn't move with my touch. My eyes were heavy, my body felt as though it were moving through mud. *That bastard drugged me* I thought just as the world went dark.

Chapter 74

The only way I could survive the memorial service for my cousin was if I were medicated. My aunt had opted to only do one service on one day, knowing how tough it would be. I was grateful. We were surrounded by family, by friends I had known all my life and it didn't make things easier. No one was placing the blame on me, but I was certain they were all thinking it. I could feel their eyes on me, pointing and whispering throughout the service and meal afterwards.

I needed more pills. I needed something to make the crazy go away. I couldn't handle my grandparents back at the house if I didn't. I looked around carefully, taking stock of where everyone was. I would go out to the SUV where my purse was, in ten minutes I'd forget about all the anxiety rushing through my body.

I walked to the door, greeting people as I did and hurried outside when no one was close by. I got to the car, luckily it was unlocked, and grabbed my purse out. I pulled the pills out of the bottom, took three of them and then stuffed my purse back under the seat.

"Jordan?" I was busted. I went rigid as I turned around slowly. "Hey." My ex-boyfriend, Zane Atler, stood across from me. He was a little older, a little more muscular and a little hotter since the last time I'd seen him. His black hair was longer and he moved his head to get it out of his eyes. He moved towards me for an awkward hug. "How are you?" I shrugged my shoulders and stepped away from him. "Wait."

"I really don't have anything to say to you, Zane."

"I know, I know. I get that, I really do. I wish…"

"Don't make this anymore awkward than it already is. I know you and Cissy were a couple and I'm truly sorry for your loss."

"We weren't…really a couple." He sighed as he looked down at the ground. "Can we talk somewhere, somewhat hidden." I laughed and rolled my eyes.

"You're kidding right? The last time I saw you, I recall you trying to rape me in public."

"I was stoned."

"And that's an excuse?"

"No." He shook his head and looked back up at me with wet, grey eyes. "I'm sorry, Joey. I just…I need to tell you some stuff. There are things your aunt and uncle need to know and they won't listen to me. I've tried."

"Why should I?

"Because we were pretty good friends before I screwed everything up. I'm asking you to forget all the stupid shit I pulled and trust me, if only for a few minutes." I stared back at him, reading his face, his body language and I didn't see anything but honest, raw emotions there. We were in the parking lot of the church my grandparents belonged to. I nodded towards a set of swings nearby in the small playground. "Thank you."

"I'm doing this for my Aunt Becky, not you." He nodded and led the way. He moved towards the swings, sat down in one and grabbed another before he held it towards me.

"First of all, I am so incredibly sorry for the torture I inflicted upon you. I…was an ultimate ass. I loved you so much and you broke my heart."

"Excuse me?"

"I loved you, but I thought you didn't love me because you wouldn't sleep with me. It never occurred to me it could really mean you weren't ready. When you caught Kylie and me together and dumped me without hesitation, it hurt, bad. I was a bastard to you, Joey. I cheated on you every chance I got. A lot of the times, I was screwing Cissy while you were sleeping." I pulled back, wanting to gasp and show my shock, but I couldn't. I wouldn't let his words get to me, wouldn't let him piss me off before he gave me the information I needed.

"And what does this have to with my aunt and uncle?"

"I'm getting to it. Always impatient." He smiled fondly at me before he looked down at the ground quickly. "Cissy has been jealous of you for a very long time, when you thought she was your friend, she was your worst enemy. She was the fuel behind my fire against you. She filled me full of lies and hatred for you. She swore you and Randy were screwing and I was an idiot and believed every word she said. I'm sorry, I should have known better and…"

"And why do you now see the light?"

"Randy Contlin. That bastard beat the fuck out of me when we got back home after…well, you know. I deserved it. I snapped on him though, spewed some of the lies I'd been brainwashed to believe and he broke my nose. Afterwards, he made certain I saw all the wrong parts of Cissy's words."

"But you've been together for what, three years?"

"No. Well, off and on, because she would be normal sometimes and then, then she'd get all crazy again. She could be an amazing, fun girl when she didn't let her jealousy get the best of her. She met this guy, said she met him online and then, I learned he was actually one of your friends. He came to visit her a lot and each time he did, she'd be all hyped up about you. She was telling everyone you were faking the cancer to get sympathy."

"What kind of person would pretend to have a deadly illness?"

"Keller James brainwashed her, just like she brainwashed me." I gasped. I knew he was referring to Keller, had that fear, but hearing his name spoken by someone from my old life, terrified me. "She was feeding him information in exchange for…well, he paid for her boob job for certain. He was the reason for her DUI's, her expulsion, everything. She told me a few times she was trying to get away from him and he wouldn't allow it. I tried to help her, Randy tried and…"

"There's no point, he's…"

"Untouchable? I've learned." He chuckled drily. "Cissy told me a month or so ago she was pregnant and Keller wanted her to get an abortion. She agreed and then decided it was too good of a card not to use against you. She told Keller she got the procedure done, but didn't. He was livid when he found out which is why she was in the state she was in when she got the DUI. She went with Becky to Illinois in hopes to smooth things over. She told him she was going to tell you she was knocked up, because she wanted to see the devastation in your face when you learned your perfect boyfriend knocked up your favorite cousin. They got into a fight before they left the house. I didn't…I didn't know they were going to break into Cissy's house. I didn't know…I begged her not to go with him, but…"

"She went anyway and…"

"I think he killed her."

"He did." I whispered tearfully.

"You saw…"

"Yes, but…"

"You have to go to the police."

"I can't Zane, it's not that easy. He wouldn't…you saw what he could do to you, to

Randy, what he did to Cissy. None of it was an accident. He is a sadistic bastard and he will kill anyone and everyone I love if I turn him in."

"But he'll go to jail."

"No, he won't. His father is the richest man in the state of Kentucky. He is the wealthiest kid in our school. He is untouchable because his father will buy off anyone and everyone he needs to, to protect his son."

"What if I went to the police and told them what I just told you."

"You will die. He will kill you. He'll kill me for talking to you." I sobbed.

"Jordan." I shook my head and stood up.

"Why was Brennan there?"

"Who?"

"Brennan Brookman? Seven foot tall guy? He showed up at the same time Zack called Cissy out. Keller aimed for Zack and when I screamed for Zack, Brennan lunged for the gun and was shot twice."

"I don't know who Brennan is. Are you sure he was a part of this?"

"He is still in ICU. He…he showed up and asked what they were doing."

"I can't answer that. I've never heard the name." I shook my head and tried to rationalize his words. Would Keller really kill someone because he knocked her up? My brain was screaming yes and my stomach clenched with the knowledge "Are you still with this guy?" I nodded. "You need to get away from him."

"I've tried."

"You have to. Does Caleb know what he's capable of?"

"Not completely."

"He needs to know."

"No, he doesn't. He can't know, Zane. Promise me you won't tell anyone else anything you've just said. I can't…I have to protect my family and friends. What Keller did to Cissy is just the beginning, he's…there's more coming I'm afraid."

"Jordan, I love, loved Cissy and now she's gone, because of this guy. I love you, your brothers are my family…I can't sit back and…"

"I have no proof, Zane but I can tell you what he's admitted to and what I know. Keller is conniving, delusional, entitled and wealthy which means he is unpredictable and dangerous. I was in a horrific car accident with my boyfriend, where kids died and when I woke up from a coma with amnesia, he told me *he* was my boyfriend and we had been together since I came to Callatin. The doctor told everyone to not feed me information, to let me remember on my own and he took it upon himself to tell a different version of reality. After that, it has been impossible to get rid of him. I hooked up with my ex, not long ago, because he is who I should be with, who I love and Keller ran his mom and family off the road, caused a huge pile up on the interstate, they could've died and he told me next time they would. Before I left for the lake house, he told me if I did anything stupid, he would make me pay and that my friend Zack would be the first person he went after. The bullet that hit Cissy, was meant for Zack. Keller was aiming for Zack and I shoved him out of the way. I didn't know Cissy was there…that…" I let out a sob and buried my face in my hands. Zane moved towards me and enveloped me in a hug.

"Don't dwell on that." He murmured in my hair. "You couldn't have known."

"I know what he is capable of." Zane rubbed my back until I stopped crying.

"Can't you come back here? What if…what if you moved back in with your aunt?"

"I can't….I mean, I won't. My doctors, my family, my life is in Illinois now and I'm not going to let some asshole bully me into running away like a coward."

"You're not a coward if you're protecting your life. You beat cancer and…"

"I don't think you're truly grasping the reality of how dangerous Keller James is. If I leave, I guarantee he will pick off everyone I know and love until I surrender to him. He knows and sees everything."

"Please be careful." I nodded my head and stood up. "We're having a small party tonight, kind of a memorial bash for Cissy. She could be pretty hateful and horrible to some people, but there were a select few who knew the real girl. You, Caleb and your friends are more than welcome to come. Randy will be there."

"I don't know if Caleb will be okay with that, after…but thanks."

"Caleb and I talked before everything happened, I saw him in town. I…get it if you don't trust me. It would just be nice to hang out with you guys again. There was a time when Caleb, Kyler and I were inseparable and you were always tagging along."

"Things change." I shrugged. "I also…I don't really want to leave my aunt alone."

"Thanks for talking to me." He stood up from the swings and gestured for me to walk back to the church. I rolled my shoulders and looked over at him.

"Thanks for talking to me." I repeated. "You didn't have to tell me any of that and I'm grateful you did." Was I though? Knowing I was at fault for her meeting Keller, they were both obsessed with me and now my cousin was dead because of it. Zane went to his car and I headed to the church. I looked up at saw Zack watching me with an angry look.

"Were you just talking to that piece of shit, alone?"

"I was talking to Zane, yes. Drop it."

"After what he did to you and…"

"Drop it." I repeated. "I am not in the mood to be bitched at, got it?" I pushed past him and he grabbed my arm and pulled me back into him.

"Please don't shut me out." His voice was barely above a whisper and my heart hurt to hear the pain it eluded to. I closed my eyes and wished my life hadn't gotten to this point. I wanted to fall into Zack's arms and kiss him stupid. I needed his strength and security, but if I did, his life was in danger. I had already lost my cousin to my ignorance, I wouldn't risk anyone else.

"I'm sorry, Zack." I murmured as I scurried into the church. I could not allow myself to be alone with him anymore. It wasn't safe.

Chapter 75

Life went on after death, which is a funny thing. I would go back to my normal, everyday routines and then be smacked in the face with the reality that my cousin was dead. We had grown apart, we barely talked or texted anymore, but it didn't mean I didn't love and miss her terribly. She had honestly been like a sister to me for so long. Unfortunately, at some point, that had changed for her. I wish I could pinpoint the exact moment. If only I knew what I'd done to push her over the edge.

We'd been home for a few days and I was expected to go back to being a normal teenage girl, to continue celebrating being cancer free and to pretend like I didn't know what my boyfriend was capable of. I also had to cut every guy not related to me out of my life, it was proving to be incredibly hard.

"How *you* doing?" Zack asked flirtatiously as he poked his head into my bedroom while I was getting ready for my band's gig. It was the first one we had done since I was diagnosed. I'm sure I looked adorable in my ratty old robe, curlers in my hair and only half my make up on.

"Zack!" I screamed as I grabbed a book to hide behind.

"Oh stop!" He laughed. "I've seen you worse."

"Thanks, asshole." I stuck my tongue out at him.

"Nice." He chuckled as he invited himself in. "Getting ready for the big gig?"

"No." I answered sarcastically as he plopped down on my bed. I should have kicked him out of my room, should have been an absolute bitch to him, but I was selfish. I was lonely and missed his company. I looked at my gorgeous friend in my mirror, he was fidgeting nervously, which was abnormal.

"You okay?"

"Huh? Yeah. Sorry." He chuckled before he looked at me through my reflection in the mirror. He stood up and stood behind me. "I know it's not much, and possibly extremely inappropriate, but I did get you something to celebrate your good news. I got it for you when you finished your last treatment, but I thought it'd be better when you were in the clear." Zack hesitantly pulled a silver charm bracelet out of a black jewelry box. I turned around as he took my hand in his and proceeded to put the bracelet on my wrist. "It's nothing extravagant, and I guess it's a little corny, but I wanted to give you something special. There's a softball glove, whatever that thing is for cheerleading…"

"A megaphone?" I giggled.

"Yeah that." He chuckled. "A microphone and this is supposed to be the ribbon for stomach cancer, it's periwinkle, which I just learned is a color. The gold ribbon is for childhood cancer."

"Zack." I gasped.

"Do you hate it? It's tacky isn't it? It's nothing like what Keller gives you, but…"

"Zack, it's beautiful and thoughtful. Keller could never give me anything like this because it'd take too much effort. I honestly think it's the sweetest thing anyone's ever given me."

"You like it then?"

"I love it." I smiled as I hugged him quickly. "And I'll never take it off."

"I only get a hug?" He pouted. I wanted to kiss him on the mouth, because it was seriously one of the most amazing gifts I've ever received, but I couldn't. I pulled away and fingered the bracelet.

"I have a boyfriend."

"That's easy to fix."

"It's really not."

"You know it's only a month or so before he leaves for Massachusetts."

"What's in Massachusetts?"

"Harvard, where he's going to school."

"He's not…"

"Jordan, he has been bragging about it for weeks. He's playing soccer at Harvard." I should've been hearing this from my so called boyfriend and then I would have pretended to be mad. Right now, it's taking everything in me not to jump for joy. If Keller was in Massachusetts, would I be done with him? Was this nightmare possibly coming to a close?

"I guess I haven't really been paying attention."

"Understandable. How are you?" He queried as he reached up and tucked a stray hair behind my ear. "You're closing into yourself." I shrugged and turned back around. He went back towards my bed and plopped down there.

"I don't know. I need to get ready. The band will be here soon and I'm not even close to being presentable."

"You are beautiful as you are, you don't need all the makeup." He muttered as he pushed himself off my bed and strutted to the door.

"Thanks for the bracelet and…" He nodded and disappeared. My heart hurt to watch him go. I looked down at the bracelet and smiled as I fingered the delicate charms. Zack was sweet and amazing. I couldn't believe he'd given me such a perfect gift.

I pushed Zack and everything else out of my mind as I finished my makeup. I stepped into my baby blue, floor length satin dress and unrolled my hair.

"Jordan." Izzy, the drummer for my band, Down Under, called as she came up the stairs wearing a red satin dress with a double split high up the leg. I scurried out of my room to greet her.

"You look hot, Iz!" I exclaimed as I hugged the leggy blonde.

"So do you, girl." She grinned as we started down the stairs. "So what did loser boy do now?"

"Huh?" She nodded to where Keller stood at the foot of the stairs.

"Jordan." He gasped as I flowed into the room. "You look amazing."

"Thank you." I smiled before I started to leave.

"Jordan." He hollered irritably. "I have flowers and a very expensive gift in my hands and you're just going to walk by me?" I stopped and moved beside him. "Please baby, just open the gift? I bought it for you to wear tonight." He handed me a perfectly wrapped present. "Please."

"I really need to go; the band is waiting on me."

"Please? Just five minutes, for me?" He pouted as he touched my face gently. I nodded my head as he grinned triumphantly and helped me to open a small jewelry box. Inside was a diamond tennis bracelet.

"Keller." I gasped. "I can't…"

"Yes, you can." He chuckled. "My girl gets only the best. Let's take this tacky thing off and…" He touched the bracelet Zack had given me and I yanked away from him.

"And then you go and ruin it. This *thing* is beautiful and an extremely thoughtful gift."

"From who?" Keller spit. "Never mind, I'm sorry, I'm sorry. My gift will look just as good on this wrist." He quickly grabbed my other hand and looked on proudly as I put the bracelet on myself. I felt Keller's hand on my wrist before it moved up to my face.

"It has nothing on you babe, you're so beautiful tonight." He kissed me sweetly. "Have fun tonight. I'll be waiting for you and watching to make sure you heed my warnings." I stumbled, but quickly regained my posture before I walked out of the house.

"Let me see that." Izzy gushed as we got into the van to head for Mencino County High School. "*That is nice.* I can't believe he just gave you that."

"It's his way of saying he's not an asshole."

"He's still an ass, he just has really good taste." Izzy continued to admire it.

"I can't believe you're still with him." Connor, our guitar player, piped up.

"No kidding, you can do better than that loser." Lane, the lead male vocalist, agreed as he kept his eyes on the road while he drove.

"What?" I asked in shock.

"Any guy who lets his girlfriend sit in a hospital room while he's out partying deserves to be dumped." Lane stated.

"Where's this coming from?"

"We've thought it for a while, we just didn't want to overstep." Connor admitted.

"Yeah we *totally* like Lance better. Why do you think we jumped on the offer to play at MHS?" Izzy admitted with a nonchalant shrug.

"Lovely, thanks for letting *me* in on the secret."

"Like you would've listened." She laughed. "He took advantage of your vulnerability from Lance and he's been using it to keep you around. He's a dog; he knows he doesn't deserve you."

"Maybe so, but he's all I've got." I shrugged.

"Why are you so afraid being single?" Lane asked. "I thought you were the most confident girl in the world."

"Far from it. Unless I'm on stage and then I'm a completely different person."

"That's an understatement." Izzy giggled.

Chapter 76

We arrived at the school early and began to set up. I was extremely nervous about seeing Lance again. After all, it had been well over a month and we'd barely spoken really. I had been avoiding every text and call from him. The worst part of this gig was that I wanted to be at the prom with Lance, not singing at it. I couldn't though, until Keller was out of the picture I couldn't acknowledge the guy I really wanted to be with.

I continued to scan the gymnasium for my ex as we began our first set and more people filtered in. I spotted Alicia and Sawyer, as they made their entrance and my friend waved excitedly at me. She rushed over at the end of our set with her boyfriend in tow.

"Lish, you look beautiful!" I gushed as I hugged her and Sawyer. Alicia was wearing a pale pink gown and she looked like a princess.

"So do you, sweetie." She grinned. "My cousin is going to flip when he sees you, not to mention my brother."

"Yeah the limo would've been a lot better if you were there instead of Miss Personality." Sawyer stated sarcastically. Alicia shot him a look. "Don't tell me you weren't thinking the same thing."

"He has a date?" I asked sadly.

"Not a very good one." Chopper remarked as he picked me up off the ground in a bear hug. "You are lovely as always. Miss Donaldson."

"And you're hot, as always." I flirted, kissing him on the cheek. I was laughing with the group, but I never stopped scanning the entrance for Lance. My face fell when he sauntered in holding a gorgeous blonde's hand. My stomach dropped as he smiled at her. Lance was obviously over me and I was a dumbass. He looked so handsome in his tuxedo and I just wanted to run and jump into his arms, but I couldn't. This was my fault, after all.

"Not his girlfriend." Alicia whispered as she stood in front of me and tried to hide the pathetic heartbroken look on my face. "She asked, he accepted, only because he didn't want to look like a loser in front of you."

"But she's…"

"Got nothing on you." Chopper interjected. "Trust me, Jo."

"I have to go." I raced back to the stage before Lance could see I was upset.

I focused on blowing the prom goers away with my performance and tried not to think about Lance and the hot girl hanging all over him. I almost lost it when Lane sang "Backwoods boy and a fairy tale princess" and Lance allowed himself to be pulled onto the dance floor. I was livid as he held his date tightly and swayed to the song that he said had been written about us.

Tears stung my eyes as I went to the side of the stage and pretended to look for something. While I was fuming, a cute girl with mousy brown hair tapped me on my shoulder.

"Hi I'm Tana Shanes, head of the prom committee." She chirped as she stuck out her hand.

"Hi, Jordan Donaldson." I greeted her, feigning a smile.

"You guys are amazing. Lance said you were fantastic. I had no clue though. I'm really glad he told us to get you guys." She talked incredibly fast and eyed her carefully, was she on something?

"Lance?"

"Lance Bowman, I thought you two knew each other."

"Yeah, I'm confused I guess."

"You shouldn't be. Lance raved about y'all. He even offered to put up the rest of the funds for what we were lacking to book you guys."

"What?"

"Yeah, I thought it was weird too, but he said you guys were the best and he was right."

"Sorry, it's almost my turn." I turned around and returned to the stage, masking my emotions perfectly. I was furious and a million different things raced through my head. Ultimately, I was convinced this was his way of getting back at me for choosing Keller over him. He was flaunting his new relationship in my face in hopes of hurting me again. Once again, I poured my emotions into my performance and tried to forget about Lance.

Chapter 77
Lance

I sat at the table with my friends, people I'd known all of my life, guys who were like brothers to me, as we all watched my ex-girlfriend perform onstage. I couldn't take my eyes off her, she was gorgeous as always. If a record producer walked into this gymnasium, right now, Jordan would be whisked off to Nashville tomorrow. I have no doubts she will be performing all over the world someday, she's that good.

When she was onstage, she wore her emotions for the world to see, it showed in her movements, her voice and in the music. It was obvious something had changed, she seemed distracted and extremely angry, but she was hiding it well. Only me, someone who knew her better than I knew myself, could see something was bothering her.

"What's wrong with Jo?" I asked Alicia innocently as I leaned across the table towards her.

"I don't know, the bimbo on your arm maybe?" She cut rudely as she glared at my date and me.

"It's just *now* bothering her?" I whipped back, unsure of why Alicia was suddenly being a bitch. Jordan and Alicia had become best friends since the start of the school year when Alicia began at Callatin, but I never thought she'd choose her over her own family.

"No j*ack ass*, it's been bothering her all night. Why do you think she hasn't come to say hi?"

"Not to mention, you took your date to the dance floor during *your* song." Sawyer added with a shrug. I looked back at the couple in complete disbelief, now one of my best friends was siding with my ex-girlfriend as well?

"She has a boyfriend and she chose *him* over me." I protested, my fists clenching a napkin in front of me.

"Who cares? Some things are sacred." Alicia snapped angrily. "Besides, dumbass, if you don't tell her how you really feel then she's *never* going to choose you."

"And using Miss Personality to hurt Joey is totally not cool." Chopper added.

"Yeah, Jordan is awesome and does *not* deserve that." Cooper threw in.

"She chose Keller over me. How many times do I have to bring up that *I'm* not the bad guy? *She* did this. She has ignored me for weeks." I argued defensively, suddenly feeling like I was under attack. My own cousin, and closest friends, were choosing to side with Jordan.

"And how many times did you do it to her before?" Alicia retorted rudely, her eyes narrowing in disgust. "No one is keeping score. Go make things better or find someplace else to hang out for the night."

"What?" I laughed nervously. "What the fuck is the point anyway, she's still with Keller."

"Maybe if you manned up, that would change." Alicia hissed, before turning her back to me. I looked back questioningly.

"Did she tell you that? What do you mean?" All of my friends turned their backs to me. I felt like I'd just been slapped in the face.

I stood up from the table, a little angry and hurt all at the same time. If I had to talk to Jordan to shut them up, then I would. I'd been dying to all night anyway, I was just worried about how my heart would react to knowing I couldn't have her anymore. I wandered closer to the stage and placed myself right in her view. I smiled up at her, praying I could win her back.

Chapter 78
Jordan

Lance smiled sheepishly up at me, but I rolled my eyes and continued to sing. For the rest of the song, I did my best to avoid allowing my eyes to settle where he was standing. A few minutes later, Lance joined his date for another slow dance. By the time our seventh set was finished, I was beyond sad and fury. I stood on the side of the stage, drinking a bottle of water and trying to calm myself before we began again.

"Jordan." Coop smiled. "Are you allowed to dance with your groupies?"

"What?" I giggled.

"It's a shame for such a beautiful girl to be standing alone during a slow song." He grinned as he held his hand out to me.

"Jordan." Lance hollered a few feet away. I pretended not to hear him as I followed his friend to the dance floor.

"Can I cut in?" Lance drawled as he stood beside us a minute later.

"No." I answered rudely. "I promised Coop a dance and *I* follow through with my promises."

"Can I have the next then?"

"No."

"Why not?"

"Go ask your date for a dance, Bowman. I'm not interested in your games."

"What? Who's playing games?" He retorted.

"Get lost."

"Back off Bo, you can have her later." Coop interjected.

"Coop!" He exclaimed in shock, but walked off without a fight.

"I need a drink." He nodded understandingly and led me away from my ex.

"Alcoholic or non?" We ducked behind some decorations and he handed me a cold beer that he had stashed behind some bleachers.

"Oh, God bless you." I breathed as I chugged it.

"That bad, huh?"

"I just want to punch him in the face. If he's trying to hurt me, he succeeded the second he walked in holding that chick's hand, the rest is just overkill."

"How do you think he feels knowing you went back to your boyfriend after a weekend with him?" Coop cut.

"Do you think that was easy for me?" I asked tearfully. "I felt trapped. I didn't know what else to do. Lance can't even fight for me, so obviously I'm not important to him."

"You are though and he does, he's just...a guy." Coop chuckled. "It's harder for us than it is for you."

"No, it's really not." I shot. "All of you guys and his family tell me how much he cares about me, but *he* never does. Why not?"

"In Lance's way, he does. He may not say the words you want to hear, but...I don't know. I guess you just have to know him *to know*." He shrugged. He pointed at a beautiful dark headed girl in a black dress across the gym. "Serena Chapel, most irresistible and dreamed about senior at MHS. Two weeks ago, she asked Lance on a date, they hung out at a party and she snuck into his truck and tried to put the moves on him. He threw her out without a second thought because the truck is sacred Jo, because of you. His house, his bedroom they're all sacred and you're the only girl who has been in them. And you're the only girl who's ever been able to rope him. And every girl hates you for it."

"I don't understand."

"Ever since Luke died, no one has been allowed in the bedroom. Hell, Chopper is the only one who's even been invited to the house. Jordan, if he didn't care about you then you wouldn't have been invited either." He shrugged again.

"I have to go." I muttered quickly as confusion set in and I escaped back to the stage. I managed to avoid Lance for most of the night and actually calmed down. I was beginning to contemplate talking to him, trying to work things out, but as I looked around the gymnasium again, I felt like I might puke. My eyes found Lance just as he was kissing his date and I lost it. Luckily, it was at the same moment we were taking our last break. I was fighting back tears, praying they wouldn't come until I reached the safety of a nearby bathroom. A slow Rascall Flatts song filtered through the speakers, making it harder to fight my emotions.

"You owe me a dance." Lance drawled with a smile as he caught my wrist.

"No, I don't." I mumbled, shaking him off.

"I have been dying to dance with the most beautiful girl here all night."

"Why are you telling me for?" I asked rudely. "Your date is over there hitting on…"

"I was talking about you." He chuckled. "I've been dying to dance with *you* all night."

"Why? You want to tell me how great your date is or rub your new relationship in my face some more?"

"What? Why would you think…?"

"Lance, I don't know what you want, but I'm not interested." I began furiously. "Why in the Hell did you make them hire us?"

"Because you are the best and I thought you might need…"

"We don't need your fucking help getting gigs. Are you *trying* to hurt me, punish me? Honestly, I chastise myself enough and you hurt me the second I saw you with someone else." I cried as I started to run away.

"Jordan." He yelled as he rushed after me. "I'm not punishing you. I didn't want to hurt you."

"But you always do. Why are we here then Lance, I don't need your pity jobs or…"

"Maybe it had nothing to do with you, Jordan. Maybe *I* needed to see you! Maybe I made them hire y'all so I could see you again, so *I* could be alone with you again! You've blocked me from your life." He exploded. I stared back at him dumbfounded. "I just wanted to dance with my dream girl at least once at my senior prom."

Tears stung my eyes as I continued to stare back at him. I could hear the CD was almost over and I knew a slow song, the last before I was to go back onstage, was starting. I knew it was wrong, but I grabbed my ex-boyfriend's hand and led him to the floor anyway. He smiled before he wrapped his arms around my waist and pulled me super close to him. I put my head on his shoulder and got lost in the moment with him.

"This is better than I ever imagined." He whispered sweetly as the song was about to end.

"I have to go." I mumbled as I started towards the stage. Lance grabbed me before I could go and planted a passionate kiss on me.

"I couldn't let my dream girl go without a kiss." He smiled. I stammered a minute before I escaped to the security of my stage again. My head was spinning. My heart was hammering in my throat and I didn't know how I could make it through the final set without falling to pieces. I wanted to run back into Lance's arms, I wanted to feel them around me, feel his lips on mine again. I just wanted him back; I wanted him to love me again. As I belted out a Carrie Underwood song, I focused on everyone in the gymnasium, but Lance. Before I knew it, we were finished.

Chapter 79

"Hey, there's an after party at my house tonight. You guys want to come?" Sawyer asked while we broke everything down.

"I don't know."

"Come on. I'll be bored if you don't." Alicia begged. "I'll bring you home, I promise."

"There'll be beer and cards..." Coop offered.

"And I still have to beat you in a game of bullshit. If you don't show, then I'll assume it's because you're chicken." Chopper teased.

"You play dirty, Chop." I laughed. The others had already agreed so I really didn't have any other choice. Keller would be livid, but I was safe because I didn't make the decision, right?

"Ride in the limo with us, *please*." Alicia begged again.

"Won't it be a little weird?"

"No, Lance and Keely left already." Chopper blurted before Coop punched him in the arm.

"He'll be at the party, but he dropped his truck off here so he could leave my house early if he needed to." Sawyer answered quickly.

"*No*, he was hoping he could take you home after the dance so you two could talk, but I don't know what he's doing now." Alicia admitted. I shrugged my shoulders and followed Alicia and Lance's friends to their limo. I started to chug beer in hopes of washing away the images I had of my ex-boyfriend screwing another girl. I was a loser for following along, I should call someone to come get me.

"*The band decided to hit an after party. Will you be around if I need a ride?*" I texted Caleb.

"*Yup, I'll leave my phone on loud. Have fun.*"

"I'm glad you're coming." Chopper grinned as he slung his arm across my shoulders and gave me a quick squeeze. I smiled and put my head on his shoulder. I missed these guys something terrible. My phone buzzed and my stomach tightened with the fear that it was Keller asking where I was, chances were he already knew though.

"*I am waiting on you, where are you? You should be home by now.*"

"*The band wanted to make a few stops. Sorry, don't wait on me, it'll be late.*"

"*You better not be with the fucking losers right now.*"

"*I am with my band.*"

"*You will regret any lies you tell me. Do not make me angry. Your friends will be the ones to pay.*" My phone started ringing and tears welled in my eyes, I would not answer Keller's call with everyone around. I couldn't risk them hearing his threats. I exhaled slowly, realizing it was Lance calling.

"I went back to look for you and Izzy said you left already in the limo." Lance explained breathlessly. "I was worried I lost my chance."

"Where's your date?"

"I left her with her friends."

"Before or after you got some?"

"Before! I wouldn't...Jordan what kind of guy do you think I am?"

"Where are you now?"

"Almost to Sawyer's. Waiting on you."

"Why?" I giggled.

"Because I'm always waiting on you, darlin'. I'm here." He hung up the phone just as the limo slowed and came to a stop in front of Sawyer's house. We all climbed out, Lance was there waiting patiently to help me out. "I have got to be the luckiest guy in the world. Not only did I get to dance with, and kiss my dream girl, but now I get to party with her too?"

"You keep talking about this dream girl, who is she and do I need to kick her ass?" I joked.

"You are so beautiful. Your hair looks great." He smiled as he referred to my short auburn pixie cut.

"Thanks." I smiled. He grabbed me in an amazing kiss.

"I'm not letting you go, even if it *is* just for tonight." He breathed as he pulled away slowly. He tugged me back to him and kissed me again.

"Get a room you two." Chopper teased.

"Mine is open." Sawyer offered with a wink. "I know y'all need to talk in *private*."

"You are changing those sheets before I climb into bed tonight." Alicia laughed. Lance grabbed my hand and led me into the small house. He made a beeline for his friend's bedroom and locked the door behind us.

Within seconds, we were all over each other. My dress was hiked up, my panties were off as well as Lance's pants. The two of us were entangled in a passionate heap for over an hour before we came up for air.

"I miss you so much, Lance." I admitted breathlessly.

"Me too." He began to kiss me again. "Not just this, although this is fucking awesome, but everything about you."

"I know." I smiled. Eventually we took the walk of shame out of Sawyer's room and found Alicia and the others in the kitchen.

"So things are good I see." Chopper teased as he saw Lance leading me by the hand. When we got into the kitchen, Lance pulled me in front of him and wrapped his arms around my waist as he stood behind me. I leaned back into him and sighed. I missed this so much.

"The sex hair is a dead giveaway." Alicia pestered, causing me to blush.

"The goofy glazed looks don't help either."

"Jo's is because she's drunk." Alicia noticed. I was most definitely drunk. I had wanted to numb the pain of seeing Lance tonight, make the whole experience a little better so I had taken a few pills Sage had given me. I was beginning to think they weren't working, but mixed with the alcohol, they were numbing everything. I didn't think alcohol would be an issue and I was too upset about Lance to care about mixing the two. I wasn't doing well at all, but I still drank another beer as we stood there and it proved to be problematic. The world began spinning.

Chapter 80
Lance

"I don't feel good. Can you take me to sleep?" Jordan slurred as she turned around and stumbled into me. She was sober earlier, wasn't she?

"How much did she drink in the limo?" I caught her, pulled out a chair and set her in it. She wobbled before groaning and putting her head on the table.

"Like two beers. She shouldn't be this bad." Alicia answered as she shot up and raced over to us. "They told her the cancer was gone. Surely they would've seen another problem."

"Alicia." Jordan giggled. "I'm fine. Cancer, schmancer, I took my pain pills and...and now I don't feel very good." Her face turned pale.

"She's going to blow." Coop laughed. I swung her up into my arms and took her to the bathroom just in time. She heaved into the toilet and I rubbed her back until she fell into me.

"Do you know what this is?" She questioned as she slapped at her wrist, showing an expensive diamond bracelet. "This is Keller's way of controlling me. It's probably got a fucking tracking device in it."

"Why would you think that?"

"Because he always knows where I am." She whispered as she looked around slowly. "He knows everything." She pushed off me and stood quickly, wavering as she did. "I have to go."

"No, you don't. Alicia texted Maddie to tell her you were staying with her."

"I can't. No, no, no, I can't. I have to go."

"Why?"

"Don't you see? Something bad is going to happen if I stay. He does this...he does it every time. I can't...I can't...I can't." Her breathing grew labored as tears rolled down her cheeks. "I spent the weekend with you, your mom almost died. I kissed Zack, Cissy died."

"You kissed Zack?"

"He'll hurt you. He'll hurt me. I can't..."

"What do you mean, he'll hurt you?"

"I can't...Alicia!" She stumbled out of the bathroom. Alicia was skidding to a stop in front of her. "Please take me home, I have to go home."

"I can't drive, I've been drinking. Everyone has been drinking."

"Where's my phone? I need Caleb to come get me...I need..."

"They're asleep. What's wrong, Jo? What did you do to cause her to freak out?" My cousin's eyes pierced through me and I immediately threw my hands up in a surrender.

"Nothing, she just started flipping out. She's scared of someone."

"Who are you scared of?"

"I can't tell you." Jordan whispered. "I need to go home. Please take me home." She fell into the floor and pushed herself into the corner, crying like a small child as she did. "He did something to my meds, this isn't right. This isn't right. This isn't right."

"Who did something to your meds?" Alicia asked.

"He will kill you too." Jordan stated with a blank look on her face. "He will kill you all and it will be my fault." She continued to repeat the words and Alicia looked up at me. Terror filled her face as she stood up.

"I need to call Caleb. I think she needs to go to the hospital."

"What if she's telling the truth?"

"About what?"

"She's terrified of someone or something, look at her."

"She said she took pain pills and alcohol, it's probably just a bad reaction. Her system is so weak from the cancer and the treatments."

"Alicia, have you ever seen her so terrified?" Alicia shook her head and pulled out her phone. "What if Zack is hurting her? What if…"

"Zack is not hurting her." She shook her head. "That's a ridiculous accusation." Keller James was an asshole, but Jordan could take him out in a second. He was a wuss, I'd seen him back down from too many fights like a coward. "Can you drive her home? Caleb needs to make the decision about taking her to the hospital." I nodded my head. I didn't want to take her home, I wanted to keep her by my side for the rest of her life. I wanted to protect her. I needed to keep her safe from whoever had her so scared.

"I'll go with you." Chopper offered. "I'll drive, you just hold her." I nodded, grateful for the opportunity to hold her a little longer. She fought timidly as I swung her up in my arms and carried her to Chopper's Bronco.

"We're all going." Coop stated as my friends followed and piled into the SUV with us. She passed out in my arms before we pulled out of the driveway.

"Did you hear what she was saying?" I asked Chopper. He nodded his head. "Do you think it's legit or do you think it was the mixture of meds and booze?"

"Jordan doesn't seem like the type of girl to let anyone push her around."

"I agree, but…"

"You probably don't know this," Alicia started hesitantly from the backseat. "But Zack is on scholarship to Callatin, his parents would never be able to afford to send him there. After some weird things started happening at school, he began a side business. He is a private investigator of sorts. A lot of my peers pay him very, very good money to get dirt on people. We've been noticing some things about Jordan, like what happened tonight, so he started following her, sort of."

"That's called stalking." I snapped. "And him trying to get the heat off him."

"I know you don't want to hear this, but Zack Bentley is in love with Jordan and he would never hurt her. He has been tearing himself apart trying to protect her. Keller cheats on Jordan constantly, which Zack has proof of, and his side chick, Sage, is who we think is doing things to Jo."

"If he has proof of him cheating why doesn't he show Jordan?"

"He has, it does no good." Alicia rolled her shoulders and reached for Sawyer's hand. "When Jordan came back to school after she lost her hair, Sage was horrific to her. Jordan would never admit it, but it was pretty brutal. There have been a lot of little things to happen and Jo just hides it and brushes it off as nothing."

"Have you talked to this girl?"

"Maddie has, Zack has just about enough to take it to Mr. D as proof of her bullying Jordan."

"And Jo thinks this girl killed Cissy?"

"No. She still hasn't really grieved, I think tonight was just that." I kissed the top of Jordan's head and held her tightly. It was obvious Zack had feelings for Jordan and it scared me to death. They were really good friends and he had more access to her than I did. He could be there for her when I couldn't be.

"Why haven't you mentioned this before?"

"You haven't exactly been in her life." Alicia shrugged. "Not to mention, we knew you would fly off the handle and try to rescue her…"

"Of course I would try to protect her."

"That's not what she means." Chopper interjected. "You are hot headed. You would go in swinging and not realize how dangerous it was."

"You knew?"

"We all did. We've been doing whatever we could to assist Zack. Sage doesn't know Drew, he tried to be stealth and get some info."

"You all did and…?"

"These kids at this school are not like us. They operate on a completely different plane. Beating the hell out of someone and telling them to leave your girl alone, would normally work, would normally earn you respect and fear. These kids aren't scared of anything, because their parents get them out of everything. We had to use other methods."

"And so you sided with Zack.

"Don't be pissed at us about this. You should be thrilled we have been trying to protect the girl you're in love with. If you see Bentley as a threat then he will be." Chopper snapped. I glared back at my friend, knowing nothing I said right now would come out the way I wanted it too. Chopper pulled in to the Callatin Academy gates and Alicia flashed her student i.d. at the guard.

"Hey Jo, we're home." I whispered into her ear. She moved slightly and when I adjusted my hold on her, she woke up. She smiled up at me, before her face went white.

"Where are we?"

"Callatin, Chopper drove you home."

"You can't be here." She shrieked as she sat straight up and looked around nervously. "I can't….no, no, no." She tried to crawl out of my lap, but I held her tightly.

"Jo, calm down."

"No, no, no…" She repeated. Chopper turned into the circle driveway and immediately slowed.

"What is that?" He queried.

"Why is the front door open?" Sawyer asked as he moved forward.

"Did you see that?" Drew yelled as he pointed to a black clad figure running from the side of the house.

"Oh my God." Alicia gasped. Before Chopper could come to a complete stop, Jordan had the door open and was jumping out.

"ZACK!!" Chopper put the SUV in park and I sprinted after Jordan. Cooper slammed past me and took off after another black clad figure strutting out the front door. Another guy was limping out behind him and Chopper barreled towards him, spearing him against the house.

"MADDIIIIIIEEEEEEEEEE!" The voice was loud and haunted. Caleb staggered from around the side of the house, holding his side. Jordan began screaming as she took in her brother's state. She dropped to her knees in front of Zack though, realizing he wasn't conscious.

"No, no, no. It's my fault. This is my fault."

"I called 9-1-1, the security guard and first responders should be here in a few minutes." Alicia interjected in a terrified whisper behind me. I hurried towards Caleb with Drew by my side.

204

"They took Maddie. I can't…I couldn't…find Maddie."

"Where did they take her?"

"I don't know. We were…" Caleb dropped to his knees, his face contorted in pain. His eyes went to Jordan and Zack. "No." Sawyer rushed into the house, yelling for Maddie as he did. The sirens of the nearby fire department rang through the night. What in the Hell was happening? I looked around at the gruesome scene. Did I go to Jordan? Did I follow Sawyer to look for Maddie or did I chase down Cooper's dumb ass who just chased after one of the people responsible for this mess?

Chapter 81
Alicia

Tears rolled down my cheeks as I looked around. I was frozen to the pavement. It was exactly like the scene Maddie had described from the lake house. I couldn't fathom what had happened or how anyone had gotten on campus to do this. I heard a scream from behind me and knew it was Maddie. I turned without hesitation and sprinted towards the sound, screaming her name as I did.

She was laying on the ground kicking and clawing at two figures. I didn't stop, I couldn't let them hurt her. Out of nowhere, I heard a low growl.

"Not tonight, bitch." I felt something hit me from behind and the whole world went dark.

Chapter 82
Keller

I was having a shit day. My girlfriend thought she could disrespect and lie to me. My roommates, people who I thought would always have my back had turned against me. They were spreading rumors about me, trying to turn my followers to them. Sage wasn't even answering my texts or phone calls and she always did, no matter what she was doing. I was done with all the disrespect. Everyone would pay for underestimating me. My phone beeped and I looked down.

"It's done, but there are complications." A text from one of my employees. These guys couldn't do anything right to save their life. It's a good thing I had taken care of the most important things myself.

I pulled my car into the driveway of my lake house. My friends were in and out all the time, it's most likely where Sage was. I'm certain she's pouting and playing pissy just to get a little attention from me. I was getting sick of her shit too.

I walked into the house and looked around. The surround sound was blaring, porn was playing on the flat screen and pot smoke filled the downstairs.

"Where's Sage?" I asked Tresden, a guy who was quickly becoming a good friend to me. Two years ago, I had put him through Hell when he entered Callatin, but he turned out to be a pretty cool guy.

"Upstairs with Adrienne, trying to get Brennan to fuck them." He rolled his eyes as he took a hit off a joint.

"Brookman is here?" I gritted my teeth. I was hoping the kid would get the hint and stay away, he was stupider than I originally thought.

"He was looking for you." Tresden started chuckling as he glanced over at me. "Did you know you have an evil twin brother?"

"So I've heard." I looked up the staircase, before I rolled my eyes and stomped to the second floor. "Sage?" There was giggling from one of the rooms and I followed the sound.

"Keller." Adrienne singsonged, she was wearing a thong and nothing more as she stumbled into my arms. "Sage won't wake up and play anymore. Brennan's so trashed and…"

"Go in my bedroom, baby. We'll be right there." I kissed her softly before she giggled and followed my order. Brennan was slumped in the corner, half awake as he tried to focus. I kicked at Sage's bare foot. She didn't move. I looked at her arm, she'd been shooting heroin again. I told her not to mess with this crap, it was too unsteady. "Sage, what the Hell? You're not going to be my girl if you keep doing this shit." I kicked at her foot again and she fell completely over. Her chest wasn't rising and falling. I fell to my knees in front of her and I cried.

Sage was dead.

"You stupid, stupid bitch." I sobbed as I touched her face. Why in the Hell did she have to be so stupid? Why in the Hell did she have to do this in my house? I looked around the room and shook my head.

"Tres!" I hollered, hoping he'd be able to get the place drug free before I had to call the cops to take her body away. Brennan grunted in the corner and an idea flashed in my head. "Brennan, Brennan, Brennan. I am so glad you showed up tonight. It's an absolute convenience that you're such an idiot." I took the cuff off Sage's arm and removed the syringe stuck in her vein. I cleaned up any remnants of the drugs littering the room. Sage was already naked but for her thong, so I pulled it the rest of the way off and tossed it in the corner. Sage and Adrienne liked bondage and they didn't disappoint now. Two ropes lay around Brennan. Perfect.

If Brennan Brookman wanted to stalk and play hero to my girlfriend, wanted to continuously get into my business, well then he was going to learn to keep to himself. No one needed to know Sage overdosed, Brennan is going to murder her.

Chapter 83
Chopper

Zack had underwent numerous surgeries and was now resting in ICU. Alicia had her head stitched up and was sleeping off the anesthesia in a hospital bed. Caleb should be in a hospital bed after his surgeries as well, but he was more concerned with Maddie. Coop had not caught anyone on his heroic chase, but came back in enough time to save Alicia and Maddie from being raped. The injured crook was sitting in a jail cell and being questioned extensively by Coop's brother. Hopefully, we had answers soon.

We all sat in Lance's living room, trying to make sense of the early morning events. I watched Jordan carefully as she rocked back and forth in an old chair in the corner of the room. Mrs. Bowman diligently did everything possible to get Jordan out of her shock, but nothing worked.

"I need to be at the hospital." Jo mumbled as she stumbled out of the chair. "I need to be with Zack. Alicia needs me. Maddie…." She began sobbing again. Lance rushed to her but she began screaming and pushed him away. The only people allowed near her were Jenn and Mrs. B. "You can't be at the hospital like this, baby. Your dad will call us as soon as he knows more."

"My dad will probably leave before anyone is okay." Jordan went for the door again. "What is that?" She scurried towards the television until she was directly in front of it. The news was on telling about a murder on the lake. They were blocking the face of the guy they were carting away in handcuffs, but Jordan began shaking. "No."

"What is it?"

"Brennan, that's Brennan."

"Who?"

"In handcuffs. Oh my God, oh my God. It's my fault. He tried to protect me. It's my fault. No, no, no…he didn't kill anyone. He couldn't. He couldn't. I have to go to the police station." She sprinted out of the house.

"We've got a runner."

"I chased one guy already today." Coop chuckled. It didn't matter because Lance was already out the door after her. Mrs. Bowman followed them out.

"Okay, so do you think this has anything to do with Zack's investigative work?" Drew asked as he looked around.

"That's what it seems like." I mumbled. "Or maybe it's all about the break in at the lake house."

"Why does Jordan keep saying it's her fault?"

"She believes it is." I shrugged. "Break ins, rapes, murder…what the fuck are we into?"

"All because someone is jealous of Jordan? I don't understand any of it."

"Maybe we should do a little recon work ourselves." Coop added.

"Excellent idea." Whoever was after Jordan wasn't just attacking her, they were going after all of us. I could handle a little bullying, but when you were physically assaulting the people I loved, I was going to fight.

Chapter 84
Jordan

I climbed up in the bed with Zack and snuggled next to him. Chances are, when he finally wakes up and realizes I am the cause of his injuries, he will never speak to me again. My heart was destroyed from Keller's games. Regardless of my choices, I would have to survive without the people who meant the most to me. Unfortunately, Keller was making sure I would take the more torturous route by obeying his orders so my friends would live. Honestly, what is worse than watching your friends, the people you love, those who know you best move on with their lives thinking you don't care? I would do whatever I had to do to protect them, even if it meant playing the part as Keller's loving girlfriend who had no friends.

I laced my fingers through Zack's and then kissed his cheek gently. My Uncle Calen had retrieved the video surveillance tapes surrounding the house. I had never known there was an alarm system on the house or surveillance, but apparently they were set up all over campus. I watched the video of the attack three times, trying to recognize someone. Even if I saw Keller though, it's not like I could identify him. It would be suicide.

Zack had been outside on a phone call when someone came out of the bushes. Zack had turned around just to see the guy about to clock him. In the meantime, a group of four headed for the house. There was a loud crash where someone had thrown something through a window. Caleb raced out of the house, Zack started yelling just as a guy punched him in the stomach. He doubled over, when he straightened blood stained his shirt. He lunged for his attacker, landed a punch and was stabbed again. At the same time, Caleb was jumped by two guys. Maddie raced out of the house, being chased by someone. She dove for her car, fumbled for the keys and screamed as they were kicked out of her hands. Caleb was screaming, kicking and punching as he tried to get to Maddie. He told her to run and she did, but two guys chased her. They tried to rape her, they had ripped off all her clothes, she was clawing and kicking when the security guard showed up and the attackers finally scattered. Alicia had attempted to save her, they knocked her out. Caleb had a lot of bruises, a broken arm, nose and rotator cuff. Zack had been stabbed a total of four times, before his attacker knocked him down enough to start kicking him in the stomach. He was truly lucky to be alive. He had lost a lot of blood and suffered enough damage that they were keeping him pretty sedated.

"How's the patient?" One of the intern doctors smiled as she walked into the room.

"Not laughing at my best jokes." I shrugged. She giggled and made her way to his I.V. bag.

"Should I move? I don't want to be in the way."

"No, sweetie, you're fine. I'm sure he'll appreciate you being there when he wakes up."

"Do you think he will soon?"

"He's been through a lot. From the injuries sustained and the reports, he fought like Hell so it may take him a bit to wake. It's not a bad thing that he hasn't really woke yet, he needs all the rest he can get."

"I just…I worry."

"Understandable." She lifted Zack's right arm to find his pulse. There was noise at the door and an older couple stood there. The woman's face fell and her hand went directly to her mouth as she gasped.

210

"Are you Jordan?" The man questioned as he put his arm around his wife. He was tall, thin and had a head full of grey hair. His eyes were the same color green as Zack's.

"Yes, sir. Mr. and Mrs. Bentley? I didn't..."

"We drove. We couldn't wait for the flight times they offered." Mr. Bentley responded with a smile. I climbed out of the bed just as Mrs. Bentley rushed to her son's side. She looked up at the doctor.

"Is he...?"

"He's good. He should wake up soon."

"Nothing has changed since we last talked?"

"No ma'am."

"Thanks for waiting on us." A short girl with wild, curly blonde hair announced with a thick New York accent when she walked into the room. She was followed by a black headed man and a dark headed woman."

"Your mom wasn't waiting." Mr. Bentley joked.

"I knew Jay should have gotten out too." The dark headed woman smiled.

"Jordan, right?" The blonde asked as she grabbed me in a hug. "I'm Kat, this is my sister Grace and my brother Jason. Please don't think I'm a stalker, I just see your pictures on Facebook and then Bubs talks about you constantly. God, you are gorgeous."

"Kat, pull it back a bit." Grace giggled as she gave me a hug as well. "She's a little intense, we're not all that crazy."

"Well, the boys in the family aren't anyway." Jason smiled as he engulfed me in a hug.

"Pay no attention to them, it's been a long car ride." Mrs. Bentley smiled, hugging me before her husband did. I'd never met any of them and was kind of thrown off by the affection. "Thanks for being here for him. It's horrible to be so far away, but I knew he was in good hands with you, Caleb and Maddie. He talks about the three of you so much."

"How are Caleb and Maddie? When your father called he said they were injured as well."

"Physically okay."

"I can't even imagine how anyone would be emotionally." Kat shook her head and looked at her brother closely.

"Do the cops have any leads? Oh, I should be asking your father this." Mr. Bentley shook his head. "Sorry, it's hard to shut the cop off in me."

"They're not really forthcoming." I rolled my shoulders before I wrapped my arms around myself. "My dad actually had to leave, so my Uncle Calen is with Caleb as they're releasing him. They should be up in a second. My uncle is a cop a few towns over and..."

"Has been harassing the sheriff's department for leads." Uncle Calen interjected as he and Caleb came into the room. "I've also been doing my own investigation." Mrs. Bentley rushed to engulf my brother in a monster hug. He didn't look at all surprised.

"Oh Caleb, are you okay?"

"You should see the other guy." He joked.

"I wish we could." Calen interjected. The room was loud as different conversations started up. I didn't want to talk to anyone, there was no point in playing nice when they would all stone me when the truth came out. I walked over to Zack's bedside and took his hand in mine again.

"I see my family has arrived." He stated gruffly. His eyes were still closed, but a smile played on his bruised face.

"Zack?" I gasped. The whole room fell silent just as he coughed and slowly opened his eyes.

"Mom." The awe in his voice melted my heart as he grinned and opened his arms right as his mom fell into them. You could see her body shaking and hear her crying. Tears rolled down Zack's cheeks as he hugged her tightly. "You didn't have to come, but I am so glad you did."

"I told her you were probably just faking to get attention." Kat teased as she wiped at her eyes. "You always do."

"Can't help the baby is more loved than the oldest." Zack responded with an evil gleam in his eye. "It took a long time for them to get it right."

"I don't necessarily think they got it right." Jason chuckled as he patted his sister on the back.

"Perfection meant they would have stopped at me." Grace smiled as she dove in between Zack and her mom. "Bubby, you scared the shit out of us."

"Not on purpose."

"How ya feel?" Kat queried as she bent down to kiss him on the forehead.

"I cannot answer with mom in the room." He whispered. She rolled her eyes and laughed before she pulled out her phone, bent down to her brother and took a picture.

"Your nieces and nephews are at home on pins and needles waiting for this text."

"And five...four...three...two...one." Jason counted. All of his family's phones began ringing. Zack grinned broadly as he turned to look at me.

"I'm the favorite."

"I see that." I giggled as he reached for my hand and squeezed it.

"Leighton is devastated she couldn't come." Kat sighed as she pulled the phone from her ear. "She is sobbing, will you skype with her in a little while?" Zack held out his hand and his sister placed his phone there. His voice changed as he talked.

"Lei lei baby, don't cry. I'm okay."

"He's the favorite uncle." Jason explained with a mock glare at his brother. "Mostly because he's the youngest and closer to all of their ages. They all adore him. Leighton is Kat's daughter, he was three when she was born. She was really colicky, if Zack would sit by her and hold her hand, she was fine. It's a weird bond."

"I'm the favorite, because I'm the coolest." Zack interjected before going back to his phone conversation.

"Good to see his ego is still intact." I laughed. Zack was off the phone a few minutes later and I leaned down. "I'm going to head out, give you time with your family."

"You can stay. Please stay." I shook my head.

"Spend time with your family. I see you every day, they don't. Cale and I will be back." He nodded as he reached out and pulled me into a hug. Caleb and I were bombarded with hugs from Zack's family before we left.

"They're, um, affectionate." I laughed awkwardly when we were at the elevator. Calen was meeting us downstairs to take us home. He was going to stay at our house for a few days, at least until dad was home. His kids were staying with their grandparents at their own home. Calen didn't want to put them in any danger by bringing them on campus.

"They're good people. Get used to it, they're a big Italian family and they love to hug. He's got a huge family."

"When have you met his family?"

"I went home with him twice when he first got here. One was because of a basketball camp we enrolled in up there."

"I never knew that." I mumbled.

"They're amazing, honestly. It was overwhelming at first. Especially when you come from a family like ours." I nodded my head. Caleb and I climbed into the elevator and I was quiet as it took us down. I wasn't coming back to the hospital. Zack was awake and that was all that mattered. I knew if I went to visit him anymore, Keller would retaliate and I couldn't allow that.

Chapter 85

Apparently, you can be the biggest bitch in the world to people and they suddenly forget when you die. Or at least, when people think you've been murdered they memorialize you as a saint. No one in this school liked Sage, not even her best friend Adrienne. She was hateful, rude, entitled and fake. These dumbasses were now turning Brennan into a monster, they were confusing the two people.

There was no possible way Brennan was capable of what they were saying. I would never believe it. I was grateful they had cancelled school Thursday and Friday for Sage's funeral. I was absolutely disgusted by the teachers' and students' fake grief. Keller hadn't been in school all week, devastated by finding his dead friend. I was determined to find a way to prove Keller was responsible for all of this. It was all too coincidental.

Despite my father's orders I didn't attend the services. Sage and I were not friends. She was a bitch to me every chance she got and the only time she wasn't was when she was too stoned to speak. Just last week she had cornered me in the bathroom and threatened my life. She attempted to barter with me to dump Keller so she could have him. I told her she could have him, but he wouldn't allow it. I also showed her some of the text messages he sent me, stating we weren't over until he said. I wanted to be done with him and he wouldn't allow it. Unfortunately, when she walked out of the bathroom fighting back tears I kind of felt bad for her.

It was also our prom weekend. People were claiming it just wasn't going to be the same without Sage there, but I'm certain it wasn't about to dampen anyone's night. I knew it wouldn't be changing mine.

I wasn't positive if Keller was even still going to prom, because we hadn't talked. I wouldn't be upset if he ditched me though, it would actually make the night perfect. I sighed when I heard Keller's voice downstairs. I couldn't get that lucky.

I was wearing a dress Keller had bought for me; a sexy black halter gown with a plunging neckline, a split raced up the side revealing skin all the way to mid-thigh. The dress was backless and it looked great against my tan skin. My hair was growing back curlier, but it was still pretty short and I used the wildness of it to my advantage.

"Damn Jo, do you ever look bad?" Alicia joked as I sauntered down the stairs. I shrugged my shoulders and complimented my roommate and her boyfriend.

"I'm so jealous of how cute you two are together." I pouted. I feigned a smile at Keller as he strutted over to me carrying gifts.

"I made sure to find the most perfect accessories for your dress." Keller opened a black box encasing diamond earrings, a necklace and a matching bracelet. I allowed him to help me put the expensive gifts on.

"Perfect."

"Wow." Maddie breathed as she looked at his elaborate gifts. "Did you do something wrong, Keller? I mean, I know how your dad likes to drop money to cover h*is* ass so I'm just thinking you picked up that trait. For you to drop over three thousand dollars on Jordan is a bit extreme, don't you think?"

"Jealous much?" Keller retorted. "My girl deserves the best and money isn't a problem."

"Don't you think she'd enjoy being your girl if you actually paid attention and showed her affection, rather than buying it for her?" Keller ignored her. He leaned over and kissed me

214

sweetly while we posed for pictures. In the limo, he was all over me and did his best to show Sawyer and Alicia we were definitely together. Keller was extremely rude to Sawyer as well; making it obvious to everyone that he thought he was better than Alicia's boyfriend.

"I'm sorry he's being such an ass. I don't know what his deal is tonight." I apologized when we sat down at one of the tables. Keller had ditched me the second we walked into the building.

"*Tonight*? He's always like this." Alicia rolled her eyes.

"We got into a fight and I think he's insecure and…"

"And so he's trying to buy you?" Alicia cut.

"No. He just likes giving me things."

"Is that why you and Lance aren't together? I told Lance he was wrong, but…" Sawyer started.

"Lance and I aren't together, because he has an inferiority complex." I shot.

"You're not exactly innocent either." I huffed, rolled my eyes and crossed my arms in front of me. I walked away from my friends. Zack wasn't here and I missed him. He had gotten an infection of some sort and was still in the hospital. I should ditch the whole prom and go watch reruns with him. If I did though, I would be putting him in danger. I let out a sigh and went to find my date. The entire night, I mostly followed him around like a pathetic puppy dog stroking his ego. Keller made a point to show off the dress and expensive jewelry he bought for me. A few times, he supposedly tripped up and told people he bought me. It wasn't an accident and it wasn't a lie either.

I went to the bathroom and when I returned I skimmed the room for Keller and finally spotted him talking to a few baseball players.

"She always comes crawling back. I throw a little jewelry or clothes her way and she's all over me. I guarantee, I won't be able to keep her off me tonight." I heard Keller bragging.

"No way." Troy Lampley laughed in disbelief. "God, I can only imagine what she's like in bed. Damn, I'd pay good money to see her in action."

"That can be arranged." Keller offered. "For the right price, I can videotape…you've seen my handiwork with Sage and Adrienne."

I was furious. If Keller wanted everyone to think he was the man then I'd take that away from him in a heartbeat.

"Keller baby, I'm ready to go." I whispered seductively as I pulled him to me. "I thought we could be alone in the limo before everyone else got there. I wanted to thank you properly for the jewelry. And I'm really hoping you don't have performance problems tonight, of all nights. Did you talk to the doctor like you promised?"

"What?" Keller laughed nervously.

"I'm sorry, but I'm really getting tired of you going limp after five seconds, it's frustrating. I have needs you know."

"Jordan." He protested as he tried to shut me up with a dirty look. He began to pull away. I grabbed a hold of his privates tightly, making it look like a triple x moment.

"You want to ruin my reputation to stroke your ego? I can play dirty." I hissed in his ear. "And frankly, I'm a little sick of this bull shit. Why won't you let me go, Keller? It's obvious you don't want me."

"I do."

"No, you want a trophy wife. That's sure as Hell not me."

"Don't make a scene." He hissed, his mouth millimeters from mine. "I will not be embarrassed in front of the entire prom. I am king of this school and will always be. You are nothing without me."

"You can hold your court asshole, I could care less. I want out."

"No." His eyes flashing angrily. "You killed Sage, you're all I have left."

"Then I have no other choice." I drawled sweetly as I leaned in and kissed him hungrily. Keller responded immediately, his hands going down to my butt. I pulled back and smacked him across the face. "*That's* for the STD you gave me." I glowered. Keller's jaw dropped open.

"What the fuck are you doing?" He asked in a low dangerous voice. I shrugged my shoulders innocently and gave him my best smile.

"The sex sucks and this just put me over the limit. It's over, sweetheart." I smiled as if I were talking to a slow child. Keller's jaw clenched as he took a step closer.

"Now is not the time for you to rehearse for your next audition, sugar." He spit through clenched teeth. "Stop drawing attention to yourself."

"If you two want to make a scene, take it elsewhere. Lifestyles of the Rich and Spoiled is not being filmed here today." Mrs. Venedy, the senior literature teacher hissed. "It's also not appropriate for your next porn video either. Understand?" I nodded my head in shock. "Time to go home kids."

"What?" Keller and I gasped in disbelief.

"Time to go home." She repeated as she crossed her arms in front of her chest. I stared back at her in disbelief, but Keller glared angrily. I turned around to leave; Keller flanked my side, gripping my arm tightly.

"You will pay for this, bitch." He hissed low in my ear. I rolled my eyes and laughed. We were out the front doors of the hotel in a matter of minutes.

Mr. James' Porsche had been dropped off at the hotel so Keller and I could leave whenever we wanted. It waited in the parking lot for us and the second we were in front of the car, he backhanded me. No one was around. Everyone was inside, there were no witnesses to the pain he was about to inflict on me. Even if there were, I don't think he would care.

"Are you happy now? Not only did you ruin *my* prom by getting us kicked out, you made an ass out of me in front of everyone there."

"You do that on your own." I retorted, only to be popped hard in the mouth again. I tasted blood, but I clamped down on it. I wouldn't let him see any weakness.

"How dare you…"

"How dare you trick me into this joke of a relationship and then refuse to let me go when you're screwing the entire school. How dare you repeatedly punish me for talking to other guys when you put your dick in anything warm and wet. I am so fucking sick of you thinking you own me, Keller James. You don't own shit."

"I beg to differ, bitch." He growled as he grabbed my hair and yanked my head back. "I *do* own you. I will make your life Hell. You disrespect me every time you go back to the lowlife plowboy. And when you do that, I cannot allow it. You *will* be punished." I could hear voices coming close; a group was coming into the parking lot. Keller slammed me against the car, pinned me there as he yanked my head back. His head dipped down low as he started kissing my neck, then my mouth until the group had passed. "You will not make a joke of me, slut."

"You are a joke all on your own." I laughed, in a high-pitched voice. Keller yanked my head back more, causing it to bounce off the top of his silver car.

"The joke is on you, babe, we're not over until I say we're over and that's not happening

216

until the fuckoff is out of the picture."

"*You're* the fuckoff." Keller's hand went back and nailed me again. My entire face stung as I fought the tears back.

"Now, help me get the plowboy out of the way and you're in the clear."

"What do you mean?"

"We can end this right now, Jordan, as long as you don't go back to Lance Bowman." He explained with a wicked smile. "But go back to him and he'll be in jail quicker than you can sneeze. I'll have him nailed for so many charges, you'll be wondering if they're for real."

"You're bluffing."

"You know I'm not. Next time, I won't miss when I aim at Zack Bentley or Lance Bowman." When had he shot at Lance? Was there something I was missing? Panic began seeping into my brain.

"Why do you hate him so much?"

"Because he's a loser, redneck, mother fucker." He spit. "And something that low will never oust me."

"That's what it is? You can't stand for him to show you up?" I gasped. Keller glared back at me; no answer meant I was right on the money. I started cackling, Keller's eyes flashed disbelief. "Unbelievable. Is that all it is? You have nothing to fear, sweetheart. Seriously, he's shown you up so many times I've stopped counting." Keller punched me in the stomach, but I didn't stop. "He's smarter than you, he's a thousand times a better person than you. He's sure as Hell hotter than you and not to mention, he does things to me in bed that you couldn't even begin to comprehend. Seriously, he could give you fifty years' worth of lessons and you'd still never amount to anything remotely close to him." Keller punched me in the face before he grabbed my arm and twisted.

"Shut your mouth." He seethed. "Take it back." I gritted my teeth and bit my tongue. Keller wrenched my arm again and I let out a cry before I fell to the ground and took back my hateful words. Keller let me up and glared until his gaggle of heiress groupies came calling his name. He dismissed me without a second thought and hurried off with them, I was grateful.

I picked myself up off the ground and looked around cautiously. Keller was gone. I was lucky I had been here all day putting the finishing touches on decorations and left my car here, just in case something happened with Keller and I needed a getaway car. I couldn't let anyone see me like this. I fumbled in my purse for my keys, found them and raced to my car. I had learned a valuable lesson recently, if Keller was able to punish me directly for my words or actions, then he would leave my family and friends alone. I could be his punching bag if it meant everyone else was safe.

I heard Alicia call for me, but I didn't turn around. I climbed in my car, blared the radio and tore out of the parking lot without a second look. I couldn't allow anyone to see the mess I'd made of myself over Keller James.

217

Chapter 86

I lay in my bed, sobbing and feeling sorry for myself. My friends were all out having a blast at prom and the after parties. I wanted to be with Zack and Lance. I wanted to be anywhere but tied to a sadistic sociopath. I was home alone, which had me terrified. Calen was at his house with his kids, dad was at a conference somewhere and no one thought we'd be home tonight.

I heard stomping in the hallway before the wooden door slammed with a thud against the wall and bounced back a little, almost hitting Keller, who stood on the other side. His normally shining emerald green eyes were clouded with rage. As he glared back at me, his movements were slow and sloppy; he was stoned.

"Keller?" I squeaked, as I clutched my phone under my pillow and scurried to the headboard, forcing myself to sit awaiting his next move. "What are you doing here?"

"What the fuck is your problem, bitch?" He slurred angrily as he stumbled over to my bed, bracing himself on the edge. I quickly moved to the opposite side, stood up and used the full size mattress for distance.

"You shouldn't be here. I don't want you here." I stated strongly. I clutched my cell phone in my hand, ready to call for help if I needed to. Not that it would do me any good though.

"Bitch!" He lunged again, this time his angry fist met my face.

"Keller!" I screamed, more in shock than anything. I flew backwards from the force and as I looked back into his vacant eyes, knew I was in trouble. The smartest thing for me to do right now would be to placate him. "I'm sorry." I whispered quietly. "I'm sorry, Keller." I slid down the side of the wall. Keller looked back at me as if seeing me for the first time all night. He knelt down and hid a smile. "When I saw you…screwing Sage and Adrienne I got jealous. Then to hear you and the guys talking…" I was pulling out all the stops. Keller was dangerous sober, he was even more so when he was pissed off and stoned. I couldn't risk his wrath.

"It's okay, I know you get jealous easily. I don't blame you."

"I'm sorry I lost my temper at the prom. I probably ruined your whole night and…"

"You did, but I forgive you." He reached down and picked up my chin. My eyes grew wide. Keller started kissing me roughly; his hands began groping and searching.

"No, Keller." I beged, pushing him away gently. "I'm tired. I was dead asleep and you scared the holy shit out of me. I'm going back to bed."

"You'll go back to bed when I say you can."

"Just leave. If you're not going to let me sleep, just go find one of your groupies." I snapped with a shake of my head, right before Keller's hand lashed out and met my cheek. Tears stung my eyes.

"I'll be fucking you tonight." He proceeded to follow up on that threat. I couldn't fight. He was stronger. I couldn't scream, no one was here. All I could do was close my eyes and cry until he passed out.

Chapter 87

"Ladies! Let's get warmed up and get rowdy!" My tall, bubbly softball coach, Mrs. Kalzoo, announced to my teammates and me as we prepared for a game a few days later. She began our team chant while the rest of us joined in, when it was over she blared the radio with a mixed CD to pump us up even more. Her tactics always worked as we used dancing, hollering and screaming to put our nerves at ease.

Alicia and I were playing catch to get warmed up in the gorgeous afternoon sun. As we tossed the ball, we danced and goofed off to clear our minds. My blonde friend and I took part in the cadence with the rest of our team and giggled hysterically.

My back was turned to the parking lot, but I knew something was going on as Alicia's hazel eyes and gorgeous face lit up. She waved excitedly.

"Oh my God." She giggled as her blonde ponytail bounced under her red and black visor. "The guys are here."

"What?" My stomach dropped, but then I remembered Keller was in another state for a baseball tournament. I was safe. The guys were just here to watch Alicia anyway, it was harmless. I turned around slowly and tried to calm myself.

"I never thought I'd be cheering for Callatin Academy." Chopper laughed. Alicia rushed over to hug Sawyer while I stood stupidly on the field watching. I sheepishly waved at Lance as he did the same.

I took to the pitcher's mound and winked at Lance in the bleachers as I did. He had a way of calming my nerves and made me want to make sure his eyes were only on me the whole time.

I looked hot in my red and black Mustangs uniform so that just left playing amazing. And I did. I pitched perfectly. It was my third no hitter.

"Wow that was better than watching the Cubs." Sawyer complimented.

"*Anything* is better than that." I cut as Sawyer shot me a funny look.

"She's a Cardinals fan or something." Lance explained with a laugh as he reached over and hugged me. "You were amazing."

"Can we take you girls to a celebratory dinner?" Sawyer asked as he linked hands with Alicia.

"*And* that girl." Chopper laughed as Carla Smithson walked by.

"Sorry, she's got a girlfriend."

"She can come too." He started to follow her.

"Someone put a leash on him." I giggled as Lance laced his fingers through mine. I smiled up at him timidly before I looked down at the ground quickly. Lance kissed my cheek as he whispered.

"You were awesome out there." I felt my cheeks turn red as we followed his friends into the parking lot. I was on a high from the game, but also because I knew we were safe. I knew it wasn't right, knew I'd probably suffer for it later, but I was greedy. I wanted every free second with Lance I could get.

"Can we change before dinner?" I asked. "I'm drenched in sweat." Lance grinned as he grabbed me around the waist and hugged me closely. "I never thought a girl in a softball uniform would turn me on so much."

"You're a dork." I giggled as I pushed him away before everyone climbed into Sawyer's Dad's black, Ford truck and headed to get pizza. We had a blast as we entertained the entire restaurant with our antics. Lance held my hand or had his arm around me throughout most of dinner; I was on top of the world because I had my boyfriend back, if only for tonight. Not only that, Lance's friends had a way of making me feel like I'd been part of their little group all of my life.

"Can we hang out a bit after Sawyer drops you off?" I nodded and smiled.

"I can take you home." Lance grinned and squeezed my hand.

Thirty minutes later, we were sitting on the tailgate of his truck in his front yard. I loved simple moments like this.

"So, I got you something." Lance smiled sheepishly as he stood up and moved to the driver's side of the truck. He pulled out a red gift bag and then handed it to me.

"Why would you do that?"

"It's nothing really. I just...I don't know." He rambled nervously. I pulled a gray army tee shirt out of the bag and looked at him awkwardly.

"Kyler is in the Navy." I stated as I referred to my oldest brother who was currently attending the Naval Academy.

"I know, but *I'm* in the Army."

"Excuse me?"

"I thought you knew. If all goes well, I leave in two weeks with Sawyer, Chopper and Coop for boot camp. I thought Alicia told you."

"No, I didn't know. Why would I know if *you* didn't tell me? The Army, Lance? Are you fucking kidding me?"

"We enlisted at the start of the school year." He shrugged nonchalantly.

"And you're just now telling me?"

"We've been off and on so much."

"You didn't think it would be appropriate to mention on our first date, maybe? Had you not come today, had we not seen each other randomly before you leave, would you have gone without telling me?" I retorted as my voice started to break. "So I would've just been calling and texting, without a reply, only to think you ditched me again? Thanks for letting me know how important I am to you."

"You know I wouldn't have done that." He began, before he quickly remembered the way he'd ended our relationship the last two times. "Okay, so maybe you don't, but I wouldn't have Jo. I would've told you, I would've said good bye. How could you think you're not important enough to me for that?"

"Hmm." I responded sarcastically as I rolled my eyes. I shook my head and looked at him sadly. "Why Lance?"

"It's something we've talked about all of our lives. Luke and I promised dad."

"Two weeks?" I asked tearfully. "What if I don't want you to go?"

"I have to. I don't have a choice."

"I am so incredibly proud of the honorable guy you are, but I also hate you for it. I don't want you to go."

"We've got two weeks left before boot camp." He shrugged with a smile. "We could spend those days wisely." I giggled as he kissed me on the nose. Keller would still be at the tournament until Thursday. We could spend time until then and in the meantime, I would figure

220

out how to make it more.

Chapter 88

It was late when I returned to campus. The whole dorm was dark and creepy as I stumbled to my room. There was a large heap in the floor in front of my door and my stomach dropped. I gasped and Keller jumped up and lunged for me.

"I came to celebrate my highlight reel with you tonight." He hissed in a low, angry voice. "Imagine my surprise when I hear you strode off into the sunset with the redneck posse, all cuddled up with the fucking plowboy."

"They came to see Alicia play and invited me to dinner."

"I forbade you to see them."

"Keller." I sighed as I pushed past him. "You have nothing to worry about, in two weeks they're all leaving for boot camp and I probably won't see any of them ever again."

"I can arrange that."

"I'm too exhausted to fight with you. Please, just let it drop for tonight."

"The Hell I will. Do you know how many people saw you all over that loser? Do you, Jordan? I had fifteen texts and just as many phone calls of people asking when we broke up and why you were slumming again."

"Lance and I are just friends. And your little spies need to mind their own damn business." Keller's hand struck out at me from nowhere.

"NO. You are not friends and you just need to obey me and stop hanging out with that scum." I inhaled and tried to control my anger, my tears.

"I'm sorry." I repeated. "I didn't mean to upset you." His hand grabbed my wrist and yanked me towards him.

"Did you fuck him tonight?" He asked, his eyes full of hurt and anger. I shook my head. It was the truth, we'd just talked and snuggled all night, but Keller wouldn't believe or understand that, I was certain. His fingers tightened on my arm and I fought the urge to wince and pull away. "Don't lie to me."

"I'm not. Nothing happened." Keller glared at me for a minute longer before he finally nodded and let go.

"I don't like hurting you. I don't like being an asshole, but you force me to be this way."

"I'm sorry, Keller. I'm sorry...you're not..." He whipped around and his face had gone red and furious. Fuck.

"I am all you will ever need, Jordan. You're just too stupid to see that. But you will. If I have to shove it down your damned throat." He was inches away from me, the angry monster barely containing itself. I nodded numbly. I was too terrified to move, in fear of setting him off. "This is your last warning. If I catch you two together, if it's even acknowledging him or his loser friends in public; I will ruin you all. I won't stop until you and all of his friends and family are punished."

"Keller." I gasped.

"I'm done playing with you." He hissed as he stormed away. "You haven't seen my wrath yet, bitch."

Chapter 89
Lance

I'd said it a dozen or more times; but this time was the final word. I was done with Jordan Donaldson. It didn't matter how much I loved her, how badly I wanted and needed her. I was nothing to her and the sooner I took the same approach, the better off I'd be.

I had left her on her front door step three days ago with the understanding we were back together, with plans for the rest of the week and she stood me up. Not only that, she ignored my calls, texts everything. When I went to campus to see her, I was informed I was not welcome. Chopper and I had even seen her and the pretty boy out one night, but she ignored us. When Chopper went to her, she turned the other way as if he had the plague. I'm tired of the bull shit. I'm tired of the games. If she wants to be with Keller James, then I'll have to get over that. It gets under my skin something awful to lose to that pretty boy son of a bitch, but she's the one who'll be miserable for the rest of her life by that choice; not me. Okay, well maybe I will be too, but she'll never know. I would rather die than allow her to see that.

"Birthday party tomorrow night." Chopper announced with gusto. "Family, friends, lots of beer and even more mud and hot girls. Please tell me you'll be out of your funk by tomorrow."

"I'm not in a funk."

"Yes, you are." Coop chuckled.

"We all understand it. Well, your part anyway." Sawyer chimed in as he took his seat next to me in our last period history class.

"Beer, mud and women seems like the perfect recipe for a bad ass time." Drew fell into the desk directly in front of me. "Seriously, we play our cards right there will be naked mud wrestling."

"As long as it's not Chopper, I'm fine with that." I chuckled.

"I'm thinking..." Drew began with a raised eyebrow and an evil grin. "Serena, Cassie and Delia."

"Throw in Sara and Katelyn and I'd pay money." Coop rubbed his hands together.

"Get Lance to ask and about half the female population would jump in just to get a date with him."

"I'll pass that around." Coop chuckled.

"Is Jordan coming?" I asked as I felt my body tense with the thought. If she was, Chopper's idea would actually come into play, but otherwise I was praying my friends wouldn't put me on the spot. I wanted nothing to do with a female, especially at this school, for a very, very long time.

"She hasn't returned my calls or texts." Chopper shrugged.

"And Alicia won't give me a straight answer." Sawyer added. "She thinks something is up with the whole scenario, but she and Maddie aren't getting any answers."

"But she's back together with that snarky little asshole?" Coop asked in almost a growl.

"Seems to be." Sawyer sighed. "Although, no one knows why."

"Doesn't matter." I lied. "Fuck her." Each one of my friends looked at me; knowing I was lying through my teeth, but none of them called me on it.

Chapter 90
Jordan

"Keller, I don't know what the big deal is." I sighed as I scurried to chase after my furious boyfriend. Not an easy feat when you're walking in stiletto heels. "A ten minute wait is nothing."

"We had reservations, damn it. *I am Keller James* and I wait for no one."

"They were packed." I reached out for his hand. "Besides, Adrienne and Cameron aren't even here yet. You're totally flaking out on your friends."

"I'll just call Adrienne and tell her. *She'll* understand."

"I'm sure she will, she totally speaks spoiled rotten, jack ass." I grumbled under my breath. We'd been in one of Smokewater's best steak and seafood restaurants for all of ten minutes, maybe. Keller had called two days ago for the reservation supposedly, but they weren't aware of it. To make matters worse, as we were waiting Chopper's family arrived, with Mrs. Bowman and the rest of Lance's friends' parents. They greeted me warmly with hugs and fussing much to Keller's disgust. I was certain that was the exact reason he was making a complete ass of himself, but I wouldn't bring it up.

I'd done exactly as he said; I'd stayed away from the Mencino High crew. I'd been an overly attentive, adoring girlfriend. It wasn't my fault Lance's friends and family were at the restaurant and it wasn't my fault they were very affectionate towards me either. I was certain Keller wouldn't see it that way though.

"Just get in the damned car so we can get the fuck out of here." He hissed low as his fingers dug into my wrist. I nodded numbly. "I need to get drunk if I'm going to be alone with you any longer." I exhaled and tried not to be offended by his comment. It stung, but I'd only be upset if someone else had uttered those words. I was seriously developing a hatred towards my boyfriend, too bad I couldn't figure out how to get rid of him. He climbed into the low slung Lamborghini while I sauntered to my side. Once inside, Keller started digging under the seat where he pulled out his stash. "Actually, I need to be ripped to deal with you, stupid bitch." Most people would be appalled by his words, his behavior as he seriously did a line of cocaine right there in the parking lot. But I was getting used to it. I dug in my purse, checked my phone and pretended not to realize what he was doing. "You look fucking hot, but it's ruined every time you open your mouth to speak." Keller had dressed me in a gorgeous teal waterfall mini dress, it was strapless of course and unnecessarily short. It was absolutely beautiful, I looked great in it, obviously, but as with anything Keller picked out for me it was insanely expensive with very little material to cover my body. I was pretty certain if I didn't monitor it, my butt would be exposed to the world.

"Son of a bitch." He growled. "You've got to be kidding me." I glanced up at him, his hand was on the door and he was glaring at the rearview mirror. I laughed, knowing exactly what had happened.

"I told you not to park like this." I stated with a roll of my eyes. I always told him not to park like this, but he wouldn't listen. No matter where we were, Keller would pull his car long ways in a parking spot, effectively taking up three or four slots saying no one could damage his baby. "Just let it go. Seriously Keller, look this guy in front of you is moving. Let it go."

"I will not be alone with you any longer than I have to be." He spit as he threw me off him and charged out of the car. "Excuse me, ASSHOLE, but we were about to leave. What in the fuck do you think you're doing? Can't you see we're trying to leave?" I jumped out of the car as well, certain I'd have to reign him in before the cops were called and his stash was found. "Move the piece of shit."

"I think I'm parking like a normal person. You're the dumbass who parked like an idiot." Lance answered in a low voice, a smile playing on his mouth as he climbed out of a green Jeep Wrangler with a little red head in tow. As soon as his eyes met mine though, the smile vanished. I felt nauseous; Lance looked about the same.

"Well, isn't this lovely." Keller laughed drily. "Should've known you'd be the dumbass to park behind me."

"Should've known you'd be the asshole to park like an idiot." Lance retorted with a chuckle as he crossed his arms in front of his wide chest. He was spoiling for a fight.

"Great." I muttered under my breath as I exhaled loudly.

"How about you move that cheap piece of shit out of my way so my girlfriend and I can leave." Lance's eyes flared and his jaw tightened. Keller shook his head and gave a humorless chuckle. "What's the matter, plowboy? Do I need to dumb it down for you?"

"It's not my fault no one taught your preppy ass how to park." Lance coughed. "Seems to me this'd be a lesson for ya." He shrugged as he turned to grab his keys out of the Jeep.

"Jordan?" Keller asked with a mischievous smile on his mouth. "Can you speak stupid hick to lover boy here? I know you understand that language well and all, tell the fuckhead to move this piece of shit." I shot him a dirty look and ignored him as I stared back at Lance longingly. "What? Do I have to dumb it down for you too? Don't be such a bitch."

"That's enough." Lance barked, as he took a step closer to Keller. "You do not talk to her like that."

"You're forgetting she's *my* girlfriend. I'll talk to her however I damn well please." Lance lunged; Keller flinched even though Lance pulled back with a laugh.

"Lance. It's okay." I tugged at his arm. "Just let it go."

"DON'T TOUCH HIM!" Keller screamed as he grabbed my wrist and yanked me back to him.

"Keller." I gasped, only because he'd caught me off guard. Lance put himself in between Keller and me, using himself as a shield. "Lance, please don't. I'm fine."

"Why don't you try and yank me around like that."

"Just move your piece of shit." Keller threw his hands up in exasperation.

"I'm not going anywhere." Lance stated in a low, threatening tone. Keller pulled back a little and chuckled.

"We all *know that*, redneck, but none of us care about your future. I just want you to move the piece of shit that you call a vehicle so MY girlfriend and I can leave this Hellhole. We would like to be alone."

"Keller." I hissed. "Knock it off."

"It doesn't look like your girlfriend wants to be alone with you." Lance laughed with a slow, sexy smile playing on his mouth. Damn it, he was goading him. I'd be an idiot not to realize how badly Lance would like to tear into Keller. Keller lunged for Lance who just stepped to the side causing Keller to slam into the Jeep. My boyfriend whipped around and glared. I just rolled my eyes and stifled a laugh. He went for Lance again, and again, missed.

"Get in the car, Keller. You're making a fool of yourself." I rolled my eyes. "Seriously, I'm over this." Keller's anger was now redirected towards me as he grabbed me and hauled me

225

to the car.

"Don't you dare talk to me like that, bitch." He ordered quietly, the whisper belying the anger and hatred in his voice. He was clutching my wrist so hard that I was certain I'd hear the bones shattering before I felt them go. "Get the fuck in the car and..."

"Step away from her. NOW." Lance growled as he came up beside us.

"Mind your own fucking business."

"I will move you myself." Keller started cackling as he placed his lower half to mine in a suggestive pose. Lance's eyes flared, his jaw clenched tight.

"Jealous, plow boy?" Keller asked as he moved to kiss me. I stood there dumbfounded not reacting at all, not even when he started to tug my dress up.

"Stop." I begged. My boyfriend's eyes flared at me again before he squeezed my arm so tight that I cried out and felt my knees weaken with the pain.

"Get the fuck in the car." Keller warned. I stood there numbly. "Get in the car, you little bitch." He repeated. Lance was in front of him in a second, placing himself in between us.

"Apologize to her now."

"Fuck you. She is my girlfriend and I will talk to her however I damn well please."

"You need to learn a little respect." Lance spit as he took a step forward.

"See what happens when you don't listen to me, Jordan? Now you start a fucking fight. I can't take you anywhere. You're such a little drama whore." He rambled as if Lance weren't standing directly in front of him, ready to pounce. Keller's eyes went back to Lance and he stepped back. "Tell you what, Loser." He began fumbling in his pants pocket and pulled out a money clip. "I'm sure you could use some more money to help out your pathetic family." Keller began pulling hundred dollar bills out of the clip. "Consider it a donation. Take this, move your piece of shit and we'll call it even." Lance took another step towards Keller, his entire body trembling with fury.

"Stop it, Keller." I hissed behind him.

"No, no Jordan." Keller laughed. "Guys like him need a little incentive. I'm sure your little poor boy here could use a little extra cash, help ends meet at the old homestead. Buy that bastard nephew of his a toy." Keller teased in an exaggerated drawl. Lance lunged, I jumped in between them.

"You're an asshole." Keller cackled as he threw the money at Lance's face. I grabbed a hold of my first love and tried to pull him back. "He's not worth it. Just ignore him." Lance's entire body was rigid and me holding his arm was doing absolutely nothing. I wrapped my arms around his waist and hugged him tightly. "Please don't do this, Lance. Please just walk away."

"DON'T FUCKING TOUCH HIM!!" Keller roared. I didn't loosen my grip as Keller charged at me. "I told you not to go near the redneck bastard and look at you!" Had it not been for Lance, Keller would've knocked me into the ground, but instead Keller plowed into his precious car. I still had a hold of Lance, but I'd moved in front of him, hiding my face in his chest repeating my mantra. "Please just walk away, Lance. Please, he's not worth it. Just ignore him." Lance's body was still rigid, like I wasn't even touching him, but he wasn't moving at least. Keller was bellowing derogatory threats towards me. I heard a horn honk, when I looked up I saw the cavalry had arrived. All of Lance's friends were hopping out of various vehicles and headed our way. Chopper was making light of the situation of course, ignoring the fighting boys and making a beeline for me.

"Aw, Jo girl you showed up for my birthday party after all!" He gushed with a huge grin as he swept me into his arms for a hug. "I've never had a wish come true. This is unreal." I forced a smile and looked between Keller and Lance warily. Keller may have been high as a kite and furious, but he wasn't so stupid as to attack Lance with multiple witnesses and potential backup.

"Let's go, J." Keller hissed as he grabbed at my arm. I ripped it out of his grip and glared back at him. "Get in the fucking car. I can't stand being around these hillbilly fucks any more. My I.Q. is dropping drastically."

"Jordan you're hanging with us right?" Chopper asked with a grin and a raised eyebrow. "We're leaving here to go mudding'."

"Really?" I responded with a grateful smile.

"Yes ma'am and nothing would be a better present than my fave girl honoring us by hanging with the paupers."

"Jordan, get in the damn car. I'm not saying it again." Keller growled. I looked back at Chopper, who was still grinning. Lance's body was rigid, but he had turned his back on the situation and was talking to his date and Sawyer.

"Alicia will be here in about five minutes." Sawyer announced. "Her, Drew and Coop are together. Coop had to work late, that's why Audrey rode with Lance." Sawyer threw me a wink, knowing I'd already jumped to conclusions about the redhead.

"I think I'm going to hang here." I raised my chin defiantly. "Alicia can give me a ride home tonight."

"You're coming with me." He grabbed my wrist this time and yanked me to the car. I was trying to free myself, but Lance started for us just as a passerby saw us.

"Unhand the young lady." An older man ordered

"Mind your own business." Keller retorted flippantly.

"Unhand her or I'll call the police." Keller's hand fell away as he held them up in a dramatic show.

"See the trouble you cause? Just get in the fucking car or we're through."

"That's easy." I laughed as I spun on my heel. Keller grabbed for me just as Lance stepped in his way. The nice gentleman did the same and Lance took a step back with me.

"You okay?" Lance asked, his eyes glued to Keller's retreating figure.

"Yeah." I squeaked. Lance went back to stand by the Jeep with his friends, leaving me alone.

"Fuck! My purse." I exclaimed as I raced to the car. Chopper was on my heels as I pounded the window. Keller stopped and unlocked the door.

"I knew you'd be back." Keller chuckled.

"I forgot my purse." I shrugged as I opened the door, leaned in and grabbed the oversized bag out of the floorboard.

"Don't be stupid, Jordan. You don't have any money. You expect the hillbilly wonders to pay for you." He laughed. "Just get in and I'll forget you pulled this shit."

"I have my own money." I stated curtly. "You're an asshole. Earlier was completely uncalled for. I should've punched you for Lance."

"You're making a big mistake." Keller hissed through clenched teeth, the monster screaming to come out.

"No. That would've been the day I believed your line of bullshit when I woke up from the accident."

"I did you a favor."

"Hardly." I laughed as I shook my head and pulled out of the car.

"I don't think you realize we're over if you go with them. We're done. You'll be no one again."

"I considered us over a long time ago. I've just been waiting on you to catch on." I flipped my hair over my shoulder and sauntered away from Keller and straight to Chopper. I couldn't get the fall back from this right? Keller had dumped me, not the other way around. I was safe, right?

"Good riddance." Chopper hollered.

"No doubt." I giggled nervously. "Boy am I glad you showed up when you did."

"You could've handled it." He laughed. "Lance wouldn't have done anything unless Keller had hurt you." I nodded as I began to dig through my purse for my cell phone.

"Who ya calling?" Chopper asked as I found my phone and pushed Zack's speed dial number on my phone.

"Zack. So he can come and get me."

"I thought you were staying." Chopper mumbled, his voice showing he was hurt by my lie.

"It's your birthday party, with your family and friends. I know you were just being polite and bailing me out."

"Um, no actually I meant it." He took the phone out of my hand and ended the call. "Alicia was supposed to ask you. I've texted and called asking you to come. You're one of my best friends Jordan, and you *are* family. Please stay."

"I don't think Lance is too thrilled with the idea." I mumbled.

"He'll get over it. It's my birthday. Besides, between you and me he's only acting like that because you hurt him. He misses you and when he sees you he thinks it is just safer to put up walls."

"I didn't mean to. The last thing I ever wanted was to hurt him, Chopper. I swear."

"You going to explain why you did?" He asked with a raised eyebrow. I shook my head. "Is Keller threatening you?"

"Jordan!" Alicia squealed as she rushed towards me. "I didn't think you were coming! I'm so excited! I thought I'd have to deal with these guys all alone." My roommate engulfed me in a hug. "I thought you and jerk boy had plans."

"You just missed him."

"Can't say I'm sorry to hear that." She joked. "Judging by Lance's face they shared words."

"Yeah, but I think he's more pissed that I'm still here." I sighed as I looked over and saw the red head was trying to calm Lance down, her tiny fingers wrapped around his left arm. I suddenly felt out of place and extremely unwelcome. What in the Hell was I doing? I was pathetic. My ex-boyfriend was on a date and like a psycho loser I was trying to horn in on that date.

I pulled away from Alicia and started for my phone again.

"Who ya calling?" Chopper asked as he pulled my phone away again.

"Zack, I'm going to have him come get me."

"Why? You said you were going to stay for my party."

"Chopper." I sighed; I fought my tears back and shook my head. "I can't."

"Yes. You can. I invited you. You're family." I shook my head again.

"I can't. Lance is on a date. It's just not right. It's not fair."

"Date?" He asked as he looked around. His eyes fell on the sight of Lance and the girl all cozy, talking quietly. He shook his head and laughed. "That's actually Coop's girl of the week. Coop's running late so she asked Lance for a ride because it was on his way. Or so she says."

"He's not on a date?" I repeated, my voice betraying my excitement. Chopper chuckled again and shook his head. "But…I'm sure he doesn't want me here. He won't even look at me."

"And that surprises you?" Chopper snapped with a raised eyebrow. I shook my head and looked away. "But it's not Bo's birthday, it's mine and I want you here, celebrating, with us. He'll get over it."

"Chopper." I sighed again.

"You're staying. Or I will be completely offended and you will totally ruin my birthday party." Damn it, he didn't play fair. I let out a sigh and nodded my head.

"I'll stay."

"Let's get inside before the parents come out to get us." Drew interrupted loudly as Coop pulled up. The group started meandering in, but Lance held back as he went to get something out of his Jeep. I held back too.

"I'm sorry about him." I murmured softly as I came up behind him. He jumped, his whole body tensed but he didn't turn around, he just nodded. "I'm sorry about everything. I…I didn't want to…I didn't mean to."

"Save it, Jordan." He sighed. He turned around and eyed me carefully. "I didn't realize this was a costume party." I pulled back and looked at him questioningly. "Sorry, I can't be your Ken doll, Barbie." Ouch. He smiled smugly at the surprise on my face and started to walk into the restaurant.

"I'll leave if you want me to. I know this isn't fair that I just show up and crash…"

"Oh shut up." He shook his head and spun around to glare at me. "Stop trying to act all innocent. We all know what a bitch you are, okay? *Me especially*. And I also know what you're trying to do, you know damn well I don't want you here, but the second I tell you to leave you'll go in there and tell everyone I won't let you stay and then you'll get the pity party and I'll be the bad guy. You'll ruin Chop's birthday for your benefit, because you're selfish and he'll be pissed off at me all night for making you leave." My jaw dropped open as I stared in disbelief. "No. I don't want you here, but I'll get over it." He started inside. When I didn't immediately follow he doubled back and got up in my face. "Do not try to turn me into the bad guy, okay? Go inside, eat dinner with everyone, do whatever Chopper asks of you, but do NOT try to talk to me again."

"Lance." I gasped, fighting the tears back again.

"Don't say my name." He growled in an uneven voice. His eyes searched mine for a second before he turned around, took my arm and started for the restaurant. I looked away, praying he couldn't see the tears roll down my face. I never thought Lance could hurt me so bad with words, with his looks or with his cold, unfamiliar touch, but he was killing me.

Chapter 91
Lance

If she thought her crocodile tears were going to make me nicer, she was dead wrong. She'd hurt me too bad, too many times for me to ease up now. I only had a week left, maybe. I prayed every night the doctor gave the okay for me to head off to boot camp with the guys. I couldn't stay another minute in this town with Jordan. I just couldn't. It hurt too much to see her living a life without me in it. I loved her. *She* loved Keller James.

"Go clean up." I ordered flatly as I steered her towards the bathroom. "You look like shit." Jordan nodded and did as I said. I didn't like talking to her like this, in fact I started to call her back and apologize, but I couldn't. If I relented my anger for even half of a second, she would weasel into that opening and I'd get my heart broke again. I couldn't afford it.

I stood outside of the bathroom waiting for her impatiently. The last hour's events were playing through my mind; my body was still tensed with the need to pulverize that cocky bastard. I would've loved to introduce him to both my fists, but I couldn't fight him in a public parking lot. I held back. Seeing the way he treated Jordan though, it almost made me forget my limits and kill him. How could she allow that? How could she stay with him when he was so hateful, so mean to her? His eyes were crazy more than a few times; I'd seen that kind of crazy before in my daddy's face. Surely, Jordan wouldn't put up with that though. If there was one thing I knew, it was that Jordan Donaldson didn't put up with anyone's shit. She'd fight back at least. It hurt even more when I started thinking she had chosen that asshole over me. I'd been so good to her, apparently she liked being treated like shit. Hell, the way I was treating her now was probably turning her on, not turning her away.

"Is this better?" She asked icily as she strutted out of the bathroom a little taller than she'd went in. Her makeup was flawless and there was no sign of her tears.

"Much." I put my arm out telling her to go ahead. She sauntered in front of me, swaying her hips for my enjoyment, I'm sure. I took a good look at her, knowing she was in full bitch mode now, but I could see straight through her act. Not only that, I noticed blue, purple, black and green coloring on different spots on her arms, her wrists, especially her wrists. I started to say something, inquire about them, but I flushed. What if her and Keller were into the kinky stuff, maybe that's why there were bruises on her wrist, she liked bondage. Maybe that's why she chose Keller over me, I wasn't exactly adventurous when it came to sex with her. She lost her virginity to me so I've always been too nervous to try anything other than missionary with her. I didn't want her to be uncomfortable or feel awkward that she didn't know what to do. And, truth be told, I was a little too self-conscious to do much else. Not to mention, we'd never been in the most private spots when we made love and I'll be damned before I let anyone else catch a glimpse of her gorgeous, naked body. My blood began to boil as I realized someone else was seeing her body and mental images of her and Keller screwing flashed through unwontedly. I closed my eyes and took a deep breath. They were gone.

"There you are." My mom exclaimed as she rushed towards Jordan and I. "I'm so glad you stayed. We've missed you so much honey." She grinned as she engulfed the gorgeous girl in a hug. When Jordan pulled away, her smile was nothing but sincere and adoring as she talked with my mother. My stomach tightened at the sight. I knew how much Jordan loved my mom and mom definitely thought the world of Jordan. I was sad we didn't work out for that alone.

My mother truly believes Jordan and I are meant to be together; maybe in a different world where Jordan wasn't a stuck up, conceited bitch who only cared about appearance and how much money a guy would throw down on her. That's not true, I know, but saying it repeatedly is the only way to keep my sanity.

"What am I? Chopped liver?" I teased as I cut into their conversation and stole a hug from my mother.

"I see you all the time, sug." She laughed as she wrapped her arms around me. "Be good to her, Lance." She whispered in my ear. "She's hurting bad. Her eyes are so sad." I nodded my head as I flicked a glance back at Jordan, but she was off making her rounds to everyone in the room.

I looked around, searching for an open chair and realized we'd been set up. Chopper grinned at me from a corner table, surrounded by everyone else. All the chairs were full, except two. A table in the corner had two empty chairs, it was the only spot open and it was meant for Jordan and me, no doubt. They're not so subtle way of making sure we sat together; that we talked. I glared, but I pulled out her chair and seated her before I did the same. I pulled out my phone and started messing with it. I would make certain I was preoccupied enough that Jordan didn't feel the need to make conversation.

She sat down across from me timidly, not looking up as she did so. I flicked a glance her direction, but it was all the acknowledgement she'd be getting from me.

"I hope they don't think they're subtle." She sighed in a low, melodious drawl. "Seriously this is blatant manipulation."

"You'd know all about that, wouldn't you?" I grumbled. Jordan huffed as she pulled out her vibrating phone. She looked down at it, then back at Chopper before she shook her head.

"I am truly sorry about this past week, Lance. I know I led you on and..." She took a deep breath before continuing. "I really thought Keller and I were over, but..."

"He threw more money at you?" I asked rudely, still not looking up at her. "I get it. I understand. I can't give you all you need, I can't spoil you like he does. No big deal. I'll probably be leaving in a week anyway. What's the point?"

"You still don't know?" I shook my head and went back to playing a word game on my phone. Jordan sighed. "Regardless, I'm sorry. I know you don't believe that and I can't say I don't blame you, but...I'm sorry." I just nodded my head. If I looked up into her face I might see she was sincere and I'd accept her apology and that was the last thing I could do right now.

"What can I get for you two?" The waitress asked as she stood at the end of our table. She was tall, lanky, red headed and somewhat pretty. I looked up at her and flashed my best smile. She may be older than me, but it didn't mean I couldn't turn on the charm and throw my flirting in Jordan's face.

"Your phone number would be great." I drawled sweetly. She winked and laughed.

"You're cute." She giggled. I flirted relentlessly as Jordan pulled away from the table, glaring back at the scene before her.

"I just want a grilled chicken salad with light dressing." Jordan stated when Callie, our waitress, turned to take her order. "And water."

"Anything else?" She shook her head and went back to her phone.

"All you're eating is a salad?" I asked in shock. This was definitely not normal Jordan behavior. She nodded her head without looking up. "Order something else. You can't just have a salad for a meal."

"It's all I need." She sighed.

"If it's about money…"

"I have money. All I want is a salad."

"Bull shit. Since when do you order just a salad?"

"It's all I've been eating. The chemo made me gain weight and Keller…"

"Fuck Keller." I hissed. "He's not here right now. If you want to eat more than a salad then order it, damn it."

"If I wanted more to eat, I would've ordered it. I need to…"

"You do not need to lose weight. If anything, you could stand to gain some weight. Order what you want, I'm paying."

"I did." She hissed as her blue eyes pierced me angrily. "Let it go, Lance." I shook my head in disbelief. She was like a pod person, seriously. The Jordan I knew always ordered steak, potatoes, a salad and a huge dessert. She would never go for just the salad. It's like Keller James had brainwashed her. And for her to think she needed to be on a diet was insane. She was about fifty pounds lighter than she'd been when we met, now she looked sick. My ire rose the more I thought about it. I was seriously kicking myself for not pulverizing Keller James now. I placed my order and looked back at Jordan once the waitress had left.

"Is he brainwashing you now?" I asked icily. She looked up at me and rolled her eyes.

"Fuck off, Lance." She bit. "I'm not hungry. We ate earlier."

"I heard you say you didn't eat earlier. Don't lie to me." I snapped in a hushed tone. "I don't know what is going on with you, but I don't like the girl before me. You're not the same girl I met two years ago."

"That's a good thing." She went back to typing on her phone. My phone vibrated and I looked down to see a message from Chopper.

"Stop being such an ass. They broke up. She said she's done it a dozen times but it doesn't count unless he does it. He dumped her in the parking lot. He threatened her, she called him on it and walked away. They are through."

My breath caught and my stomach dropped. They were officially over now? She was single. My heartbeat sped up as I thought about the possibilities. I'd been telling myself that I didn't care about her, that I didn't still love her, that her being with Keller James was what was best for both of us, but I was kidding myself. Honestly, I would never stop loving her and I was greedy, I wanted every minute I had left as a civilian to be spent with her.

However, I wasn't sure if it was worth risking my heart for her again.

Chapter 92
Jordan

Lance slid his phone across the table. I looked up at him and his muddy brown eyes had changed to sadness.

"Is that true?"

"Yes. You're an asshole." I responded with a forced smile.

"Not that part." He growled. "Are you and Keller through?"

"That's what he said." She shrugged nonchalantly. "What does it matter though?"

"It doesn't." He pulled his phone back to him and began messing with it again. He couldn't stand to look at me for more than a few seconds and I didn't blame him at all. I'd been a cold hearted bitch to him lately. Well Keller had left me no other choice and no matter how much I wanted to explain, to tell him everything, I couldn't risk his life.

"*Give Him time. U hurt him bad. He won't trust u again easily.*" Chopper had texted me.

"*We barely have a week. Maybe I should just forget about it.*"

"*Do u luv him?*"

"*Stupid question.*"

"*Then don't forget about it. Only hurting yourself.*"

"*Trust me I know.*"

When our food finally arrived, I looked at Lance's plate in dismay. He'd curtailed his order to appease me. If he ordered steak, it was rare, today it was extremely well done. He normally ordered a baked potato with just sour cream, but today he'd gotten loaded mash potatoes without sour cream and heavy on the butter. I looked back at him, but he wouldn't make eye contact. I dug into my salad, grateful for the reprieve.

"Want some?" Lance offered me a fork full of steak. I shook my head. "I know you do." I shook my head again. "I know that salad won't fill you up." I let out a sigh and shot him a dirty look.

"If I take a bite will you shut up?" I asked rudely. He shook his head as he left the fork dangling for me. I let him feed me and then shot him a funny look. Afterwards he began cutting his food and putting parts of it on a plate.

"Lance. Stop. I'm not a child."

"You need to gain weight and I know you're hungry. I know that salad is just some stupid demand of Keller's. Fuck that. You will eat when you're around me."

"It's a good thing I'm not around you much then." I answered flippantly as I finished off my salad. I was still hungry, but I wouldn't admit that to him. I did take a few bites he offered, but I tried to snub it as much as possible. I didn't want him to think he was right. We were quiet for a few minutes and I couldn't handle the awkwardness I was causing.

"You're mom said you're the valedictorian of your class." I started with a smile. Lance nodded. "That's awesome. Congratulations. I'm so proud of you. I can't wait to hear your speech."

"No."

"What?" I gasped. "Why?"

"I turned it down. I'm not really a public speaker."

"But I can…I could help you write it."

"Writing is not the problem." Lance stated roughly.

"But it's…"

"I'm number one in a class of two hundred. I still wear the cords on my gown to appease mom." He shrugged. "Titles aren't important to me."

"As opposed to me, the Callatin girl." I snapped.

"I didn't say that." He sighed in exasperation.

"Do you want me to leave Lance?"

"It's not my call."

"I don't care. If you don't want me here, then I'll leave. I don't want you to be uncomfortable."

"As I said before, Chopper wants you here. It's not about me."

"Answer the question." I mumbled softly, but Lance ignored me as they started cutting the cake.

"So," Alicia interjected with a reassuring smile as she and Sawyer slipped into seats beside us. "Have you decided what we're doing for Maddie's bachelorette party?"

"Her sister has planned the bridal weekend." I answered with a grateful smile. "I thought we could just bar hop or maybe just go to my aunt's lake house. I don't know what she's going to feel up to doing though. She's pretty uneven from everything that happened."

"I think it would help her to forget a little. She could definitely use a break from the wedding and school stress."

"I know, she's teetering on the edge."

"All I know," Sawyer began with a toothy grin. "Is that I love her choice of bridesmaid's dresses." He slid a wink at Alicia.

"I modeled it for him since he won't be here to see me in it." Alicia rolled her eyes playfully. "Will Kyler be home?"

"He called this morning to say he was approved and would be here for sure."

"That's awesome. When does he go back?"

"The Monday after." I responded sadly. "But it'll be nice having us all together for that little bit of time."

"Hopefully I'll get to see him. I bet Zack is stoked too."

"He is. I texted him after I hung up with Ky and he called back whooping and hollering. He's already got a huge party planned."

"I can't wait." Alicia laughed. "Zack definitely knows how to throw a party."

"That he does." I laughed.

"How's Zack feeling?" Sawyer queried, his eyes flitting to Lance questionably.

"Sore, but still his cocky, butthead self." I laughed.

"Have you seen him?" Alicia asked with a raised eyebrow.

"A few times." I looked down at my plate. I usually snuck out of the dorms before class started, pretending to go for a run and would go to the hospital then. I knew Keller wouldn't question my workouts. I couldn't stay away from Zack though. Most of the time, he was sound asleep and didn't know I was there. The fewer people who knew I was visiting him, the better.

"I would have thought you'd be there every free second."

"I want to, I just…I don't want to bother him and his family."

"Maddie said his mom is trying to pull him out of Callatin. She thinks he's in more danger here than he was in New York."

"They won't let him. Keller's dad threatened to sue and make them pay back his scholarships. Zack doesn't want to leave." I fought back the tears pricking at my eyes. I'd heard this conversation. Their son was only in danger because of me and I was doing my best to be low key so he remained safe. If Zack left Callatin, I would never forgive myself or Keller.

"What does Keller's dad have to do with it?" Sawyer queried.

"He's on the board and is one of the biggest donors, whatever he says is law, no matter how ridiculous."

"Explains where his son learned it from." Alicia grumbled. I nodded and looked away again.

"We should get back over there and let you guys finish eating." Sawyer muttered as he grabbed his girlfriend's hand and tugged her away. They stopped to get pieces of cake and Lance followed. He grabbed a huge piece for me and watched like a hawk as I ate. He was treading on dangerous ground.

"Those bastards." I cursed twenty minutes later as Lance and I walked out of the restaurant. I hadn't realized everyone else had left before us, Lance had been talking to his mom while I went into the bathroom. When we got to the parking lot, only Lance's Jeep was familiar. Lance chuckled to himself and shook his head.

"Does it surprise you?" I dug through my purse and searched for my phone again. I pulled it out and looked back at Lance.

"I'll just call Zack to come get me." I sighed. "There's no need to make this anymore awkward and torturous than it already has been."

No, if you want to go home, I'll drive you, but I won't ever hear the end of it if you flake out on the best part of Chopper's birthday party."

"Lance." I sighed. "I would love to go to Chop's party, but this is too much. I know you don't want me here, especially don't want to have to cart me around and they're forcing the issue. Zack can just grab my car and be here in fifteen minutes."

"Then you call and tell Chopper I had nothing to do with your decision."

"You have everything to do with my decision, Lance. I won't lie to him."

"You don't have a problem lying to me."

"That's not fair. I…"

"Just stop. If you want to go home, I'll take you to Callatin. If you want to go to the party, I'll take you there." Lance started to the Jeep without me, his posture rigid.

"I'm not exactly dressed to go mudding." I pouted as I scurried after him.

"It looks like Alicia left you something on the front seat." He nodded towards a duffel bag. "Any other excuses?"

"Stop it!" I exclaimed as I grabbed his arm and forced him to turn around and look at me. His eyes were wide, waiting for me to finish my tantrum. "Stop being indifferent about this shitty situation. Please. I don't like this either. I'd rather die than hurt you any more than I already have." He started to retort, but I held my hand up. "I'm asking you right now, it doesn't matter what anyone else wants, just you okay? Do you want me to go to Chopper's party or not?" Lance shook his head before he closed his eyes and exhaled loudly.

"Of course I want you to go, Jordan." He admitted softly. "But I shouldn't." He ran his work-roughened hands over his tanned face. "You are entirely too important to me and my friends for you not to go. It just hurts too bad to be around you, because I want you, but I can't have you."

235

"You *can* have me, Lance. You already do." Lance shook his head again.

"Don't do this, okay? This night will go a lot smoother if you don't pull that shit." I nodded my head and started to the passenger side of the Jeep, Lance followed.

"I thought you got a truck." I murmured, desperately looking for any way to change the subject. Lance's old truck had been completely totaled in our accident.

"I did. This is Luke's mudding Jeep." I looked up at him quickly trying to gauge his feelings on that, but he wouldn't look me in the eye. "I don't like taking it out. I don't like for anyone else to ride in it but me and the guys…"

"Then I'll call Zack." I sighed as I stopped abruptly.

"I didn't mean…" He looked directly into my eyes. "I was pissed off Audrey rode with me. She maneuvered her way in and that wasn't cool. I didn't mean you. You're probably the only girl, that's not family, that I don't mind riding in it."

"Lance, it won't hurt my feelings…"

"I know." He responded with a sad smile. His hand started towards my face, but he quickly pulled it back. "I want you to go. " I smiled and turned back around to open the door of the car, but Lance was already there opening it for me. I mumbled a thanks and Lance nodded as he grabbed a towel out of the back and placed it on the seat. "Don't want to ruin your clothes." He shrugged.

"They're just clothes." I whispered quietly as he helped me inside. I squeezed his hand and fought the urge to lean in and kiss him, no matter how badly I wanted to.

Lance crossed in front of the Jeep and climbed in on the driver's side. I dug through Alicia's bag searching for something to throw on. I really hoped there was a pair of shoes, but no such luck.

I hate these shoes." I whined as I bent down to pull them off. Lance was quiet and when I looked up, I realized it was because he was watching me, his hand hovering on the ignition.

"Um," He stammered as he leaned back and began fumbling behind his seat. "Here's a shirt, if you want it." He handed me a black tee shirt with Jason Aldean's picture emblazoned on the front. "I went to the concert the other day and I won it." He looked down at the ignition for a second.

"I knew he was playing." I had begged Keller to take me for months, but he wouldn't. He's not a big country music fan to begin with, but he was certain it was social suicide to be caught dead at a concert.

"Yeah, well you *could* have gone." He spit evenly, trying to hide the anger in his tone. "I bought you a ticket, but seeing as how…"

"You bought a ticket for me?" I gasped. He nodded.

"He's one of your favorites. As soon as I found out he was coming to St. Louis I got tickets. It was a surprise, but…"

"I fucked it up." I slipped the tee shirt over my head. It smelled of Lance and for that reason alone, I would hang on to it for the rest of my life. "I wish…"

"No big deal. There'll be other concerts and I'm sure you did something more exciting anyway." I hadn't, but I nodded my head. Keller had been MIA that night for four hours so I'd been at home listening to the radio and doing homework.

"The cooler has Jack and Coke already mixed up." He opened it and pulled a Styrofoam cup out. "Plus beer. You want one?" He handed me a cup. I nodded my thanks and looked back at the cooler as he grabbed a cup out for himself. There were at least eight Styrofoam cups made up.

236

"Did you make those up for someone else?" I asked awkwardly. "You're not meeting…"

"No. They're all for me." He shrugged nonchalantly. "Would it matter if I was meeting someone?"

"Of course it would." I breathed. Lance started the Jeep and put his hand down on the gearshift before looking back at me sadly. "Lance." I covered his hand with mine before I leaned towards him and caught him in a kiss. "I love you." I whispered against his mouth. He stared back at me for only a second before he put the car in reverse and pulled out of the parking lot.

Chapter 92
Lance

It would be so easy to steer off to a side road and tug Jordan across the console and into my lap. I was having an incredibly hard time focusing on anything but the thoughts that kiss dredged up. My groin was on fire with need, the desire to feel her in my arms, to be inside of her, but I knew it wouldn't end well. It couldn't. It hadn't so many times in the past and I'd be a moron to fall back into the patterns. Of course, I'm a blessed idiot for *not* saying a word after an amazing kiss like that one.

Here I was sitting next to an incredibly hot girl who was barely dressed and definitely willing to sleep with me tonight and I couldn't do it. I wanted to. I wanted to so bad, but I couldn't.

"There's a plastic bag here if you want to put your stuff in it, so they don't get ruined." She nodded her head and took it out of my hand. She bagged up her stuff, slid it under the seat without saying a word. She leaned over and flipped on the radio, turned up the volume when she realized it was a Tyler Farr song playing. She sang along as though I wasn't even there. I was mesmerized. I always was when she got lost in the music, she was utterly breathtaking.

I turned down the road that led us to the empty creek bed and fields we'd be playing in tonight. The sound of her voice, the empty road and the memories I was lost in began to take hold of me and I finally pulled the car down a field road. Jordan looked back at me. I put the Jeep in park and turned to look into her ocean blue eyes. If I focused on just that, I could probably forget everything else. Her eyes spoke volumes to me, always pulled me in to her heart.

I leaned over and dragged her to me, capturing her mouth with mine in a second. I touched her face with one hand as I let my tongue play with hers. The kiss betrayed everything I needed, wanted from her. I could tell myself I just wanted to ease the fire in my crotch, be done with it, but I needed her far more than just for sex. I feared I always would.

"It's just sex. NO attachments." I grumbled as I let my mouth trail down her neck. She nodded eagerly as she took control and climbed into my lap.

"I don't think that's possible, Bowman." She mumbled softly as she straddled my lap. "But I'm willing to try. If that's all I can have of you, it's what I'll take." She was willing and eager as she took control, for the first time and she'd never been more beautiful. I couldn't stop kissing her, a sure sign this went a lot farther than sex.

When we'd both finished she lay nestled in my arms panting into my chest. I kissed the top of her sweaty head and let my hands caress her long, smooth legs. I could feel the urges firing up again as could she, I heard her giggle before she reached up to kiss me sweetly.

"I'm greedy, Lance." She breathed huskily into my ear. "I want more. Can I have more?" Her tongue ran along my earlobe, then down my neck as she nibbled a few times. She was an expert, she knew which buttons to push, within two minutes she was climbing in the back, and I was following like a fool.

"It's about damn time." Coop bellowed as he hurried over to the Jeep when we finally arrived at Chopper's birthday party. "We're riding with you." His date, Audrey, was in tow. She was grinning at me, but glaring at Jordan when she thought I wasn't looking.

238

"We're not starting yet are we?" Jordan asked sadly. "I'll ride with Chopper." Her eyes flicked to mine.

"There's enough room for all four of us." Jordan smiled back at me. Chopper was hollering and motioning us to where he was standing with the rest of our normal crew.

"What are you drinking, Bo?" Audrey asked giddily as she moved a little too close to me. She grabbed the cup out of my hand and started to take a drink.

"Don't take a man's alcohol, woman." Coop snagged the cup before her mouth touched it. Audrey shot my friend a dirty look before she sauntered over to the Jeep and the red igloo cooler in the back.

"Then I want one for myself. I hate beer."

"Whoa!" I hollered. "Back off the cooler. Those are mine. "

"It's Jack and Coke; it's a man's drink." Coop chuckled.

"She's drinking one."

"Jordan can handle her liquor." Coop retorted with a roll of his eyes and a laugh.

Audrey huffed and shot Jordan a dirty look before she turned on her heel and started back towards the party.

"You need another one, Jo?" I asked loudly for Audrey's benefit. The girl had been throwing herself at me all day and I wanted to make certain she knew I wasn't interested. She was here with my best friend.

"Please." She smiled. I grabbed a cup out of the back and handed it to Jordan who was still sitting in the front.

"Wanna go see Chop?"

"You can go ahead." She shook her head. I looked at her questioningly before I realized the only shoes she had were heels. I smiled and walked to her side of the truck. I opened the door and turned around.

"Hop on."

"What?"

"Hop on; I'll give you a piggy back ride."

"Lance."

"You don't really want to walk barefoot through all these rocks and God knows what else, do you?" She shook her head and grinned.

"But um, my dress is pretty short and…"

"The tee shirt is pretty long, darlin'." I laughed. "Unfortunately, it covers your assets."

"Unfortunately?" She raised an eyebrow. She climbed onto my back and I carried her over to Chopper and set her down on the ground gingerly. For the next thirty minutes, we just hung out with my friends and I completely forgot Jordan and I weren't together anymore. No matter how many times I chided myself for it, I couldn't help it. I kept my distance though; I didn't touch her constantly no matter how badly I wanted to. It still felt natural, felt right we were there together.

When we finally all climbed into our vehicles and started throwing mud and having a blast, I'd forgotten everything. The girl before me was the one I'd fallen in love with. She was squealing and laughing, pointing out the best mud pits. She loved every minute of it and I was pretty sure I was falling more in love with her by the second.

Audrey leaned forward to talk to me every chance she got, begged me to let her drive more than one time and I kept saying no or just ignoring her. When we finally got stuck late into the night Coop and I hopped out, Jordan took the steering wheel and we tried to maneuver out

239

before anyone realized what happened and came to attack.

"Things are good I see." Coop commented with a knowing smile.

"We're stuck."

"I meant between you and Jo." He rolled his eyes. "Don't think I haven't noticed the looks you've been giving her."

"Does it matter? If she doesn't ditch me first, then I will when we leave for boot camp in a week."

"It doesn't have to be like that. It's not what either of you want."

"I don't know what she wants Coop. I only know what I want."

"Then maybe you should find out what she wants, because seriously man, the puppy dog faces are getting old." I rolled my eyes and punched Coop in the arm.

I looked up in the driver's seat where Jordan grinned back at me and threw a playful wink. I couldn't help grin back. She was gorgeous, even covered in mud. I had it bad for that girl and only time would tell if I was the fool.

Chapter 93
Jordan

"Let me give you a friendly warning sweetheart," I started sweetly in a whisper to Audrey as I had half my attention on her, the other half on Lance's directions from the rear of the Jeep. "You will stop throwing yourself at Lance right now or I…"

"You have no claim on Bo." She laughed as she leaned forward. "*You* have a boyfriend."

"So do you." I smiled. "You are with Coop, not Bo. Lance won't touch you because of that and if you're thinking of dumping Coop, well you should know Lance won't give you a second look if Coop says to stay away. And I can *guarantee* he will. Now, if you continue to hit on Lance or you hurt Coop in any way, you'll answer to me."

"What are you going to do, buy someone to beat me up?" She cackled.

"No, honey. I'll take care of you myself. If you don't believe me ask Kelcie or Remy." Her eyes grew wide just as we got unstuck.

"You want to stay in the driver's seat?" Lance asked as he started towards the passenger side.

"Are you serious?" I practically squealed. Lance laughed and nodded his head.

"You can drive darlin', I know you're dying to."

"I hope you plan on getting muddier kids." I smiled with a sly glance. "Momma don't mess around." Once everyone was buckled, I took off like a shot and covered everyone in the Jeep and anyone nearby in mud. Audrey didn't believe my warning though, every time she leaned forward to talk to Lance I'd slam the gas down and throw her back or make sure I maneuvered the Jeep just enough to drench her. There were many times she ate mud. After the third time Lance would just look at me, laugh and shake his head in disbelief.

This girl is something else." Coop chuckled as he started climbing out of the Jeep an hour later. "Damn Jordan, I don't think there's a clean spot on the Jeep *or us*." I just grinned back at Coop. He laughed again. "Definitely a keeper Bo, but I think I've mentioned that a time or two."

Neither Lance nor I responded to his words and Coop just shook his head. He and Audrey hurried towards the group that had already formed around Chopper. Lance and I were slow to follow.

"What were you and Audrey talking about?" Lance asked nonchalantly as we started for our friends.

"You. I told her to back off or I'd make her myself."

"Why would you do that? Are you going to threaten every girl who shows interest in me?" He asked incredulously, with a hint of anger in his voice.

"First off, she's supposed to be on a date with Coop and she's throwing herself at you. That's not cool. I don't want Coop to get hurt. Second of all, yes. Until you're mine again, I'll stalk you." Lance laughed and shook his head at the last part, knowing I was joking. Well, maybe a little I was.

"I might just play hard to get so I can see that." Lance teased.

"Whaddaya say about a dip in the lake?" Chopper interrupted as he made his way towards us.

"I say it sounds like Heaven." I giggled. "I think I have mud in some very hard to reach places."

"I'm sure Bo will help you get nice and clean." Chopper grinned with a jab in the ribs to Lance.

"Aw, I was hoping you would." I flirted.

"Let me in on that." Drew interjected as he rushed towards us.

"Sorry birthday boy special." I teased as Drew put his arm around my shoulders and pulled me into him.

"So I have to wait for two whole months?" Drew asked in almost a whine. I nodded my head and laughed as I moved away from him and towards Lance.

"Give it up, Drew." I heard Chopper warn as I looked up at Lance. He smiled at me as he nodded towards the Jeep; I followed like a puppy dog. In no time, we were part of a convoy headed towards the public lake. It was closed at this hour, of course, but we'd done this sort of thing often. We'd be in loads of trouble if we ever got caught, but we would cross that bridge if we ever got there. It helped that Cooper's big brother was on the police force and worked third shift, it kind of meant we were invincible.

"Will you take a picture with me?" I asked Lance sheepishly once we pulled up to the secluded spot. He nodded reluctantly, but didn't say a word. I first snapped a picture of him, then held the camera out as I snuggled up to him and took another photo.

"Oh, wow." I gasped as I looked at the picture. "I look worse than I thought. I'm a drowned rat."

"No, you're beautiful." Lance murmured softly as he turned my face up to his. "You're always beautiful." His eyes implored mine; I was lost.

"Kiss me, Lance." I begged in a husky voice. He made no move, just continued to stare at me for another minute.

"I can't." He pulled away and put his hand on the door handle.

"You can. I want you to." I whined. "I'm single. Remember?"

"I've been down this road before." He got out of the Jeep.

"What about earlier? You can't..." I started as my voice began to break. I fought back the tears, took a deep breath as he walked away, ignoring me. When I climbed out of the car, you'd never know I'd been upset five seconds prior. I busied myself taking pictures of everyone, knowing it could be the last time we were all together for a long time to come. The boys were all graduating soon and heading off to boot camp, Drew to college.

"I don't think this dress was meant for lake water." I giggled as I emerged from the water, the dress looking like it might fall apart at any second, and it definitely didn't leave much to the imagination.

"It was meant for you definitely." Drew breathed, his tongue hanging out of his mouth as he blatantly stared at my breasts. Chopper hit him in the arm, but Drew didn't budge.
"As if you're not staring." Lance walked in front of me with a towel.

"Cover yourself." He growled as he wrapped the towel around me forcefully. My eyes were wide with hurt at his gruff tone. He grabbed my hand and tugged me towards the Jeep.

"Are we leaving?" I asked bewildered. Lance didn't answer, but everyone else started heading to their cars as well. Lance grabbed Alicia's bag out of the back and shoved it at me before he climbed into the driver's side.

"Change clothes. Now." He hissed as he turned his back.

"Did I do something wrong?"

"You can see EVERYTHING in that dress, Jordan." He spit as he fought with himself not to look down and check out the merchandise.

"And that bothers you?"

"It does when all my friends can see what I should…"

"No one was looking."

"Drew was."

"Drew doesn't count." I laughed dismissively as I started to pull the dress over my head.

"Jordan."

"What Lance?" I sighed in exasperation. "You've seen me naked a hundred times and it has never bothered you before." I was completely exposed and he just stared as if I were killing someone in front of him. I pulled the Jason Aldean shirt on over my naked chest and then stood up and pulled my wet panties off, before pulling a pair of Alicia's boy shorts on. Lance watched the entire time, his hands on his hips. "Is this better?" I hurried to the Jeep and plopped into the passenger seat.

"No. Damn it Jordan, now I know you're not wearing anything under your clothes." He growled in a husky voice, his breathing uneven as he turned around and walked away from the Jeep. He started towards the lake again. I cursed as I climbed out and hurried after him.

"What in the Hell is wrong with you?" I asked irately as I grabbed his arm and turned him towards me.

"I can't do this, Jo." He admitted sadly, as he turned back around and stared out at the sky. "I thought we could hang out all day, as if we were friends, as if I didn't have feelings for you. But I can't. I just can't fucking do it."

"Then don't." I reached out and touched his arm softly. "Please don't. I'm miserable knowing you're five feet away from me at all times and I can't touch you."

"Why do you have to play these games?" He exploded.

"Games." I repeated flatly.

"Games." He spun around and looked at me. His eyes were so full of hurt and rejection that I couldn't hold back anymore, I rushed to him and wrapped my arms around his waist.

"I'm not playing games, Lance." I looked up into his face, he was looking down at me and I could see the fight he was having with himself. I hoped his heart won out as I reached up and kissed him. He didn't push me away, instead he pulled me closer and kissed me hungrily. He picked me up and continued kissing me as though he were terrified I'd run away if he put me down.

Headlights panned across us and brought us back to reality. The SUV kept driving, but it had killed the mood. Lance put me down gently before he hurried off to the Jeep.

"We better go before they think we ran off and got married or some stupid shit." He started for my side, thought better and just hurried to the driver's seat, leaving me to open my own door. It was his way of proving a point, apparently, since he was normally quick to open all doors for me.

I tried to talk to Lance, but he was a rock. He turned up the radio and dismissed me. Once we arrived at Alicia and Drew's house, he hurried inside. It didn't matter though, his friends made certain we were always thrown together, always within two feet of each other. Everyone was out on the back deck enjoying the night air, laughing and talking. I went inside to the bathroom and when I came out Chopper was waiting for me in the kitchen.

"Did you and Lance talk?"

"Lots of talking." I answered drily as I pulled a beer out of the cooler.

"And?"

243

"And he's over me. He just wants sex."

"That boy will never be over you, love." Chopper bellowed with laughter. "He will love you until the day he dies."

"You're wrong, Chopper. I've practically thrown myself at him and he's blown me off every time. Except for the quickie on the way to the creek."

"Just don't give up, okay?" He asked with a tilt of his head. He reached out and grabbed my hand in his and squeezed. "I leave in a week and I need to make sure you two are good."

"One week." I sighed sadly. "It just doesn't seem right. Lance hasn't heard anything yet, I take it."

"Not that he's said." He pulled me in for an encouraging hug. The boys had all enlisted in the Army at the beginning of the school year with delayed entry. After our car accident, Lance was put on a medical hold. According to Chopper and Alicia he'd gone to all their doctors and taken all their tests and passed; now he was just waiting for Uncle Sam's okay on whether or not he would still be able to join. "And don't worry; he won't leave without saying goodbye to you."

"I don't think you're right about that." I leaned into him while we walked back out of the house. "You look good, by the way. You've always looked good, but you can tell you've been busting your ass. How much weight have you lost?"

"Fifty pounds?"

"What? You didn't have that much to lose, did you?"

"I'm barely under the max weight. They're going to have a field day with me."

"You'll be fine. I would never have guessed you had that much weight to lose." Chopper shrugged nonchalantly as he slid his arm across my shoulders.

"I think you're one of the first people to notice my weight loss."

"People don't like to talk about anyone but themselves." I joked, he chuckled and nodded. I was upset none of his family and friends had commented on it though. They should have been his biggest support system. Chopper was one of my best friends so I stuck close to him, so I could fight the urge to be glued to Lance's side. Before long though, Chopper, Lance and me were the only ones left standing.

"Isn't this cozy?" Chopper asked with a wide grin on his face. "Now you two can talk."

"Stop, Chopper," I pleaded, trying to hide the thickness of my voice. "He doesn't…"

"She's the same girl she was before Lance. She remembers everything. And she and Keller are over for good this time." Lance's eyes flitted to mine. I shifted uncomfortably under both boys' scrutiny.

"I did notice." Lance mumbled. "But just give it a rest, Chop."

"No, I won't. You two will talk or I'll go in and lock you out of the house."

"I'll just go home." Lance rolled his eyes as he started to get out of the chair he'd been sitting in.

"You need keys for that."

"I'll just beat the Hell out of your roly poly ass for them."

"Bring it big boy." Chopper laughed.

"It doesn't matter." I interjected quietly. "I told you earlier, he doesn't care. Why do you insist on making things more awkward?"

"Because you're wrong. You two are my best friends, Jo," Chopper came towards me and took my hands in his. "And I just want you to be happy, but right now you both are miserable without each other. You both still care about each other, no matter what either of you

244

say right now." Lance and I sat quietly averting each other's eyes. Chopper released a loud breath and shook his head in disgust. "How many times today did you forget you weren't together anymore? It was as if nothing ever changed between ya. It's impossible for you to not be together and not be Lance and Jordan. You're meant to be together."

"We're seventeen." I interjected.

"Who fucking cares?" He spit. "It's obvious to everyone but y'all. You can't be around each other without…"

"Then we won't be around each other." Lance snapped.

"Shut up." Chopper groaned in exasperation as he leaned back and pierced us both with angry eyes. "You're single. She's single. Stop being an idiot. Just risk it."

"I love you, Lance." I didn't need to look to know Chopper was giving Lance an I told you so look. "And I miss you. I am miserable without you." Lance was quiet. Chopper stood up, squeezed my shoulder and went inside.

"I miss you too." Lance mumbled. "But it doesn't matter."

"It does to me." I argued as I looked up at him through watery eyes. "I'm sorry about everything. I really didn't know and then when I did it was too late. I'd done messed everything up."

"You didn't…"

"I did." I sighed. "That first night we were together again, I was clueless but something kept pulling me to you. And you were so sweet and I liked the attention; the way you looked at me. I thought I'd never been looked at like that before. I was a bitch to you Lance, and it backfired on me because the first time you kissed me I started remembering. When we made love, more came back. Then, after that, I was using you, well not totally, I just wanted to remember my life before the accident. I love having you around, love how you take care of me, but all those times we hooked up, I had no intention of leaving Keller because…because I thought I could do better than you."

"You can."

"Lance." I groaned. "Keller's Jordan could because that's what he brainwashed me to believe." I moved closer towards him slowly. "But she was delusional. Being with Keller means I have to play a part, I can't be the real me without consequences. Even though I know you are who I want. I will never find anyone like you. I'll never feel like this about anyone else. But I hurt you and I was horrible for using you and I apologize for all I've done to you."

Chapter 94
Lance

Jordan was mere inches away from me now. Her hand reaching out to touch my knee. Her voice sounded so sincere, so sweet that I reached out and covered her hand on instinct.

"I missed you." I repeated. "And I'm sorry for all the crap I pulled that even allowed Keller to trick you."

"You had no way…" I put my hand up to her mouth.

"You know what I mean." She nodded her head and leaned into my hand before she straddled my lap in the chaise lounge I was sitting in. "God you feel so good."

"I can feel better." She smiled coyly as she leaned down to kiss me hungrily. "You. Make. Me. Feel. So. Good. You always know where to touch me."

"I can't." I stammered. Any protest was gone as she rocked against my erection. I was done. I couldn't say no to her, just like before, I was weak when it came to Jordan Donaldson. It wasn't long before we made love on my cousin's back porch. I didn't care if anyone came out to find us, I just wanted to be in her. I couldn't see sex with anyone else being this phenomenal; couldn't imagine needing anyone else like this. So no matter how badly I knew it would hurt when she left me in the morning, or when I left next week, I discarded those thoughts and focused solely on Jordan and the amazing things her body could do to me.

Chapter 95
Keller

I was so sick of having to chase my damn girlfriend down every night. I was disgusted by the scene that played out today, she humiliated me but she's damn lucky none of our friends were there. Had she pulled that in front of anyone but the townies, I would punish her for a long time to come. As it is now, I'll let her slide with a warning.

Tresden, Ted, Cole and Tanner were all waiting in the car for me. We were headed out to meet up with the rest of our group, but I was going to coral my girlfriend first. It looked bad if she wasn't at my side some times. People might get the wrong idea about us. I told them she'd gone over to her roommate's to stay the night, but had called begging me to come get her; she missed me of course.

When we pulled up to Alicia's house I wasn't surprised to see the driveway full of crap, mud covered vehicles. I was enraged to see Lance Bowman's vehicle there though. The front door was locked and no one answered when I knocked so I started towards the back of the house.

I heard Jordan's voice and when I turned the corner, I felt like I'd been hit with a semi-truck. My girlfriend was completely naked, her breasts covered by the plowboy's nasty hands, his dirty mouth was all over hers. She was riding him, with no shame, no hesitation like she does with me. The girl I was in love with was screwing that worthless SOB and I wanted to puke. I stood there staring in disgust, watching as the porn played out in front of me.

"God, you're amazing." She panted. "I love you." I was too enraged to hear Lance's reply. I spun on my heel to head back to the car; no way was I touching that bitch now. Tresden stood behind me silently gawking at the scene. There was no chance of me leaving quietly now, not when I'd been humiliated and there was a witness. I took a deep breath and turned back around.

"Bravo." I jeered sarcastically as I began clapping my hands. "You deserve an Oscar for that one, hon." I made my way slowly towards the two of them. At the sound of my voice, Lance had immediately flipped Jordan under him, protecting her from view. "But you have it all wrong."

"What do you want Keller?" Jordan demanded drily as she fought out of Lance's grip. She had no issues with her naked body as she stood up and started to redress herself.

"The deal was to exact revenge on the loser, not fuck him." I fumed aghast. She narrowed her eyes and shook her head. "That's the only reason I agreed to this; you swore it was just revenge. You've gone too far."

"Keller, get lost." She snapped icily as she stepped into a pair of shorts. Lance's entire body was rigid as he glared between Jordan and me. "Seriously, you're being ridiculous."

"No, *you* are. This is unacceptable, Jordan. How am I supposed to forget that you let the plowboy put his disgusting dick inside of you?"

"We're over, Keller. You ended it, remember?"

"That was all part of the plan. You weren't supposed to go off and fuck him." I exclaimed in disbelief. "I thought feigning amnesia was enough punishment, but you won't let it die." Jordan's mouth dropped open as Lance's head swung to gawk at her. "The plan was for you to get back at him for dumping you like he did. I was all for it because he needs to learn not to fuck with a Callatin girl, but we never talked about you sleeping with the piece of shit."

"Keller, I don't know what you're doing, but you need to stop." She warned in an icy, slow southern drawl.

"This is over. I won't allow you to exact revenge on the hick anymore, not if you can't keep your legs closed. Look at this," I pointed back to Tanner and Tresden who were now both watching with amusement. "Do you have any idea the image you're portraying to these guys? Everyone at school is going to know you're a whore like your mom was."

"You bastard!" Jordan screamed as she tore off the deck and ran for me. "You worthless piece of shit! You fuck anything that walks and have the nerve to call me a whore because I'm sleeping with Lance, when I love him?"

"Love?" I cackled. "Oh Jesus Christ, Jordan, give it up! How in the Hell can you think anyone would even come close to believing this crap? You're a Callatin girl, the best of the best, and he's at the *very* bottom of the gene pool."

"Why are you here? You said I couldn't dump you, no matter how hard I tried, but YOU DUMPED ME, with an audience. We are over. Why in the Hell are you still harassing me?"

"What are you talking about?" I laughed. "Like you'd ever dump me. Seriously, how many times a day do you call or text begging for some alone time with me?" Jordan's eyes were narrowed, her fists clenched tightly at her side.

"Leave Keller. I'm done with your shit."

"Enough with the theatrics. Let's go." I thundered as I took her balled up hand and tugged her towards Tresden.

"Fuck you."

"I'm not touching you after you screwed that lowlife." I hissed as I spun on her. "You'll be lucky if anyone touches you with a ten foot pole after this shit gets out. You were damaged goods before, now you're just trash." Lance was behind her; looking as though he were ready to kill me, but unsure if I was telling the truth about Jordan's motives. I started laughing.

"You're pathetic, plowboy. You can't honestly believe a girl like Jordan would ever want anything to do with you, do you? You're pond scum. You'll be a nothing for the rest of your life."

"Leave Keller." Jordan snapped as she took a step closer to me. "You're done. You can spout all the lies you want, even if Lance believes you, it won't change the truth." My eyes flitted to hers as she smiled wickedly. "The plow boy is a thousand times better than you in every aspect. I LOVE him. I despise you."

"Knock it off, it's not funny anymore."

"It was never *funny*, Keller. You tricked me and you manipulated me so I wouldn't leave. It's over. I'm done with you."

"You will *never* be done with me." I hissed as I got up in her face. "I own you, remember?"

"You fucked with the wrong girl this time." She spit in almost a whisper. "It's over." I laughed and shook my head as I pulled her into me. When she pushed away, I grew aggravated and yanked her around the corner.

"Let go of me." She demanded as she tried to pull free. "Let go of me now, Keller. We're over." When I continued yanking her behind me, she grew pissed and started screaming obscenities.

"Let her go, James." Tresden insisted as he tried to pull Jordan away from me. "She doesn't want to go."

248

"Stay out of this, Tres." I warned.

"What in the Hell is wrong with you, Keller?" She screamed, feeling a little stronger with Tres in between us. "How in the Hell could you sit there and lie like that? How could you tell Lance I was just trying to get back at him?"

"It's the truth." I laughed. "Why are you acting so innocent? Everyone would've figured it out sooner or later. Hell, I already told these guys because it's the only way you could survive Callatin. If everyone thought you were for real about that plowboy and his loser friends, you'd be fish food."

"Stop lying. So help me God, if he believes you…"

"Oh, he does." I replied with a smug smile. "Why do you think he let me manhandle you? The good ole boy wouldn't have let that slide any other time, but now he knows what a psycho, vengeful bitch you are." I barely felt her hand making contact with my face. My eyes grew hooded as I glared back at her. "And now everyone else knows you're a whore too. You're so finished, Jordan and I'm the only one who can save you now."

"The. Hell. You. Are." She growled.

"Tell you what, fuck me like you just did the plowboy and maybe then I'll take you back. Hell, Tres and Cole will even go get him, so he can watch what it's like when you're really getting off."

"He sees me *really* getting off all the time, you're the one who has only seen me fake it." I smacked her across the face, just as I grabbed her hair and yanked her back.

"Keller!" Tres snapped as he attempted to intervene. I shoved him back before I got up in her face again.

"I can be your fantasy or your worst nightmare. Which is it going to be?"

"*Fuck you.*"

"Very well. I will go after you, the plowboy, all his little friends and both of your families. By now, you should take my threats seriously. How's Zack healing?"

"This is between you and me."

"Nope." I argued with a low chuckle. "If you won't listen to reason, then I have to make you *see* reason, babe. I don't fight fair when I want something bad enough. You are mine. You will always be mine." She shook her head. I tugged on her arm again. I was sick of this crap and I was quickly losing my high. I needed more pills, needed more liquor to deal with her drama. "Let's go."

"Fuck. Off." She snapped as she planted her feet in the ground. When I tried again she put up a fight, got a little louder. I could see the plowboy's shadow from the back porch's security lights. I smiled back at her wickedly.

"Keller, let her go." Tres repeated. I spun around and glared at him.

"I don't mess in your business, you don't mess in mine."

"It's okay, Tres, I'm not worth it. Ask Brennan what happens when you interfere in Keller's life." Jordan stated evenly as she watched my reaction. Tresden's eyes flew to hers before he looked back at me questioningly. I rolled my eyes and looked back at her.

"Jordan, you can cut the act, okay? Lance is long gone. It's better this ends now, you're becoming obsessive. Paying off those kids for the accident, faking the amnesia and whatever else you've dreamt up for your soap opera is way *too* far. The kid looked like he'd been whooped, like you'd destroyed him. Isn't that what you wanted?"

"What?" She gasped as she started to back away. "Tell me you didn't. Tell me you didn't pay off those kids…tell me you didn't set that up." She was in panic mode now, shaking her head and looking around frantically. "You sick son of a bitch."

"Stop acting innocent. It was all your idea." I looked back at Tres and Cole who were panicked as well. "It was her idea."

"Keller." She started in a hoarse whisper as tears rolled down her face. "You almost killed Lance and me. You killed those kids. You...I...You killed Cissy and..."

"Shut the fuck up you self-righteous bitch." I bit. "Everything I've ever done has been to appease you. Whatever your whim, I granted." Jordan was shaking her head repeatedly. I grabbed her arm and propelled her towards the car where the rest of our group awaited us. Jordan darted away from me quickly and sprinted towards the back yard. I took off after her, leaving our friends to watch in disbelief.

I was really getting sick of her theatrical side. In fact, when we were alone again I'd make certain she never pulled this crap again.

Chapter 96
Lance

I needed to walk. Needed to clear my head. Needed to punch the fuck out of something, but trees were all there was and I didn't feel like breaking my hand with my stupidity.

If Keller's taunts were true, than I was a bigger fool then I'd ever given myself credit for. I couldn't believe him though. I couldn't picture Jordan; my first love, the girl I'd taken virginity from, the girl who'd bend over backward for anyone, who loved my family and friends from day one, I just couldn't see her being that vengeful and spiteful towards anyone; let alone me. Especially since she knows I love her.

Keller's Jordan; the girl after the accident, if she had really become the girl she'd been pretending to be, well then, I could definitely see that girl doing all this to get back at me. Anymore, I wasn't certain who I was dealing with.

Jordan had come unglued with his comments. If I could just look into her eyes, I would know the truth.

They were still arguing, but they were leaving. The best thing for me to do is to keep walking and clear my head. I couldn't think with the remnants of Jordan's scent on my skin. If I could just last this week, then I'd be shipping out and leaving her behind. I'd be gone for three months, about, and that would be plenty of time to purge her from myself. After that, who knew where I'd be going, I could only pray it was far away from her though. I loved that girl with all my being, I wanted to be with her for the rest of my life, but I was a dreamer. Jordan deserved better than me, more than the future I could give her. I couldn't picture myself without her, ever, but obviously she doesn't feel the same way. Hell, if she felt half of what I did we wouldn't be dealing with Keller James in the slightest, she'd have gotten rid of him a long time ago.

"Damn it, Keller!" Jordan screamed shrilly, her voice breaking the serenity of the woods. "Leave me alone!" I couldn't hear Keller's response, but I'm certain there was one, the guy had to have the last word. "I can't believe you! Leave me alone!" Jordan's words were so full of venom that I spun on instinct and headed back towards her. I hadn't known the girl long, but I'd learned one thing about her; the angrier she was the quieter and slower her southern drawl became, now her accent was nonexistent. I'd only seen it one other time; when she was so angry at me, because she thought I'd cheated on her. She was so angry, so terrified of losing me that she flipped out and all her manners were gone. I heard the same anger and terror in her voice now; was it over me? Probably not. Was it because Keller was crossing the line? Probably. I don't like the way he talks to her, the way he handles her and if needed, I'd slam him in the face for that alone. No one deserves to be treated like that.

I was closer now, coming to the edge of the woods that lined my aunt and uncle's property. I could see Jordan was distraught as Keller gripped her arms tightly. He was talking to her; his face and body were rigid. Jordan's knees looked like they were ready to buckle, as if she was only standing up on sheer determination.

"You've done enough. I don't know why you won't let me go. I don't love you. I don't want you."

"Yes, you do." Keller growled through clenched teeth as he tugged her towards him. "What in the Hell has he done to make you believe that load of shit? Before your accident, we…"

"Were friends. I remember everything. I know you lied to me. I just don't understand why."

"Because you belong to me. We belong together. *Together* we run Callatin."

"And without me, you still will."

"No, I won't." He shook his head. "I need you Jordan and you need me. You are nothing without me."

"You're wrong." She sighed as her posture relaxed. "Just let me go, please."

"No, I will not lose to that backwoods asshole."

"You've been putting me through absolute Hell for months because you can't stand to lose to him? You killed someone because of a competition with him?" She asked incredulously. Killed someone?

"I don't lose." Keller snapped evenly. "Now stop being such a stupid whore and get in the car. It looks horrible that I have to come pull you out of a fucking townie party. That's bad enough, then to let Tres see you fucking that prick..." Keller let out a loud breath and shook his head. "It's unacceptable. You are nothing but a manipulative, self-centered bitch who will do anything to claw her way out of her loser mother's memory." Jordan's hand was quick to react as her palm connected with his face. Keller pulled back with hooded angry eyes and just laughed. "You will never be any better than her, J. You're just as fucking crazy as she was, right? You look in the mirror every day and think that, don't you? Bouncing from one extreme to the next, claiming all the attention wherever you go. That's the real reason you're with the cow fucker, because his friends bow down to you. Same with Bentley and Maddie? It's all so pathetic, just like..."

"Don't finish that sentence." Jordan hissed in a low southern drawl. Now that was the girl I knew. "Do NOT finish that sentence."

"Pathetic." Keller finished with an evil grin. "You're a psycho, pathetic WHORE." I couldn't hear what he said next because my rage was roaring in my ears as I started towards them. Whatever it was caused Jordan to launch herself at him, her fists flying wildly. I heard a roar; I wasn't sure where it came from. I just had a gut feeling trouble was coming.

Chapter 97
Jordan

I had flipped my lid. No really. I was screaming and my arms were flailing wildly. I was fighting like I was in a grade school girl fight. I knew better, but I was so furious that I wasn't thinking straight. I only wanted to hurt Keller James, to shut him up. I couldn't hear his voice any longer or I would implode. Maybe, I already had.

"You're headed nowhere fast, Jordan." Keller had murmured softly. "You'll be forgotten just like her. The difference is that you're going to be taking everyone you supposedly love down with you when you go. I wonder which will be more painful, you staring at Lance and Zack's lifeless bodies, or them seeing yours. Regardless, I'll be standing over your grave laughing when it happens too." That's when I lost it. I don't know what part of it set me off more, but I knew he'd gone after my family and friends in the past; well I didn't have actual proof, but I was pretty certain he had. Maybe if I beat the Hell out of him he'd back off?

I felt strong arms wrap around my waist, felt myself being pulled away from Keller. I continued to scream at him, I flailed trying to get back at him.

"Joey, stop." Lance breathed in my ear. "He's not worth it." I calmed until I saw Keller lunge for us.

"Get your hands off her." Keller hollered. Lance swung me behind him and placed himself in front of me.

"I think it's time for you to leave."

"Get your hands off my girlfriend."

"She's not your girlfriend." Lance retorted with a smile in his voice. "I do believe you dumped her, besides the lady has told you repeatedly in the last fifteen minutes to leave her alone. Since you won't listen to her, maybe you'll listen to me."

"Fuck. Off."

"You first." Lance laughed as he turned around to me. "Come on darlin', let's get you inside." His voice was low and soothing as he wrapped his arms around my body and led me towards Alicia's house. I was worried Keller might attack, but Lance didn't seem to be.

"This isn't over." I heard Keller growl behind us. "Get back here, Jordan."

"It is over." I mumbled and Lance repeated it.

"Keller, we're ready to bounce." I heard Tresden say behind us. "And honestly, you look pathetic trying to force her to come with us." Keller let out a growl and then a slew of derogatory curse words came next. He took a swing at Tres, but he ducked and laughed at Keller. I'm certain he would pay for later.

Lance sheltered me with his large body as he led me into the house and downstairs to the basement. Everyone else was passed out in various places in the house, Chopper was asleep on one of the couches nearby, but he was dead to the world.

"Lance, I'm sorry." I flung my arms around his waist. "Please don't believe any of his horrible lies. Please don't." I felt like the world was closing in on me at hyper speed. I couldn't handle it if Keller had won again. I couldn't lose Lance. I couldn't.

Chapter 98
Lance

She was trembling in my arms. She was blubbering and sobbing uncontrollably. I instinctively wrapped my arms tighter around her, rubbed her back and tried to soothe her fears away.

"Lance, I love you. I can't lose you. Keller was lying. Please. Please."

"Sshh Jordan." I murmured. "He's gone. It's over. It's over." She stopped babbling and sobbed into my chest.

Twenty minutes later when she'd finally stopped shaking, stopped crying, I pulled away from her. She clutched my shirt.

"Jordan," I began softly as I took her face in my hands. "I know you better than Keller does and I know you are not capable of such manipulation. I know he was lying. I didn't believe him for a second."

"Liar." She muttered with a sad smile. "If you didn't believe him you wouldn't have left me alone with him."

"I guess you know me best." I pulled her in for a hug. "But, once I thought about it more, I knew. And I'm here now, right?" She nodded her head and hugged me tighter. "Let's get some sleep." I lay down on the couch and pulled her down beside me. If everything fell apart later, if Keller's words were true, well, at least I got to hold her tonight.

Chapter 99
Jordan

I let out a sigh as I woke up in Alicia's basement ensconced in Lance's muscular arms. I snuggled in closer relishing his warmth, terrified this amazing dream would crash around me shortly. "I love you." I breathed as I kissed his neck softly. Lance smiled and pulled me in tighter.

"I love you." He murmured against my hair.

"I need to get going." I lied sadly. "I have a lot of stuff to do today." I had homework, finals to study for, a paper to write, laundry to do along with a lot of housework for my dad and brother. But, honestly, I was embarrassed about my screaming fit with Keller the night before and how I'd basically cried myself to sleep in Lance's arms.

"No." He gasped as he looked down at me. "Stay with me." He pulled me in tighter to him. "Please spend the day with me."

"Get me a change of clothes and I'm yours." I grinned as I stretched up to kiss his neck again.

"Taken care of." Alicia announced as she tromped down the stairs with a cup of coffee and a plate of food. "You can borrow something of mine. Just meet up here tonight and we'll drive back to the dorms together."

"Thanks Lish." I smiled as I flipped over, still in Lance's arms. "I really don't want to move just yet." Alicia and I talked while Lance held me on the couch until everyone else started to drift downstairs. About forty-five minutes later I ran out to Lance's Jeep to get my purse. I dug through its contents and pulled out my phone. I was sucker punched the second it announced my voicemail messages. Keller had started leaving angry voicemails around two in the morning. His words were slurred and sloppy, in short, he was drunk or high and livid and that was so not a good combination. I knew he was pissed when he left here, but the voicemails sounded worse as he let out a slew of threats. As soon as I was inside, I sidestepped Lance and hurried to take a shower; if anyone could see the fear Keller put in me, it would be Lance Bowman. I knew spending the day with Lance was dangerous, but avoiding Keller was a necessity. He needed to calm down, but it was more possible he would just get angrier and have a better chance to exact his revenge.

When I came out thirty minutes later, Lance was on the phone looking overly stressed.

"What's wrong, buddy?" He asked softly. "Calm down, Wyatt and say it again, slowly. I can't understand you." He listened carefully, his face a mask of worry. "Wyatt, go get your mom or Nana." Lance's body went tense and he spun and hit Chopper in the arm before he held his hand out for his keys. Chopper scurried to a drawer in the makeshift kitchen, grabbed out the keys and dropped them in Lance's hand. Lance's body had gone completely still. "What do you mean they won't wake up?"

Each one of the boys jumped up and headed towards the door. I took Lance's keys out of his still outstretched hand. "Wy buddy, I'm on my way. Can you try to wake up Nana again? Then call me right back, okay?" Lance started towards the door at a furious pace, immediately dialing his phone again. "Jen. Go to the house. Wyatt called and said there was a tornado and mom and Jess won't wake up. He says it smells funny." My stomach clenched as we all raced to the cars. Lance climbed into the passenger seat, still talking to his oldest sister. "No wait until we get there, unless Rob's with you. Call and tell Wyatt you're outside though. We're on our way now."

It was only a ten minute drive from Alicia's house to Lance's farm, but in the strained silence, it felt like days. As I turned onto his long, gravel and dirt driveway I could see damage to all of the animals' fences. Cows and horses were roaming free. The dogs were nowhere in sight. Lance let out a curse. We skidded to a halt in front of the house, pulling up next to Jess's car, which had all the windows busted out; when I looked over at Mrs. Bowman's car, it had suffered the same fate.

"What the fuck?" Someone murmured as smoke rolled out of the back of the house. Lance raced inside just as Jess and Rob's truck roared down the drive. Chopper and Cooper sprinted inside as well. Wyatt tore out of the house. I ran towards him and scooped him up in my arms. Jenn and Rob got out of the truck and hurried towards their family, but Cooper was dashing outside waving his arms wildly.

"Go, get away, go! There's a gas leak!"

"Lance!" I screamed as I put Wyatt down and sprinted towards the house. Drew grabbed me and Wyatt, pulling us back at a fast pace.

"They'll make it out, if you go in there, they won't." Seconds later, Chopper and Lance both tore out of the door with Jess and Mrs. Bowman thrown over their shoulders. There was a loud whoosh before flames shot out of the back of the house. There was a loud explosion and the house splintered every which way. The force knocked all of us down to the ground and we could only stare in disbelief.

Sirens shrieked down the driveway and we were surrounded by the red and blue lights of the fire department. A couple of the guys rushed to us while the others went to the blaze. They took Jess and Mrs. B away, looked over the cuts Chopper and Lance had received and corralled us out of the way and towards the barn.

"How did this happen?" Rob questioned slowly. "How does a house explode?"

"The car windows were shattered before the house blew up." Coop stated angrily. "Someone did this." His eyes flitted to me quickly, before he looked back at Rob. "I called it in, Connor should respond soon."

"What...who would do that knowing Wyatt, Jess and mom were inside?" Rob shook his head in disbelief.

"Bo said Tim has been lurking around lately." Sawyer commented. "I guess he came looking for money, threatened to take Wyatt from Jess and she blew him off and told him to get lost or she'd file an order of protection. Retaliation?"

"Who is Tim?" I queried.

"Wyatt's dad. He's a piece of shit who bailed as soon as he found out. He used Jess for money and continuously comes out when he's in a bind. Jess got the order of protection, obviously it's just a piece of paper that doesn't mean much." Drew explained. I nodded and swallowed hard. Maybe I was overreacting, maybe Keller didn't do this and they were right. I could pray for that anyway. I didn't want to be responsible for this devastation.

"We should try and patch the fence." Coop instructed solemnly as he stood up and stretched. "We'll need to get those animals in before dark. The cows might be okay overnight though."

"No, we can get em all by tonight." Chopper disagreed with a shake of his head as he came up to our group. "Dad's on his way. He was getting a group together from church to help patch things up."

"Make sure you get pictures of everything before it's fixed." Rob added. "There won't be an adjustor out here until tomorrow sometime. They won't pay if it's already fixed."

"I've got my camera in the car." Alicia interjected as she went towards the driveway. Everyone began moving around, springing into action to keep their mind off the destruction we'd witnessed. I looked around the farm. The barn had been vandalized, doors and wood broken, fences splintered, animals released. Lance's home was over a hundred years old and had been in his family the entire time. All their memories, all thei history was blown to bits in a matter of seconds. I wrapped my arms around myself in a hug as I looked for Lance.

He stood near one of the fire trucks, talking to a police officer and a firefighter. He was standing strong, answering questions and being the man he needed to be for his family. It broke my heart to see him having to shoulder such responsibility. Mrs. B and Jess had been taken by ambulance to the hospital, they were unresponsive when Chopper and Lance took them out. They were breathing, but couldn't be woken. Jenn and Wyatt had followed the ambulance.

I watched Lance carefully as I noticed a convoy of cars coming down his driveway. People were coming to help. He looked up, then his eyes flitted to mine and he gave a weak smile. My heart hurt. If Keller was responsible for this mess...he couldn't be, right? My head didn't want to believe what my gut was screaming.

Chapter 100
Lance

"Are you okay?" Jordan murmured as she slid beside me and wrapped her arms around my waist. I nodded, knowing voicing the word wouldn't be believable. She looked down the driveway to see a green Tahoe added to the mix of vehicles. "There's Caleb."

"You didn't need to call your brother to come get you." I mumbled embarrassedly. "I could've taken you home."

"I thought you could use some help." She shrugged.

"Your brother hates me."

"No, he doesn't. He just hates seeing me get hurt. Besides, he called to check in and when I told him what happened, he offered." She leaned into me and kissed my cheek. Maddie, Caleb and Zack climbed out of the SUV and looked around. Jordan went to greet them and I followed suit, grabbing her hand in mine.

"Thanks for coming out." I extended my free hand towards Zack and Caleb.

"Just tell us what you need done." Zack offered. "Although, I am a city boy so I should definitely steer clear of those monstrosities." He pointed at the cows and horses behind me. Jordan laughed and rolled her eyes.

"Go see Chopper, he'll direct you." Jordan pulled away from me slightly as she looked up at Zack sadly. "Please don't try to do too much."

"Stop mothering me." Zack grinned as he winked at her.

"I can't help it." She looked at her brother. "You too, I get you want to help, but you're on restricted duty for a reason."

"Thanks for thinking of me before Zack." Caleb laughed sarcastically as he tilted his head and looked at his sister questioningly. Jordan quickly turned and gave me a small smile.

"Where do you want me?"

"Right beside me so I don't go insane." I whispered as I bent down to her ear. She squeezed my hand and nodded.

Within the hour, the farm was a flurry of activity as people from the community, friends and family, gathered to help clean up the destruction. I was grateful. I really was, but I needed time to myself to process this mess.

"Will you be okay for a few minutes? I'm going to check on Maddie and the others." I nodded my head, grateful she could read me so well. She scurried out of the barn and I watched as she went.

I should've been here. I should've been here protecting my family. Without dad here, that's my job. Mom, Jess, and Wyatt could've been killed or seriously injured. As it is, Wyatt will have nightmares for a while. How in the Hell can I leave for the Army when this could happen again?

I hammered away patching yet another hole in the main barn. Whoever had it out for us had destroyed all the horse stalls as well as the chutes. I'd chased off just about anyone who'd come in to help. I needed time by myself. Lucky for me, everyone realized that and didn't linger long.

The pounding was somewhat helpful, but my fury was still bubbling over. If I ever saw Tim again I'd be hard pressed not to murder the jerk. I guess I should be grateful he had enough restraint to hurt us financially and with the dogs rather than having murder on his hands. Of course, as Jordan so quickly pointed out, sometimes animal abuse gets a more severe penalty than murdering a human. Sad, but true. What kind of sick bastard goes after dogs anyway? Poor Flash. My old basset hound had been found dead right under my bedroom window, a bullet to the head.

"How's it going?" Caleb asked as he came inside the barn carrying some more wood. He put it down nearby, grabbed a plank and brought it over to me.

"Been better."

"No shit. I'm real sorry about this. It's pretty fucked up. I can imagine that beating the Hell out of wood and nails is only some consolation. I was ready to explode after the…attack and this is much worse."

"If it weren't for all the people around…Hell, if it weren't for Jordan, I'd have done gone insane."

"She's pretty good at that, if she's not the one driving you there." Caleb snorted as he held up the plank, while I hammered it into place.

"If that ain't the truth." I laughed. "But I wouldn't trade her for anything in the world."

"Good to hear."

"Can I ask you something?" I sat up and looked at Caleb. Last night's scene had been bothering me since it happened. Keller had gotten pretty rough with Jordan and she didn't retaliate, I couldn't understand why. "Has she ever said Keller hits her? Have you ever witnessed anything…?"

"No, but I have concerns. I don't have any proof, otherwise the mother fucker would be in jail."

"If he does hit her…he got pretty rough and mouthy with her last night. I have never seen Jordan cower from anyone, but she did with him."

"I would like to think Maddie and Alicia would know if he was. They're together constantly, after all. I will keep a better eye on the situation. I know Zack's been doing some investigative work and hasn't seen anything." I nodded my head and returned to hitting the nail into the plank. Picturing Zack and Keller on the other end of the hammer made me feel a lot better.

"They broke up last night." I added.

"Good. Hopefully the SOB stays away." I nodded in agreement; I'd actually been praying the same thing last night and most of today. Their whole relationship had me worried, because Caleb was right, Keller was definitely doing something to pull Jordan down. I was clueless as to what though.

"I'll talk to Chopper. Feel him out. They've gotten pretty close lately."

"Much to Keller's chagrin." Caleb laughed. I nodded and the two of us continued to work together in an easy silence. Thoughts of Jordan were now flitting around my head and I mentally kicked myself for falling all over again. I knew it was safer to stay away from her, I just couldn't. I was leaving for boot camp in one week and not only did I have to worry about my family's safety, but now I was terrified of what would happen to Jordan once I left. Keller James would have free aim at her then.

"Maddie ordered pizza for everyone." Jordan announced timidly as she walked into the barn to see Caleb and me working together easily. "It's almost eight. Everyone's finishing up. We've tracked down most of the animals, there's still a few loose, but we're better than we were."

"Thanks." I smiled with a nod. Caleb and I finished the last stall we were working on while Jordan watched from a nearby bench.

"Heard anything about your mom or Jess?"

"They're at Jenn's. They'll stay there for a few days until I get this all cleaned up. There's a few make shift apartments that ranch hands used to use in the back of the barn, I'm going to work on those so we have someplace to stay until we get this crap figured out."

"Will you stay at Jenn's too?"

"No. I'll stay here."

"No." Jordan argued firmly as she stood up.

"Jo, I'll be fine."

"I don't care. I'll worry about you. Stay with me."

"In the dorms?" She made a face.

"He can stay with me or we'll both stay here." Chopper interjected as he walked into the barn. The poor guy was covered in sweat and dirt, but he didn't seem to care as he flashed Jordan a flirtatious grin before he looked back at me. "Everyone but us is gone."

"Are y'all going to eat or not?" Jordan sighed in exasperation when she realized my sleeping arrangement conversation had been closed.

"Yup, we're finished for now. It's as good as it's going to get until I get some better boards at the lumberyard tomorrow." I stood up, dusted myself off and placed my tools back in the oversized Craftsman toolbox.

"You've got to see this!" Coop laughed as he stood at the barn door motioning for us to come outside.

"And for your entertainment…city boy meets his country love." Maddie announced with a flourish and a giggle. Zack was being chased by one of the horses. If he stopped, she stopped, if he turned, so did she. He couldn't get away from her.

"Aww, Zack. That's Cinnamon. She's harmless." Jordan giggled. "Looks like horses can't resist the Bentley charm either." She stepped out to help him. She was a natural when it came to anything and easily coaxed the Paint back into the fence.

"That is why I'm a city boy." Zack bent over and gasped for air. "Crazy freaking animals."

"She just has a crush on you, Z. Just like all the other females of the world."

"I'll show you a crush." Zack growled as he lunged for Jordan and picked her up off the ground. She squealed with laughter. My stomach clenched with envy. The bond and flirtations between them was blatantly obvious. It was hard to see another guy get that same adoring look she usually reserved for me. Zack put her down and she immediately reached for me, rushing to my side with a grin. She laced her fingers through mine as we walked back up to the house. For now, that was good enough for me.

Chapter 101
Jordan

"What were you and my brother talking about anyway?" I asked quietly as I slowed our pace so we were back further from our group. He shrugged his shoulders innocently before he let go of my hand and slung his arm over my shoulder and pulled me into him.

"You and how amazing you are." My stomach clenched with guilt at those words. If he knew the truth, he probably wouldn't feel that way right now, he probably wouldn't even touch me.

"Lance." I sighed.

"I don't know what I'd have done if you hadn't been with me today, Jo." He admitted softly as he gently placed a kiss on the top of my head. "Seriously, you've kept me sane." I stopped and took his hands into mine.

"Are you okay though? Really okay?" He nodded his head and looked away quickly.

"I'm furious and disappointed in myself for not protecting them. I'm upset about Flash and the other dogs, but I'm really just grateful it wasn't worse. It could've been. God, I keep imagining that he could've kidnapped Wyatt for ransom, you know? Could you imagine?" Tears sprang to my eyes at the thought and I shook my head.

"Can I stay with you tonight?" I begged in a broken voice. Lance shook his head.

"It's too dangerous. What if they come back? I can't let you get hurt."

"Then stay with me." I pleaded. "Lance, we can stay at my house. I don't have to stay at the dorms, dad can just write me an excuse. I won't let you stay here without me."

"Jordan." He sighed.

"Lance." I mimicked as I raised my chin defiantly. "Seriously, I'm not budging. I stay here or you stay at my house. Either way we will be together tonight." Lance gave a small smile as he shook his head. He pulled me in closer and planted a passionate kiss on my mouth. I felt my knees go weak.

"I love you." He breathed in my ear. "I'll stay with you tonight." I grinned like a fool at his words and gave him an excited hug before we went to the trucks to eat with our friends.

For the next three days, I avoided Keller at school and the dorms. After practice, I would rush off to change and then join the others as we headed back to Lance's house to finish the repairs. Keller's goal had been to keep me away from Lance I'm certain, but he'd only succeeded in making sure I was with him even more.

On the third night, Lance and I were asleep in my bed when I awoke to the sound of heavy footsteps coming up the stairs. My bedroom door opened and I could make out Keller's profile in the darkness. My stomach dropped. I took a deep breath and rolled over to face Lance as I kissed him softly. He reciprocated by pulling me tighter and giving me a full out kiss.

"I could get used to waking up like this." Lance chuckled. "You're spoiling me darlin'." I let out a soft sigh and snuggled into him before I heard Keller leave the room. He had finally ended our relationship and it didn't matter what he thought now, it was over. Lance and I were back together.

Chapter 102
Lance

"Mr. Bowman, Mr. Cooper, the Principal would like to see you in his office." Miss Blather advised primly as Coop and I walked into our sixth hour class. I shot my friend a weird look before nodding at the teacher.

"Yes ma'am."

"What the Hell is this about?" I asked my friend as we walked back out of the classroom and towards the principal's office. In a matter of minutes, all my close friends gathered in front of the door.

"This doesn't bode well." Drew stated with a shake of his head. "You know the fucking drug dogs were here today, right?"

"You got a stash we don't know about?" Sawyer hissed under his breath.

"Hell no, but why else would we be called in, right now?"

"Maybe we're getting a reward." Chopper joked with a shrug of his shoulders as he opened the door and followed the rest of us in. One by one, we were called into the office; but no one ever came out. I was the last to be called and my stomach was in knots.

"Mr. Bowman." Principal Gaithers greeted me gruffly as he nodded towards a seat. The Deputy Sherriff stood near the doorway. "As you are probably aware, we had a visit from the County police today for suspicious activity and anonymous tips to the hotline."

"And what does that have to do with me and my friends?" I queried calmly.

"Why don't you tell me?"

"I don't know what you're talking about, sir."

"If you come clean, the penalty won't be as severe. Your friends already have."

"Tricking me won't cause me to lie, as I'm sure my friends didn't do either."

"We found an impressive amount of drugs and paraphernalia in your locker."

"It wasn't mine." I shrugged.

"Compiled with what was found in your house a few nights ago and the anonymous tips to the hotline, we believe it is yours. You have the chance to save your friends here; the rumor is that you're the big wig, running it all. Come clean and only you will be punished." The arson inspector had found a very large amount of various drugs in what used to be my bedroom closet. Coop's brother was on scene when it was found and assured the inspector it wasn't mine. They both decided that if I or any of my friends knew about the stash we would have gotten rid of it quickly with the amount of police combing the grounds. County police should not have been advised of the find, nor should they be responding to this situation either. The high school was the City's territory. The only reason why my house fell in city limits was because the police chief was my next door neighbor.

"That's ludicrous." I laughed as I shook my head. "My mother would beat the Hell out of me if I so much as attempted to sell drugs, let alone do them."

"Your brother…"

"Leave Luke out of this." I growled.

"Are you going to fess up or not?"

"There's nothing to confess. You know me, sir, you know my family. You both do. You both know my friends and their families and you know none of us would do this. We may drink beer, but we don't do drugs. None of us would risk our upcoming enlistment. We're all clean. You can drug test me now."

"Very well, you and your friends are expelled pending further notice."

"What?" I exploded just as Sherriff Jamison put handcuffs around my wrists.

Chapter 103
Jordan

"Jordan?" Miss Aimes stopped me in the hall and motioned for me to follow her into her room before the rest of the class started pouring in. "Your father needs a word with you."

"Now?" I asked. It was very rare for my father to bother me during the school day unless it was an absolute emergency. I hadn't heard from Lance since he'd left my house at six o clock this morning, which was unusual. I'd get at least one text a morning from him or Chopper, but nothing from either of them. My heart skipped a beat as I feared the worst; something had happened to my boyfriend and best friend. I scurried down the hall to my locker. I dropped my books in the large silver contraption and then started for my father's office. It was three buildings over and quite a long walk, it'd be even longer now since I was terrified it was bad news. I checked my phone again. I sent a text message to Lance, Chopper and Sawyer. At least one of them should answer, right?

"Any idea why I've been called to see your dad?" Zack questioned as he sidled up beside me, his hand brushing mine. I shook my head.

"That's where I'm headed too. I haven't heard from Lance or Chopper all day. Now I'm worried."

"They wouldn't call me in too, if that were the reason." Zack laced his fingers through mine quickly and squeezed my hand. He held on for a few seconds before he let go.

"I'm worried." I whispered. "Something is not right." Maddie, Caleb and Alicia came into view, all heading for the administration building as well. "Why would we all be called to the office at the same time?" Just as quickly as the words escaped my mouth, the culprit smacked into me. Literally.

"Hey guys, where you headed?" Keller grinned.

"Out for a walk. How about you?" Zack replied coolly.

"Ditching." Keller shrugged. "You want to come, J? I've got room."

"No thanks. I have too much studying to do before finals next week."

"Your loss."

"Not really." I smiled sweetly.

"Still pissed at me, I see. Tell me you'll be over this by graduation, there are a lot of parties my girlfriend should be attending with me."

"I'm. Not. Your. Girlfriend. Anymore." I hissed. "You dumped me."

"I would never dump you." He laughed incredulously. "I love you, babe." I rolled my eyes and walked off.

"We're through, Keller." I called over my shoulder. He shot me a wink as he watched Zack and I scurry towards Caleb and the girls.

"I'm proud of you."

"You'll be even more proud when I wipe that fucking smirk off his face. He's responsible."

"For what?"

"For us getting called to the office. I just know it."

"You're overreacting. Keller doesn't have that kind of pull."

"You're fucking blind if you believe that." I spit. I didn't acknowledge the others, I was too furious to be social.

We sat outside my dad's office for almost thirty minutes before all five of us were called inside. My dad sat at his oversized mahogany desk looking like he had one foot in the grave already. Keller's father and two other board members sat in the large, leather-backed chairs near the window and two county sheriffs stood near the desk.

"What the fuck?" Zack murmured beside me.

"Come in, kids." Mr. James ordered with a fake smile. "Have a seat."

"Dad?" Caleb asked as he looked over at our father for help. My dad shook his head and sat back in the seat, his face full of disappointment.

"He is not your dad at this moment. He is your headmaster and as such, you will show respect." Mr. James hissed from his seat. I never did like that man.

"I've called the five of you to my office today on the account of numerous anonymous tips of some illegal activity you are taking part in."

"Illegal activity?" I repeated sarcastically.

"You will not speak until spoken to young lady." Mr. James spit hatefully. I clenched my teeth and fought back the words on the tip of my tongue.

"As per the anonymous tips, the Sherriff was granted a search warrant. I'm sorry kids, but I have no other choice but to expel you from school."

"What?" Caleb exploded. "For what? You haven't even told us what we've done wrong. I can guarantee they didn't find a damn thing when they searched any of us."

"One of you, has a prior record in dealing drugs."

"That was bogus then," Zack interrupted tersely. "And if that's what you're accusing us of, it's bogus now too."

"Dealing drugs?" I repeated. "You're kidding right? Are we being punked or something?"

"This is not a joke. It's a matter of the law and that's why the Sherriff's deputies are here now, to take you all away."

"This is ridiculous. My father will not stand for this." Maddie shot up our of her seat, looking every bit the heiress she is. "Mr. James, you know me well enough to know this is a bogus charge."

"Madeline, it's breaking my heart to see this happening to you. I know you're a good girl, from a great background, it just seems you've fallen into the wrong crowd. Your friends are bad news."

"Talked to your son lately?" Maddie spit back sweetly. Mr. James stiffened before he redirected his attention to my father.

"If you come clean now, you will not serve any jail time. The boys at Mencino have already ratted you all out as the suppliers for this little...little drug ring. If you tell us who your main provider is, all your contacts, then you will be reprimanded in the smallest amount."

"But still expelled from school right?" Zack snapped rudely. "My father is a detective for the NYPD, has been for twenty plus years. I have two brothers and three cousins on the force as well, so don't insult me by trying to pull one over on us."

"With such a background, I'm the most disappointed in you." My dad commented. "I thought giving you a chance here would straighten you out and yet..."

"I took your son and daughter down with me?" Zack shook his head in disbelief. "This crap isn't going to work on me, or them, so just stop. We have done nothing wrong. This is bogus bullshit and you know it. If it weren't for the suits pulling your strings over there, we wouldn't even be here."

"Mr. Bentley, I suggest you shut your mouth." Mr. James growled sternly as he stood up.

"Zack's right." I interjected. "We have way too much to lose to even consider doing that crap. Maybe you should look a little higher up on the Callatin food chain before you accuse us."

"It all points to you, actually, young lady. Well that and your friend, Miss Bowman. I told them not to let kids from the public school transfer over, maybe now they'll see our reasoning." Mr. James smiled. "You and Miss Bowman are the link between the Mencino High School boys, you being the charlatan of the group."

"You..." I hissed as I jumped out of the chair. Zack grabbed me and yanked me back down.

"That's what he wants. Ignore him."

"We're not done yet, kids." Mr. James laughed. "Not only do we have evidence of the drug ring, but you're also being brought up on charges of bullying. Miss Donaldson and Mr. Bentley have also been rumored to have been making sex tapes, having sex on school grounds and..."

"With each other?" Zack laughed. "I wish."

"Am I seriously in a bad after school special?" Caleb asked in disbelief. "Seriously? I'm with Jordan, are we being punked?"

"This is not a joke." Mr. James growled.

"I'm begging you to confess. It's the only way to save your futures." My father begged in a pleading voice, his face going whiter in the few minutes we'd been in the room.

"There is nothing to confess." Zack responded. His green eyes flew to Mr. James' cocky figure while he reached down into his backpack and pulled out his phone. "But I do have some pictures you and the police would probably like to see, sir. Maybe you'd like to see the extra curriculars your son has been participating in."

"Attacking the innocent will get you nowhere." Mr. James chuckled with a shake of his head.

"You may take them now." My father stated to one of the police officers. I looked back at my father in disbelief, back at my friends as if one of them would say something to get us out of this whole mess.

"Not before I call my father." Maddie spit angrily as she reached for her cell phone.

"There will be time for that later."

"The Hell there will be." She hit the number three button on her phone and got her father immediately. After one minute, she had hung up and Mr. James' phone began to ring. He ignored it of course and then my father's phone immediately went off. "Daddy is on his way." Zack shoved his phone in front of Mr. James' who tried to yank it away, my father turned his head and the police officers weren't paying attention so no matter how hard Zack tried to show them what he had on Keller, none of them wanted to see it.

The next thing I knew I was getting hard metal slapped on my wrists. This had to be the worst moment of my life.

Chapter 103
Lance

"No fair! Lance gets conjugal visits?" Coop whined as he jumped off a bench and hurried over to the front of the cell we'd been put in. I looked up to see Jordan being ushered inside. How did she know we were even here?

"Grab my ass one more time, Rico Suave and I'll make sure I'm guilty of the charges this time." Jordan swung out of reach for the young Hispanic cop who was ushering her. She pierced him with a deadly stare and jerked away from him again when he made a play for her. When he threw her against the bars, I flung myself towards them only to be stopped by the steel cage.

"Don't get so feisty, Chica." The cop laughed. "I like them feisty. Maybe I'll bail you out just for the fun of you owing me."

"My knee in your sorry lack of a crotch going to be feisty enough for you?" Jordan retorted as she pulled her leg back.

"Jordan." Zack hissed. "Don't. Maddie's dad will make sure that jerk needs to find a new job after today. Then, you can kick his shit."

"You rich kids are funny. You think just because you come from money that you're above the law? Too bad you learned the hard way."

"Only one person in here is loaded beyond belief, Mikey." Coop advised drily. "And none of us believe we're above the law. You know this is a load of crap."

"I did, until I saw the group you were running with."

"Oh yeah, because we look like a bunch of thugs." Jordan answered sarcastically as Mike pushed her into the cell next to ours, before handing Maddie and Alicia through as well. Zack and Caleb were pushed into ours by another cop.

"Maybe you guys can all figure out how you're going to get out of this one." Mike stated with a shake of his head as he and the other cop sauntered off.

"What the fuck?"

"We've been set up." Jordan spit in a low menacing tone.

"No shit." Drew retorted. "Mom's going to stroke when they tell her Alicia and I are both in jail."

"Well, at least your dad's not the one who sent you up the river." Caleb snapped drily with a shake of his head.

"We'll be out in an hour. Tops." Maddie promised as she looked at the expensive silver watch on her wrist. "My dad is on his way and these charges will disappear in no time."

"They have no proof." Chopper added. "No proof at all. I can't believe…"

"If they do have proof I'd sure as Hell like to see it." Zack sauntered over closer to where Jordan had fallen against the wall. Her face was buried in her hands and she was obviously crying. "How about you, J?" Zack knelt down to where he was level with her. "If they've got sex tapes, I would love to see them. Maybe it'd jog my memory since I don't remember making them." I gripped the bars tighter, my teeth and gut clenching.

"Shut up." Jordan hissed through clenched teeth.

"Oh come on, Jordan." Zack chuckled. "Don't get so pissed. We all know this is bogus ass bullshit and we're going to walk. The whole sex thing sealed the deal."

267

"What sex thing?" Drew asked. "What tapes?"

"There are no tapes." Jordan growled, but she wouldn't make eye contact with me.

"As per Mr. Donaldson, Jordan and I are involved in some serious sexcapades all over the campus, we made some porn even. Apparently, not only are we drug lords but we're starting a sex ring too." Zack laughed. "As I said before, I'd sure like to see this proof."

"Shut up, Zack."

"What the fuck are you talking about?" I growled as I got up in Zack's face. I was already enraged over this whole situation, but to hear Jordan and Zack had been screwing too. I was ready to obliterate someone or something.

"Down, Bo." Chopper scurried in between Zack and me.

"He's kidding." Maddie interjected. "It was one of the bogus accusations made. Makes me think Jordan is the target." Maddie's head turned towards Jordan inquisitively, but she was staring out of the cell, not making eye contact with anyone.

"Sadly, Jordan and I have never hooked up." Zack admitted with an exaggerated sigh. "I would DEFINITELY remember that."

"Knock it off, Zack." Maddie sighed with a menacing glance. "Jordan is scared."

"Well she shouldn't be." Coop went towards the side of the cell the girls were on. "You either, Lish. This is bogus ass bullshit, to quote Zack. As soon as Connor gets here, we'll be out."

"My dad will get us all out." Maddie interjected as she went to sit beside Alicia.

"My mom is going to stroke." Alicia sobbed into her friend's shoulder. "She's going to hate us." Maddie tried to calm Alicia down while Sawyer watched helplessly between the bars. I felt his pain. Jordan was obviously near a meltdown and I couldn't even touch her. Zack was still bent down looking at Jordan, trying to get her to talk to him, but she was in another world.

"I'm sorry, Jo." I mumbled in a choked voice. "I'm sure this is my fault somehow. If I find out…"

"It's not your fault, Lance. This is all my fault. Everything is *my* fault." She repeated it over and over, never looking at anyone. There were protests of course, but they were ignored.

An hour later Connor, and his partner, Shane sauntered into the hall between the cells. Connor looked pissed off; Shane just shook his head and laughed.

"Never thought I'd see the day." Shane tisked. "Someone get a picture of this? I think it's going to be on my desk. I'll put a caption underneath…Mencino County drug lords busted." Shane bellowed with laughter. "Which one is the pimp again?"

"Knock it off, Shane." Connor chuckled. "Who'd y'all piss off this time, little brother?"

"Obviously some conniving little bitch." Coop retorted. "I'm seriously traumatized from this day. I think Drew was hitting on me."

"In your dreams, Coop." Drew remarked. "I would find a way to get through the cell to Jordan before I touched your ass."

"To who?" I asked as I took a step in front of my cousin.

"I'd take Coop." Drew sighed as he backed off. "But only because I couldn't run from you in here."

"Glad to see the big house didn't bring y'all down." Chopper laughed as he shook his head and headed towards the open cell door. "Sorry kids, but lead me to the nearest bathroom I have got to pee like a Russian Racehorse."

Jordan was the last to leave her cell, a dazed expression still on her face. I hung back and waited for her. I slid my fingers into hers and squeezed.

"Prison time makes a man have urges, you know?" I teased in her ear. She shook her head and laughed. "There's the smile I love. What's wrong babe?"

"Uh, do I need to spell it out for you?" She asked drily as she held up her hands to encompass the police station.

"It's a hoax. We all know we're innocent."

"I'm not."

"What does that mean?" I asked, my overactive imagination certain she was talking about the sex tape.

"I know who did this."

"Who?"

"Isn't it obvious?" I shook my head and pulled her to the side. She looked around at all the people in the waiting room and shook her head. Maddie's father was amidst all of the parents, motioning for us to close in on him.

"Unfortunately, these officers believe evidence is everything. You're all out on bond, the charges have not been dropped. No one seems to believe the unbelievable coincidence of this whole situation. I've got a court order for the anonymous tips transcripts, caller id, etc. By the end of the week, you'll be absolved."

"But what about Boot Camp?" Coop asked. "We leave this weekend. What if the charges aren't dropped?"

"I've never lost, son. If it takes that long, so be it. I'm sure the courts will allow you to continue with your enlistment."

"So what does this bond thing mean?"

"It means our parents put things into hock to get us out." Coop answered with a shake of his head.

"It also means we shouldn't leave town anytime soon." Drew added bitterly. Tears ran down Jordan's face as she started towards her father. His face was pale, his hair had more grey running through it than the last time I'd seen him and his face was pinched. He wouldn't look at either of his children as he started for the door.

"Jordan." I called as I snagged her hand. "I can take you home."

"No, you won't." Mr. Donaldson snapped angrily as he finally looked at his children. "Caleb, Zack, Jordan you will walk straight to the vehicle, without another word. Do you understand?" All three of them nodded. "Madeline, if you're headed back to campus I expect the same out of you."

"I'll be riding with my father." She remarked tartly. Mr. Donaldson nodded his head, his lips pressed in a fine line as he followed his children out of the police station.

"You're the devil, Lance Bowman." Coop joked as he slapped me on the back.

"Give it time, honey." My mom commented as she came up behind me. "Unfortunately he doesn't have faith in their upbringing like we all do. I know none of you are capable of such atrocities. Especially, Jordan. Unbelievable."

"Thanks mom." I stepped out of the building and watched Jordan climb into the front seat of the Callatin Academy SUV. She wouldn't look up as she did.

Chapter 104
Jordan

The car ride home was eerily silent. None of us dared to move. Once we were inside the house, my father angrily directed us to the living room where he preached to us for two hours about the error of our ways. Not once did he ask if it were true, never did he believe we weren't capable of this ridiculous accusation. That hurt worse than anything.

"I'm confiscating your cell phones." He held out his hand to me, then to Caleb. "Your parents have been notified, Zack. As soon as the judge allows it you will be shipped back to New York."

"Why are we being punished for something we didn't do?" Zack asked belligerently. "This is ridiculous. I realize I'm not your child and that your disappointment shouldn't bother me this much, but it does. You don't know me. You obviously don't know Caleb and Jordan, either. Especially if you can sit there on your high horse and not once, ask what the Hell is going on."

"You're on house arrest, Zack. Go up to the spare bedroom. You will only leave for school and practices. Same goes for all of you. No visitors. No phone calls. Nothing. You are cut off from the world until the judge says otherwise."

"Apparently, the judge has already spoken." Zack retorted as he started up the stairs.

"To your rooms. Now." My father shouted without looking at either of us. Caleb and I didn't protest, we just followed orders.

"How can you keep silent?"

"Talking won't do any good. We've already been convicted." Caleb replied. "Jordan and I are pros, Zack. He never believes us. He believes the puppet masters first and foremost."

I left the two boys to talk it out in the hallway as I hurried into my room. I knew Keller was responsible for all of this. The only way it would go away was if I went back to him. Maybe I should just have faith in Mr. DeMarina's abilities though. Maybe he could save me from this Hell that Keller had created for me.

I opened my laptop, knowing my dad hadn't thought of taking that from us yet. It would only be a matter of time before he realized it was contact with the outside world. As soon as I signed on my instant messenger was flashing in the corner

"You okay?" Lance questioned.

"Grounded for life. No phone and I'm sure the laptop will go soon."

"Did u talk to him? How can he believe this BS?"

"My thoughts exactly. There's no point in wasting my breath, he's a sellout."

"I have faith in Maddie's dad. Last time he worked magic."

"I'm sorry you've gotten in so much trouble since you met me. I'm pretty much a bad luck charm for you."

"None of this is your fault."

"Says you."

"Please don't blame yourself when I can't talk you out of it. I love you, Jo."

"I love you, too. I need a shower. I'll message you later, okay?"

"Please don't tell me you're taking a shower and then log off, that's just cruel."

"LMAO thanks for the smile." I signed off the computer, closed it and stuffed it in my messenger bag. Hopefully, if dad didn't see it he would confiscate it.

Chapter 105

A few hours later, I went downstairs to get a bottle of water. The house was silent and it made the large place seem even more haunted than normal. I almost ran into my father as I padded into the kitchen. I should turn around and wait for him to leave. I do not want to deal with his disappointment. I was angry enough at myself for both of us.

I didn't say a word as I pushed past him and walked to the refrigerator. I grabbed a water and turned back around. He gasped and my eyes involuntarily flitted to his face. He was a ghostly white, almost blue. His fingers gripped a chair back tightly right before he collapsed to the ground with a sickening thud.

"Caleb!" I shrieked at the top of my lungs as I searched frantically for my cell phone. Damn it, dad had taken them hours ago. I screamed for help and prayed neither of the boys had fallen asleep yet. I looked around the kitchen for the cordless phone and found our cell phones resting on top of the microwave. "Daddy? Daddy, answer me." He was silent, still, and I couldn't find any breath coming out. I shrieked for Caleb again, finally hearing thundering feet on the stairs before I lunged for my cell phone to dial 9-1-1.

"What happened?" Caleb asked breathlessly, his face almost as white as my father's.

"I don't know. He just collapsed." I sobbed as the operator picked up the phone. I explained the events and watched in disbelief as Caleb and Zack started CPR. I fell against the cabinet, barely aware of my tears as I watched the scene play out. When would this ridiculous drama end?

The ambulance arrived and everything flew by in a haze before we plopped down into the waiting room to hear from the doctor. I could not lose my father. He may be an ass, but Caleb and I couldn't survive without him. My aunt could not lose her daughter and brother in the same month. Seriously, this could not be possible. I was having a nightmare. I had to be.

"It's all my fault." I whispered as I hugged myself. Caleb moved towards me.

"Do not blame yourself."

"If I had…"

"He brought it on himself, Joey. It's the job, all the perks, aren't really perks at all." I shook my head and turned away from my brother. Caleb gave me a lopsided hug before he walked outside for some air. He'd managed to get a call in to Maddie so I'm sure he was really headed to the parking lot to wait for her.

Zack knelt in front of me and put his hands on my knees. I looked down into his worried face. "It's going to be okay, babe." He pulled me into him for a hug and then sat beside me in the chair. I instinctively snuggled in, resting my heavy head on his shoulders. With Zack everything was safe, comfortable, it all just felt right like maybe I'd been here a million times before. It was really nice to feel that now.

"If I hadn't gone downstairs…I could've lost my daddy too." I murmured as a sob racked through my body.

"It doesn't do any good to think about that, J." He played with a strand of my hair. "You just thank God for the way it panned out and pray things keep going your way."

"Did you get that from a card?"

"Nope." He chuckled. "My Grandma actually."

"It's nice." I sighed, my eyes closing. They were so heavy from the exhausting day I'd already had and Zack playing with my hair was not helping at all.

"I hope whoever pulled this crap on us gets a wakeup call from this. Seriously, their payback could've caused more damage than they intended."

"Maybe this is what they intended."

"No one could be that cold blooded." I shrugged my shoulders knowing Keller James could indeed be that cold blooded. He had no heart, no morals and I'm sure no remorse for almost killing my father.

My phone buzzed and I flipped it over, only because I was waiting on a call from my Grandparents. Alicia's face flashed next to a text message. *"Wyatt is missing!"*

"What?" I gasped as I immediately hit the phone icon. Alicia instantaneously answered.

"Jo, I know you're in trouble and...but Wyatt is missing. He just walked out of the door at some point in the middle of the night. Aunt Sarah went to check on him and..."

"He couldn't have gotten far. Do you think...?" My voice broke just as the doctor came out of the emergency room doors. Zack pried the phone from my fingers and gestured for me to talk to the doctor.

"Alicia, sorry, it's Zack. Mr. D had a heart attack, we're at the hospital."

"Miss Donaldson, your dad is going to be fine. He had a massive heart attack and after running some tests, we're going to have to perform surgery to remove a large amount of blockage."   "Now?"

"In the morning. He'll be kept overnight in ICU though." I nodded and looked around helplessly.

"Can we see him?"

"For a few minutes, he's pretty weak and out of it."

"Thank you." He nodded and went back behind the double doors. Zack stood up and enveloped me in a hug as I repeated the doctor's words.

"They're going door to door looking for Wyatt now. She said she'd call you when they hear something."

"I need to..."

"You can't be two places at once, but you need to be here." Tears rolled down my cheeks as I nodded my head. He was right. I pulled away from him and went back to the plastic chairs waiting for Caleb to come back in. "Do you want me to holler at Cale?" I nodded and Zack scurried outside. I pulled out my phone and called Lance. It went straight to his voicemail.

"Lance...my dad, my dad had a heart attack and we're at the hospital with him right now. Alicia called about Wyatt. I want to be there...please call me when you find him." I was blubbering when Zack walked back in with Caleb and Maddie.

"They'll find him. He'll be okay." Zack promised as he wrapped me in another tight hug. I wish I had his confidence. I was certain Wyatt would only be okay if I made a phone call that I didn't want to ever make.

Chapter 106

Caleb went in to see my dad and I stayed in the waiting room with Zack and Maddie. I fidgeted with my phone, warring with myself to make the call. What if I was overreacting? What if Wyatt legitimately just went for a walk? What if Tim had him?

My phone began ringing and I knew my suspicions were right when I looked to see Keller's arrogant face flash in front of me. I scurried out of the hospital doors before I answered.

"Hey babe, how goes it?"

"It goes."

"Shame about the kid. Hope they find him before it's too late."

"Keller." I sobbed. I heard him chuckle on the other end.

"You can help with that, you know?"

"My dad had a heart attack. You almost killed him and now, now you're kidnapping."

"You did that. Not me. I have warned you repeatedly and you blatantly disobey me. This is all your fault, J. If the kid dies, his blood is on your hands."

"No! Please, please don't hurt him. I'll do whatever you want, Keller. Please just let Wyatt go back home."

"Say it."

"I love you, Keller." He made a funny noise. "I only want you."

"Say it again." He repeated in a rough voice.

"I love you. I only want you."

"Good girl, I'll see you tomorrow." He hung up the phone and I fell onto a bench and sobbed. Five minutes later my phone sounded with Lance's ringtone.

"He's home?" I questioned as I answered.

"Yes. Yes, he's home. He's okay."

"What happened?"

"I don't know. He's pretty tired and out of it. He said he thought he heard you outside and went to find you. He never did and then he realized he was lost. He's unfamiliar with Jenn's subdivision. He also said some guy stayed with him until we found him, but there was no one there."

"Lance." I gasped as I cried harder.

"Do you need me there? I can be there in five minutes."

"No. No, I think we're headed home. I just...I needed to hear your voice and know Wyatt was okay. Go to bed, it's been one Hell of a day."

"That's an understatement." He chuckled. "I love you darlin', call me if you need me."

"I will. I love you too." My heart broke when he hung up the phone. Chances are, I would never hear those words from him again. Keller would stop at nothing and that meant no one was safe anymore. I was alone and always would be.

Chapter 107

Thursday morning Keller was downstairs waiting for me when I finally descended, it was our first day back to school since my father's heart attack. Maddie and Caleb had already left, Zack was lingering to walk with me. When he came down to find Keller waiting he took one look at me, shook his head and rushed out of the house in a huff. I couldn't blame him. I only wished I could've followed him.

Needless to say, I got a very cold, very hard shoulder from Alicia, Maddie, Zack and Caleb. None of them wanted anything to do with me. I couldn't blame them. I knew what I was doing was wrong and maybe someday they'd understand I had no other choice.

The second I stepped into my dorm room after softball practice Maddie locked the door behind me.

"What in the Hell is wrong with you?"

"I'm tired?"

"Don't play stupid. Why are you back with Keller?" I shrugged my shoulders and began moving around my room to find clothes so I could shower.

"It just kind of happened."

"How did that just kind of happen? You hate him."

"I don't hate him." I sighed. I continued to dig through drawers and avoid eye contact at all costs. "He came over last night once we were back from the hospital and it just kind of happened."

"What about Lance?" Alicia asked quietly, her arms crossed in front of her chest self-consciously.

"So, in other words, Keller took advantage of your vulnerability."

"No."

"This is ridiculous. You don't love him, you hate him. He's a controlling asshole who treats you worse than dog shit."

"Not to mention you and Lance were supposedly back together."

"Lance never said that."

"Yes, he did." Alicia argued, her face twisting in anger. "Was Keller telling the truth? Were you playing Lance?"

"Keller's an idiot." I slipped, my eyes widened and I backed up. "We had a fight, I ran to Lance and Keller got pissed. He lied to get back at me, that's all. I would never do that to Lance."

"You're doing it right now." Maddie shouted in exasperation. "Seriously Jordan, you're like a tennis ball and you're totally screwing Lance in the ass right now."

"Such language." I clucked with a shake of my head. "No big deal. Lance leaves in a few days."

"He still doesn't know. Regardless, it doesn't make this right."

"I can't help it okay?" I snapped on the verge of tears. "I can't change it. I wish Lance wasn't getting hurt in this. I hate that most of all, but I have no other choice."

"Yes you do! It's your life." Maddie exclaimed. I shook my head and hurried out of the room.

275

"No. It's not." I mumbled. I cried into the shower and tried to forget about everything. All the bad things would stop now. My friends and our families could be safe, could live happy, normal lives now.

The next day, all charges against my friends and me had been thrown out due to improper police procedure. It was a miracle, Maddie's dad said, but we would take it. We were all back in the good graces of our schools and my father was feeling a thousand times better. All because of Keller.

The boys would be leaving for boot camp tomorrow morning. There was a huge going away party at Chopper's tonight. I'd talked to Lance via IM a few times. He'd gone distant within a day or two, Alicia had apparently clued him in. Any time I asked if he was leaving, he'd never give me a straight answer.

"Lance is here." Alicia nodded towards the stands during our softball game. He was by himself, surrounded by a sea of prep school kids. He looked extremely uncomfortable, but his eyes were intense as they watched me. He flashed me a smile and I gave a sheepish wave back. "You going to talk to him?"

"After the game." I stated with a nod. "Too much to say right now."

"He deserves an explanation."

"He won't understand."

"Do you even understand?" Alicia retorted. I shook my head and opened my mouth to say something else, but Coach Kalzoo interrupted. I'd never been more relieved in my life.

It was hard to concentrate on the game when the love of your life is watching you as if he's ready to rip your clothes off and kiss you stupid at any given second. I'd almost forgotten I had another boyfriend, until he showed up during the ninth inning.

When the game was over, if Lance tried to get near me, Keller pulled me away to something else. As we headed to his Porsche I looked back to find Lance. He gave me a sad smile and wave, before he shook his head and walked off.

I wanted to cry. I wanted to run after him and tell him to hide me away forever. I couldn't because Keller was watching and Keller was very, very angry.

Chapter 108
Chopper

"I didn't think we'd see you tonight." I greeted Jordan as she walked into my backyard with Zack, Caleb and Maddie in tow.

"It's your last day as a free man." She teased as she flashed a gorgeous smile and took a tentative step towards me for a hug. I cocked an eyebrow and nodded my head. I love this girl to pieces; she was the only girl I'd ever been so close with. She was one of my best friends, which was a big accomplishment considering the others were male and I'd known them all since birth.

"Didn't think you cared." I muttered drily as she wrapped her arms around me tightly.

"That's a silly thing to think." She hugged me tighter. After the disappearing acts she'd been pulling lately, it wasn't really that off the wall to think she didn't give two shits about us. As much as I didn't want to believe that, it was extremely hard not to think it.

"Not really."

"Do you want me to leave?" She asked as she pulled away.

"I didn't say that." I shrugged nonchalantly. "The more the merrier." I greeted the others before pointing out the alcohol and excusing myself.

"Chopper?" Jordan called in a hurt voice.

"I'll catch you later Joey, I've got stuff to tend to right now." It wasn't a complete lie, but it'd work for now. I didn't hate her. I couldn't hate her, but the way things stood now, it looked as if she'd been playing my boy for a fool and using the rest of us in the game, or maybe she was too embarrassed by all of us. I don't know which. Unfortunately, the girl wasn't very forthcoming in the details. Maddie and Alicia were her roommates and they were clueless as to what in the Hell was going on with everything.

"What did you expect, J?" I heard Zack ask. "You play his best friend like a violin every chance you get."

"I don't." I heard her protest.

"You do." Zack snapped. I didn't like being a jerk to her, but it was against my code of conduct not to be, she'd broken my best friend's heart. It was because of her that he wasn't here tonight, even though he'd never admit that.

I went to mingle and separated myself from the Callatin crew as long as I could. They're good people, but the whole Jordan situation had me scratching my head. Maybe if she drank enough I could get the truth out of her. It was breaking my heart that I wasn't hanging out with her tonight, I missed her already and that probably wasn't a good thing.

Chapter 109
Jordan

"What's the fucking point of me being here if no one will talk to me?" I asked Zack bitterly as I chugged my beer. He shrugged his shoulders and shook his head.

"Don't act all innocent." He snapped with a humorless chuckle. "You brought this on yourself."

"Fuck you."

"I'm not going to sugar coat it for ya, babe." He admitted with another roll of his shoulders. "Never have, probably never will. You claim to be madly in love with Lance Bowman, but every time you two get back together, you blow him off for Keller the jackass. So don't be surprised Lance's friends think you're a bitch."

"I didn't have a choice."

"And why is that?" Zack queried as he turned to look me dead in the eye.

"None of your business. And Lance has constantly screwed me over and they never had a problem with it."

"Jordan, stop blaming him. He's been all about you and you've been all about fuckhead." I shot my friend a dirty look and turned my back to him. Zack just laughed. "No one else will talk to you, so you're stuck with me."

"This is ridiculous. I'm ready to go home. I don't care if…"

"Quit pouting." Zack sighed in exasperation. "It's really unbecoming."

"And you're really an asshole." I spit as I spun back around to glare at him.

"And you're being a spoiled rotten princess. Keller has definitely brainwashed you."

"What would you know?"

"I know this isn't you." He took a step towards me and got up in my face. "I also know you genuinely have deep feelings for Lance and his friends so I'm not exactly sure why you've been treating them all like dog shit. But, of course, I know when Keller James comes into the picture you tend to treat everyone that way. So, why don't you tell me what in the Hell he's got on you to make you act like this."

"Quit being ridiculous, Zack." I laughed nervously. Drew and Coop were walking behind us headed to the keg so I swooped in between them and linked arms. The rest of them may have been acting pissy towards me because of what I'd done to Lance, but Drew wouldn't. Drew cared about himself first and, maybe, others later. But, first and foremost, he had a huge crush on me and I'd use that to my advantage if I had to.

"Hey boys." I flirted. "How's it going?"

"Better now." Drew replied as he winked at me.

"You always know the right things to say." I sighed as I leaned into him.

"I'm going to go see if Chop needs anything." Coop pulled away.

"Coop?" I whined. "Come on."

"Sorry Jo." He shrugged.

"No, you're not." I bit as I crossed my arms in front of my chest. Okay, so maybe I was acting like a spoiled princess. I let out a sigh as I put on my best pleading face. "Is Lance leaving with you guys tomorrow?"

"No." Coop answered with a sigh and a shake of his head. "But only because he and his family went up to St. Louis tonight. He wanted to spend some fun time with Wyatt and Ella so they got a hotel room with a pool and…"

"So he was cleared." Coop nodded his head. "And he's not going to be here tonight. So he left without saying goodbye to me." I didn't care how good of an actress I was, there were some emotions that I couldn't mask and one of those was the hurt Lance had a habit of causing me. Tears filled my eyes.

"It's not like he won't be back in ten weeks."

"Only to leave again." I harrumphed.

"It didn't have to be like that." Coop looked back at me intently. "In fact, I'm pretty sure…never mind."

"I know I'm a bitch Coop, but I didn't have any other choice."

"Then maybe you should've explained that to Lance. Or *maybe* you should explain it to us." Drew interjected with a shrug.

"I can't."

"Then we can't help you. You pretend to be upset about this Jo, but maybe that's all it is, an act. I know for Lance, it's not."

"It's not for me either." I protested loudly. Tears rolled down my cheeks. I didn't know what hurt more, the fact that Lance was gone and I didn't get to apologize and say bye, or the fact that his friends, who I thought were mine as well, were practically shunning me. "Forget it." I waved a hand in the air dismissively. "I came to say goodbye to my friends, to tell y'all how much I'll miss you, but it's nice to know the feeling is not mutual." I spun on my heel and stalked off. I was pretty certain I was in no condition to drive because I'd been throwing beers back all night but I didn't care, at this point, I only wanted to get the Hell away from any living, breathing thing.

"Jordan!" Coop hollered. I ignored him and kept walking. Drew caught up to me within seconds and directed me inside the house where no one else was.

"Let's talk."

"Let's not." I snapped. "I'm ready to go home."

"No, you're really not." He grabbed my wrist and pulled me to him. "They may all act pissed, but this isn't easy for any of us, okay? We have an obligation to Lance, but the truth is, every one of us feels the same way about you. We've had this talk repeatedly, had it before the party started actually. It's not easy, but we've known Lance longer and you're not exactly treating the rest of us like we're of any importance."

"It's better that way." I sighed tearfully.

"Is it really?" He asked softly. I nodded my head.

"It's probably best if I go now." I whispered.

"Nope. I'll drive you home if I have to, but you're not driving. How about we see if Zack's ready, he's been holding off so he could be DD."

"Whatever." I murmured. "But I really don't want to deal with anyone right now."

"And just remember, I'm not leaving yet." He added with a flirtatious grin. I rolled my eyes and laughed.

"Should that make me feel better?"

"I wish it did, but it did make you smile." He grinned as he threw an arm around my shoulders and steered me back out of the house.

"I'm going to say my goodbyes." I murmured sadly as I tucked my arms around my chest self-consciously. "I'll hate myself if I don't."

"I'll go look for your boy." Drew stated with a nod as he gave me a one armed hug and kissed the top of my head. He headed off towards Zack and I started towards Sawyer and Alicia. Luckily, they were all gathered together in a huddle so my goodbye would be short and sweet.

Chapter 110
Chopper

"Here comes Jordan." Alicia announced softly as she nodded behind us. "I hate this. I really do. Does she even know Lance is gone?"

"I told her earlier." Coop answered with a sad nod. "She started crying."

"See? That's what doesn't make sense. If she's upset he's gone why in the Hell is she with Keller James?" Sawyer asked abruptly. "Seriously, I don't care how good of an actress she is, she can't fake what I've seen."

"I agree." Alicia sighed. "Something's up."

Our entire group grew silent as Jordan came close enough to hear, making the whole situation awkward. She looked terrified and sad all at the same time as she took a step towards us.

"I came to say bye." She murmured. "I'm ready to go home and I...I didn't want to leave without saying bye." She took a deep breath and looked at me first, then Coop and then Sawyer. "I know I've been...horrible to all of you recently and I wish I could explain it, other than just saying I'm a bitch. Meeting you guys two summers ago was one of the best things that could've ever happened to me. I love all of you guys and I'm going to miss you when you leave. I hope you don't hate me, although, I understand if you do. I just wanted to say that before you left."

"Aww Jo." Coop engulfed her in a hug. "We don't hate you. We're hurt, I guess. We love you, too."

"You're our family." Sawyer hugged her too. Jordan was grinning from ear to ear as tears slid down her cheeks. Her eyes darted towards me, but I stayed where I was. I wanted to hug her, tell her I loved her too. Because I did. Maybe a little more than I should, to be honest. Sometimes I thought my feelings were dangerously close to more than friends, but I would never put either of us in that situation. Jordan talked with the others a little longer while I watched from the sidelines but when she started to leave, I grabbed her by the elbow.

"Let's go talk, you and me." I snapped as I led her inside the house and straight into my bedroom.

"Um, Chopper." She started.

"What in the Hell is your problem?" I asked angrily. Her eyes grew wide, I'd never raised my voice to her in the past and I imagine it would be a shock to anyone, especially to her. She didn't say a word, she started to, but closed her mouth quickly. I crossed my arms in front of my chest and glared at her.

"What's *your* problem?" She countered as she mimicked my pose and raised a defiant chin. I narrowed my eyes and shook my head. She let out an exasperated sigh and uncrossed her arms before looking down at the floor quickly. "Come on Chopper, it's your last night home for a while. Do you really want to spend it fighting with me?"

"Cut. The. Shit." I growled. Her eyes widened again and I felt a twinge of guilt at the sadness that filled her pretty blue eyes. "What in the Hell is your deal?"

"Chopper. Please." I shook my head and glared some more. It wasn't exactly easy for me to be intimidating. I was by all means a lover, not a fighter. A big teddy bear until you hurt my family, and then the grizzly bear came out.

"I ain't falling for your bull shit anymore, Jo. I'm done." She still didn't say anything.

Just stood near the doorway and fidgeted nervously as she tried to fight back tears. "What the fuck is your problem? I put my boy out on the line, pushed him out on the limb because I thought you were genuine and you didn't just knock him off, you cut down the damn tree."

"I was…"

"Shut up and listen to me." I spit. She pulled back in shock. "This girl you've become, or maybe always have been, is a manipulative, cold hearted bitch and I don't like her." Tears rolled down her cheeks, but I wasn't stopping, I couldn't. "I hate her." Jordan raised her chin again and stared straight at me. "The girl you are with Lance, you were with Lance, I love her. *She's* my best friend. I don't know who the Hell you are. I don't know who the Hell is real, honestly."

"You know the real me."

"Do I?" I laughed. "And which girl is that? The girl you are with the pretty boy asswipe or the girl you are around my friends and me?"

"How can you not know?"

"Easy." I replied evenly. "You are this amazing, down to earth, super cool girl who is my best friend sometimes and then the asswipe comes around and you can't even acknowledge me? Friends don't do that to each other."

"You don't understand."

"You're right. I don't. So why don't you enlighten me." I leaned back against the wall and waited.

"I can't."

"You won't. There's a difference."

"Chopper." She sighed. "Please, just let it go. I'm sorry."

"I can't just let it go!" I yelled as I pushed myself off the wall and got up in her face. "Do you have any idea how much Lance loves you? Do you know how big of a deal that is? I can only pray that I will someday find my perfect match like you two already have, but between the two of you, you fuck it up every chance you get. What the fuck?" I yanked at my hair in frustration, took a step back and turned around before pivoting right back in front of her. "You will never find anyone better than Bo, Jordan. Never. He's a good guy; he'd bend over backward for anyone and *for you*, he'd walk through fire. He's been through Hell and lived to talk about it and it's a damned miracle that he's not a fucking suicide bomb waiting to implode."

"I know that." She whispered.

"Obviously, you don't. Who fucking cares that Keller James can buy you ten new cars and God only knows what else? He treats you like shit. He's a damned, druggie asshole who cheats on you, but for some reason, you keep going back to him and leaving Lance holding the bag."

"It's not…"

"Then tell me why."

"I can't." She cried.

"Then get the Hell out of my house." I growled. Her eyes went wide again as she looked up at me in complete shock. "Get the Hell out of my house. Get the fuck off my property, out of this party. Get out of my life. Out of all of our lives. I won't sit back and let you destroy my best friend any more than you already have. I put you on a pedestal, we all did, but you don't deserve one bit of acknowledgement from any of us. You are a cold hearted, gutless bitch for the games you play with Lance. Leave."

"Chopper." She sobbed. "Please. Don't."

"LEAVE." I hissed as I got up in her face. She stood there trembling, tears racing down her perfect cheeks as she stared back at me in disbelief. She just shook her head back and forth. "Then tell me why you ignore us when you're around your little boyfriend? Tell me why you refuse to let him go, but you throw Lance away without a second thought. Explain to me how you can bald-faced lie to me, to Lance, to all of us about how much you love Bo, then turn around, and go back to the pretty boy? You turned us all against Lance, made us all think you were the injured party in everything when, in reality, you didn't give two shits. The only person you care about is yourself, princess."

"I can't." She repeated in between sobs.

"Then for the last time, LEAVE!" She didn't move so I took a step forward and she flinched as if I were about to hit her. Another step and she actually ducked. I almost gaped, but I shook my head as I started to grab her by the arm. She flew back before I could.

"No." She gasped. I stopped.

"I'm not going to hurt you, Jo." I stated flatly. "You're doing a good enough job of that on your own. You're not welcome here anymore." I walked out of the room. I didn't care if she left or not. I'd said my peace, she had no rebuttal and that hurt like Hell. I bee lined out of my room and straight to the refrigerator for the bottle of vodka I had chilling.

I was seriously in love with that girl. She was perfect for Lance and the two of them apart would lead a miserable life, but together they were phenomenal. The sad part, our whole little group hinged on them. I feared their destruction would tear us all apart in some way. Bo would be the first to go and it would be pure devastation. Therefore, I wasn't sure what hurt worse; the premonition of losing another brother, the pain of losing both my best friends, or that my heart was broken in a bazillion pieces because I'd bought everything that girl said hook, line, and sinker.

I was just as much of a fool as Lance Bowman was.

Chapter 111
Jordan

The world was closing in on me. There was a roaring in my ears. I couldn't stop crying. I couldn't catch my breath. My stomach hurt. My heart had just broken into a hundred pieces in the floor. If Lance had ripped my heart out by leaving without saying goodbye, well then Chopper had just done the fucking Mexican hat dance all over it.

I could never have imagined Chopper, of all people, could hate me so much. I thought he was my best friend. I loved him so much, like he was another brother and he'd basically just…stabbing me in the heart and letting me bleed out would've been kinder than hearing what he thought of me.

Who can blame him really? I deserved everything he said and more. I was everything he called me, *and more*. What I'd done to Lance and the guys, to my friends, because of Keller James, was cold and cruel. I was lucky any of them still talked to me. Damn lucky Keller wasn't all I had left. Well, I guess, he kind of is now. He'd successfully cut everyone else out of my life, like he wanted.

I was grateful for the beer bottle I still clenched in my hand; I just wished it were full. I chugged the remainder down and tried to settle my emotions. I was hurt, devastated really, because I wasn't just losing Lance, who I truly believed to be my soul mate, but I was losing him as a friend as well. Not to mention, Chopper as my best friend. I was losing the guys. I would no doubt lose Alicia and she was one of two girls I was even remotely close with. Then there was Lance's family. God, his mom was everything I ever fantasized my mom being and I thought of her as my mom, really. And Wyatt. Seeing his disappointed face would kill me. If there were any of my heart left to break, he would do it.

The more I cried, the more pissed off I got. I was livid at Chopper for telling me off and telling me to leave. More than anything, I was furious at Keller James for winning.

Jordan Donaldson didn't lose and tonight would not be the first time for that. I'll be damned if that SOB dictated my life anymore. I was done.

Chapter 112
Chopper

Five long pulls from the bottle of Vodka and my mood had not changed. My whole body was shaking from the confrontation with Jordan. My urge to go back and apologize was growing stronger with every drink. Damn it.

I stood with my back against the kitchen counter, staring at the table as I thought about all the parties we had here over the years. How many times as kids we would gather around that table scarfing down mom's pancakes; Luke was always the first done, always the one to eat the most with a big, goofy grin on his face. I laughed to myself as I thought about the last time we'd done that, two weeks before Luke left, the goof ball was the exact same way at fifteen that he was at five. I missed him something fierce.

And just like that Luke's goofy face disappeared and Jordan slid into view, sitting as close to Bo as possible, looking up at him like he hung the moon. She'd never been there for a sleepover, that my mom knew of anyway, but she was always bellied up to the table with us as if she'd been there all our lives. She was one of us. I closed my eyes and shook away the thought that I'd just lost another friend and it hurt just as bad as Luke's death.

"Fuck you, Chopper." Jordan slurred as she stumbled into the kitchen. Her face was red and puffy from crying, tears stained her face, snot ran from her nose, and yet she was still beautiful. She narrowed her eyes at me before she ripped the Vodka bottle out of my hand. "Fuck you. I'm not leaving."

"I said you're not welcome here anymore. Don't make a fool out of yourself, Jo. Have some dignity."

"Fuck you." She repeated in a low southern drawl as she took a very, very long pull from the Vodka bottle. She watched me closely when she finished, she didn't even shiver as the liquor went down. I raised an eyebrow and looked back at her warily. This might get ugly. "Don't you dare tell me where I can and cannot go. I will leave whenever the Hell I want."

"Sorry princess," I spit. "But you're wrong."

"No. You're wrong." She hissed. "*I love you. I love Lance Bowman.* I love all of you stupid bastards and that is why I've done everything I've done these last few months. I was protecting you dumbasses." I pulled back a little and waited. If she was about to spill everything, I wasn't about to ruin it. "Don't you see Chopper?" She turned around and walked to the kitchen table. She pulled out a chair, plopped down on it and buried her face in her hands. "Don't you get it? All the bad shit that's been happening to us? To you guys? To Lance? It's all my fault! The bogus charges that got us arrested, that brought Lance into jail on more than one occasion, *I* did that."

"What do you mean, *you* did that?"

"It's all my fault. Lance's house…." She was sobbing, gasping for breath and there was a not so subtle group clamoring at the sliding glass door trying to listen or see what was happening. I grabbed her by the arm and hauled her up and into my bedroom.

"Talk."

"Ever since…I didn't know…" She rambled as she plopped down in front of my bed and slid into the floor. She buried her face in her hands again as she sobbed uncontrollably and talked gibberish for about five minutes. I finally grabbed her face in my hands and forced her to look at me.

"Stop." I ordered as I stared deep into her blue eyes. "Breathe." She inhaled, and then exhaled like a child. "Go slow and tell me what you're trying to say."

"I didn't know Keller was so conniving. I didn't." She mumbled softly. "Before Lance he was controlling, but...I never..." She took a deep breath and shuddered before she looked back up at me. "He warned me repeatedly to stay away from Lance, that I belonged to him and he wouldn't be showed up by a townie, but I thought he was bluffing. He wasn't. I didn't realize...I started noticing things at random, once I got my memory back and realized how manipulative he was. It was little things at first; my dad's reputation, Caleb's drug charges and then he brought Lance into it when he had Sage claim that Cale, Zack and Lance all gang raped her. There were more, Zack and Alicia were accused of cheating, Maddie of stealing and so on. I'm sure there's a lot I don't even know about. I mean, he told me the other night, the last night Lance and I were together, your birthday party...he told me he paid off those kids in the truck, the ones that died. He said I wanted him to, that I told him to...he blamed me. When I think back, the whole thing when I almost got kicked out of Callatin for dating the TA, I'm pretty sure he was behind my fall and then he was my savior. As long as I'm good, as long as I'm with him he won't hurt anyone else."

"And you think he was responsible for Lance's house..."

"I know." She murmured before she started sobbing again. "I found his wallet and I hid it." Her eyes went down quickly. "Lance would've killed him and I couldn't have that responsibility. I...I was afraid Lance would blame me and..." She was gasping for air again before she stopped, took a deep breath.

"Are you kidding me?"

"No." She sobbed. "God Chopper, if Lance ever found out...he'd hate me even more and..."

"It's not your fault."

"YES. It is. If I'd have just listened to Keller. If I stayed away from y'all and..."

"Keller is not your damned boss." I growled at her.

"Yes he is. If I don't listen to him then bad things happen. My dad almost died, Chopper. Lance's house was destroyed. Cissy died. Brennan is in jail for murder. He shot Zack, he tried to kill him twice. He kidnapped Wyatt."

"None of that was your fault."

"It's all my fault. Wyatt...five minutes after I took Keller back, Wyatt was found."

"Have you told Zack or Caleb any of this? You need to go to the police or..."

"I could tell the police, but they're not going to believe me over Keller James. He's so good at manipulating people and...I would be risking everyone else."

"Jordan." I sighed as I fell down in the floor beside her. I slid my arm around her shoulders and pulled her into me as she continued to cry. I didn't know what else to do, I was absolutely helpless. And I felt like the biggest ass in the world for yelling at her the way I did. The poor girl is terrified of the repercussions of her actions and I was a bastard. I believed her. However, I didn't believe Keller James was capable of murder and arson. It's possible she was overreacting to the situation, but there was no doubt she believed she had to protect all of us. "I'm sorry, Jo."

"Shut up." She grumbled with a shake of her head as she wrapped her arms around me and squeezed. "I deserved everything you said and more. If I'd just explained everything to Lance then...how am I any better than all I've bitched at him about?"

286

"Had you told Lance then…well, I don't think it'd be pretty for Keller."

"He could've…there's so much worse that Keller is capable of. Chopper, if he really paid those kids…Lance could be dead." She started crying harder, gasping for air as she tried to grapple with the horrors she was probably only now realizing.

"But he's not, okay? It's going to be okay."

"No. It's not. When Keller finds out I was here…"

"Does he hit you?" I asked softly. She stiffened immediately.

"No. Do you really think I'd let some jackass hit me?" She retorted, without looking me in the eye. My stomach dropped as I pulled her into me, she was lying through her teeth, but I wouldn't push her. It was too much already.

She cried it out until she fell asleep on my chest from sheer exhaustion. She didn't even stir when I picked her up and placed her in my bed. I looked around my room for my phone, finally found it on my computer desk.

"We need to talk." I texted Lance. It was close to four in the morning, but I had a feeling he was still wide-awake. We all knew we wouldn't be getting much sleep today, too much lay ahead in our future that was scary and uncontrollable. Sure enough, my phone beeped with a reply.

"You better not be pussing out on me."

"Never lol it's about Jo."

"She there?"

"Yup."

"She okay?"

"Right now, yes."

"Then that's all that matters. I don't need to know anymore. I have to get her out of my head."

"I understand. I'll catch you before we board the plane. It's important."

"Heavy stuff? Lol Can't tell me now?"

"Too much to say via text and I can't talk right now."

"K. See you in the morning."

"In a few hours if our drunk asses wake up lol"

"Good night?"

"Wasn't the same without you."

"Whatever lol later." I put the phone back on my desk and looked at the gorgeous girl passed out in my bed. She was my best friend and had fallen asleep on me before, but tonight I could hold her one last time before everything changed.

Chapter 113

Jordan was gone when I woke up barely two hours later. There was a note taped to my computer desk, but that was the only sign she'd ever even been there. I was sad I hadn't woke up, but it was probably for the best. It cut out the awkwardness.

"Hey buddy." My mom greeted as she poked her head in the door. "You getting around?" I nodded my head and sat up. "We should be heading out soon. Everyone will be here shortly; the other boys are waking up too."

"Thanks for letting us have the party last night, mom." She grinned back at me and nodded before she came into the room. She sat down on the bed and hugged me quickly.

"You boys needed it. We don't know when you'll all be together again, right?"

"We'll always be friends."

"No doubt about that." She laughed. "I just meant, life and reality take you in different directions, down completely different paths than you could've ever dreamed of and it may be hard for you all to get together at the same time."

"I know. It's probably my biggest fear."

"Although, I'm pretty sure you'll all come back home to live and thrive." She smiled. "You're all pretty much mama's boys."

"That ain't no lie." I chuckled. "I love ya, ma." I kissed her cheek.

"And I love you. I'm pretty proud of you. You're an amazing young man...with great friends. I'm proud of all of you, really. And I'll miss you guys like crazy."

"And we'll miss you." I smiled. My mom gave me another hug before she stood up and started out of the room.

"I've got pancakes on the griddle, for old time's sake." I grinned from ear to ear and laughed. "You're the best." She nodded, blew me a kiss and shut the door as she left. I stood up and grabbed my clothes out for the day. Then I went over to Jordan's note on the computer screen.

Chopper,

I learned not to leave my notes on the bed the hard way...you wouldn't find it until you were thirty if I had. Ha ha. Thanks for last night. You're amazing as always and one of my best friends, I'm truly blessed to be able to say that. I'm sorry for the way I've been towards you, Lance and the guys...it's inexcusable and I hope you truly forgive me because losing any of you is like losing a family member. I wish you the best of luck in boot camp and know that I'll be missing you all like crazy. Please tell Lance the same. I hope you'll write if you can and let me know how y'all are doing. I can't wait for the day you guys are done, come home to party, for real with me again!! I love you, I'll miss you and you suck for leaving me behind!!!

Love, Jo

I chuckled as I read it again before I headed to the shower. I only wish I could've told her the same to her sweet face.

Chapter 114

"Put your big boy pants on kids." I joked as we all congregated on the steps to the MEPS building in St. Louis where we'd all be finishing our final paperwork before boarding a plane to boot camp. We'd gotten lucky and would all be flying out to Ft. Benning, GA for basic training together.

Drew and Alicia had come along with us, Alicia for Sawyer and Drew just because. To be honest, I think he felt a little guilty, if not regretful, of his decision not to follow through on our childhood pact. I couldn't blame him though and none of us ever would for choosing a full basketball scholarship to a university in lieu of the Army.

"There's Lance." Alicia announced sadly as she clung to Sawyer's hand. Lance grinned and gave a little wave as he and his family sidled up to the rest of us. We all said our goodbyes...we were all one big family. There were picture, of course and lots of crying, and not just from the females in the group either.

"How was the party?" Lance asked

"Pretty amazing for some of us." Drew cocked an eyebrow at me. I shot him a wry look as I shrugged my shoulders.

"As I said last night brother, we missed you."

"Jordan didn't." Drew shot.

"Actually, she did." Coop interjected. "She was a little upset, to say the least, that you left without saying goodbye."

"Not worried about it." Lance shrugged nonchalantly. All of us looked back at him in surprise, he just rolled his shoulders again.

"So then you don't care Chop moved in on her?" Drew asked bitterly as he shot me a dirty look. My jaw dropped open just as Lance took a swing at me. I ducked, pretty impressive moves for a fat boy like me, actually.

"Whoa! What the Hell are you talking about?" I yelled. "Bo, nothing fucking happened."

"Then why did she leave your room at five this morning? After saying, she was ready to leave at midnight? No one could find either of you for hours. And her note said you were amazing last night." I could see Lance's entire body go rigid, his jaw clenched in time with his fists at his side.

"Drew, you jack ass. I was amazing for hearing her out last night. That girl wouldn't give me a chance if I was the last man on earth." I chuckled with a shake of my head. "What the fuck, dude? Why would you stir shit like that?"

"I saw her..."

"Yeah, she fell asleep in my room. She's like my little sister. Unlike you, I wouldn't have taken advantage of the situation."

"What?" Drew started as he took a step forward. "Sorry. I was upset that...I wasn't thinking. I'm sorry, Lance. I'm sure he's right."

"Is that what you wanted to talk to me about this morning? Tell me you hooked up with her."

"Fuck no." I sighed in exasperation. "She talked last night." I raised my eyebrows meaningfully. "We'll talk later, because I'm not broadcasting it to the world."

"Drew, I can't believe you thought Jordan would hook up with Chop before she'd hook up with me." Coop bellowed with laughter. Lance relaxed and Drew shook his head. He repeated his apologies again and hung back with his family.

Three hours later, we were leaving MEPS and loading onto the MetroLink bound for the airport. Luckily, we'd all been separated in the seats, but I clung close to Lance.

"What's up?" He asked with a resigned sigh.

"Jordan talked." I answered with a shake of my head once the Metro started forward. "And you're not going to like it."

"I know she played me, you don't have to…"

"Au contraire mon frère. She isn't playing you. According to her, she withdrew to protect you. To protect all of us."

"It sounds like bull shit to me."

"Me too, but then I realized it made sense." I rolled my shoulders and leaned back into the seat before I began to relay everything Jordan had told me. Unfortunately, the more I talked, the angrier Lance got. He was gripping the seat in front of us so tightly, I thought he might rip it apart.

"He's hurting her?"

"She says no, but I think that's the only part she lied about. I walked towards her and she flinched, she freaked out like I was going to hit her." Lance closed his eyes and inhaled deeply.

"So you're telling me she believes she has to stay with that bastard, take his bull shit to protect us? Why wouldn't she tell me any of this?"

"She thinks the attack on Zack was because of what he knew. She wouldn't risk your safety any more than she thinks she already has. I don't know if Keller is really doing all of the shit that's happened, but she is convinced he is. She did what she thought was best. She's terrified of what he's capable of."

"And we're boarding a damned plane, about to go to boot camp for ten weeks and she's…still there with that SOB. I can't…"

"You have no other choice but to board the plane, Bo. I pulled Caleb's cell number from Jordan's phone and texted him before I laid down this morning. I told him what I suspected and that Keller was threatening Jordan. He'll take care of her."

"You're sure he got it?"

"He didn't reply, but it was also four in the morning. He'll take care of it. Of her. Of that bastard." Lance nodded his head before he leaned forward and buried his face in his hands.

"I feel so helpless." He mumbled in a quiet voice. "How could I not see this?"

"She didn't want you to? You didn't want to? I don't know. None of us saw, not even Lish or Maddie and they live with her."

"What do I do? I went to say goodbye to her, but that jackass wouldn't let me near her and so I just…I got pissed and…I didn't tell her goodbye even though I swore I would."

"Write her a letter?" I shrugged with a grin. "You can have it finished and I'm sure someone at the USO will mail it out for you." Lance nodded. Once we got to the airport, we had a little time to kill and we managed to find a pen and some notebook paper for him. It wasn't perfect, it wouldn't ease his turbulent emotions, but it would help a little and it would help Jordan a lot, I'm sure.

Regardless, the damage was already done and all we could really do was pray Jordan was safe while we were gone and that Lance could right everything in the short time we had home before we left again. I was certain Zack and Caleb could protect her, but only if Jordan would let them and she was never one to do that very easily.

Chapter 115
Keller

This hacker software is the best investment I've ever made. It was a good thing I was still awake when the text from an unknown number went through Caleb's phone. So Jordan talked, did she? So someone believes I am threatening her and she feels forced into our relationship? What a joke. I had already snuck into his room and deleted the message. I didn't need anyone else prying into my business. Bentley was bad enough but he'd backed off after the attack, which was the point of it.

I would find out what all Jordan had said and then I would twist her words easily. Her reputation is nonexistent anymore so no one would believe her. However, she would pay for lying. She would suffer in unimaginable ways for her betrayal.

THE END

About the author

Melissa Logan is a single mother of five; three boys and two angel babies. She is a Veteran of the U.S. Coast Guard, an author, an employee of the U.S. Postal Service and an online fitness coach. In her spare time she loves to workout, read, write, photography and spending time with her family. Melissa was raised in a small southern Illinois town and currently resides there today with her children.

Other books by this author

Callatin Academy #1 New Beginnings
Callatin Academy #2 Trust Me
Callatin Academy #3 Crazy Girl
Callatin Academy #4 Backroad Reality
Callatin Academy #5 Plastic Princess

The Brittany Files: Crossroads
The Brittany Files: Hostile
The Brittany Files: Twisted
The Brittany Files: Blindsided

Available in print at Amazon.com

Connect with this author

You can friend her on Facebook at the following:
www.facebook.com/melissa.logansanders
www.facebook.com/authormelissalogan
www.facebook.com/melissasandersfitness

You can find her on Twitter @melissalogan79

Made in the USA
Columbia, SC
05 November 2022

70508097R00161